PRAISE FOR
Manly Wade Wellman

"A superb writer."
Michael Moorcock

"From pulp magazines to Arkham House to 'The Twilight Zone,' Manly Wade Wellman is a legend—and one of the finest regional fantasists of his day."
Greg Bear, author of *Darwin's Radio*

"Like nothing you've ever read before."
Karl Edward Wagner, creator of Kane

"When you read about tribal celebrations—and tribal interactions—in the Hok stories, remember they were written by somebody who had seen and participated in similar things. It was clearly written by a man who grew up knowing that kill or be killed wasn't just a phrase. Manly was doing something very different here: he was giving a realistic description of life in a state of nature."
David Drake, author of *Lord of the Isles*

"One of science fiction's few authentic, legitimate artists . . . entertaining, familiar in a racial-memory sort of way, and educational, [but] also comforting and uplifting . . . stories that somehow feel exactly right. There are some brilliant and evocative stories waiting up ahead for you."
Mike Resnick, author of *Stalking the Dragon*

"Wellman is a writer as good as he is prolific, and his output is so varied that anyone interested in the fiction of the supernatural is sure to find something enjoyable."
The Reader's Guide to Fantasy

"Wellman's stories are not only first-rate fantasies and marvelously entertaining, they have a truly unique warmth to them."
Gahan Wilson for *Realms of Fantasy*

THE PLANET STORIES LIBRARY

Sos the Rope by Piers Anthony
Steppe by Piers Anthony
The Ginger Star by Leigh Brackett
The Hounds of Skaith by Leigh Brackett
The Reavers of Skaith by Leigh Brackett
The Secret of Sinharat by Leigh Brackett
The Sword of Rhiannon by Leigh Brackett
The Walrus & The Warwolf by Hugh Cook
Infernal Sorceress by Gary Gygax
The Anubis Murders by Gary Gygax
The Samarkand Solution by Gary Gygax
Death in Delhi by Gary Gygax
Almuric by Robert E. Howard
Template by Matthew Hughes
The Swordsman of Mars by Otis Adelbert Kline
The Outlaws of Mars by Otis Adelbert Kline
The Dark World by Henry Kuttner
Elak of Atlantis by Henry Kuttner
Robots Have No Tails by Henry Kuttner
Worlds of Their Own edited by James Lowder
The Ship of Ishtar by A. Merritt
City of the Beast by Michael Moorcock
Lord of the Spiders by Michael Moorcock
Masters of the Pit by Michael Moorcock
Black God's Kiss by C. L. Moore
Northwest of Earth by C. L. Moore
Before They Were Giants edited by James L. Sutter
Battle in the Dawn by Manly Wade Wellman
Who Fears the Devil? by Manly Wade Wellman

STRANGE ADVENTURES ON OTHER WORLDS
AVAILABLE EXCLUSIVELY FROM PLANET STORIES!

FOR AUTHOR BIOS AND SYNOPSES,
VISIT PAIZO.COM/PLANETSTORIES

Publisher's Cataloging-In-Publication Data
(Prepared by The Donohue Group, Inc.)

Wellman, Manly Wade, 1903-1986.
  Battle in the dawn : the complete Hok the Mighty / by Manly Wade Wellman ; cover illustration by Kieran Yanner ; [introduction] by David Drake

   p. ; cm. -- (Planet stories ; #30)

  Stories previously published separately in Amazing Stories and Fantastic Adventures, 1939-1942.
  "March 2011."
  Manly and the Stone Age / by David Drake -- Battle in the dawn -- Hok goes to Atlantis -- Hok draws the bow -- Hok and the gift of heaven -- Hok visits the land of legends -- Love of Oloana -- Day of the conquerors -- Untitled Hok fragment -- Autobiography.
  ISBN: 978-1-60125-289-0

  1. Prehistoric peoples--Fiction. 2. Neanderthals--Fiction. 3. Atlantis (Legendary place)--Fiction. 4. Adventure stories, American. 5. Fantasy fiction. I. Yanner, Kieran. II. Drake, David. III. Title. IV. Title: Hok the Mighty.

PS3545.E52858 B28 2011
813./54

COVER ILLUSTRATION BY KIERAN YANNER

BATTLE IN THE DAWN: THE COMPLETE HOK THE MIGHTY BY MANLY WADE WELLMAN

MANLY AND THE STONE AGE
   by David Drake 6

CONTENTS
BATTLE IN THE DAWN 10
HOK GOES TO ATLANTIS 50
HOK DRAWS THE BOW 86
HOK AND THE GIFT OF HEAVEN 122
HOK VISITS THE LAND OF LEGENDS 148
THE LOVE OF OLOANA 198
THE DAY OF THE CONQUERORS 207
UNTITLED HOK FRAGMENT 256
AN AUTOBIOGRAPHY
   by Manly Wade Wellman 258

PLANET STORIES is published bimonthly by Paizo Publishing, LLC with offices at 7120 185th Ave NE, Ste 120, Redmond, Washington, 98052. Erik Mona, Publisher. Pierce Watters, Senior Editor. Christopher Paul Carey and James L. Sutter, Editors. Special thanks to Jeremiah Rickert and Bill Thom. *Battle in the Dawn: The Complete Hok the Mighty* © 2011 by David Drake. "Manly and the Stone Age" © 2011 by David Drake. Planet Stories and the Planet Stories planet logo are registered trademarks of Paizo Publishing, LLC. Planet Stories #30, *Battle in the Dawn: The Complete Hok the Mighty*, by Manly Wade Wellman. March 2011. PRINTED IN THE UNITED STATES OF AMERICA.

Manly and the Stone Age
by David Drake

I met Manly briefly in 1970 before I was sent to Viet Nam. When I returned to The World in 1971 we became friends, sharing family dinners regularly (generally with Karl Wagner) and even going to England together. We chatted about many things over the years, not least books and writing.

Manly was bedridden for the last ten months of his life. I was the only person besides Frances whom he saw regularly during that time (Karl didn't have reliable transportation) and we became much closer. I heard still more stories then, because Manly was consciously using me as a repository for his memories.

I wish I could remember everything Manly told me over those fifteen years, but of course I don't. What I say below is informed by that long friendship, however.

The most important thing to remember about the Hok stories is that Manly was born and raised to age seven (1903-10) in the village of Kamundongo, Angola, where his father ran a medical mission. Manly's brother Paul was the first white child born in the community, and Manly was the second. He grew up speaking primarily Umbundu because the only whites for fifty miles in any direction were his family members.

Kamundongo wasn't technically a stone-age community: the natives had metal which they'd bought from traders. I have one of the knives Manly brought back, a hardwood handle shaped like a flattened hourglass with a short, angled steel blade at one end (something like a gracefully handmade box cutter).

Village society hadn't changed significantly since Europeans brought metal to the region, however. One day a leopard attacked the village goats.

A playmate of Manly's was watching the herd; he killed the leopard with his spear.

Even in his last months of life, Manly was enthusiastic as he described the feast the village gave the hero, the songs of praise chanted in his name, and the way everybody tasted a bit of the meat of the dead leopard. When you read about tribal celebrations—and tribal interactions—in the Hok stories, remember they were written by somebody who had seen and participated in similar things.

Manly always said that Hok was what he thought might have been the original of the Hercules myths; he makes the kinship explicit in the final story of the series, "Hok Visits the Land of Legends." However, speaking as a writer (and not based on Manly's own comments), I'm pretty sure that the first story, "Battle in the Dawn," was written as a stand-alone. The remaining stories followed at a considerable distance (eleven months; the first two stories of John the Balladeer—which *were* written as a series—were separated by only six months) and all have "Hok" in their titles to make clear the series relationship. I strongly suspect that positive reader comment on "Battle in the Dawn" led Manly to write more about his hero.

The tone of "Battle in the Dawn" is quite different from that of the later stories. It was clearly written by a man who grew up knowing that kill or be killed wasn't just a phrase: in Kamundongo, it had been present reality. There are accounts of leopards who ignored the goats to take the herd boy, and if Manly's little friend hadn't been quick, the story might have had a very different ending.

I think it's significant that the Hok series—and particularly "Battle in the Dawn"—appeared in *Amazing* and *Fantastic Adventures*. These (extremely successful) Ziff-Davis pulps appeared to target an unsophisticated but fully adult readership.

The—literally—savage brutality descried in "Battle in the Dawn" would not, I suspect, have been acceptable in any other SF magazine of the day. Stories in Weird Menace pulps like *Terror Tales* were often written around scenes of torture, but Manly (who never wrote Weird Menace, despite the fact that the field paid very well) was doing something very different here: he was giving a realistic description of life in a state of nature.

Though Manly had grown up in a savage village, his descriptions of prehistoric men and animals were based on the best academic texts available to him. To the end of his life he maintained a deep interest in human emergence, and his personal library included *The Age of Mammals* by Henry Fairfield Osborn and *A History of Land Mammals in the Western Hemisphere* by William B. Scott, the most authoritative sources of their day.

Having said that, Manly went through the University of Wichita (now Wichita State) on a football scholarship. He frankly admitted that though he had a BA, he would have had the same straight C grade point if he'd never attended a class.

Though Manly wasn't an academic, he *was* very smart and he had an intuitive understanding of many things based on his personal observation. For example, when Karl and I claimed on the basis of current medical thinking that cocaine didn't have long-term negative effects, Manly (who'd been a police reporter) strongly disagreed. Manly was absolutely right, as I can see in viewing the wreckage of several acquaintances now.

Not surprisingly, there were occasional errors in the way Manly used scholarly texts. In "Hok Visits the Land of Legends," he describes Dinoceras (Uintatherium) as an omnivore. Nothing in Manly's own copies of Osborn and Scott even hint at the possibility, and my attempt to find *any* suggestion that the creature wasn't an herbivore has been unsuccessful. My suspicion is that he meant the contemporary Archeotherium, a giant, pig-like Enteleodont. The error makes no difference in story terms.

And in one case, the error occurred because Manly did follow the best scientific opinion: Piltdown Man appears in "Hok Visits the Land of Legends." It wasn't until the 1950s that scientists finally accepted that Piltdown Man was a hoax. It was decades more before workmen in the (British) Natural History Museum found the hoaxer's equipment in a closed-off fireplace in the office of the Keeper of Geology.

Incidentally, the original publication of "Hok Visits the Land of Legends" has an asterisk at the point where Hok meets Soko, but the footnote apparently dropped out in the typesetting. Manly isn't around to ask what he intended there, but from context it was probably a discussion of why scientists believe that Piltdown Man was more arboreal than either Cro-Magnons or Neanderthals.

The Hok stories are in all senses pulp fiction, and certainly they have the pulp virtues of action and color. When you read them, though, keep in mind that they contain a great deal of truth, both personal and scientific.

I learned a lot from Manly, and I continue to learn from him. You can too.

Dave Drake
March 2009

DAVID DRAKE, *perhaps best known for his Lord of the Isles series, is one of the most prominent authors of military science fiction. He has written or co-written over 60 books in a wide array of fantasy and science fiction subgenres, and edited or co-edited about thirty anthologies and collections. Visit him online at* **david-drake.com.**

Battle in the Dawn

Prologue

Stone-Age Europe was spacious, rich and uncrowded; but there could be only one race of rulers.

Homo Neanderthalensis must have grown up there from the beginning, was supreme and plentiful as the last glaciers receded. His bones have been found from Germany to Gibraltar, and his camps and flints and fire-ashes. We reconstruct his living image—burly and stooped, with a great protruding muzzle, beetling brows, no chin and no brow. Perhaps he was excessively hairy—hardly a man, but more than a brute. Fire was his, and the science of flint-chipping. He buried his dead brothers, apparently believing in a hereafter, even a deity. He could think, perhaps speak. He could fight, too.

When real men first came through the eastern mountain passes or out of the great valley now drowned by the Mediterranean, battle ensued. The invaders were *Homo Sapiens,* in body and spirit like us, their children. They could not parley with the abhorrent foe they found; there could be no rules of warfare, no truces or treaties, no mercy to the vanquished. Such conflict could die only when the last adversary died.

It must have been a struggle generations long. Was it not full of daring, despair, sacrifice, triumph? Was not the conquest the greatest, because the most fundamental, in the history of the race? No champions of mankind ever bore a greater responsibility than those first little bands who crossed, all unaware, the borders of Neanderthal country.

With one such band, at the moment of such crossing, our story begins—

Chapter I
The Land of the Gnorrls

The southern country had come to hold too few game herds, too many hostile bands of fellow-hunters; hence the family's spring migration, many days' journey into the north which these days grew warmer than their fathers had known it.

The particular bright morning found the whole nine scattered. A foolish deer, grazing too close, bounded away with a javelin in its shoulder, and the swiftest runners led the chase with the rest trailing behind. So from horizon to horizon and beyond, the pursuers went, with flecks of blood to point the way across rich green meadows, and hunger to quicken moccasined feet. The sun had reached zenith and passed when the first of the hunters, gaining the top of a little knoll, saw that the prey had fallen and died just beyond.

That first-comer was the eldest son of the wandering household, and the tallest and swiftest. He was as strong as the leopard whose pelt he wore for a single garment, and his smooth young skin showed tanned and healthy with good outdoor living. His lion-tawny hair had been cut shoulder length and was bound back from his shrewd face with a snakeskin fillet. His chin, plucked clean of beard as custom decreed with bachelors, jutted squarely. His mouth was wide and good-humored beneath a straight nose, and his gray eyes opened widely, clearly. In one hand he swung a stone-bladed axe, and a loop at his shoulder held the mate to the javelin that had pierced the deer. His name, and he hoped to make it great, was Hok.

Pausing thus, Hok grinned triumphantly for just the half of an instant. Then his eyes narrowed and his lips drew tight. Something dark and shaggy crouched on the far side of the fallen animal. A bear? Hok's free hand flashed backward, twitching the second javelin from its strap.

Behind came the patter of other feet, and a comradely panting. That was Zhik, a younger half-brother and favorite companion. Not as tall as Hok, nor as old by three years, the stripling nevertheless was sturdy and handsome. Hurrying from behind, he poised a spear of his own.

At that moment the shaggy thing rose from the side of the deer, rose on two legs to face them. It was not a bear.

Barely thirty paces separated the youths from the creature that disputed their right to the meat.

It had hands and feet, coarser and larger than Hok's own; it was a head shorter than he, but broader, it wore no clothes, and coarse hair thatched shoulders, chest and knotted limbs. Then its eyes grappled Hok's across the intervening space.

Shrewd were those eyes, in a broad, shallow skull like the skull of a hairy lizard. Fire was in them, and intelligence and challenge. The two bright crumbs of vision, under their coarse brows, did not falter before Hok's gaze as would a beast's. Meeting the stare, startled and fierce on his own part, the hunter-youth was aware only vaguely of the rest of the face—out-flaring nostrils, a sagging lip, a hideous rank beard and forelock, ears that seemed to prick like those of a wolf.

Zhik drew in his breath, as if setting himself for the cast. "Wait," interposed Hok quickly, he did not know why.

A third human figure had come from behind the Chief, their father and head of the party, a hunter still vigorous and swift but unable to match forever the pace of these two eldest sons. He, too, balanced a javelin ready, and at sight of the creature before them his heavy, fulvous beard gaped open in amazement.

As for curiosity itself, this last reenforcement daunted it. Slowly, clumsily, it backed away. They saw that it moved with knees bent, back hunched, arms hanging forward like an ape's. Its eyes still turned to Hok, and it was at him it blurted a sudden guttural sound of defiance. Then, turning upon broad, flat feet, it made off with awkward speed. It dropped into a fold of the meadow, remained invisible for moments, then reappeared beyond, well out of javelin range, to plunge into a thicket.

Zhik, the youngest, recovered his high spirits first. "*Gnorrl!*" he shouted after the fugitive, in imitation of its throaty cry. Hok laughed, and repeated, "Gnorrl!" A new word was born into man's language, a word that would be used often and fearfully in days to come.

All three moved forward, tensely cautious. It was as though they expected the slain deer to spring up, alive and savage. But it was dead enough. The Chief turned it upon its back, then drew a knife of ground buckhorn. Hok knelt to help him open the belly and peel the hide, but Zhik gazed searchingly around the horizon for long moments.

"That Gnorrl left a bad stink here," announced the Chief. "Let us drag the meat away." They did so, but still smelled, or fancied that they smelled, the vanished monster.

The rest of the party came up as the butchery went on—first Asha, latest wife of the Chief, a plump, handsome young woman in a doe-skin tunic, with a naked boy-baby straddling her hip; next Barp and Unn, half-grown sons of Zhik's dead mother, carrying on their unwilling shoulders part of the camp luggage; after that Eowi, full sister to Hok, a slim and agile maiden also loaded with bundles; finally Asha's other child, the little girl Nohda, old enough to walk but not to carry any burden save her clout of hare's fur and a necklace of red seeds. As these arrived, they helped in cutting up the meat. Under the Chief's direction the four quarters, the loin and the tenderloin, the heart, the liver and the kidneys, were detached and wrapped in the new hide. The ribs, head, shins and entrails remained for hyenas and ravens.

By now it was mid-afternoon, and the party went no further than a willow-fringed creek before the Old Man uttered the laconic order "Camp." At once Hok and Zhik produced axes and cut long, supple willow poles. Several of these were thrust into the ground and bent together for central lashing. Over them Asha and Eowi drew the tent-cover of sewn hides. Barp and Unn gathered kindling and heavier wood, and the Chief reverently produced from his belt-pouch the long, charred fire-spindle. A piece of soft, punky wood served as hearth, and upon this he twirled the spindle-point, crooning the while the ancient prayer to the fire god.

When a bright blaze had been kindled, the meat was apportioned. The Chief got, as was his right, the tenderloin. Next choice, steak from the rear quarter, went to Asha. Hok's turn came third, and he cut slices of liver and impaled them on a green willow withe. As he put them to the fire, his sister Eowi came and squatted beside him.

"What happened?" she asked. "None of you have told, but—"

"Gnorrl!" cried Zhik, whipping himself erect and standing at gaze.

They all saw it then, far down the stream. It had crept up to watch them, and at the chorus of bewildered shouts from the campers it now shrank back into a little clump of bushes—a broad, repulsive shagginess that blended into the leafy shadow.

Hok had dropped his liver into the fire and had sprung to where javelins were planted, tip in earth, for a quick snatch. His back tingled and crawled, in the place where, with his long-ago ancestors, a manelike strip of hair had bristled. His eyes measured the distance to the bushes. He ached to throw a spear.

Eowi came to his side again. She had rescued his dinner from burning, and was touching it with a gingerly forefinger. "I know now without being told," she said softly. "That was the danger. What was it, a man?"

"No," returned Hok, his eyes still prodding the clump. "It was a Gnorrl. Zhik made the word."

The Chief was laughing loudly and carelessly, for the sake of the frightened children. After a moment, the others joined in his merriment. Barp and Unn whooped bravely at the silent bush-clump, waving their axes and exhorting the Gnorrl to show himself and be slain. Hok returned to his cooking, tried a lump of liver experimentally, and finally ate with relish.

But as the sun drew to the horizon's edge, Hok's uneasy mood came back upon him. The Chief and Zhik betrayed something of the same feeling, for they brought wood in great billets and built the small fire into a large, bright one. Hok sought serenity in toil, looking to his weapons. Did not the edge of his axe need retouching to make it sharper? With a bone chisel he gouged away at a tiny flake of flint.* But this aided neither the appearance nor the keenness of the weapon. He started suddenly.

It had grown dark as he handled his gear, and he thought that something heavy and stealthy moved outside the patch of firelight. He felt as he had felt in childhood, when his mother, the Chief's first wife, still lived and told of how her dead grandfather had moaned outside the tent to be let in.

The Chief, who likewise felt the need for occupation, tightened the already perfect lashings of his javelin. "We shall sleep outside tonight," he decreed. "Zhik, too. The women and children in the tent, and a big fire kept up until morning. One of us will watch."

"Well said," agreed Hok. "I am not sleepy. I shall watch first."

It developed that Zhik was not sleepy, either, but Hok was the elder and had made first claim. The Chief then raised his voice, calling "Silence!" At this customary signal for bed-preparations, Asha, carrying her baby, entered the tent. Eowi and little Nohda followed, and then Barp and Unn, who took their places at either side of the doorway. The Chief and Zhik lay down by the fireside.

Hok, left to his vigil, fought hard against the perplexing sensation of being watched. He tried to say that these were fancies. The chill at his backbone came because it was a spring night, and he had come farther north than ever before. The uneasiness was because of the strangeness. Any prudent hunter did well to watch, of course; if the Gnorrl came . . .

It did not come, and at last he grew sleepy. The stars overhead told him that night's noon was at hand. He nudged Zhik into wakefulness, and lay down.

He dropped into sound slumber, for moments only as it seemed—then started to his feet with a wild, tremulous wail for fear and pain ringing through his head. Catlike, he commanded himself upon the instant of rousing, could see, stand and clutch at his javelin.

It was dawn. The crying came from the direction of the tent. Something huge and dark was carrying something small that struggled and screamed. The Chief, too, was there running with axe uplifted.

But a shaggy arm drove like a striking snake. Hok saw the Chief spin and fall heavily. The Gnorrl—it was that, of course—fled with its prize.

When Zhik and Hok had gained their father's side he was dead. His skull had been beaten in, as though by the paw of a bear.

---

* The flint weapons of these early dawn men were quite excellently chiseled, done with painstaking care, and an amazing accurateness. They were far superior to the rough, crude hand axes of the Neanderthal. Their edges were sometimes razor sharp, and their shapes ranged from perfect spear tips, to a variety of axes (to which handles were cleverly attached) to slim-bladed knives and even double-edged tools.

Chapter II
Blood for Blood

The others were out of the tent by now. There was considerable hysterical weeping, notably by Asha, who had lost baby and husband in almost the same instant of time. Hok, bound by racial custom not to speak to his stepmother, told Eowi to comfort the distracted woman. In the gray dawn he and Zhik reconnoitered.

A look told them everything. Strange, enormous tracks behind the tent, a slit in the side covering—the Gnorrl, plainly, had crept up here. By guess or scent it located the sleeping place of Asha's baby son. A single strong rip with a sharp flint would give egress to a hand. The Chief, the only camper awake, had been slapped to death like a fly—the strength of the Gnorrl must be enormous. Had Hok pursued blindly, he might have died as well.

The brothers looked pallidly at each other. "You are the Chief now," Zhik said.

Hok had not thought of that, but it was true. He, with manhood barely upon him, must be leader, defender and father of this handful. The realization steadied him, and he made plans for the space of two breaths, while Zhik waited expectantly.

"I am going to take up the trail," said Hok at last. "Stay here and bury him." He gazed down at his dead father. "Heap stones, to keep the beasts away. Then break camp. Keep your weapons in hand, and have Barp and Unn do the same. Yes, and Eowi too, and Asha when she stops crying. Be ready to fight for your lives."

"I understand," nodded Zhik.

"When you are ready to march, wait here and watch. I will make a damp-wood fire. When you see its steam, come and find me there."

Zhik nodded as before, started to ask a question, but tactfully paused. Hok knew what was on his mind, and issued a final command.

"This trail leads north. If I make no signal by noon, you will know that I will never make signals again. You, Zhik, will be the Chief. Lead the others south."

"South?" echoed the younger brother. "Where there is danger?"

"Maybe the danger is less than what we have found."

He turned away without waiting for further comment from Zhik. He saw to his javelins, slung them in place, thrust axe and knife into his girdle. Neither speaking nor looking back, he strode quickly out of the camp, picked up the spoor of the raider and followed it at a trot.

The footprints of the Gnorrl betokened a long, wedge-shaped sole, point-heeled and splay-toed. Its greatest weight was at the outer edge—Hok remembered how grotesquely the legs had bowed. From force of habit he gauged the length and tempo of the stride, the considerable bulk supported on these strange feet.

The sun was well up by this time, and he glanced quietly but expertly around. The country was all rolling meadow, well grown with grass and heather—rain must fall plentifully. Far to the north he saw wooded heights, from which a river wound its way. He made out distant dark spots at the brink—wild cattle drinking, and a rhinoceros or two, proof of the good hunting to be found. Upon his right, the east, ran at an angle the silver thread of the creek beside which his people had made camp, and he could descry a little ravine through which it ran to join the river.

The track before him doubled back toward the creek and into the ravine. Cautiously Hok approached, his javelin poised. He did not enter the cleft, but scouted along its lip. Where it opened at the riverside he picked up again the tracks of the Gnorrl. A gout of blood showed beside them and, farther on another.

The trail led him along the sand of the river's brink to where, winding upstream around a rocky height, it was lost to view. He paused a moment under the high rock before turning the corner. Breeze brought him a tiny wreath of smoke.

"The Gnorrl uses fire," he said to himself. "It cooks."

No question what cooking it did this morning. More blood spotted the track at juncture of bluff and river. Here were many footmarks of varying degrees of freshness, easily classifiable as made by three pairs of feet—two large, one smaller. Hok slipped gingerly around the point of the bank.

Just beyond the steep slope of rock curved away from the water. It made a crescent-shaped open space, tufted here and there with grass, almost entirely enclosed by the bluff and the river. At the center point of the bank's inward curve, at twice Hok's height above the sandy soil's level, opened the wide mouth of a cavern. A tall man, standing on its floor, might touch the roof by jumping, and across the opening from side to side would take four considerable stretchings of the legs. A jagged shelf extended above this grotto, filling it with shadow, and an ancient water channel descended diagonally from the cavern's lower lip to the ground, making a natural runway up which two men might mount abreast. The air was full of the musky odor Hok had first known beside the slain deer.

This was the den of the Gnorrl.

Hok's heart drummed partridge-like within him, but he advanced without hesitation. His nose curled with revulsion at the stench. He got a better view of the cavern, and from its shadowy interior came forth new wisps of smoke, laden with the smell of roasting.

He gained the foot of the runway—deep and narrow and not as steep as the bank to left and right. It was worn as smooth as Hok's palm; the feet of Gnorrls must have trod it for uncountable years. Hok set up a fierce yell, beating with his javelin shaft on the stone.

"Hi, hi! Gnorrl, Gnorrl! Come out, baby-killer!"

He heard movement in the cave overhead. A deep rumble made reply. Hok laughed scornfully: "Gnorrl! Come out and eat a javelin!"

Something crept into view at the lip of the opening—a dark, coarse hand, matted with hair, that grasped the shoulder of rock beside the deep-worn runway. Above it peeped the low, bearded face of the Gnorrl.

It looked like the one Hok had seen yesterday, the one that had wanted to fight for the deer's carcass. This time he refused to shrink from its biting gaze. "Come out, Gnorrl!" he urged. "Show me your body!"

As though it understood, the thing rose into view. It swung a stick abruptly; from that stick's cleft end a stone whizzed, over Hok's instinctively ducking head. The Gnorrl charged down after the missile, lumbering swift as a rhinoceros.

Hok let fly with his javelin. The upward angle was strange, but he knew his weapon. There was a hum in the air, an abrupt *chock* as the stone point drove home, and the Gnorrl fell on its face. It came sliding down the sloping way. Almost at Hok's feet it subsided quivering, blood from its gasping mouth soaking the sand.

A coughing roar sounded from above, where another Gnorrl had appeared. This was a female, almost as thickset and fearsome as her fallen mate. She saw at once what had happened. Her voice shrilled into a scream as she dashed vengefully down the narrow way.

Hok snatched his second javelin from behind his shoulder, but there was no time to flex and throw. He quickly planted the butt-end in the sand, dropped to one knee, his right hand supporting the shaft at an angle. Even as the she-Gnorrl launched herself through the air, her great hands crooked like talons for the grapple, he point-blanked the flint head into the center of her gross breast. The force of her own assault impaled her, and Hok, releasing the javelin sprang lightly to one side. She floundered down, the blood-gushing point springing into sight between her hairy shoulder blades. Hok caught hold of the shaft just at the lashings and with a wrench pulled it clear through her body.

She still lived, trying to squirm around and clutch his ankle. He danced away, laughed, and stabbed through her eye into the brain. As she sagged into death he freed his javelin a second time and sprang across the carcass of the male to mount upward to the cave.

Inside the dark chamber crouched a halfling male cub of the Gnorrls. Its frightened face was greasy with eating, and one hand clutched a gnawed morsel. Hok darted a glance at the fire and the interrupted cooking. That one glance was enough. He set foot on the floor of the grotto, watching the young Gnorrl.

It chattered at him like a crazy monkey. Monkeylike, too, it was fuzzy of body, nervous of movement. Hok chuckled harshly. The young Gnorrl understood, tried to retreat. In a far corner of the grotto opened a small inner cave. Hok let the thing win almost to that hiding; then, still chuckling, he darted his javelin.

Just before noon, called by Hok's damp-wood smoke signal, Zhik and the others arrived. They found their new leader seated at the foot of the runway, scrubbing his weapons with sand.

"The Gnorrls are dead, all," he told them. "I have thrown all their bodies into the river."

"Is this their cave?" asked Eowi, her eyes round.

"No," replied Hok. "It is our cave now. Get green wood, burn and drive away their smell. In this good game country we stay."

Chapter III
Skirmishing

The grotto, with its water-worn sides and floor of hard-trodden earth, was more than large enough for all the surviving members of Hok's family. In odd corners the new tenantry found the possessions of the slain Gnorrls. Near the runway were heaped throwing stones, to be flung by hand, or with a cleft stick, as Hok had seen and survived. A horizontal crack, like a natural shelf, held other stones, rather roughly chipped into tools and weapons. These included hide-scrapers that Asha and Eowi appropriated, also several almond-shaped flints, like haftless axes, to be held in the hand.

Gnorrls, too, were learning something about the weapons of the strangers. On the morning after the first night in the cave, Zhik went for a brief scout down river and returned to say that Hok's three victims had washed ashore in the shallows not far away. Barp and Unn slipped off to see the corpses, and returned shuddering. From the shelter of a willow clump they had seen half a dozen living Gnorrls moaning sadly over the dead. Eventually, said the frightened boys, these grotesque mourners had carried the bodies away.

"They are like men," commented Zhik. "They weep for the slain and take them away to bury them. The Gnorrls worship."

"They are evil," growled Hok, and dutifully boxed the ears of Barp and Unn, warning them to avoid all contact with Gnorrls.

Other clues to Gnorrl-life turned up in the cave, and from them Hok and Zhik deduced that the shaggy people lived in rock-sheltered communities during winter, rather wretchedly and scantily. Warm weather would set them roving in small groups again, even as true men loved to do. It had been only chance that the last three Gnorrls idled in these winter quarters.

If this was an established stronghold of the things, they would want to come back, and there would be trouble; but Hok felt that the odds lay with the defenders. The Gnorrls would have to gather upon the open half-moon of sand below, in fair view, and could scale the runway only a pair at a time. The ledge above the grotto precluded attack from that quarter. Wisdom and watchfulness would do the rest.

Accordingly the young chief announced that whenever he and Zhik were absent, Barp and Unn must keep faithful watch at the river's brink, where they could see up and down stream, while the women held themselves ready at all times to hurl spears or stones against attackers.

The next adventure with Gnorrls was Zhik's alone. He and Hok, hunting for meat, went in opposite directions across a plain on which grazed deer and cattle. When the brothers met later in the day, Zhik was minus a javelin and trembling with rage and excitement.

He had stalked a wild cow, crept through high grass and pierced her heart with a javelin. Then, before he could come up to her, the nearby thickets had vomited Gnorrls, and he had been forced to run for his life.

It was the last lone hunt of either young man for many months. Not only did they roam together thenceforth, but they made more preparations at the cave. From leg bones of deer and bison they cut serviceable points, which they bound to straight shafts. Thus they made plenty of good javelins for throwing or stabbing. These they stacked near the runway, ready for instant use. Hok instituted target practice for Barp and Unn and the women.

But the feared attack did not come until autumn's frosts made the mornings white. It was then that the Gnorrls tried to take back their ancient shelter.

They made a rush early in the dawn. Only Asha was awake, and had gone down to fill a skin water-bag. The hairy ones were upon her in a triumphant yelling wave. Even as Hok and Zhik started to wakefulness on their pallets at the lip of the grotto, they saw their stepmother beaten to death with stones and ragged clubs, and her limp body dragged backward out of sight beyond the shoulder of the bluff.

The girl Eowi, who had been on guard but had gone into the rear of the cave, rushed back and hurled the first vengeful missile. It was one of the bone-tipped javelins, and it split the broad face of a Gnorrl as he gained the very foot of the runway. He sat down, howling through a sudden mask of blood, and his blind wriggles blocked for the moment a concerted charge. Meanwhile the open space below seemed thronged with the enemy, and into the heart of them Hok and Zhik threw spear after spear. No need to take careful aim at such close quarters; four of the besiegers were down in as many breaths, and the rest gave back. The occupants of the cave shouted their defiance, and Barp threw a lucky shaft that pierced the shoulder of a Gnorrl slow in retreating.

Screaming loudly, the wounded monster sprang into the water and wallowed there. Again the cave-holders yelled, as at a good omen.

Five human battlers were in action—Hok, his three brothers and Eowi. The Gnorrls numbered six times as many, and seemed to have some sort of attacking order. One or two growled commandingly, and made gestures as if to show

how few were the enemy. A volley of stones spattered the defenders, and Unn yelled in startled pain. There was another dash for the runway.

This time it was almost taken. Barp, Unn and Eowi threw their javelins too quickly and, although the casts took toll, a flood of Gnorrls came scrambling up the narrow channel in the rock. Hok and Zhik, who had reserved their casts, now skewered each Gnorrl, but the others swarmed over the fallen and up to the very level of the cave floor. It looked like defeat, destruction. Desperately Hok slashed with his axe of flint, hewing down the foremost attacker. Then it was Eowi who turned the tide of battle.

She had snatched a blazing stick from the breakfast fire, and ran to thrust it into the snarling face of the next Gnorrl.

That move was genius, or luck, or both. Had the Gnorrl been killed outright, he would have fallen, and his comrades behind rushed trampling over his body to the conflict. But as the flame kindled his rank beard, there went up from his great mouth a hideous howl of pain and terror. He toppled backward on the slope of the runway, flung out his thick arms and grappled those behind him. Crazed with fear and agony, he tried to fight his way back through the press. Two or three other Gnorrls slipped and fell. Zhik, greatly daring in his extremity, sprang upon the fallen bodies, spurning them with his moccasined feet and thrusting with a javelin at those beyond and below. A moment later the whole attack was demoralized and the Gnorrls, dragging some of their wounded, fled wildly back to the river, then along the edge and out of sight beyond the bluff.

Hok and his people waited cautiously while the morning sun lifted itself in the sky by the breadth of a hand. Then they descended to the ground and reconnoitered. The Gnorrls were not to be seen up or down river, nor on the meadow below the bluffs. On the sand lay nine of the creatures, dead or dying. Three of these had fallen upon the runway and had slid to its foot. Hok and Zhik finished the last struggles of the wounded with judicious axe-blows and hurled the bodies into the river, where they drifted quickly away.

The only loss on the side of the defenders was Asha, whose corpse had been borne away by the retreating Gnorrls—for what purpose Hok well knew. He grimaced in revulsion at the idea, but reflected that his stepmother's flesh was a repast dearly bought. Lesser mishaps were a deep cut on his own cheek, which he could not remember sustaining, a wrenched ankle for Zhik, and a big bump on Unn's forehead from a flung stone.

The following day a heavy snow fell, and the Gnorrls menaced them no further. Undoubtedly the strange aborigines of this northern meadow-country found another shelter from the cold. Once or twice, when hunting on fair days for snow-bogged elk and bison, Hok and his brothers saw Gnorrls at a distance and were interested to see that the natural sagginess of the things was augmented by crude mantles or skirts of skin. However, there was no more fighting, no close contact even, during all the season of snow.

Several times in midwinter the cave-dwellers found themselves on the shortest of rations, but all of them were young and vigorous, and all lived to see the spring.

Hok, sauntering southward with Zhik, saw something else.

"Smoke," he pronounced, pointing afar in the direction whence they had come a year ago. "Fire—of men, like ourselves." He looked at his brother sidewise. "You can be chief for a time—and Barp and Unn have grown. They can help hunt and guard."

"Why do you talk like this?"

"I am going south," replied Hok. "Where there are men, there will be women. I want one."

Chapter IV
The Capture of Oloana

It was one of the smallest pools in the wide, dense-grown forest, a blob of shiny dark over which boughs and vines laced greenly. The girl turned over lazily upon its quiet surface, swam three strong, slow strokes to the brink and waded out.

Her golden, glistening body, its curves at once strong and graceful, would have intrigued even critical modern eyes. She shook herself, like the handsome wild thing she was, and drops showered from her like rain. Then she donned her single garment of soft doeskin, that looped over one round shoulder, covered her young bosom's swell, fitted her waist and dropped like a short skirt to mid-thigh. Her slender feet slid themselves into sandals of well-tanned bison leather. On her right arm she fastened a sort of bracelet, strung out of small gay shells. Finally she rummaged in a belt-pouch, brought out a shallow-toothed comb of deer-horn and, leaning back against a half-rotten stump, began to arrange her great, damp cloud of blue-black hair.

Oloana, daughter of Chief Zorr and beloved of his giant lieutenant, Kimri, feared nothing. The huntsmen of her little tribe had long ago driven the beasts before them, even in this northern edge of the forest. As for human menace, who would dare so much as look at her, for all her new ripeness of beauty?

Yet someone was looking. He lounged easily in a tree-fork overhead, lithe and motionless as a leopard in ambush. Unlike Oloana's dark folk, he boasted a head of hair the color of a lion's mane. His face, clean of beard, was ruddy rather than sallow brown, and a scar across one young cheek added sternness to his undeniable good looks. He wore moccasins instead of sandals, and the fashion of his axe, dagger and javelins was strange to the people of that forest. He was Hok, who had come south to find a woman.

His gray fighter's eyes sparkled with honest relish, and his wide mouth spread wider in a grin of approval. His big hands opened and closed, as though eager to seize what he saw. Noiselessly he rose erect on his perch, twitching a javelin from his shoulder-loop. The long shaft whizzed in the air, and thudded into the stump beside the girl.

Oloana screamed in panic, tried to spring away—in vain. The sharp flint point had pinned fast the edge of her skirt. Even as she struggled to tear loose, a happy laugh rang out above her. A long-limbed, bright-maned demon fell out of the branchy heavens, lighted easily upon moccasined toes, and caught her by the elbow.

"You are mine," he announced, in a language similar to her own.

She screamed again, and struck at him. Her fist rang on a chest as hard as wood. He laughed the louder, plucked away the tight-wedged javelin as easily as Oloana would have gathered a wildflower. Still struggling and shouting in fear and rage, she felt herself whirled lightly up and across his shoulder. Then he ran.

For another, deeper shout answered Oloana's appeal, to be echoed by more shouts. Her people, the dark forest men, had heard her and were coming. Hope came to the girl and added fire to her battle for freedom. Hok chuckled and fled the faster.

Still more loud came the pursuing cries. Racing figures could be seen among the thickets behind—black beards and brandished weapons.

"No javelins!" bellowed one great voice, the voice of Zorr, Oloana's chieftain father. "You might kill her. Run him down!"

"We have him!" howled back the gigantic Kimri, who was to marry Oloana. "He's running toward the ravine!"

It was true. A narrow, ancient creek had cut deeply into the loamy floor of the forest, and there the ravisher must perforce come to bay. Oloana ceased her cries, fiercely exulting over the imminent reckoning. She heard Hok's sharp gasp of surprise as he spied the ravine, a good five times the length of a man across and nearly double that in depth.

But he did not slacken his pace. Once more the stolen girl screamed, screamed in new and mortal terror, as Hok raced to the very rim of the chasm and sprang out over it.

For one heart-smothering moment Oloana stared down at the rock-torn current far below. They must fall; be crushed—but her captor's free hand had seized a dangling vine. Their weight carried them flying onward, upward, while the far bank rushed to meet them. Hok's feet found the brink, clutched solid footing, and he paused to look back.

The black-beards were lining the other bank, cursing and raving. Several lifted their spears. Hok laughed and swung Oloana's body before him.

"Do not throw!" commanded Zorr anxiously. "Cross after him!"

"None of you dare the leap," taunted Hok.

"I will follow!" screamed Kimri, towering among his fellows.

"Follow, then," laughed Hok and plunged anew into the forest, dragging Oloana by the wrist.

For eternities, it seemed, he urged her to match his tireless lope. She ceased to struggle and drag backward—her strength was nothing to his. They came into strange country, beyond the northernmost limits of Zorr's latest northern foray. Just as the girl wondered if her captor would never grow weary, he came to an abrupt halt.

They stood in a little clearing among birches, with a trickle of water crossing it, and to one side, a rocky hummock with a yawning cave entrance.

"We camp here," said Hok, Oloana's eyes threw black hate-fire and her bosom heaved as she probed her mind for names bad enough to call him.

"You dared to steal me!" she flung out.

"You are a woman," he replied, as if that explained everything. "I am a man. My name is Hok."

"A man?" she echoed scornfully. "With no beard?"

"With my people, men without mates pluck out their beards. Now I shall grow mine."

Her voice trembled with rage and contempt. "You have the face of a boy. Kimri will crush your skull like a toadstool."

"Let him try," said Hok. "Come into the cave."

"I won't. Not with you."

He lifted her from her feet and carried her in. She screamed once more, though help was far away, and her flying fists glanced from his chest and face like hailstones from a cliffside. Setting her carefully upon the floor of the cave, he barred the door with his own great body.

"You are beautiful," he informed her. "What is your name?"

She sprang at him and bit his shoulder. Snorting, he pushed her away.

"We had better rest," he decreed. "Both of us."

Deep night found a fire blazing at the cavemouth. Hok had speared a grouse in the clearing, and was grilling it on a twig. When it was done, he offered the choicest morsel to Oloana.

She shook her head, her eyes bright with tears. "When will you let me go?" she pleaded for the hundredth time.

"I have said that you are mine. I am a chief in the country to the north. We will go there."

"Go there?" she repeated. She began to edge toward him.

"What is your name?" demanded Hok once more.

"Oloana," she breathed, coming closer. He gazed in happy surprise.

"Oloana. That is a beautiful name. When we—"

Out flew her hand. She caught one of his javelins from where it leaned at the entrance to the cave. Whirling it, she plunged the point straight at her heart. Hok's hand, still clutching a shred of his supper, threw a haunch more swiftly. The deflected point glanced off across the base of Oloana's throat, leaving a jagged thread of crimson. A moment later Hok twisted the weapon from her hand.

"You might have killed yourself," he scolded.

She burst into new tears. "I hate you. As soon as you let me go, I will try again."

Hok took from his shoulders the javelin-strap. Pulling her wrists together, he bound them.

"My feet are free," she cried and, springing up, darted from the cave and leaped across the fire. Before she had run half a dozen steps he overtook her and dragged her back. This time he bound her ankles with his girdle-thong. She lay helpless but tameless, and glared. Hok hugged his knees and studied her with worried eyes.

"I wanted you the moment I saw you," he said plaintively. "I thought you would want me, too."

She spat at him, rolled over and closed her eyes.

"Sleep then," he conceded. "I shall sleep too."

In the morning he woke to find her propped upon bound hands, her eyes turned unforgivingly upon him.

"Let me untie you," he offered at once.

"Do," she urged bitterly. "Then I can kill myself."

"You must be thirsty," he said. "I will bring some water."

In the clearing he plucked a dried gourd from a spreading vine. Deftly cracking it, he cleansed the withered pulp from one cuplike piece and filled it at the stream. Carrying it back, he offered it to Oloana. She neither moved nor spoke, but when he held it to her lips she drew her head away.

"You do not eat or drink," he said. "You will die."

"Let me die, then."

Hok gazed at her perplexedly. Things were not going as he had hoped. What would life be like, with a sullen, vengeful woman who must go always tied lest she run away or kill herself? Suddenly Hok saw an awful vision—Oloana still and voiceless, with blood flowing from her heart where nested his javelin. So vivid was the mental picture that he dashed the back of his hand to his eyes.

"I hate you." Oloana snapped at him.

He rose and stooped above her. His hands caught the leather that bound her wrists, his muscles suddenly swelled, his breath came in a single explosive pant. The cord broke. Bending, he hooked fingers under the thong at her ankles. A heave, a tug, and that, too, tore apart.

"Run away," he bade her dully.

She rose to her feet, amazed.

"I thought I had you," he tried to explain, "but even when you were tied, I did not have you." His brow creased at his own paradox. "You hate me. Run away."

"You don't want me now?" she challenged him.

His hands grasped her shoulders. Their faces were close to each other. His stare fastened upon her sulky mouth, as full and red as a summer fruit. How sweet that fruit would taste, he suddenly thought. His face darted down upon hers, their lips crushed together for a whirling moment. Clumsy, savage, unpredicted, it was perhaps the first kiss in human history.

Still more abruptly, Hok spun and fairly raced out of the cave, out of the clearing, into the forest away from Oloana's black eyes and fruit-red mouth.

Chapter V
The Capture of Hok

But he did not run far. Somehow it had been easier to run yesterday, even when encumbered by the struggles of Oloana. Hok lagged. His troubled young eyes sought the ground. His feet took him where they wished.

The day and the distances wore away like rock under falling water. Hok did not eat. Twice or thrice he drank at singing brooks, then spewed out the water as though it were brakish. Once he saw a wild pig rooting in a thicket and by force of habit reached back for his javelins. Then he remembered that he had left them leaning at the door of the cave. He had left Oloana there, too. He could get more javelins, but never another Oloana.

It was nearly evening. He walked slowly down a game-trail, less watchfully than he had ever walked since childhood. Before he knew it, something huge and swarthy flashed from behind a broad tree-bole and flung itself upon him.

On the instant Hok was fighting for his life. One glimpse he caught of that distorted, black-bearded face before they grappled—it was Kimri, the giant who had sworn to follow him and take Oloana back. He was an adversary to daunt the bravest; but Hok had faced Gnorrls, which were more horrible. Smaller but quicker than Kimri he locked his arms around the huge body in a python-tight underhold. His tawny head burrowed with canny force into Kimri's shaggy cascade of black beard, driving under the heavy jaw and forcing it upward and back.

The dark forest man's huge muscles began to sag as Hok increased the leverage. Hok's heel crooked behind Kimri's. Hok's entire weight came suddenly forward. Down they went with a crash of undergrowth, Kimri beneath, while his lighter opponent's oak-hard fingers drove through the beard-tangles, finding and closing upon the throat beneath.

But a flurry of feet drummed down upon them as they strove on the ground. Two sinewy hands clamped under Hok's chin from above and behind. He bit a finger to the bone, heard his new assailant howl, and next instant was yanked bodily away from the prostrate Kimri. As he tumbled he tore free, whirled catlike to get his feet under his body, and rose swiftly to face a second black-beard, shorter and older than Kimri. But something darted forward to quiver a thumb's-breadth from his head—a long, lean dagger of chipped flint.

"Move!" the newcomer dared him. It was Zorr, Oloana's chieftain-father. "Move—and die!"

Hok stood motionless. Kimri struggled up, wheezing and caressing his bruised throat with shaking fingers. He gulped welcome air into his great lungs, then seized his fallen axe.

"No!" barked the father of Oloana. "The rope!"

At the voice of authority, Kimri dropped his axe and jerked from his girdle a coil of rawhide line. Quickly he flung a loop of it over Hok's shoulders and ran the rest of it round and round, pinioning the prisoner's arms to his body.

The chief lowered his dagger. "Where is Oloana?"

Hok shook his head.

"Answer!" roared Kimri, and struck Hok's mouth with his horny palm. Blood sprang to the bruised lips as Hok curled them in scorn.

"Coward's blow," he mocked. "Untie me, and I will take the head from your body like a berry from a bush."

"Where is Oloana?" demanded Zorr again.

"I do not know. I set her free."

"You lie," raged Kimri. "Tell us where you have hidden her."

"I say that she is free," insisted Hok.

"Tell us," Kimri repeated, "or we will kill you."

"You will kill me anyway," said Hok.

Kimri's beard bristled, and again he clutched his axe. As before, the chief intervened.

"It is nearly night, Kimri. We will camp. He can think until morning." He studied Hok narrowly. "Tomorrow, if his mouth is still empty of the words we want, we will stuff it with hot coals."

Kimri grunted acquiescence, and the two herded their prisoner through the trees for nearly a mile. In a grove at the top of a brush-faced slope they came to a halt, shoved Hok violently down at the base of a big tree and tethered him between two gnarled roots with the free end of the rawhide. Then Zorr kindled a fire with rubbing sticks, chanting a ritual similar to the one Hok's people used. The forest men produced flitches of dried venison from their belt-bags and began to eat, talking in low tones.

Darkness came. The two dark men stretched and yawned. Kimri rose, larger than ever in the fireglow, and came to the big tree. He examined the knots in the cord and gave the prisoner a kick.

"Tomorrow you will talk," he prophesied balefully, and returned to the fire. Zorr built it up with hard wood. Then the two lay down and fell into quick, healthy slumber.

Hok listened until the men by the fire began to breathe regularly and heavily. Then he tried his bonds, cautiously at first, lastly with all his strength; but the rawhide had been passed many times around him, and was drawn tight. He could not make it so much as a crack.

Forced to lie still, he thought of Oloana and her resentful beauty, of how he had not tamed her. With the dawn his enemies would awaken and question him again. Zorr had hinted of fire-torture. He, Hok, could truly tell them nothing, but they would never believe. If he were lucky, he might goad them into finishing him off quickly.

He dozed fitfully at last, started awake almost immediately. What was that? . . . He felt, rather than heard, the stealthy approach of light feet. The ash-choked fire suddenly cast a bright tongue skyward, and Hok saw the newcomer—a woman, crowned with clouds of night-black hair. Oloana had tracked him down.

She bent to look at Kimri, at her father. Another tongue of flame rose, and by its brief glow she saw where Hok lay. Immediately she tiptoed toward him. Her right hand lifted a javelin—his javelin, brought from the cave.

Kneeling, she slid her other hand across Hok's chest to where his heart beat, beneath two crossed strands of rawhide. He looked up into her deep eyes and grinned mirthlessly. If she but knew how she was cheating her father and her lover, if she could foresee their rage when they would find him slain and beyond torture! The flint point came down. He braced himself to meet it. Then—

The rawhide relaxed its clutch upon him. A strand parted, another and another, before the keen edge of the javelin-point. He was free. Wondering, he rose to his feet, chafing his cramped wrists and forearms. Oloana, close to him in the dim night, cautioned him to silence with a finger at her full lips. Then she beckoned. Together they stole away toward the edge of the bluff.

Oloana, going first, brushed against leaves that rustled. A roosting bird squawked in sleepy terror and took noisy flight.

Next instant Kimri's awakening roar smote their ears. Oloana ran like a rabbit down the slope, while Hok swung around to meet the clumsy rush of his late captor. A collision, a clasping hug, and again the two who wanted Oloana were straining and heaving in each other's arms. Loose earth gave way beneath their feet. They fell, rolled, and went spinning over and over down the declivity.

At the bottom they struck with a thud, flew sprawling apart, and rose to face each other. The giant hung back from a new encounter, his hand groping for his dagger-hilt. But then he flinched and stiffened. In the gloom Hok fancied that the wrath on the hairy face gave way to blank surprise. A moment later the huge form pitched forward and lay quivering.

Oloana, revealed behind him, wrenched the javelin out of his back. She made an apologetic shrugging gesture with her shoulders.

"I knew that you would win," she stammered, "but I—wanted to help."

From the trees above rang Zorr's shouts for Kimri. Hok extended his hand for the javelin, but Oloana held it out of his reach.

"No," she pleaded. "He is my father. Let us run."

Toward dawn, back at the cave where they had parted, Hok again coaxed fire from rubbing sticks. In its warm light the pair relaxed, their shoulders to the rock.

"Oloana," Hok now found occasion to ask, "why did you follow me? I thought—" He paused.

"Yes," she nodded shyly. "I, too, thought I hated you. But, before you left me, free and alone, you—" She, too, fell silent.

"What was it?"

"This." Her round arms clasped his neck. His lips groped for hers. It was, undoubtedly, the second kiss ever to be achieved.

"Tomorrow we start north," he said, after a time. "My people are there. You will like my brother Zhik, and my sister Eowi." He frowned. "Yet there are things you will not like. The Gnorrls."

"Gnorrls?" she repeated. "Are they animals?"

"No. Not animals."

"Men? Evil men?"

"They are not men, but they are evil. Like the spirits that trouble sleep."

"I shall not fear them," she said confidently.

"You, Hok, will fight and kill them."

"Yes," he agreed, "I will fight and kill them." Then he paused, wondering how he would manage it.

Chapter VI
The Capture of Rivv

Hok and Oloana had not much time in the days that followed to discuss or dread the Gnorrls. As a matter of fact, Hok forgot the creatures, as much as any man could forget, having once encountered them. But when, in sight of the familiar plain and the bluff-bound river he saw on a ridge a cautiously peering hulk that was neither beast nor man, the old hate and revulsion came to him—came almost as strongly as though for the first time.

It was then that Hok, clutching Oloana's wrist with a crushing strength that surprised even her who had seen him grapple the giant Kimri, half growled and half quavered a command never to stand, walk or sleep without a weapon in reach; never to relax guard; never to stir from the home shelter alone. Oloana then knew that if her mate feared anything, it was the unspeakable Gnorrl. Solemnly she promised to obey and strictly she kept that promise.

Approaching the old rock-defended camp by the river, Hok's trained eye glimpsed footprints that told him of the presence of his kind. When he and Oloana drew into sight at the narrow entrance between rock and water, young Unn, who was standing guard, first sprang erect with poised javelin, then burst into an uproar of welcome. Others dashed into view—Eowi, Barp and Nohda, all larger and lovelier to Hok's sight than when he had left them. There was a gay reunion in the open space before the cave; Hok introduced Oloana, with the simple declaration that she belonged to him and must be respected as much as his own right eye. Eowi smiled shyly but winningly at the strange girl, and cemented a friendship with a present—the finest of the scrapers captured from the Gnorrls.

When the first hugs and shouts had subsided a trifle, Hok suddenly stiffened to attention. Two figures—living human figures—crouched in the shadow of rock.

"Who are these?" he demanded at once.

"Oh," replied Eowi, with the carelessness employed in speaking of chattels. "Zhik found them."

"Zhik?" Hok had missed his brother. "Where did he find them?"

"Here he comes," interjected Barp. "Let him tell it himself."

Zhik trotted into view, bearing the hide and choicest parts of a slaughtered goat. He whooped at sight of Hok, and the two exchanged affectionate fraternal roars and buffets. Then came once more an introduction of Oloana, and finally Zhik's explanation of the strangers.

He called them to stand forth—a middle-aged man with a great slate-colored beard, and a slim young girl, several years Eowi's junior and as dark in complexion as Oloana. The man's name was Kaga, and the girl was his daughter, Dwil. Zhik considered them his property, by right of discovery, capture and defense against the Gnorrls.

"Two days after you left," he told Hok, "I was hunting, and saw four people—these two, another man and an older woman. I did not know if they were friends, and I kept out of sight. They were new in the country, for they did not watch for Gnorrls. Before they knew it, Gnorrls had risen out of the grass and bushes—nine." He held up that many fingers to illustrate.

He went on to say that the second man, foremost of the quartet of strangers, had been seized and literally plucked to pieces by three Gnorrls—his arms and legs had come away in those terrible paws, like flower-petals. The others ran. The oldest woman had gone next, being overtaken by two of the pursuing monsters, and had died under their rain of blows. Before the last two could win to safety, a stone hurled from a Gnorrl's cleft wand knocked the gray-bearded man down. His daughter had rallied beside him, facing hopeless odds. She meant, it seemed, to die in his defense.

"But the Gnorrls did not know I watched," continued Zhik, a trifle complacent in memory of his scouting skill. "I jumped up, and let them have both javelins, one after another. I wounded two. A rock came my way, but it went to pieces in the air, and it only cut me." He laid a finger on his temple. A scar showed that had not been there when Hok had left. "After that the girl—Dwil—threw her javelin, and it went through a Gnorrl's arm. That was three down in less time than I have told it; the others ran before they were well aware of what had happened, and carried away their wounded and the two they had killed."

He told how he had gone up to the fallen man and the girl. She had been most suspicious, and drew a stone knife, which Zhik took away from her. Then, as her father regained consciousness, Zhik possessed himself of their other weapons and obliged them to return with him to the cave. There they had been assigned most of the community chores—wood-carrying, water-fetching and so on.

Hok talked to Kaga, whose language like Oloana's was understandable. He learned that the unlucky four had been searching, as had Hok's own people a year ago, for new and uncrowded hunting grounds. They had friends, far to the south and east, who waited for them to return and report.

"You have friends?" Hok repeated. "You will stay here." For he knew that the Gnorrls would be quite enough to fight at one time; he wanted no human adversaries in the neighborhood.

"Yes, you will stay here," seconded Zhik. Then he looked at Hok, at the manifestly happy Oloana, and finally at Dwil, who lowered her eyes. Zhik muttered to his brother: "I want to ask you something."

"Wait," said Hok, with all the authority he could muster. His own courtship of Oloana had been so brief as to be almost instantaneous, and he had by no means repented at leisure; yet he wanted to be sure before advising Zhik, or permitting him to mate with this captive girl.

"You are growing a beard since you got Oloana," Zhik added. "It looks well."

"Wait," said Hok again, and his brother sighed dolefully.

Hok asked to hear more about the Gnorrls, and learned that they were more numerous by far than a year ago. Not a day passed but what Gnorrls were sighted, sneaking through thickets or among boulders, watching all that their human foes did, but seldom offered fight. Zhik did not like this, nor, when he heard of it, did Hok.

"They are planning something," said the older brother. "They care for their dead—means that they worship, as we do. If they worship, they think. And they are many, where we are few."

It was early in the summer that Barp and Unn, rambling together in search of marmots, came back in a scamper to gasp out what they had seen—a group of Gnorrls overpowering a human stranger. He, a slim youth whose budding beard was dark, was patently unused to Gnorrls. They had stalked and surrounded him almost effortlessly. But the novelty of the tale was the forebearance of the captors. Instead of tearing their prey to pieces, they had bound him with long strips of tough bark and dragged him away northward. Hok frowned and pondered. Then he asked Barp and Unn if this was not a joking untruth.

Both lads protested earnestly, and offered proof of their adventure. Unn, stealing in the wake of the Gnorrls and their prize, had picked up something that might have been torn from a man's belt during the brief struggle—a pouch made of striped cat-skin. Hok took the article, opened it and made an inventory. There was a hank of split-sinew thread, three or four flint flakes, a bone awl ground to a slender point, with a spiral line incised around it. At sight of this last item, Oloana cried out sharply and ran to clutch at the splinter of bone.

"My brother!" she exclaimed.

"What?" grunted Hok. "What about your brother?" Zhik and Eowi both came near to listen.

"It is his," replied Oloana. "I made the awl for him. The man the Gnorrls took is my brother—Rivv, the son of Zorr."

Hok pursed his lips. "He must have followed us here. He should have kept his eyes open."

"The Gnorrls did not kill him," said Barp again. "I wonder what they will do with him."

Oloana was looking only at Hok. "Go," she said suddenly. "Follow him."

"Huh?" ejaculated her husband. "Follow your brother?"

"See if you can get him away from the Gnorrls."

That began a discussion that did not end with supper or with bedtime. Hok pointed out that Rivv had come north to avenge himself on Oloana's abductor—which meant Hok; Oloana answered that Rivv meant only to help her. Hok argued that the Gnorrls probably had killed Rivv; Oloana made reply that, had they intended to do so, they would not have bound him and carried him away. Hok complained that Rivv was of a strange and enemy people, and Oloana flashed back with considerable heat that she herself was of that same race.

The night long there was little sleep for anyone within earshot of the two, and in the morning the debate came to a conclusion that feminists might regard as epoch-making—the woman had her way. Hok made over temporary command to Zhik, took his weapons and a few slices of dried meat, and left camp to follow the brother of Oloana.

Chapter VII
Rescue from the Gnorrls

He picked up the trail where Barp and Unn had said he would. It was easy to trace, and as he went northward he saw, in one or two spots, the clear-made tracks of the Gnorrls. Among them were distinctive narrow prints of a true man's foot.

Thus guided, he crossed a little range of hills and came late in the afternoon to a place where a year ago he had mentally set up the boundary of his hunting grounds. A sloping height rose beside the river that poured down from the north, and to the west were trees. Between the rising ground and the river at the east was a very narrow strip of sandy beach that had once been part of the river bottom. At the southern end of this strip lay a long jumble of boulders, washed there in ages past by a greater river, now choked with sand and coarse weeds.

The Gnorrls had taken this low, narrow way and he followed them, observing as he did so that the water had once risen here to considerable height, but that it had fallen and now ran swiftly in its narrow channel, almost in rapids. Emerging from the pass, he saw that the northern face of the rise fell nearly perpendicularly, and then beyond a small meadow began semi-wooded country, with thickets and clumps of trees and brush.

At that time Hok may have been close upon the heels of the Gnorrl band, which would be hampered by its prisoner; but he went no farther into strange country, camping before sundown on the sand at the northern end of the tunnel between river and height. The next morning he resumed his hunt, but moved slowly and with a caution that may have been greater than was necessary. Thus, he did not approach bushes, groves or other possible hiding places of Gnorrls without an examination from all sides. His second night out from home he spent without a fire, climbing a tree for safety from possible wolves or cave-lions. The following day he spent in a treacherous and foggy swamp, and barely emerged before it was nightfall again. This time he camped in a sort of burrow made by the uprooting of a great tree, and in that shelter he dared build a fire.

Dawn almost brought disaster, for it was a fearsome scream that brought him instantly erect, awake and alert as the wild instantly are, to face the leap of a tawny, spotted sabertooth.

He had no time to more than seize his javelin, drop to one knee, and present its point to the charging monster.

Braced against the ground behind him, it impaled the great cat from breast to spine.

Scrambling from beneath its great weight, he wrenched his spear from the carcass and then stared down in awe. Fearsome things in this Gnorrl country.

At noon of his fourth day he moved cautiously over an open plain, sparsely covered with grass and heather, and bearing scant sign of game. It was a poor country up ahead, he guessed, and he could not blame the Gnorrls for wanting back the pleasant territory he and his were now holding.

The lips of a valley lay northward, apparently formed by a curve of the river on a lower reach of which his people camped. Toward this depression led the tracks of the Gnorrls he followed—they must be within it. At once he dropped down and began an elaborate creeping approach, flattening his long body in the heather. After a time he saw a Gnorrl, then several more, emerge from the valley and strike off westward, as if hunting. He waited for them to get well away, then resumed his lizardlike advance.

The sun dropped down the sky, and down, as Hok drew nearer to the valley. He paused at last—he heard a noise, or noises. That was the kind of noise made by many throats and tongues; more Gnorrls must be in the valley. At length he won to the brink, gingerly parted a tussock of flowered stalks, and gazed down a rocky incline upon the floor of the valley.

It was full of Gnorrls.

The steeps that made up this slope of the valley fringed a great rounded level space, a sort of vast enlargement of the guarded camp ground which Hok's own people had taken from the Gnorrls. In ancient times the river had been higher and wider up here, too; this had been a bay or even a lake. Now a big dry flat was visible, and this unlovely people gathered upon it, to make fires and rubbish-heaps and stenches.

The Gnorrls sat, singly or in family knots, around small, ill-made hearths. Some of them toasted bits of meat on skewers of green wood, some chipped and knocked at half-finished flints, women chewed the fleshy surfaces of hides to soften and smooth them. Little Gnorrls, naked and monkeyish, romped and scuffled together, shrilling incessantly. Some of the old males grumbled to each other in the incomprehensible language of the race, pausing now and then to wag their unshapely heads as though in sage agreement. Over all went up an odor, so strong as to be almost palpable, of uncleanliness and decay and near-bestiality—an odor that had something in it of reptile, of ape, of musky wolf, as well as something like none of these.

Hok tried to judge how many there were. Like most intelligent savages, he could count up to a hundred—ten tens of his fingers—but beyond that was too difficult. There were more than ten tens of Gnorrls, many more. With something of a pioneering spirit in mathematics, Hok wondered if there could not be a full ten of ten-tens; but there was not time to count or add or compute, even if he could marshal the figures in his head.

Thus he estimated the situation, as a good hunter and warrior should, half instinctively and almost at first sweeping glance. His second glance showed him the specified item he had come to note and to act upon.

Close to the foot of the declivity, but well to the left of where Hok was peeping down, stood a little gathering of Gnorrls, all full-grown males, and in their center a tall figure. This one had a smooth dusky skin, a lean body, an upright head with a black young beard—Rivv, no other. He stood free, though Hok thought he could make out weals upon chest and arm that bespoke recently-loosened cords. One big Gnorrl held Rivv by the wrist. Another held out something to him.

Hok stared, absolutely dumbfounded. By all mysteries of all gods and spirits, known and unknown, the Gnorrl was trying to make Rivv take a javelin! Why? Hok almost thrust himself into view, in his amazed eagerness to see more. Then it came to him.

The Gnorrls had puzzled it out. Man, fewer and weaker than they, had one priceless advantage, the javelin and the art of casting it. That was why Rivv had been seized and kept alive. The Gnorrls meant to learn javelin-throwing. Rivv was to teach them.

To Hok's distant ears came the voice of Rivv, loud even as it choked with rage: "No! No!" And the Gnorrls understood his manner, if not his words. Their own insistent snarls and roars beat like surf around the captive, and the Gnorrl who offered the javelin thrust it into Rivv's free hand and closed his fingers forcibly upon it.

Far away as he was, Hok could see the glitter of Rivv's wide, angry eye. For a moment the prisoner stood perfectly still, tense, in the midst of that clamoring, gesticulating ring of monsters. Then, swift as a flying bird, his javelin hand rose and darted. The Gnorrl who held Rivv's wrist crumbled with the javelin in his breast.

For one moment the other Gnorrls stood silent and aghast, their snarls frozen on their gross lips. In that moment a loud yell rang from on high. Hok sprang erect on the bluff, waving his javelin.

"Rivv!" he trumpeted. "Rivv, brother of Oloana! Run! Climb here!"

As if jerked into motion, Rivv ran. So, a breath later, did the entire squatting-place. Rivv dodged through his ring of captors and headed for the height.

"Climb!" yelled Hok again, at the top of his lungs. Rivv climbed.

He was active, but the rock was steep. He had barely mounted six times his own height when the first of the pursuing Gnorrls had reached the foot of the ascent. Stones and sticks of wood rained about Rivv, but by some unbelievable fortune none of them hit. He gained a great open crack in the face of the bluff, and swarmed up more swiftly. The Gnorrls were after him, scrambling like monkeys for all their bulk. But Hok, falling at full length above, reached down a great hand, caught Rivv's shoulder and dragged him up by sheer strength.

"Who are you?" panted Rivv, staring at his rescuer.

Instead of answering, Hok carefully kicked a great mass of stone and gravel down upon the climbing Gnorrls. To the accompaniment of fearsome howls, both men turned and ran.

It was a splendid dash on deer-swift feet given the further impetus of danger behind. Nor did it cease until, long after dark, Hok and Rivv came to the edge of the swamp and there made a fire. They talked long, and before they slept they touched hands, shyly but honestly, in friendship.

Chapter VIII
Alliance

The midsummer dusk was thickening, and the half-moon of open space in front of Hok's cave was filled—with skin tents along the curve of rock, with cooking fires, and with men and women and children. Most of them were strangers, quiet but suspicious, dark of hair and sallow of skin in contrast to the tawniness and ruddiness of Hok's brothers and sisters.

At a central place, small so that men might draw close, sat three grave figures. Hok, the host, was youngest and largest and most at ease. Opposite him, his long fingers smoothing his beard, was stationed Zorr, Oloana's father, who had last viewed Hok as his prisoner. The third man was the heavy, grizzled Nukl, head of the clan from which Kaga and Dwil had come.

"This meeting is a strange thing," said Zorr weightily. "It has never happened before that peoples who hate each other have met and eaten food and talked together."

"Yet it must be," rejoined Hok, very slow and definite in his defense of the new idea. "I sent your son, Rivv, back to you with the word to come. He and I are friends. He vouches for you. This is good hunting ground, as you yourself have seen."

"I think the meeting is good," chimed in Nukl. "Kaga and Dwil came from you to say that you were a true man, Hok. They said that there would be country and game enough for all of us."

"Why do you do this?" Zorr demanded. "It is not usual that a hunter gives away part of his good country for nothing."

"There are the Gnorrls to fight," said Hok. Every ear within sound of his voice pricked up. Men, women and children paused at eating or chattering, to listen.

"I have told you about the Gnorrls, and of how Rivv and I saw that they intended to return and eat us up," went on Hok. "My people have killed many, but there are more Gnorrls than we have javelins. You, Zorr, bring four men with you, and Nukl has five, counting Kaga. My three brothers, whom I sent north to spy on the Gnorrls, and I myself make four. With the women and boys who can throw spears, we number three tens. That is enough to fight and beat the Gnorrls."

He felt less sure than he sounded, and perhaps Zorr guessed this. The southern chief pointed out that his own people came from the south, where Gnorrls were not a danger.

"But too many hunters live there," argued Nukl on Hok's side. "The game is scarce. You, Zorr, know that. Once or twice your young men and mine have fought over wounded deer."

"There will be no reason to fight for food here," added Hok. "Men need not kill each other. If anyone wants to fight, there will be Gnorrls."

"The Gnorrls never troubled us," reiterated Zorr.

"But if they come and eat my people up, will they stop here?" asked Hok. "They have learned that man's flesh is good, and they may come into your forests, looking for more."

Nukl sighed. "I think that I will have to stay. Zhik, the young man who is scouting up north, is going to take Dwil, the daughter of my brother Kaga. Kaga wants to stay, and I should help him if he is in danger." His eyes shone in the fire light. "Anyway, Gnorrls have killed two of my people. I want some of their blood for that."

"That makes the southern forest less crowded," pointed out Zorr. "Plenty of room and game for my people."

But Hok had gained inspiration from what Nukl had said. "Zorr," he replied, "your son, Rivv, has asked for my sister, Eowi. She wants him to have her. I shall give her to him—if he remains with me."

Zorr stiffened, almost rose. He muttered something like a dismayed curse. Hok continued serenely:

"Two of your children will be here when the Gnorrls come. Also, if Oloana is spared, there may be a son, a child of your child—"

"I shall help you against the Gnorrls," interrupted Zorr, savage but honest in his capitulation. "When does the fighting begin?"

"When Zhik warns us," replied Hok gravely. "It may be many days yet."

And the remainder of the summer went in peace. Hok and his new allies hunted successfully and ate well. Once a lone Gnorrl ventured close, to be speared and exhibited to the strangers as an example of what they must face sooner or later. The greatest item of preparation was the fashioning by every person in the three parties of new javelins—sheafs and faggots of javelins, some with tips of flint, others armed with whittled and sharpened bone.

With the first chill of autumn, Zhik and his two younger brothers came loping into camp, dirty but sound. With them they brought the news that Hok had long awaited with mixed attitudes of anxiety and determination. The Gnorrls were on the march. Up north in their country a blizzard had come, and it had nipped the brutal race into action. They were advancing slowly but steadily into their old haunts in the south.

"We are ready to meet them here," said Zorr at once, but Hok had another idea.

"No, not here. A day's march toward them is the best place."

Quickly he gave orders. Only the children remained at the camp before the cave. Barp and Unn were ordered to take charge there, but teased and begged until at the last moment Hok included them in the expeditionary force that numbered full thirty men, women and boys. In the morning they set out northward.

Hok, pausing at a certain dam-like heap of stones, lifted his palm to signal a halt. Then he gazed as if for the first time at the rocky slope beyond the narrow level between it and the swift waters.

"We shall fight the Gnorrls here," he said definitely, and almost added that he was sure of winning.

Zorr and Nukl moved forward from their own groups, coming up at Hok's elbows. They, too, studied the ground that Hok was choosing for battle. "How shall we fight them if there are so many?" Nukl asked.

Hok pointed at the slope. "That leads to the top of a bluff," he said. "The Gnorrls will come from the north side, and will not climb, but will enter the pass between it and the river. They can come upon us only a few at a time, and we will have these rocks for a protection."

"How do you know that they will choose the pass?" was Zorr's question. "They may go to west, and through those trees."

Hok shook his head. "Before they come, we will set the trees afire—the sap is almost out of them. And the Gnorrls will go east, into the pass."

Zorr and Nukl glanced at each other, and nodded. Then Zorr addressed Hok again: "It sounds like a good plan, better than any other. What shall we do?"

"Zhik says that there are more than ten tens of Gnorrls. A few of us shall meet them on the plain beyond here, and make them angry. Then those few will run and draw them into the pass. After that it will be as I say." He gestured toward the crown of the slope. "You, Zorr, shall be the leader there, with most of the men, to throw javelins upon the Gnorrls when they are close together and rushing into the narrow pass."

"But you?" prompted Zorr.

"I shall go, with my three brothers, to meet the Gnorrls."

"Me, too," said Rivv, who had come forward and overheard part of the discussion. "I can run almost as fast as you."

"Very well," granted Hok over his shoulder. "You, too, Rivv. Now we must camp. First we will get ready, as far as possible. Are the women here with the extra javelins?"

"They are," Nukl answered him.

"Then I want some—as many as ten—laid midway between here and the far end of the pass." He turned around. "Oloana!" he called. "Bring the javelins that you have."

She came obediently, and they went together to lay the weapons at the point he had chosen. For a moment he studied them, then on inspiration picked them up and thrust their heads into the earth, the shafts pointing almost straight upward. "They will be easier to the hand," he commented.

"Why do you do that?" asked Oloana.

"You will find out," said her mate, rather darkly. Again he raised his voice. "Zhik, are you back there? You and Dwil take more javelins to the north end of the pass, and stick them there as I do here."

Zhik shouted comprehension of the order, and shortly afterward went trotting by with Dwil. When the two rows of spears had been set in place, all four young people returned to the barrier of stones. It was nearly evening. Hok, Zorr, and Nukl, as chiefs of their respective bands, kindled fires with appropriate ceremonies. Then there was cooking and discussion. Hok repeated his defense plan for all to hear.

"The women will stay back of these stones," he concluded, except those who go, before battle, to set fire to the trees. I do not want anybody to run, unless the Gnorrls get the upper hand. Then those who are able must try to get back to the cave. The Gnorrls will have a hard time capturing that."

All nodded understanding, and both Zorr and Nukl spoke briefly to their own parties, in support of Hok's arrangement.

"When will the Gnorrls be here?" Hok then asked his brothers, for the benefit of all listeners.

"Tomorrow," replied Zhik. "Probably before the sun is high."

"Good," said Hok. "We must be awake by dawn, and take our places for the fight. Tonight we shall sleep, and be strong and fresh."

But as the camp settled to repose, he could not sleep. Neither Oloana nor Zhik could induce him to lie down. For hours after all had dozed away, he sat in the brisk chill of the night, on a large stone of the barrier. Now and then he weighed his axe in hand, or picked up a javelin and felt its shaft for possible flaws. When he did close his eyes, he slept sitting up. Four or five times he started awake, trembling from dreams that the enemy was upon him.

Chapter IX
Conquest

The Gnorrls were up betimes the next morning, stretching, grumbling, fighting for drinking room at the creekside. A light frost patched the ground, and necessitated building up of the fires that had burned low overnight. There was considerable bad feeling here and there, because some who had brought abundant food would not share with those who had little or none; but three or four of the largest and oldest sternly curbed all debate, even striking with clubs those who persisted. At length the advance began.

The formation was simple, but it must have been arranged and commanded by the wisest of those dark psyches the workings of which no human being can understand or even imagine. The fighting males of the horde went first, in a single line, close-drawn and several deep. In front walked the chiefs—perhaps their chieftainship was one of tradition or election, perhaps physical superiority, perhaps chance. All bore weapons—clubs, stones, or cleft sticks with pebbles in place for casting. Some carried the rough spears they had made in imitation of the javelins that had wrought such havoc among the Gnorrl-people.

Behind this wave of armed males came the females and the young, in a completely disorganized mass. Possibly they were held in that position as a supporting body in case of defeat; more probably they attended simply as curious watchers of the triumph that seemed already achieved. Sometimes the half-grown cubs of this rearward body would scamper forward as if to join the fighting males, but they were always driven back with warning yells and sometimes with missiles.

That the Gnorrls were able to communicate, to think ahead, and to obey their leaders can be demonstrated by the fact that they maintained their formation and their forward advance while the sun mounted higher and higher toward the top of the sky. The morning was considerably beyond its halfway point when, pushing through a belt of scrubby willow that marked the dry bed of an old creek, the foremost of the Gnorrls came out upon a plain with the river to the left and a bluff beyond.

First of all they saw a great cloud of murky vapor above the trees that grew to the right of the bluff—smoke. Tongues of flame flickered among the branches. The Gnorrls faltered in their advance. Through that woods they had intended to go, and to kill men, their foes and persecutors on the rolling meadows beyond. Now they must go far to the west and so avoid the fire, or negotiate the narrow pass between bluff and river.

Even as their strange minds comprehended the new factor in the campaign, and before they could grapple with it for answer, a loud and mocking whoop sprang up from the quiet ground before them. A tall, tawny man in leopard skin rose into view from behind a bunch of dried thistles, so close to their ranks that several Gnorrls marked and recognized his features—it was Hok, their foremost tormentor. A moment later an answering yell, from several throats at once, echoed from a point due east. Almost at the river bank four more young men popped up from a little hollow in the earth.

The Gnorrls blared their own challenge, a fearful blast of rage and menace. Before it swelled, Hok had cast one, then the other of his javelins. The second was in the air before the first had struck down a leader of the Gnorrls, and it flew beyond its fellow to pierce the heavy paunch of a warrior in the ranks. Then Hok yelled again, in derision and invitation, and began to run—not back toward the burning trees or the face of the bluff, but almost parallel with the front of the Gnorrl array.

As he did so, his companions by the river threw their javelins, four in a volley and then four more. At that close range, barely forty paces, there was little chance of missing. Every javelin of the eight took effect, and four or perhaps five of the stricken Gnorrls died on the spot or within moments. An earth-shaking howl of execration went up from the army of brute-men, and the whole left wing of it charged full at the four audacious javelin-casters, who turned, laughing, and fled. The right wing had crumpled up on itself to follow and overtake Hok, who still raced along the front of the line. A rain of ill-aimed missiles fell almost upon him, but the range, though short for a javelin in good hands, was too great for accuracy with stones or clubs. As the Gnorrls lumbered with deadly intent upon him, came almost within reach, Hok swerved to his right and made for the pass.

For him, at least, it was a chase that taxed him to the utmost. Zhik, Rivv and the two younger lads ran easily away from their pursuers, but Hok, who had fled at an angle to draw the right-hand portion of the massed Gnorrls after him, had a near thing of it. So close did the swiftest Gnorrls win to him that they stretched out huge, eager hands in readiness to clutch him. But at that point he, too, turned into the straight line toward the pass and ran in earnest, four flying strides to three of the best Gnorrl.

Zhik and Rivv had reached the point where the bluff rose, and a moment later Barp and Unn caught up. There, at the head of the narrow lane between rock and water, they came to an abrupt stop, and the Gnorrls as they ran heavily thought that these amazing adversaries were calmly plucking reeds or saplings that grew there in a clump. But the reeds were javelins, and Hok stopped as he ran, to let them hiss over his back. Two of his closest pursuers fell in mid-leap, somersaulting and writhing. That gave him a moment to run slower, whirl around, shout new insults and make again a gesture of invitation to the conflict. Three more of those nearest him collapsed before javelins thrown by the men at the head of the pass. Then Hok had joined his companions, and they were dashing along beyond the bluff.

That the Gnorrls were not cowardly was plain from their headlong and unfaltering charge against the shrewd javelin-volleys that had found more than a dozen targets; but they could be cautious as well. The moment the leaders reached the head of the pass, they stopped, as any sagacious wild thing should. Their instinct demanded that they investigate before plunging blindly in.

As they peered down the narrow strip of beach, on which the flying backs of Hok and the others shrank and shrank with increasing distance, more Gnorrls caught up, paused and peered, too. Then the rest arrived, in a swarm that closed in upon itself, pushing, cramping, chattering, eager to know what went on ahead.

Upon that clot of life, that gathered while the leaders studied the situation during a dozen breaths' spaces, fell destruction. From the crown of the bluff overhead came javelins and more javelins, and the yells of triumphant marksmen who take pride in seeing their casts fly home. Zorr, Nukl and nine others were hurling shafts as swiftly as they could seize them from the great scattered store at their feet.

The fire took effect in the midst of the packed throng, and for a moment or so the Gnorrls in that central position were all that experienced and comprehended what was happening. They did considerable screaming and milling before the outer edge of the pack, which could move in defense and retaliation, understood and peeled away and dashed with a fine show of courage at the foot of the bluff.

The Gnorrls could climb, even where human hands and feet might fail at the steep ascent; but it was foolish and vain to advance against the defenders above. Laughing boisterously in their security, Zorr's and Nukl's men centered their attention upon this scaling party. Not a javelin went wrong, and only one Gnorrl reached the brink of the level space above. Him they allowed to mount up and up, after the others had been picked off or had retreated. Mouthing his inarticulate war-cry, he scrambled pluckily up among them; and every man of the eleven stabbed home in his hairy body.

In the meantime, Hok and his four companions had come to a halt once again, midway down the pass. Their saucy yells and capers stung the pursuers into motion as before. There was a great struggle to rush down the narrow way, so much of an effort to be first that half a dozen or more of the Gnorrls were thrust by their fellows into the rapid water, where they were whipped howling away and under, helpless to fight to shore. Meanwhile, the fugitives waited only until the rush was well under way before snatching more javelins from where they seemingly sprouted and sending them singing into the face of the attack. So narrow was the front, so close together the Gnorrls, that half a dozen casts raised a veritable heap of bodies, damming for a moment the onset of the others. And yet again the decoy party, not one of whom had suffered as much as a scratch, turned and fled, distancing all pursuit.

The Gnorrls stubbornly followed, while javelins from in front and from the height above claimed lives and lives. A new blizzard of flint points seemed to pour from a heaped barrier of rocks. To this they charged panting, and now their enemies did not run. They thrust and hacked from behind their defense, and more poured down from the slope, striking from the flank. Women at the rear screamed encouragement and threw javelins. When the supply was gone, they threw firebrands and rocks.

One who fights thus hand to hand remembers little about it afterward, nor cares to. He is only glad when it is over. It does not make much difference even to realize that he has won.

Hok would not hold his head still as Oloana tried to lay a broad green leaf upon the gash that showed the bare white bone of his chin-point.

"How many are killed?" he asked once more.

"Zorr, my father, is only stunned," she replied. "For a time we thought that Rivv would be our chief."

"I am your chief," Hok reminded her. "Nukl is dead?"

"Yes, and Kaga. Perhaps Zhik will lead that party after this."

"I think that Zhik will limp always," Hok's voice was low, but Zhik, sprawling nearby, overheard.

"I shall not limp always," he shouted defiant. Then he shut his mouth and gritted his teeth as Dwil dragged strongly upon his ankle. She, too, turned a protesting face toward Hok.

"The leg bone is broken," she conceded, "but I will put sticks on each side, and hold the break shut with clay. My people know how to cure lameness of this sort. He will walk before winter is over."

"Kaga is dead," said Oloana again, "and I think three more of those who were on the high ground. They charged and killed many Gnorrls, but the Gnorrls were able to get at them. They had no barrier of stones." She smoothed down the leaf. Hok's blood was thickening under it and would hold it in place.

Barp, spitting blood from broken teeth, was returning from a survey of the pass.

"How many are dead?" asked Hok.

"I do not know. Very many. Far north I could hear the others crying like rabbits in the snare."

"I am glad that some were left alive," said Hok suddenly. "They will always be afraid to come back here, and will tell other Gnorrls, and the young ones who are born after them, of how terrible we are."

Barp did not share this approval of the situation. "I want to fight Gnorrls again some time," he said, rather wistfully.

Hok put out his hand to cuff affectionately the lad's untidy head. "Wait," he counseled, "You have many years. There is enough game country for all of us who are left alive, but more men will come. When this country is crowded, you and others can go north and capture new ground from the Gnorrls."

"And when the Gnorrls are all killed?"

"That will take a very long time," said Hok, "but when the Gnorrls are all killed, men will own everything."

Hok Goes to Atlantis

The Legendary Land of Atlantis

All peoples and continents have memories of it, so it must have existed—fair, lost Atlantis, the land that was the greatest in all the ancient world for strength and beauty, and was swallowed by the maw of ocean.

Where did that bright country once rise? An island in the mid-Atlantic, of which only the mountaintops show today as the Azores and the Canaries? In the heart of the Sahara, near the peaks called Atlas? In the Gulf of Mexico, teaching Aztec and Maya to pronounce the mystic word Atl?

Or was it the vast rich valley between the continents, the warm, green country that glaciers never touched, that existed when our fathers, the first of the true men, were wresting Europe from the bestial paws of the monstrous Neanderthalers? That valley is filled with blue water today, and is called the Mediterranean—the midst of the Earth. Its forests and meadows are drowned; but from them may have come the people who bore and cradled culture in the nations around that inmost sea-nations "like frogs around a puddle," as said Plato, who also knew of Atlantis.

Tremendous as was the glory of that lost land, more tremendous still was her doom. It beggars imagination, the rush and triumph of ocean, breaking the barrier and filling the sunken basin that was like an inverted continent, drowning forests, cities, nations. How could even one escape from the judgment? Yet some one did, and told his children of what he had seen and escaped, and they told those who came after them, down to the present day. How else could we know?

Who was that survivor of Atlantis? He must have been a mighty man. He may even have been the hero we remember as Hercules.

Chapter I
The Horsemen and the Valley

The wolves had been chasing Hok for three days.

Hok had become great, in body and in fame, since the days when he, barely past his boyhood, entered the northern game-lands and purged them of the inhuman Gnorrls.* Maturity had made him taller than ever, and more bull-strong and leopard-swift and lion-tawny. He wore a short, soft beard, like the fiber which his wife, the lovely Oloana, beat from autumn grasses and wove into baskets and pouches. He ruled a fighting tribe of valiant hunters and handsome women, and also was respected and deferred to by the allied clans of his brother Zhik and his father-in-law Zorr. His hunting grounds yielded fat game, and there were still Gnorrls to fight if the time passed heavily. Yet Hok had not outgrown his enthusiasm for exploration; and so, telling Zhik to command for him, he had gone away on a spring jaunt to the south and west, into country he and his did not know.

And the wolves, a good forty of them, picked up his scent and hunted him through the forest for three foodless, sleepless days and nights.

Now they gave tongue exultantly, for they were driving him toward a great cliff, against which he must come to bay; but Hok, who ran like the deer and fought like the lion, also climbed like the ape. He scaled the rocky wall nimbly, laughing backward at the famished howls of the pack, and dragged himself to the brow of the cliff in the bright morning. Standing erect, he gazed afar into a valley.

But such a valley! It stretched down and down, gently but ceaselessly. He gazed into sloping meadows, with groves beneath them, and water-courses, and broken country, for the distance of many marches—falling down, down, down, gently but steadily. As for the valley's other side, it was lost in far blue

---
* Stone age men called the Neanderthal beast-men Gnorrls.

mist, as though it were hidden beyond a piece of the sky. Things were green and fresh, and Hok heard birds, saw the cautious motion of game in tall brush. It must be a good hunting land. If he had not cast away his two flint-headed javelins at the wolves—it was always that way when you had nothing to throw. Here came some horses toward him, around that thicket.

No, not horses—men! . . .

No, not men—but not horses, either!

Hok's bright beard stirred with excitement. He shaded his blue eyes with a wide, hard palm. Surely the things had hoofs—four each—and horsey tails. But why did the heads and shoulders of men thrust up from each? And then Hok saw, and wondered still more. The horses were normal, and so were the men—but the men were riding upon the horses, as baby monkeys ride on their mothers' backs.*

It was almost too much for the cave-man's simple mind. To him, a horse was a toothsome creature that yielded much meat—no more. He had never thought of riding one. Yet, whatever his surprise, he did not fear. He moved forward to the rim rock that jutted above the valley, and gazed.

Hok was naked except for leopard-skin kilt and moccasins of tough bison hide. At his girdle hung a pouch and a sheath that carried a finely worked dagger of deer-horn. He bore, too, a stone-headed axe, chipped of blue flint, its keen edge a full span in width. His body was tanned and superbly muscled but, save for his hair and beard, it showed as smooth as a peach. Not even in those fierce days was one apt to see a bigger or better specimen of manhood.

The horsemen came close toward him, then halted their animals at a signal from their leader. There were as many of them as there had been hungry wolves below. Most of them seemed swarthy and bearded, and wore strange clothing, either pale or shining. If it was of leather or fur, Hok had never seen such beasts as yielded it.

The leader came forward by a horse's length—a trim, smooth-faced individual, in a close-fitting garment that seemed to be made of huge fish-scales.

"You on the rock!" came a clear challenge, in a tongue not too dissimilar to Hok's own. "Who are you?"

"Aye," growled a deeper voice from the party of riders, "and tell us your people, and the name of your master."

"I am Hok," shouted back the cave-man. "My people are those who hunt to north and east, beating back the hairy Gnorrls. I have no master."

"The fellow flouts us, he is a madman," grumbled the deep voice, and its owner sidled his horse out to join the leader. This second speaker was squat and black-bearded, and even at the distance Hok saw that he was fierce of face and sharp eyed.

"If I am mad," Hok threw at him, "I may come down and make you fear my bite."

---

* From some such introduction to mounted men must have come the first conception of the centaur.

With an oath, the bearded one lifted himself in his seat, whirled a spear backward, and launched it at the defiant Hok, who stood still to watch the course of the weapon. It was a sure cast, but not too strong, according to cave-man standards. As it came at Hok, he swayed his big, lithe body sidewise, shot out his right hand like a snake, and seized the flying shaft by the middle. Whirling it end for end, he sped it back the way it had come, with all the strength and skill of his mighty muscles behind it. Forty throats whooped, in startled anger as the black-beard spun off of his beast, transfixed by his own weapon. Hok's answering shout of laughter defied them. It had all happened in two breaths of time.

For more than two breaths thereafter, the company hesitated. To them it seemed that the spear had bounced back from Hok and punished its hurler—a feat of magic. None cared to attack magicians in those times. Again the leader spoke:

"I did not order my man to cast at you, and I do not take up his quarrel. Come down and make peace."

Hok did not stir.

"Come down," came the invitation a second time. "I swear by my honor, and by my god, the Many-Legged Ghirann, that you will find only profit."

Hok felt sincerity in that oath. He scrambled down the face of the inner bluff, and strode forward. The leader trotted out to meet him, and Hok grew sure of what he had been suspecting that the leader was a woman, young and of a certain sturdy beauty. Her jaw was square and her nose straight, and her hair and eyes were dark. Around her throat was a collar-like string of sun-glowing lumps. Hok's own blue eyes met her dark ones, and he tossed back his lion's mane of hair.

"Hok, you call yourself?" said the horsewoman. "I am Maie, a chieftainess of Tlanis. Now, by your act, we ride one short. Will you make our band whole again?"

"If I refuse?" he suggested, hand on her bridle-rein. "If I become your enemy?"

She smiled, without showing her teeth. Her tight lips could be hard, he saw.

"You cannot fling back all our spears, Hok. Be wise, take the horse and tackle of him you slew."

A man was leading the sturdy, shaggy brown beast forward. A gourd at its withers danced and gave forth liquid sounds. Hok, who feared not Maie or all her followers, was thirsty enough to let this item persuade him.

"I seek new sights and peoples," he consented. "I will ride with you." And he vaulted upon the proffered animal, confidently though a bit clumsily. "Where do we go, warrior woman, and on what errand?"

Like him, the mounted troop had been exploring. When she heard from him that beyond the rimrock was a great steep cliff, and only trackless forest beyond that, Maie gave a signal to turn. "We will ride back five days to our own place," she said, "and if you are indeed a stone-chipper and cave-dweller, we can promise you your fill of strange sights."

They rode away. When they made camp that night, at a grove of palm-like trees with a spring at the center, Hok had learned to manage his mount in a way that bespoke his great courage and aptitude. There were other wonders harder for him to fathom. The drink in the gourd—wine, Maie called it—was at once fiery and refreshing; the weapons of the man he had supplanted were of strange bright material, neither stone nor bone, but tougher and keener than either, and called bronze by his new companions. Their clothing, too, was partially of that material (Hok was a little scornful of the idea of armor) and partially of woven threads of plant fiber or animal fleece, a fabric like Oloana's grass baskets, but finer.

On the next day he rode beside Maie at the head of the party. The slope took them down and ever down, and as they descended the country grew richer and warmer. Hok, used to tough-grassed meadows, hardy bushes and cone-bearing trees, gaped with wonder upon feathery palms and shrubs with bright flowers a foot across, on clusters of red and yellow fruit, on broad-leafed, sky-aspiring groves, in which played gay-plumed birds and chattering monkeys. Yet his wonder was tinctured with a ghostly sense of familiarity, as though within him stirred the memory of his own dim ancestries, spent in such an environment.

He also learned about the people of Tlanis.

They lived, said Maie, in a stronghold near the ocean, and had neither to hunt nor to steal for sustenance. This great valley, many days' journey across, was full of subject tribes who provided food and other necessities for their rulers in Tlanis. Hok heard in half-comprehending wonder that other animals besides horses were kept captive, and fed fat for leisurely butchering; and that fields were planted with seeds, to bring forth vegetable stores that Tlanis gathered far more surely and easily than the women of Hok's people gathered fruits and nuts in the forest.

He was full of questions, that lasted even to the fifth and final morning of the ride. Maie answered them all.

"And now, great wielder of stone," she asked him at length, "are you not convinced that our way of living is better and softer than yours, among caves and wild beasts?"

"I think," he replied, "that soft living makes soft men."

"But is there not an advantage?"

"I cannot yet say that, Maie."

She smiled as she heard him speak her name. "You might say, at least, that you like me, Hok."

"I do not know yet if I like you," he replied. And no more he did, although he had loved and wanted Oloana within the first instant of seeing her. This woman, Maie, was beautiful and wise, and so far had treated him with more than fairness; but Hok reserved judgment upon her.

He looked again at the collar of gleaming yellow objects she wore. They were beads curiously worked and engraved, and strung on a thread or wire of the same substance.

"What are those?" he asked Maie.

"They are gold."

"What is gold?"—And she sighed, as though she must give up trying to instruct him.

They rode in silence through a lush, sweet-smelling forest, and before noon came out in open country.

A height of rock and earth rose against the horizon. It extended to left and right, beyond reach of the eye, and beyond it shone, or seemed to shine, a bright blueness—water, more water than Hok had ever seen.

Directly ahead of the riders, lifting from the level of this barrier, appeared a broken peak. From its top floated a wispy plume of dark smoke as of a great beacon fire.* And beneath the barrier, at the point where the peak crowned it lay heaped and clustered strange mineral shapes, of various angles and sizes and plans, but somehow ordered in their relationships. Hok stared.

"What things lie there at the foot of the cliff?" he demanded.

"They are houses," said Maie. "Walls and palaces and streets. Did I not promise you wonders? Yonder is the city of Tlanis, which rules the world.

---

* The volcanic character of the rocks at Gibraltar, and across the straits in Morocco, suggests that a great volcano once rose there, shutting back the ocean from the sunken valley which now holds the Mediterranean.

Chapter II
A Summons from Cos

To describe the city of Tlanis, words and comparisons are needed which were utterly strange to Hok as he rode with his new friends down the broad paved trail.

Built at the "end of the world"—that is, under the lee of a mighty barrier that held back the high-piled wastes of the ocean—it was far below sea level, nestled against the steep slopes and lower ledges of the great natural dam of volcanic rock that kept the valley from being flooded. On the landward side, a great artificial wall of stone, cut and mortared, defended the place, with green meadows, orchards and grain-fields close to its foot. Within mighty gates of hewn logs, each a cunning interlacement like a giant's mat-weaving, were squares and clumps of houses, one and two and three stories high. The passage-spaces between—Hok must learn to call them streets—were faced with flat slabs of stone, and thronged with men, horses, litters, wooden-wheeled carts. Maie pointed out to him the various classes of citizens, the laborers, merchants, soldiers, farmers, nobles, beggars.

The city rose on a succession of broad ledges or terraces. Each of these was strung with buildings, a lengthwise street or two, and occasional ramps to other levels. Passing upward, the company came to the market level, in which great arcades and small shops were filled with foodstuffs, fabrics, weapons, utensils, jewelry and other wonders, over which merchants and customers chaffered in yelling multitudes. Hok listened to Maie's explanation of commerce, but the idea of money—pieces of metal, sun-yellow or moon-white—he could not grasp. Maie's gold beads he understood. They were ornaments, such as women prized. Beyond that, gold was nothing—not good to eat, too soft for weapons.

"I think that some of these people work too hard, and others too little," he announced. "That man with the curly beard and the red cloak, whom you call a rich merchant, is too fat. So is that other, who comes and talks to him. They are short-breathed and flabby-muscled. I have a son at home, a little boy, who would live longer than they in the forest."

"This is not a forest," Maie reminded him. They mounted to a higher level, where only soldiers marched or lounged on the street, and dwelt in the sturdy barracks buildings of stone and timber. Here, Maie ordered her horse and Hok's to be led away.

"Come," she said to him. "I will show you places of delight in this city."

They went down a ramp on foot, passed through a howling market—the voices were too shrill to please Hok—and came to an open-fronted, palm-thatched shop with tables, benches, and the scent of food and wine. At Maie's motion, Hok entered, and they both sat down. A slender youth with curly hair brought them steaming portions of meat and vegetables on clay platters, also metal mugs of wine.

"Thank you," Hok said cordially to the waiter. "It is kind for you to give a stranger food and drink."

"Strangers must pay, like others," was the reply, and Maie took coins from her belt-pouch.

"Why is gold given for food?" demanded Hok when the waiter had gone. "It is a matter too deep for me."

"I am afraid you hate gold," smiled Maie.

"All except the beads you wear. They are beautiful."

"You like them?" And at once Maie undid the collar from her neck, and held it out. "They are yours."

Hok was about to refuse, with thanks, when it occurred to him that his wife, Oloana, would demand a present when he returned to the caves. And so he accepted the present, and fastened it around his corded wrist, where it hung like a bangle.

"I have many such beads," Maie told him. "I am rich, I have lands and servants and warriors."

"I never before saw a woman who led fighting men," said Hok.

"My father had no sons, and when he died I became a chief in his place. Is that strange? Will not your little son, of whom you spoke, be chief after you?"

"I hope he will," replied Hok, "but he must earn and prove his right to lead, when he is a man. No son stands on his dead father's legs with us."

The two ate and watched the passing market-crowd. Many a gaze answered theirs, admiring and appraising the stalwart tawniness of the cave chieftain. Hok listened as Maie continued her explanations of the government, the organization and life-ways of Tlanis.

"I still think it is bad," he said, when she had finished. "From what you say, many are poor—some even hungry—in this big sunken valley, which to my notion is the fullest and finest place in the world. There must be food enough for everybody, almost for the taking."

"But there can be no taking without paying," Maie assured him patiently. "All this belongs to our rulers—to Cos."

"Who is Cos?"

"The master of Tlanis, and of the great valley. Of all the world."

"He is not my master," replied Hok doggedly. "I never heard of him. But he must be tremendously big and hungry to eat all the good things I have seen."

"He is a great man, and his appetite is good," admitted Maie.

"But to feed this one man, many go hungry and wretched," argued Hok.

"He has soldiers to feed, and slaves, and more than fifty women," Maie elaborated.

"Fifty women!" cried Hok, and shook his head in refusal to believe. "One is enough for any man."

Maie was thoughtful. "Cos does not think so," she said. "He is always taking more. Just now he wants me, he has asked me to enter his palace. I will be his favorite if I will leave off adventuring and exploring, and give myself to him."

"You love him?" asked Hok.

"My family is great in Tlanis. Since my father died, I have become chieftainess of many men, horse and foot, with other property. Yet, if I accept Cos, I may be even greater."

"Why should you want to be greater?" demanded Hok, and Maie seemed unable to answer. "I do not know if I like Cos," Hok went on. "He takes food from others, and to starve is a bad death. He should go hungry himself, to learn how it feels."

As they finished their food and wine, a tall, lean man in a long robe came up to them. He had a face like a wise eagle, and a tag of beard on his chin. "Greetings, Maie," he said in a high, disagreeable voice. "Cos has heard that you are in Tlanis."

"The ears of Cos are long, priest," replied the young chieftainess.

"He wonders why you do not come to make report to him of your explorations, instead of sitting in a wine-shop with a great bull of a stranger."

"Call me bull, and I will gore you," said Hok, getting up and kicking back his bench.

The eagle-faced man turned pale and shrank away, while Maie hastily interposed. "Do him no harm, Hok; he is a priest, full of wisdom and authority."

"Does the authority allow him to insult strangers?" demanded Hok. He glared wrathfully, and the priest slunk away. Maie stared at her guest from the wilderness. Her dark eyes were full of light, half fearful, half admiring.

"Come," she said. "Cos has spies who have told him of us. He is jealous. We had better both go to see him. Are you afraid?"

Hok feared nothing, and said so. They left and climbed again, to the highest level of the city, a grand terrace overlooking the rising clumps of houses, the wall at the foot of the height, and the fertile valley beyond.

This terrace was carpeted with green grass, and tufted with trees and flowering bushes. Hok wondered still more when he learned that all this planting was by man's labor, as in the fields of grain and vegetables below. Among the shrubbery loomed a great cube of a building, white-pigmented with lime, which Maie called a palace; to one side was a wall, with a gate. The two came to this gate, were admitted by a sentry in armor, and entered.

They stood in a courtyard, paved with white gravel, and completely surrounded by spike-crowned walls, with the blue sky above. At the side where the great building abutted, was a canopy of striped fabric, raised on poles against the warm sun. Beneath the canopy was set a chair, of carved and gilded wood; and upon that chair, flanked on either side by a dozen sentries braced to attention, sat Cos, the master of Tlanis.

Chapter III
Defiance and Doom

Hok stared at Cos, and was deeply disappointed. This man, who ruled more land than one could cross in many days' journey, and more people than one could count in weeks, who could hold back supplies of food from the mouths of hungry tribes, he had already judged as unkind. Now that Cos was in view, Hok saw plainly that he was neither brave nor strong; and courage, strength and fairness were, to Hok, the criterions of chieftainship.

Cos was flabby and bunch-bellied, with sleek, soft calves and biceps. His beard, trained into black curls, cascaded down his bare, dark chest. In the midst of the gleaming thicket of hair showed a plump red mouth, like a spoiled fruit—the mouth of an idle sensualist. His eyes, set as close as a spider's, had shifty lights, detracting from the proud power of brow and nose. He wore bracelets, fillet, and girdle of hammered gold, and his kilt and sandals were embroidered with small glittering stones of red, blue and green.

Maie bowed before him with ceremonious respect. "Hail, Lord of Tlanis," she spoke. "I am come from my explorations, to give you news of unknown wild lands toward the north. Men live there, and other creatures. I have brought with me one such man, himself a master of peoples."

"With whom you prefer to loll and drink," Cos added poutingly. His spider-eyes wandered to Hok. "Give account of yourself, stranger."

Hok did so. Cos listened, with disdainful hostility at first, then with almost greedy interest. As Hok told about his enemies, the hairy, half-human Gnorrls, Cos exclaimed delightedly, and began to ask questions.

"I have heard a little about this race you call Gnorrls," he said at last. "You say they are very strong creatures? And cunning, though less wise than men? . . . Good. I will send soldiers to encounter them."

"To kill the Gnorrls?" suggested Hok.

"Hmmmmm.... No. Not kill them. Capture them. They are strong beyond human strength, and wise enough to learn, but not to overthrow. I will have them brought here, for slaves." Cos licked his loose lips over the prospect of conquest, as a hungry man might relish the thought of good food. "And now, cave-man," he went on, "tell of your own people."

Hok amplified his first remarks about his kinsmen and followers, living and hunting in the country they had wrested in fierce combat from overwhelming spawns of Gnorrls. Cos listened eagerly, as before, then shook his gold-circled head. "I do not think I will enslave your tribe," he said.

"It is well not to try," Hok assured him.

"They would make bad slaves, I am sure," continued Cos. "They are proud, wise, fierce-tempered." He mentioned those characteristics as though they were faults. "No, not for slaves. My men will kill them all, and take their country."

It was briefly and plainly said, even for that age of scant diplomacy and frank statements. Hok glared at this evil, greedy wielder of great numbers and wealth. He wished that he had not told of his people. Anger grew against himself and Cos. Into his throat rose a deep growl of challenge.

"I will go to prepare my people for war," he announced, and turned toward the gate. Cos made a finger-wagging motion. The line of sentries at his left deployed, spears at the ready, to cut off Hok's departure.

"Stay where you are, chief of the stone-chippers," commanded Cos. "My own soldiers will bear the news of war to your land. Be thankful if you yourself escape."

Hok's anger burst like a hurricane. "Unsay those words!" he roared. "Otherwise, you will not live to speak others!" And his big stone axe, stirring in his bulky fist, lifted its blue head like a threatening snake.

Cos grinned, and made another languid motion. The guardsman at his right elbow moved forward.

Hok swung to face this new challenger. The man was beard-tufted and lank, with not half of Hok's volume of muscle; but he threatened the cave-man with a strange device.

It looked like an apple or melon, a round smooth sphere of bronze. From a small hole in it protruded what looked like a twisted, blackened rag, hanging free as the soldier poised it in his ready right hand. The left hand lifted something else—a smouldering saucer of oily fool, like a lamp, not more than a hand's breadth from the dangling tip of the rag.

"Have a care, stone-chipper," chuckled Cos in his curly beard. "If you threaten me, I will sweep you away with the weapon of thunder and lightning."

"Thunder! Lightning!" echoed Hok, in unbelieving scorn. "Do not lie. Only Sky-Dwellers wield such things."

"Ah," said Cos, "and I am as great as the Sky-Dwellers. Ghirann the Many-Legged made their secret of destruction mine."

"It is true, Hok," muttered Maie fearfully, close to his ear. "The lightning-stuff is made by the slaves of Ghirann's priest—it has long been known and used in Tlanis."*

But Hok did not show the slightest fear or hesitation. He addressed the soldier: "I will take that fruit-thing from you, and your hand and arm along with it."

"Oh, show the fool," snapped Cos, and the soldier, dipping his fuse into the fiery saucer, lifted and flung the bomb.

Maie shrieked and sprang frantically away; but Hok, still holding his axe in his right hand, shot up his left, caught the flying missile as it came toward his face and hurled it instantly back, as he had hurled the spear a few days before.

There was a fearsome roar, a blinding flash, a cloud of soot-black smoke; and through it Hok could see that Cos had been knocked from his throne-chair, his beard half singed away, while four of the twelve men on his right hand sprawled, burnt and broken, in death.

"See!" yelled Hok. "I have given you back your evil magic!" And he charged at the overthrown Cos.

But the rest of the sentries rushed at him from either hand. They levelled bronze-tipped spears at his heart as they closed in. Hok emitted a short, fierce spurt of laughter, and swept the blade of his axe horizontally in front of him. Its keen-flaked edge found and shore away the heads of three spears, and he sprang into the gap thus made. His swooping weapon bit through a helmet, and through the skull beneath it to the nose-bridge, and as he strove to wrench loose the wedged flint, the others were upon him.

"Take him alive!" roared Cos, starting to his feet; and a score and more of hands clutched at Hok's body and shoulders. He strove and cursed, kicking and buffeting. With one full-armed swing of his fist he smashed a bearded jaw, with a grasp and a wrench he dislocated a shoulder. But the soldiers were too many for him, and in the end he lay prone on the gravel, his wrists and ankles bound by the belts of the sentries.

Cos now dared grin and exult. "The hero of the forest lies at my feet," he sneered. "So will his people, when my soldiers march upon them. Take him away."

"Where, master?" panted a sentry.

"Where but to the sea-barrier above?" replied Cos. "Let him enter the dwelling of Ghirann our god, whose food is the blood of the wicked and proud—Ghirann the Many-Legged, the Terrible, who has waited over-long for sacrifice from Cos, his brother!"

"Not Ghirann!" ventured a shaky voice—Maie, who had stood apart and marvelled at the strength and fierceness of Hok. "Stop and think, Cos! Might not the courage of this prisoner merit a better death?"

"He would merit a worse one, if I could invent it," growled Cos. "Take him away, soldiers, and let me hear this night that Ghirann has feasted full upon his blood and body."

---

* Ignatius Donnelly, in his interesting work, *Atlantis*, offers an interesting collection of legends about explosives among Atlanteans.

Chapter IV
The Cave of Ghirann

Up the face of the cliff above the city ran a sloping way, cut slantwise, like a crossbelt on a giant's chest; and up that way the detail of soldiers shoved and dragged the bound chieftain. Hok could not tear loose from his bonds, and so he stopped trying. Philosophically he looked out across the scene below—the huddled city, the cultivated lands beyond, and the valley afar, all groves and plains and slopes. Surely this was the land of fruits and dalliances, a paradise where winter never came—and it was ruled by Cos, the selfish and cowardly tyrant.

Hok's greatest regret at the time was that he had not fleshed his stone axe in the scornful face of Cos. . . . Regretting, he was borne to the top of the great barrier-cliff under which Tlanis nestled.

Even though Maie had told him that the sea flowed higher by far than the tallest roof in the city, it was a surprise to come out upon a rocky shore, with the limitless blue waters beating almost at one's feet. The top of the mountainous barrier now appeared as a vast extending causeway, losing itself in foggy distances to either direction, with the sea close at hand on one side, the valley far below on the other. The slanting upward trail had taken Hok and his captors well beyond the position of Tlanis, so that the peak now appeared at a distance. In the other direction they proceeded, toward a square-built stone hutch or house.

Hok, as he hobbled along, gazed once to landward. He realized, for the first time, how deep the valley truly was—a sort of sky-pointing cavern. No wonder that things were always green and warm here, he mused.

And then the sentries were hailing someone who came from the square stone house.

It was the tall, eagle-faced priest in long robes, with whom Hok had come close to quarrelling in the wine-shop. He grinned sardonically when he saw the prisoner and heard the report.

"I knew he was meat for Ghirann when first I saw him," he informed the guards, fingering his tag of beard. "Leave him in my charge." To Hok he said, "Come with me, you meat for the god."

Hok, his ankles hobbled with a leather thong, raged unavailingly as the priest shoved and chivvied him along the rocky shore to the stone building. From the doorway came another man to meet them—a filthy, tousle-haired creature in a red kilt, with vacant eyes and a twitching, slobbering mouth. Hok gazed with loathing; his own people were accustomed, for the sake of mercy and practicality, to kill the feeble minded.* But this creature, apparently a favored companion of his new guard, danced and gibbered, gnashing long yellow fangs.

"Is this Ghirann, who is to eat me?" Hok demanded of the priest. "It is to be expected that the people of Tlanis would worship a crazy man."

The priest turned pale with anger at the slur, but then smiled harshly. "Ghirann has touched his mind, and made him holy,"** he explained. "There is always such a one, in the service of the god. But Ghirann himself, the Many-Legged Hungry One, will appear even more strange to you—for the little time you will see him."

With the scrawny hand of the priest urging him forward and the mad acolyte jigging and twittering, Hok came to the house, but was pushed around it instead of entering the curtained door. Then he saw that the stonework was only an augmentation of a rocky protuberance, apparently the mouth of a cave. A smaller opening, full of blackness and closed by a grating of wire-bound wood, faced away from the sea.

"You will go in there," said Hok's captor. "The cave runs far back, into the salt water. And Ghirann lives within, silent and hungry."

"Free me of these bonds," said Hok, "and I will face and fight Ghirann, or any other living thing."

"You would resist a god's hunger? I overlook the blasphemy," said the priest; and, to the madman, "Open."

The grating was drawn back, and Hok pushed in, so violently that he fell full-sprawl upon wet, smooth rock. To the imbecile's giggle was added the bitter, superior chuckling of the priest. Then the grating fell in place again, and was fastened with a heavy bronze hook.

Hok lay still, trying to pierce the gloom with his eyes. That the hole was closed up suggested that Tlanis did not care to have its god emerge—it might devour worshippers as well as sacrifices. When would it appear? Hok gritted his teeth and his beard stiffened. Would he, who had come safe out of the

---

* The splendid physical proportions and large skull capacities of the Cro-Magnon skeletons have led scientists to conclude that the Stone Age Spartans, Hok's people, systematically destroyed the weak in body and mind, thereby improving the breed.

** This belief is common today, among many ancient peoples.

clutches of tiger, lion, bear, wolf and Gnorrl, be eaten at last by a monster called the "Many-Legged"? If only he were free, to fight for his life with his mighty hands. . . .

He could see now, a little, as his eyes grew accustomed to the darkness.

The cave was large, extending downward rather than up, and the water of the sea filled its bottom so that the ledge on which he lay was none too spacious for his stalwart, helpless body. At some little distance a bluish glow of light showed. Apparently there was a seaward mouth to the cavern, just now under water.

Hok surged with all his strength against his bonds, until his muscles cracked; but the belts and thongs were of stout make, doubled and tripled. Horses could not have burst them apart. He tried to roll toward the water, hoping to soak the leather and so stretch it; but at the very lip of the ledge were wooden pegs, driven deep into the rock. Over them he could not hoist himself.

He turned his attention to the wooden pegs, as a possible cutter or ripper, and scowled. Many years of water-washing had smoothed them, rounded them. No escape there; he rolled back toward the better light under the grated doorway, and studied his bonds.

The soldiers had tied his wrists in front of him, and then had encircled his arms and body with other bands, so that he could not get his strong teeth to the fastenings. His ankles and thighs were similarly fastened together. Drawing up his knees, Hok studied the twisted belt that was drawn tight just above them. Then he grinned, and in inspiration.

Into that belt had been sewn a rough red garnet for ornament. Hok, by straining, extended his wrists a hand's-breadth from the bonds that held them to his body. He drew up his knees, closer and closer. The wrist-clamping leather rasped against the red stone. Again—again—

Hok had begun to pant by the time he had scraped through the cord on his wrists, but the other bonds were easy to unfasten then. He did not go to the grating at once, but lay at the rim of the ledge, thrusting his arms between the pegs to cool the chafed skin in the water.

And he could see well enough in the cavern's dimness to realize that he was not alone.

First a ripple of the water; then a blotting away of the blue patch of light, as though a bulk crowded in from the sea; and finally a churning of the surface, a great curved lump of darkness, a thrash of many cable-like limbs—and Ghirann came stalking through the shallows in search of his prey.

Hok, rising on his knee, saw the god of Tlanis plain.

Limbs as pliable as snakes and as strong as spear-shafts bore Ghirann wrigglingly forward. Above, and centrally, rode a puffy bladder of a body, as large around as Hok's arms might clasp, liver-dark and smooth. Intent, bright eyes seemed to probe Hok with animous hunger. Ghirann was of a ghastly, baleful dignity, that has impressed younger cultures than worshipping Tlanis.*

---

* The octopus is represented in the votive art of ancient Crete, pre-Spanish Mexico, and Japan.

The god charged, with a churning splash, and Hok did not retreat.

There was grim grappling on the ledge. Ghirann's legs became arms, embracing Hok's bare flanks and shoulders, clinging to his flesh with a multitude of round red mouths. In such an embrace had many a luckless victim perished; but Hok was free, and full of battle. His strength was perhaps as great as that of any adversary Ghirann had ever encountered. He wrenched himself free from two of the tentacles, and drove back Ghirann with fierce kicks against the flabby body. Ghirann splashed into the water again, but with two mouth-lined cables still clung to Hok's waist and thigh. Other tentacles made fast to some anchorage under water. Then Ghirann began to drag his prey from the ledge.

Hok cursed at the drawing pain of the suckers on his flesh, and braced himself against the row of wooden pegs. Ghirann's dragging arms drew tight across the wet surface of the rock, bent at the angle of his lip. It was a tug-of-war, and a stern one; Hok, with something of embarrassment, knew that Ghirann was stronger than he. When his braced limbs relaxed, he would be whipped into the water.

He clung to a projecting point of rock on the floor, with all his strength. It held for a moment, then started from its bed, as a loose tooth starts from a jaw. Again Hok cursed, but suddenly broke the curse—the yielding of that rock had provided him with a weapon.

The fragment was big, heavy, and had a rough edge. In his great hand he poised it, like the haftless axes of the Gnorrls. Sighting quickly, he struck at the nearest clutching arm of Ghirann, where it was drawn taut against the rock. He felt the tough tissue yield, and struck again, harder still. The tentacle parted like a chopped vine. Hok laughed fiercely in joy of battle, and struck with the edged stone at the other arm that held him. It, too, smashed in twain, and he was free.

Ghirann bled darkly in the water, but started erect upon the six limbs left him. He loomed above Hok like an immense spider above a stinging wasp. Crouched low on the ledge, his rock-weapon ready, Hok could see the under-center of Ghirann's body, in the midst of those writhing legs. In that center, like the heart of some nightmare flower, was Ghirann's mouth, a hooked, ravenous beak, opening and shutting viscidly.

Ghirann came on again, and Hok hurled his edged stone. It struck and obliterated one of those unwinking eyes, but the god of Tlanis barely faltered. Hok, too, rose erect, retreated a step, and found himself against a rough wall of stone. He tore fragments from it, with desperation of strength, and hurled them in a volley. That gave Ghirann pause, though his tentacle-tips still came gropingly after Hok.

The cave-man laid both hands to a lump of stone, twice the size of his head, and fully half his weight. It would not come from the wall. Hok dragged and wrenched, and then Ghirann made another rush, enveloping him with tentacles.

The monster pulled strongly, and Hok held himself to the wall by the projection he had clutched. Another pull, that Hok thought would fetch his shoulders from their sockets—and then he was flat on the ledge, being dragged along by the gripping tentacles. But his hands were full of weight—the big rock had broken from its place, by Ghirann's strength as much as Hok's.

With a supreme flexing effort, Hok rose erect on the very brink of the ledge, all twined from ankle to armpit with the snakes that grew from Ghirann's body. But that body lay below him, against the stone floor. Straight at the remaining eye Hok brought down the great missile he had lifted, driving it with all his massed brawn.

And Ghirann, the Many-Legged Hungry One, deity of Tlanis, was smashed like a worm.*

When Hok, pushing away the slack tentacles of his dead enemy, turned toward the landward opening, he realized for the first time that he had an audience. The long-robed priest stood there, his eagle face vacant with awe that now turned to terror. Hok strode to the wire-bound grating, and smashed his way through as a bull smashes through a cane-brake. The priest who had thought to feed him to a sea-monster fell nervelessly on his knees, with bony hands lifted to plead for mercy.

---

* See the myth of Hercules, and his conquest of Geyron, the six-legged man-monster, in a land far to the west of Greece.

Chapter V
The Wise Stone and the Thunder Secret

"Do not kill me," stammered the bony man. "I did not know your strength, great lord, or your courage! I crawl before you—"

"I do not kill, except in battle or for food," Hok interrupted contemptuously. "Yet I think you will die, without my help. This Tlanis affords strange ways for men to get their livings. Your living, I take it, was from those who worshipped the god Ghirann. Now that I have pounded him to death, you will go hungry."

"No, no," the priest made haste to say. "You have killed a god, you yourself are godlike. I will serve you, mighty one, as I served Ghirann. Give me your commands."

"First of all, get up." Under the blazing eyes of his erstwhile captive, the priest rose, trembling and fawning. "Now, then, there is one secret that I would learn."

"Anything," was the quavering reply, but the priest was stealthily plucking at something under his robe. Hok made a quick grab, drew back the folds, and possessed himself of a long bronze dagger, which he thrust into his own girdle. He went on speaking, as though there had been no interruption:

"What I would know is this thunder weapon which Cos, your ruler, says comes from Ghirann."

The priest rolled his eyes and shook his head. Hok showed his teeth, and offered to draw the dagger.

"But it is Ghirann's secret," protested the lean one.

"I have killed Ghirann, and his property becomes mine," replied Hok, stating a law that governed the cave folk.

"Thunder would blast us both," the priest wailed. "Come, the Wise Stone will advise us."

"The Wise Stone?" echoed Hok, once again mystified. "Now, how can a stone be wise?" And he allowed the priest to lead him into the house. The half-witted attendant scampered away before them, toward the path that led cityward.

Inside were couches, stools, and various great stone chests and jars. From one of the latter, the bony priest drew something like a stick with a lump at one end. That lump was huge and shiny. This he carried forth into the daylight.

Hok examined the object. At some time in the past, a stout stem or branch had been split, and a piece of stone inserted. Later, when the division had healed to clasp and hold the lump, the stick had been cut away well below, to make a handle the length of a man's arm. The stone itself was an angular ovoid, thrice the size of Hok's big fist, and of a semi-transparent whiteness. It glowed and flashed, too, as though from fires within. Hok had never seen its like, but he failed to show the awe with which the priest hoped to inspire him.

"What is this stone's wisdom?" he demanded, and touched it with his forefinger. There was a tallowy feel to it, though it looked clean enough.

"It holds visions within itself, and tells the future," was the deep-toned reply.

Hok laughed. "Then it lies, and so do you. The future cannot be told, but is what men make it."

"I will show." The priest held the thing up by its wooden shaft, like a torch toward the sun, and stood thus for some time; then he carried it back into the hut, Hok following. With his free hand, the priest drew the curtain of heavy woolen fabric across the door, shutting them into darkness. "Look!" he bade.

The big stone now shone softly, as with diluted moonlight.*

"It casts light upon things to come," came the priest's hollow whisper. "Within it unfolds a picture. I see you blasted by fire, and all the world with you, because of your blasphemy and disbelief—"

Hok, staring over the other's shoulder, saw nothing but the moon-glow of the stone. "Stop that babbling!" he growled, and, putting out his hand in the dark, snatched away the Wise Stone by its haft. "I count this thing as no more to be feared than Ghirann. Like Ghirann, it shall be smashed."

Surprisingly, the priest laughed, with a scorn to match his own. "Try it," he dared Hok.

"I will," and Hok thrust aside the curtain and emerged into the light. He turned toward the stout rocky front of the house, swung the stone against it like a hammer. The priest laughed again; for the clear crystal lump remained unchipped, while a sizeable niche showed where it had struck.

Hok studied the phenomenon with a scowl, then drew the bronze knife he had appropriated. With the stone firmly clenched in one fist, he pressed the metal point hard and fair against it. His muscles poured pressure upon the contact. He heard an audible clink, saw the point bend; but not so much as a scratch marred the Wise Stone.

---

* Diamonds are often phosphorescent in complete darkness.

"Well!" he said, and drew a breath. "It is very hard. I will keep it—for a club, since it cannot be chipped into an axe. Lead me to the thunder secret."

And the priest did so, because he must.

He conducted Hok along the barrier, between sea and sunken valley, toward the peak that gave off a veil of smoke. As they drew near, Hok saw caves in the lower slopes of the peak.

"Is the thunder made there?" demanded Hok.

"Yes—by slaves and prisoners," was the answer. "They must make much of the stuff, for Cos needs it to rule his people, and to conquer others."

At the entrance to the largest cave, they paused to look in. There, under two heavy-faced overseers, toiled many squatting men and women, all naked and miserable-looking. Some stirred messes of black-looking muck in pots of clay and stone. Others spread the muck carefully on the hearth of a fire that gave both heat and light to the operations. Still others were rubbing dried flakes of the material into meal, between pestle and mortar.

"Is this the thunder stuff?" Hok asked. "I still do not understand." He sniffed, and wrinkled his nose distastefully. "It smells like rotten eggs in there."

"That comes from one of the materials used," the priest told him. "Come, I will show you that also."

They skirted the peak, and looked into a smaller cave. It gave into a long tunnel, full of the sharp eggy smell Hok had noticed. The lower end held a little soft rose of light.

"That way leads to the heart of the smoking mountain," the priest said.

"Fire?" suggested Hok.

"Smoke, on which the deeper fire reflects. From those depths comes a part of the thunder weapon. See."

A skinny, wretched-looking slave came up, gasping from heat and foul vapors. He bore a shoulder-pole, with baskets slung to either end. Those baskets were full of yellow fragments, duller than gold. Hok, bending to examine, sneezed and stepped back. The priest found himself able to smile maliciously.

"That yellow cake from the mountains entrails is mixed with black wood, which we make by roasting willow."

"You burn it?" Hok tried to elaborate, but the bony head shook.

"No, burnt wood has no life. We roast it black, in clay pots."

Hok stared after the slave. "Black willow wood, and that yellow dirt! Are thunder and lightning made from those?"

Again the head shook. "Not entirely. The yellow and the black, placed together in equal proportions, make up only a fourth part. There is another thing, which we add—little grains and crystals, coming from the heaps of seaweed that rot along this water's edge.* Three times as much of that as the yellow and black together—the whole stirred and melted in water, then dried

---

* Saltpeter can be produced in beds of desiccating kelp and other sea plants rich in nitrates. The priest's formula has not been too far improved upon—25 percent of charcoal and sulphur combined, with 75 percent of saltpeter, has made a powerful explosive for later ages than his.

and ground. It is the thunder, speaking loudly and killing many at the command of its master."

"Yet I have seen it strike such a master," growled Hok, remembering how he threw back the bomb at Cos's guardsman. "Well, the more I hear of the weapon, the less I like it. With it a woman can stand safe and slay a warrior, but not cleanly, as with a spear-throw. This," and he flourished his diamond-headed club, "is more to my taste and understanding."

"What is your will now?" asked his companion as they turned from the mouth of the cave.

"To depart from this insane place," Hok was beginning to say, when his eye caught a figure, hurrying along the rocks toward them from the direction of the slanting runway and the priest's house.

It was the mad attendant. He skipped, gestured and grimaced, but the sounds he made were unintelligible. Both men questioned him—Hok roughly, the priest nervously. All he could do was point to the landward rim of the barrier, and they all three went to peer down upon the city of Tlanis.

Nearest to them though still far below, was the green, flower-rimmed terrace that held Cos's white palace and courtyard. It appeared black and crawling with humanity, which bunched up suddenly, then split into little struggling groups. Hok had seen battles too often to mistake this one, even from a distance above it.

"Fighting," he said, and the priest gaped. "Yes," went on Hok, "someone has roused his friends and attacks that fat spider, Cos."

"But who would dare?" demanded the priest, of the unanswering sky. His imbecilic companion whimpered to attract attention, and put out a trembling finger to Hok's wrist. He plucked at the gold collar fastened there. The priest understood the gesture.

"Ehhh!" he ejaculated. "He has been down to the city—he has seen. It is the woman, Maie—she has power and popularity. For some reason she has rebelled against Cos."

Chapter VI
War in Tlanis

Had the priest been as wise in human thought as he deemed himself, he would have known Maie's reason for rebellion. It was simply that she had never welcomed the insistent love-profferings of her ruler. Had she been less handsome, Cos would have ignored her. Had she been less powerful, he would have taken her. Things being what they were, he had wooed her for many moons without ceasing and without making real progress.

Hok's defiance in the gravel-strewn courtyard, with his capture and departure for the sacrifice, had been the occasion rather than the reason for what happened. Maie, who had first begged for the cave chieftain's life and had been refused, turned and hurried from the courtyard. Cos had called commandingly for her to return, and, as she passed the sentry and vanished from his sight, he made up his mind that there should be no further flouting of him. He called for a messenger and issued orders.

Meanwhile, Maie reached her own dwelling, a sprawling stone house on the level below the palace. In the front room she sat alone, trembling with emotions she found hard to analyze. She kept envisioning the blond giant who had walked by her side to Cos's audience, and had departed in bonds. She thought of his engaging ignorances, his strange philosophy of life, his puzzling questions and his definite statements. He was the strongest man she had ever known, and the most honest, and the most handsome. And she loved him—at least she assured herself that she did. Perhaps she really did. Such things were so hard to know.

In the midst of this, a slave came to her inner sitting-room to say that an armored man was asking for her at the door. She went, inquiringly, to find that the visitor was the courier from Cos.

"You are to come with me to the palace," he announced. "Cos wants you. Today you become his chief woman."

Maie shook her dark head, her mouth too dry to speak. The long, frustrating consideration of whether she would yield to the master of Tlanis was now up for a decision; and she was deciding against it.

The courier frowned. "You cannot disobey your master."

"Cos is not my master," said Maie at once. She was quoting Hok, and it was treasonable. The courier put out a hand to seize her arm and drag her along.

Maie screamed. At the sound of her voice, a soldier of her own following dashed around the corner of the house. In his hand was a chopping-sword, like a very long-bladed bronze cleaver. He cut down the courier with one stout blow, and faced his mistress across the wilting, bloody body that lay on the outer threshold.

They were lost, they both knew—a representative of Cos had come on his master's errand, and had been resisted and killed. There was only one thing for Maie's retainer to say, and he said it immediately and sturdily: "Mistress, I shall not desert you." To this he added: "No, nor will the other men."

"But we are few against Cos," objected Maie. "Drag this body out of sight, and let us think."

Fate granted them scant time for thinking. The event had been seen by a lounger, who ran to report to others, and even as Maie and her servitor bent above the bloody form, the foremost of a curious throng came in view of the doorway.

Once again Maie screamed. Others of her household ran out, thinking to protect her from some danger. The mob, already numerous, but unarmed and not particularly vicious, was daunted. Maie took time to exhort them.

"Do not betray me, people of Tlanis," she begged. "Cos sent an evil fellow to threaten me. My man came to my defense—there was nothing else to do. Am I to blame?"

"Not a whit!" shouted a citizen in the forefront of the gathering, a man with a loud voice and a secret grudge against the ruler of Tlanis. A murmur of agreement went up, and he was emboldened to speak further: "Would that Cos lay dead here instead of his slave!"

"Well said, friend!" responded one of Maie's armed men heartily. This soldier was an opportunist, and saw a chance of real resistance against the fate that would soon move against him and his comrades. "Who else is for us and against the tyrant?"

Had a philosopher been present, he might have spoken learnedly about the spirit which sways mobs, all unprepared, to one common fierce impulse. But there were no philosophers—only loiterers and poor laborers, most of them with valid grievances against the cruel, greedy man up yonder in the palace. They began to speak out, bravely, and to roar for blood and vengeance. Maie, more frightened than ever, tried to calm them—she had never quite thought of actual rebellion; but the affair had passed quite out of her hands.

Some of her soldiers, ready fellows without too much forethought or discipline, had plunged zealously through the press of people, and shouted for volunteers to storm the palace and do justice on Cos, the monster. The air was rent with the shouts of those who were anxious to comply—some for sympathy with Maie, who was neither unknown nor unrespected in the community; some for hate of Cos, who had been arbitrary and oppressive for years; and some for the chance of loot and excitement. They drew daggers, flourished sticks and cobblestones. Others, drawn by the commotion, ran in from byways and adjoining squares and streets, then joined the group without real realization of what the disturbance was about.

The mob, with Maie's soldiers at its head, tramped loudly along the main thoroughfare and came to a small party of Cos's guardsmen at an intersection. This detachment mistakenly called on the mob to stand. There was a brief, cruel clash, and the men of Cos were slashed and pounded to pieces without exception. Citizens, exultantly blooded, caught up the armor and arms of the slain. "On to the palace!" went up a concerted cry. Maie, the cause of the business, was already forgotten.

She ran, a lone and lithe figure, up a ramp and away toward the terraced height where Cos sat awaiting her, all unaware of the danger below. Pushing past the sentry at the gate, she came into the courtyard and faced Cos, who had summoned a barber to trim his singed beard. He looked at her with a sort of tigerish zest, that had very little of love in it.

"It is time you came here," he grumbled. "Hereafter there will be no misunderstanding between us. I am the master, and you—"

"No time for that," she panted. "Danger comes—men, armed and angry—are after your blood."

"Huh!" He stared stupidly at her, and pushed away the barber. "What are you talking about?"

"Listen!" she bade him.

He listened. There was a sullen mutter, growing to a roar, from the levels below.

"What trick is this?" snorted Cos, jumping up. His sentries also pressed forward, listening. The threatening note in the racket was unmistakable, and all pressed out into the open, Cos prudently coming last. They moved toward the edge of the terrace, to peer down, when the answer to Cos's question came on fagged but scurrying feet.

A soldier dashed up from the city below. He was a mass of sweat and blood, his armor cut and smashed, his spear lost. He almost fell at the feet of Cos.

"Master, master!" he gurgled. "They fight, they kill your servants, they cry out for your life!"

"Rouse the town!" thundered Cos; but it had already risen, and more of it against the tyrant than for him. The conflict was loud enough to convince any ear. Cos turned upon Maie.

"This is your doing," he accused and put out a hand as if to clutch her shoulder.

At that moment there was a multiple scamper of feet, a chorus of howls, and the first of the revolutionists mounted the terrace. They saw Maie in the grip of the tyrant, and their angry shouting made the air shake. A spear sped at Cos, to be narrowly deflected by a guardsman who struck it aside with his own weapon. Then, at Cos's shouts, the soldiers of the palace poured forth, and battle joined on the very lawn in front of the ruler's dwelling.

Again forgotten, Maie ran for the second time. There was only one avenue of possible escape—the slanting way up the barrier to the sea above. And she took it because she must.

But before she had mounted far, cries rose behind her. The soldiers of Cos had begun to turn back the rebels, and some could be spared to pursue the woman who was being blamed for it all. The pursuers gained, for Maie was only a woman, and badly spent. She doubted if she could reach the top—yes, she was almost there—but her way was barred, by a fierce, towering figure.

He lifted a missile, a great piece of stone, and hurled it.

It buzzed past her, and clashed on armor behind. A moment later the giant had run down, and seized her to help her along.

"Are you hurt, Maie?" asked a voice she knew.

"Hok!" she whimpered gladly. "Oh, Hok!—" And her weary arms sought to embrace him, the rest of the world forgotten; but he thrust her away and up to the head of the slanting trail.

"No time for that. We have fighting to do."

Chapter VII
When Hok Came to Bay

As Maie had mounted upward, pursued by a leash of Cos' soldiery, Hok had seen, understood, and prepared. Quickly he had gathered as many big rocks as he could find, heaping them at the very top of the sloping trail. Now he began to hurl them. The heavy missiles, propelled by all his oaken strength, made themselves felt even through hammered helmets and linked breastplates of bronze. One or two of the foremost pursuers fell, badly hurt. The others paused, and Hok launched his chief dissuader—a rounded boulder, a leg's length in diameter.

A heave and a shove started it, and down trail it bounded and plunged, sweeping three men along with it.

The others flung spears at Hok and Maie. The girl took a bronze point in her upper arm, but Hok dodged one shaft, caught another as was his wont, and threw it back to transfix an enemy. That was enough to halt a second volley. The soldiers hung back, cagy and nervous. Hok flourished his diamond-headed club.

"Come and fight!" he taunted them. "You are easier to kill than flies!"

More were approaching from behind, but those at the forefront tried to shove their comrades back. It caused a press not many men's lengths beneath the place where Hok stood to hold the trail. Thus things might have hung in abeyance for an indefinite time; but Maie, behind Hok, looked up from cherishing her wound. She screamed.

"Hok! The priest! Beware—"

Hok spun around. The eagled-faced man who had served Ghirann had crept up, his robes kilted in one hand, a bronze axe in the other. He struck, but not soon enough. Hok stooped under the downward sweep of the axe, caught him at the waist with an encircling arm. Plunging back toward the trail, he found the soldiers rushing up toward him.

He hurled the priest, like a billet of wood. The man's body mowed two men from the head of the trail, then flew from the path into the abyss. A shriek trailed upward as the wretch vanished. But others had gained the top of the barrier, were deploying to attack Hok as hunters might attack a lion or bear.

Hok made a lightning decision, shot out a hand to catch Maie, and ran swiftly back toward the mountain. His flying feet outdistanced the none-too-eager servitors of Cos, and there was considerable margin between him and his enemies as he gained the mouth of the cave where the thunder weapon was made.

At his roars and club-flourishes, the score and more of toiling slaves wailed and scurried out like rats surprised by a hungry ferret. Hok motioned to Maie.

"Into the cave," he directed quickly. "It is full of the thunder stuff. We can fight off nations."

They ran in, gazing around in the light of the fire. Maie uttered a despairing groan, and shook her dark head.

"It will not serve us," she said. "Look!"

Lifting her unwounded arm, she pointed to the great heaps of powdered black material that almost filled the back of the cave. "The thunder dust is loose, not in round balls," she said. "We cannot throw it. I might have known that Cos would not let the weapon be finished anywhere but in his palace—up here an enemy might come and gain advantage over him."

"We can still defend this cave," said Hok, and sprang back to the entrance. His big bulk almost filled it.

The first rush of men was upon him, and his heavy diamond club hummed as it struck once, twice, smashing two craniums. The bodies fell across each other, and Hok caught up a weapon in his left hand, one of the cleaver-like swords of Cos' bodyguard. He flailed at the oncoming band with both weapons, cutting a third man almost in half and breaking the arm of still another. The rest gave back. They had to.

"Spears!" roared someone, and Hok dropped the wise stone from his right hand in time to snatch yet again a whistling shaft, reverse it, and send it through the body of its hurler. Then he dropped to one knee, quickly dragging the bodies of his dead into a protecting heap in front of him. The press of soldiers—there were at least sixty or seventy by now—again drew back, staring in panic. About Hok and his dead hung a certain atmosphere of uncertain, superhuman horror.

"He is invulnerable," muttered one.

"Yes—was he not sent to be eaten by Ghirann? Could not even Ghirann finish him?" And the murmurs grew.

Then there was more commotion, and into the heart of the group hurried a figure with gold on head and arms, with a dark face and a lopsided black beard—Cos, the tyrant. His men below had beaten the undisciplined throng of rebels and was driving it through the lower levels of the city, and he had come aloft to see what happened on the barrier. His eyes blazed as he stared into the cavern, and saw Maie staunching the blood on her arm.

77

"Who hurt the woman?" he bawled. "I want her."

"You can never have me," Maie cried back to him.

Cos gestured angrily. "Why do you all stand like fools? Go into the cave and fetch her out."

"They are sick of trying," Hok informed him.

Cos gave new orders: "Throw no more spears. Capture Maie alive, but cut that big savage to pieces."

"He is a devil," protested a white-faced soldier, who felt that he had had more than enough of fighting with Hok.

"Do you fear him more than you fear me?" demanded Cos angrily. "Charge him!"

A full dozen obeyed. Hok, meeting them, was hard put to it to defend himself against a rain of blows, much less speed returns. But help came. Maie, catching up a hoe-like tool from the floor of the cave, rushed pluckily. She came to Hok's right side, and with a sweeping stroke brought down a guardsman. Others turned blindly upon her, striking and stabbing, and Hok in turn belabored them. Once again there was a reeling backward from the cave-mouth, now half-blocked with bodies. Cos, safely out of reach, was again able to see what had happened, and he cursed wildly.

"Fools! You have killed her!"

It was true. Maie, the fair chieftainess whom a ruler had coveted, lay dead. Her body was stabbed through with spears, her head was bitten open by a chopping-sword. There was silence. Hok and Cos gazed at each other above the heap of mangled bodies, as fixedly as though they were the only two men left in the world.

"You have been the reason for her death," said Cos, in a cold voice of accusation.

Hok wagged his bright-thatched head. "That is a lie, as is almost every word you speak. It is you who made her die. A quick death, and now she is happy with the Sky-Dwellers—safe out of your hands, Cos the liar and coward."

"Ghirann shall punish you," gritted the ruler of Tlanis.

Again Hok made a sign of negation. "Can Ghirann punish his punisher? Look yonder in that cave, that is half-full of water. Ghirann, whom you called your brother, lies pounded to nothing. And I did it—I! Hok, who brings woe to you and yours!"

Somebody moved through the crowd to Cos's side. It was the red-kilted imbecile who had been a servitor of Ghirann and Ghirann's priest. The foolish head was wagging, to corroborate Hok's story.

Cos turned back to the cave chieftain. His soft red mouth broke open in an ugly grin.

"Your life is forfeit, stone-chipper, before you bring more calamity on us," he said in a voice that choked. His hand reached out, the fingers snapped. Someone gave him what he wanted—a bomb, with hanging fuse. Another offered a blazing lamp to kindle it.

But a frantic chorus of protests rose. "No, master! No! Throw nothing! He will seize and throw it back!"

"That is the truth," Hok assured Cos. "I have been doing it all day."

The tyrant of Tlanis gazed wildly about him. "Someone must charge him," he said. "Charge and hold him, so that he cannot catch the thing. Who goes?"

Only one dared rush upon death—the madman, who was too foolish to fear. He leaped forward and at Hok, grappling with monkeyish strength. For the moment Hok was busy tearing him free, then swung the Wise Stone against the idiot head. In the meantime, Cos laughed as Death laughs, ignited his fuse, and whirled the bomb backward for a cast.

Hok saw, and with his left threw something on his own account—the bronze chopping-sword he had caught up. It sang in the air like a deadly insect, and struck home. Cos remained briefly upon his feet, but of his head remained only the black beard, the grinning red mouth. The rest flew away like a nut falling overripe from its tree.

In death, his hand still moved to throw the bomb, but it went high. Diving beneath it, Hok landed in the thick of his enemies.

The lump of explosive intended for him went sailing, all a-sputter, into the cave he had quitted.

He broke a skull, another, with the Wise Stone. As he whipped it up for a third blow, he heard a voice shriek:

"Fly! Fly! The cave is full of thunder dust—it will take fire—kill us all—"

And Hok, remembering that the bomb had fallen in the one place where it would wreak the most damage, stopped fighting and ran. He clove a way through the press as a knife speeds through water, and began to run northward along the causeway. So did some others. But it was too late.

The bomb exploded. Then came a greater explosion—the great hoard of thunder dust. Then a third—the volcano itself. And the doom of Tlanis was sealed.

Chapter VIII
Home Is the Hunter

Hok had thought only of getting away. The soldiers of Tlanis had thought only of returning to their city under the barrier. This difference of desire resulted in his escape and their destruction.

As Hok raced northward along the rocky shore, the voice of the bombarded mountain bellowed behind him, filling the earth and the sky with noise. The shock of the first explosion made him stagger, the shock of the second threw him flat. He scrambled up again, shaking off the dizziness. The air was suddenly full of pungent vapors. The volcano was spewing smoke and fire.

For the cave-full of explosive had acted as a greater bomb than any man of that age could conceive. It drove deep into the heart of the mountain, liberating a rush of red-hot lava.

The warriors of Tlanis dashed along their sloping trail to the levels below. Thus hidden under the overhang of the barrier's height, they did not see the destruction that was upon them until the immemorial sturdiness of rocks dissolved and dashed them down, forty or fifty of them at once.

For the new upward rush of the subterranean fires had split open the slopes of the hollow mountain. Water from the sea flung itself upon a world of molten rock, fluffing away into live steam. The tortured rocks and slopes shook and writhed, like a huge animal in pain, then disintegrated.

Probably many in Tlanis—the merchants, the nobles, the soldiers, the beggars—died before they knew that the wall above them had changed from stone to water, and was descending to crush before it overwhelmed. Others did see, shrieked and ran. They were overtaken and obliterated before they could reach the gates. Tlanis, built for an age, was being washed away like a scattering of leaves in a spring freshet. The blue teemings of ocean, crowding through the widening rent in the barrier, deployed to flow out and down valley.

Hok, still running like an antelope, realized that the waves no longer beat against the shore at his left hand. They raced to his rear, to the south, scrambling and fighting like live things to find and pass through the hole where the mountain had burst. The sand-plugged stones under his feet ground and gritted together. They, too, would go before long.

Hok's mind, trained to face and deal with danger, told him that he had best get away from this sea-assailed rampart. He did not slack his windy speed, but his eyes quested ever and again to the right, the landward. And eventually he found what he sought—a sloping ledge that dropped away, like that other one now disintegrated and drowned, that had given descent toward Tlanis. Hok raced down it, sprang at the end into a lofty treetop, and swarmed down to the brown soil of the valley. He resumed his running, ever to the north and the higher ground. At length he came out on the brow of a rise, and stopped to look.

The sea had taken possession of the valley's bottom. It rushed in a fierce, foul torrent, full of uprooted trunks and leafage, masses of turf and muck, the bodies of trapped animals, either slack or struggling—yes, and the bodies of men. Overhead flew screaming clouds of frantic birds. Beyond all this Hok could see the barrier, its gap now torn as wide as the whole of City of Tlanis had been, and widening. There was the greatest swirl, through which still burst the angry jets of steam and smoke from the riven volcano.

The water rose visibly as he paused. He dare not stop to see more.

But, as he turned away to run still farther, a sound broke forth beside him that made him jump, then turn gladly. It was a whinny, the voice of a horse—one of the horses of Tlanis, a servant and worshipper of man.

It came trotting to him, trailing a broken halter—a trembling brown beast with wide, worried eyes, glad all over to see a man still alive, already trusting Hok to avert danger and death for them both. Hok held out his open hand, and the animal put a soft nose into it.

"Shall we go together?" asked Hok, as though the beast could understand. He thrust the handle of the Wise Stone into his belt, seized the end of the halter, and vaulted upon the willing back. Then, with drumming heels, he urged his steed away to higher ground still.

On he rode, until the poor horse panted and stumbled, and the sun dropped down. The day was dying, and Hok took time to remember that at mid-morning he had first set eyes on Tlanis. A day's adventure and strife beyond imagination—and would he live to see the sun again?

Horse and man camped because they could budge no further, among hills that gave like buttresses upon the slopes of mountains. Hok slept, exhausted; but twice he awoke, shuddering, from ill dreams, and the gray dawn showed him that all the upward slope over which he had galloped was drowned, with the sea come in to fill, from horizon to horizon, that vast valley which had known the rule of Cos and the worship of Ghirann. The water still climbed after him.

A second day he urged his horse to the slope, and a second day the sea crept in pursuit, but more slowly. At noon of the third day, he was aware of no chase. The sea was finding its depth, was content with its conquered lands.

He came to a forest of pines and beeches, a forest he thought he knew. Not far away would be his own country.

At once he dismounted from the brown horse. He drew off the halter that was its badge of servitude, and started away on foot. There came a clop-clop of hoofs. He was being followed.

Turning, he faced the animal. "Go and be free," he bade it solemnly. "I cannot take you to my people. They do not use horses, except to eat."

The horse gazed as though it understood, but made to follow again. Hok shouted, and it came to a halt.

"I tell you to go another way," he said sternly. "My country is bad for horses. Not only men will eat you, but lions, bears, tigers, Gnorrls. You are safe from me, because you helped me escape. But not even I can protect you."

Again he walked away, for a good hundred paces among the trees. Then he glanced back. The horse remained where his voice had last halted it, as though it was loath to bid him goodbye.

When Hok returned, after some days, to his home in the bluff-surrounded cave that fronted the half-moon beach and the river from whose brink he had driven the Gnorrl people, all his tribe came to stare respectfully.

"You have not been gone more than a moon," remarked Zorr, his father-in-law. "Yet you have many new scars. Was there a fight?"

"There was a fight," replied Hok. He felt like deferring the story until he had rested.

Oloana came forward, curiosity mingled with the adoration in her eyes. "What is that thing on your wrist, the thing that shines?" she asked.

Hok undid the string of beads.

"It is gold," he said. "A woman called Maie gave it to me."

"A pretty woman?" demanded Oloana quickly.

"Not as pretty as you," Hok assured her, with something like marital diplomacy. "She is dead. I kept her gift for you. It is to be worn on the neck."

Oloana donned the bauble, and asked other questions, but Hok never had much to say about Maie, then or later. Today her name, as Mu or Mou, or Maya, is a name of mystery.

Zhik arrived from the hunt, to greet his brother heartily, and to him Hok presented the bronze dagger that he had taken from the priest of Ghirann. For himself he kept, forever after, the Wise Stone in its wooden handle, as a war-club hard enough to crush the toughest skulls of man or beast.

And finally he came to his cave, and sat alone by the fire in the entrance. It was quiet there, and he began to yawn. A patter of feet sounded from the gloomy interior. There emerged a plump little entity, with a shock of hair as pale as frosted barley grass. In one chubby fist was clutched a toy spear of wood.

"My son," said Hok.

"Father," came the solemn response. "Will you tell me a story?"

Hok drew the boy to his knee.

"I will tell you," he began, "a story which you must remember as a great marvel. When you have children, tell it to them, and they will tell it to their children. It is the story of Tlanis, the home of many strange and wonderful things, and of how the sea drowned it and them."

Hok Draws the Bow

Foreword

They all died long ago, at the hands of our ancient ancestors in the bitterest and most final war of all human history and prehistory, but we still wonder at their grotesque remains—the Neanderthal Men that were not men, but somehow a different and rival race. Fierce and cunning and horrific, they had to be exterminated if our fathers would live in the Europe they found thirty thousand years ago.

The Neanderthaler was gross and shambling and hideous, prototype of ogre and troll; but he fashioned and used tools with those great meaty hands of his, built fires, cooked meat, joined with his fellows in great bands for war and hunting. We know that he worshipped, for he buried his dead with provisions and weapons for use in an afterlife. We do not think he had art, but we cannot be sure. And no man can say into what pattern fell his thoughts, for they were not such thoughts as we think.

His skull was primitive, thick, almost browless: but what it lacked at the front it made up in a great swelling occiput, and its whole tissue approximated in size and weight many modern brains. What would be his ethics, impulses, his likes and dislikes? The only surety is that they differed from our own—were so different that when our true forefathers, the tall handsome hunters of the Upper Stone Age, met such hairy ogres, they could not make treaties or agreements. It was war, and to the death.

It was a long war and desperate. Not only was there close and awful combat, to the last drop of blood and the last ounce of strength; there was brilliant thought and planning and courage, and inventions mothered by sternest necessity—inventions that seem simple enough to us now, but which then changed the fate of whole continents and epochs. We wonder about such matters, cannot help wondering, imagining, making mind-pictures of how things may have fallen out in that grim youth of the world.

And so—another adventure of Hok the Mighty, chief of cave-dwelling hunters, as he strove against the abominable beast-folk he called Gnorrls.

—M. W. W.

Chapter I
The Strange Warrior

"Ha!" cried Hok, for the love of battle was strong in his breast. Now he lifted the first of his javelins and, scarcely aiming it, he sent it in a short arc to the chest of the closest Gnorrl. Hok was shouting now, and the battle cries of his tribe rang from his lips.

He had come on them accidentally, and it had been contrary to his nature not to offer them battle, though they outnumbered a hundred to his one. His legs planted apart, he sent the second javelin spinning through the air. "Remember Hok!" he called.

They were Gnorrls, right enough—hairy, burly abhorrent—but they were not acting like Gnorrls. Instead of charging in a howling mass, they formed into a skirmish line and closed in, twenty or so very cannily.

Noticing this strange behavior, Hok grew wary, and even in battle, his eyes became thoughtful. He had left only his stone axe with its span-wide edge, his poniard as sharp as a sting, slung in the girdle that held up his clout.

At the very first moment he drew away from them. Clean-limbed, long-legged, deep-chested, his tawny hair flowing behind him, he was a famous runner. He was less bulky than they, and he towered above their tallest by the height of his proud head. His moccasined feet touched the snowy ground like a stag's hoofs, and as he ran, his face grimaced in disgust.

Anyway, he would soon be clear of their swiftest—those bandy legs and heavy bones could not begin to match his hunter's lope.* Even though they had surprised him as he roamed among the crusted drifts near to their stamping grounds, they could never catch Hok, strongest and swiftest of men.

---

* Comparison of skeletons shows that the Neanderthal man was heavy and clumsy, and certainly no speedy runner.

BATTLE IN THE DAWN

But even as he drew far ahead, his blue eyes snapped with the cold fire of desperation. For he was running down a long, gentle slope, tufted with leafless thickets above the snow crust, and at the bottom was a winter river—but not frozen! Here the channel was narrow, and the current raced too rapidly even for the ice-spirit to clutch. Before many breaths' space he would be there—would have to swim that blood-stopping water—no, that would be impossible!

Because the Gnorrls lumbering behind him were not pursuing alone. Along the river-bank to right and left other parties appeared, closing in. He could not break either way, and if he sprang into the water their hurled stones would smash out his brains before he could flounder across. Hok was trapped!

Knowing that, he turned and faced the beast-men as they converged upon him. The fear of the Gnorrl still touched his heart, as from his first boyhood encounter with them; but not they nor smarter creatures could have guessed it from his challenging glare, the flash of teeth in his beard, the upward whirl of the war-axe in his great cobble of a fist. So formidable was his coming to bay that the three bands of Gnorrls wavered, snarling and jibbering, even as they came together and formed a half-circle to trap him with his back to the racing torrent.

"Come on and fight, Gnorrls!" Hok roared at them and saved the rest of his breath for the last and grimmest struggle that he thought was upon him.

But at that instant something buzzed through the air from behind him, like a huge wasp, and the centermost Gnorrl of the half-circle suddenly stiffened, dropped his club, and fell limply on his back. The shaft of a javelin sprouted from the thing's gross, shaggy chest. And the others, who had wavered, now stopped in their tracks and burst into a chorus of dismayed whines and wails.

Hok flexed his muscles—he was for leaping straight at the line, smashing his way through. But again there was diversion from across the river to his rear.

A voice made itself heard, a human voice that roared in gutturals—it seemed to be imitating the Gnorrl language in mocking defiance. Hok had insulted Gnorrls like that in the past . . . but the half-human monsters were more dismayed by the voice than by the spearcast. They began to stumble backward, breaking their formation. More shouting at them from over the river and they actually turned and fled. Hok leaned upon his axe, and was grateful to whoever had so strangely rescued him.

"Hai, you chief of men!" bawled that same rescuer. "You are safe now! Walk upstream a few paces—there is a broadening, and ice enough to cross! Come to me! I will wait here for you!"

Hok had time and safety now, he turned and looked.

Three ten-tens of paces away,* with the river and much other width between him and Hok, stood the figure of a tall, lean man in a muffling mantle of bison-pelt. Hok scowled in mystification. Three ten-tens—had the stranger thrown a javelin so far and so straight? Even so shortly after deadly peril, Hok was able to feel chagrin that he himself could not do much better, if at all. He salvaged the weapon that had pierced the now dead Gnorrl. Then, obeying the words

---

* With Hok's people, as with many more recent savages, the term "ten-ten" signified a hundred.

and gestures of the man beyond the river, he trotted to where the ice would bear his weight and bring him across.

The other came to meet him—strangely roan-red of hair, with the beard plucked clean from his square, shallow jaw in token of bachelorhood. Hok met the gaze of two eyes, brilliant but close-set, that seemed to sneer. But Hok was not one to forget his manners.

"Who shall Hok thank for standing his friend against those Gnorrls?" he asked formally.

"I am Romm, the free hunter, wandering to see new and pleasant countries," was the airy reply. "Your name is Hok? Are you not the chief of that tribe that lives to southward along this same river, the man whom the hairy folk—the Gnorrls, as you name them—call the Slayer From Afar?"

Hok's jaw must have dropped in wonder, for the stranger laughed without particular abashment. "Oh, I know the language of the creatures," he elaborated. "I have long observed them, you might say. Come, Hok, you stand my debtor for saving your life. Will you not invite me to visit your camp and tribe?"

It was badly requested, but again Hok did the polite thing. "Come," he said, and turned downstream along the river. Romm followed, and the two began to travel toward Hok's country.

On the way, Romm did most of the talking—an incessant recounting of the wonders he had seen in many countries to south and east, of his love-successes with stranger women, his cleverness in hunting and battle. Yet, for all his verbosity, he remained a figure of mystery not easy for Hok to estimate or classify.

"You have learned the language of the Gnorrls," Hok found time to remind him. "When you yelled at them across the river, was it to frighten them?"

"In a way—yes," grinned Romm. "At any rate, they left you alone."

"It was as though you had given them an order," pursued Hok.

"In a way—yes," repeated Romm, with more of his characteristic mockery. "An order—it seemed like that. But you thank me too much, Hok. Perhaps you are more useful to me if you remain alive."

Hok opined weightily that any good man was more useful when alive, and Romm laughed and laughed. One thing Hok did not mention about the rescue, and when they camped that night in a little cedar-rimmed hollow, Romm himself brought it up.

"How did you like my javelin-casting?" he inquired.

"It was well done," responded Hok, who found it harder and harder to maintain his gratitude toward this rescuer of his.

"Well done!" echoed Romm. "Can you say no more? But I can cast a javelin farther than any living man."

Hok said nothing. It had been his private opinion for years that he, himself, was the best javelin-thrower in the world.

On the next day, shortly after noontide, they reached Hok's stronghold. Hok led the way in, by a narrow runway between high bluff and swift water, and Romm followed him to the lip of a lime-shaped beach made by a backward curve of the bluffs. The only other way out was a ladder-like trail that slanted to the top of the high ground.

From the clump of conical huts, made of woven willows and clay daub, came Hok's people to greet their chief and stare at his guest—thirty huge-limbed hunters, with their women and children; some ninety or a hundred in all. Some were tawny like Hok, some were brunettes from further south who had gathered under the mighty chieftain for leadership and protection; but none of them had ever seen a roan-head like Romm, who rather gloried in the attention he drew.

"This is Romm," Hok introduced him. "He saved me from some Gnorrls—he speaks their tongue, and may help us fight them."

Romm replied with another of his ready chuckles that did not invite anyone to share his mirth. "What if I do not care to fight Gnorrls?" he asked, for all to hear. "Men of the riverside, does this big chief of yours waste your strength in useless war?"

In the forefront of a knot of hunters stood Zhik, the brother of Hok, two years his junior and a sub-chief of the clan. Like Hok in color and features, he was only a finger's breadth smaller all around. He took a slouching step forward, scowling.

Romm did not appear to notice. His bright, narrow-set eyes were questing elsewhere among the onlookers. "You have handsome women here, Hok," said he.

Hok followed Romm's gaze, and saw that it had found a comely woman with black hair and a golden-tanned skin. She had come from Hok's own residence, the grotto in the bluff behind and above the huts. Now she turned her back, in modest dislike of Romm's searching regard. Hok's nostrils twitched and an icy light kindled in his own eyes. "That is Oloana, my wife," he warned Romm bleakly.

"Mmmmm—yes." Romm was not abashed. "Women are won by fighting of their men, is that not so? If someone fought and beat you, Hok—"

Zhik growled and spat in the sand, and made a leaping stride that brought him within reach of Romm. "Hok, I do not like this stranger," he snapped. His hand darted to his hip, swift as a conjuror's, and came away with a beautifully ground dagger of deer-horn. "Let me slit open his narrow belly and see how his blood discolors the ground."

"I am your guest, Hok—in your protection," said Romm hastily, and Hok thrust Zhik back with the heel of a hand against his chest.

"It cannot be, Zhik," he said; then saw that Romm, for all his claim of hospitality rights, had drawn from his own girdle a little hand-axe with a narrow, chisel-like blade—a weapon that could drive to the brain with a single flick of the wrist. Hok's other big hand shot out like the paw of a cat and struck Romm's wrist so that the axe was knocked to earth.

"No fighting," commanded Hok. "Romm, it is best that you make no enemies here. My men are skilled with weapons."

"With the javelin?" asked Romm, who seemed to have conquered his momentary nervousness. "They do well with that, I suppose—and you, of course, surpass them all?"

"I, too, am thought skillful at javelin," Romm informed the gathering. "It would be sport, I think, for Hok and me to cast javelins against each other to see who made the farthest throw—two out of three trials."

Eager for diversion, the tribesmen applauded. Hok gazed at his guest, so ready with challenges and evidently so confident of victory. Could he, Hok, afford to take up such a defiance? Nay, could he afford to refuse?

"Let javelins be brought," he directed some halfgrown boys. "We will go to the meadow beyond here, and Romm and I will match our skill."

He led the way up the slanting path that mounted the bluff.

Chapter II
The Javelin-Throwing

The clan gathered quickly—men who happened not to be hunting, women who could drop their work, children in winter garments of rabbit-fur and soft deerskin. At Hok's direction, two of the biggest boys stepped off a hundred paces in the snow, planted a branch of cedar, then a second hundred paces and a second branch, and finally a third.

"A fourth ten-ten mark, too," requested Romm, who was squinting along the shaft of a javelin. Hok stared, and Romm snickered. "Perhaps three ten-tens of paces is your limit, Hok, but I can do better."

Hok raised his great voice, so that the distant lads heard him. "Pace off another ten-ten!" he yelled, and all who watched murmured together in wonder. Who had ever cast a javelin four ten-tens of paces?*

"Will you try first?" said Hok courteously to his rival, who grinned in some secret mockery and chose one of the javelins scattered upon the snow. He threw off his bison-wool robe, caught the shaft by its balance, took his stance carefully, and threw it. High in the air twinkled the shaft, a dazzling streak against the cloudless blue of the sky. It climbed a great slope of space, skimmed smoothly into its downward path, and drove into the snow well past the middle of the third hundred paces.

A watching lad quickly stepped off the distance, shouted the result to a nearer comrade, who passed it on to the gathered watchers. Two ten-tens and sixty-eight paces—a more than adequate throw. But Hok had done as well in the days before he had come to his present growth and strength. Dropping his lion's skin, he stood forth in the crisp bright air with only

---

* These may seem great distances for javelin-throwing; but the strength and constant practice of the cave men must be considered.

a clout and high moccasins. Disdaining to choose among the javelins, he caught up the nearest, set himself with left foot forward and left hand lifted as though to point. A quick flexing of all his sinews, a driving of his strength in behind the launched weapon, and it went singing like a locust along the trail of Romm's attempt.

Every eye followed the course of the missile, and the younger men chorused a cheer as they saw it rise to a greater height than Romm's had attained. The javelin angled downward and into the snow—beyond the first throw of Romm.

Jubilation on the part of all the very prejudiced watchers as the boy paced the distance and hooted it back—two hundred and eighty-nine paces. Only Hok was silent, reserved. Romm laughed with the others, but in his secret manner that was becoming such an irritation.

"You have beaten me—once," he acknowledged cheerfully. "I thought to allow you that much. But two more trials remain."

He fumbled in a belt-bag and produced a piece of buckskin cord, as long as his arm and very thin, round and even. Then he selected another javelin and, while Hok and the others gazed in mystification, began a strange activity. He hitched one end of the cord around the javelin, just rearward of the balance, and then wound the rest in tight, even spirals, around and around, until only the other end of buckskin remained clear. This part was split, and into the opening Romm hooked his thumb.

"This is a trick of my own devising," he chuckled, and grasped the balance of the weapon. Again he took his stance, drew back his arm and launched the javelin. At the same moment, his thumb jerked strongly upon the cord.

That violent pull unwound the wrapping, almost instantaneously. It spun the javelin as a fire-drill is spun between the palms. As the shaft took the air, it yelped rather than sang—tore up and up and up into the sky, as though it would never come down. Hok's eyes, following that amazing journey, widened apprehensively . . . and then the boy was reporting that the distance was three ten-tens and thirty-two paces.*

The murmur of the watchers became a hubbub. Nobody had ever seen such a throw, nor had they heard of one, even in the legends of their grandsires. Hok made himself stand and speak calmly, but he breathed deeply as he put out a hand and fingered the string that still dangled from Romm's thumb.

"There is great strength in that buckskin," he pronounced, and Romm laughed yet again.

"You did not think that such a cast was possible," he taunted Hok. "Do you give up the trial, big man, or will you continue and be beaten?"

All pricked up their ears. Nobody had ever dared speak thus to Hok. Out of the group of young hunters that stood nearest moved Zhik as before, and he sauntered dangerously, like a panther on the hunt. His hand clenched on the hilt of his dagger.

---

* Anyone who has even pegged a top with a cord will understand the method of Romm's casting; a spinning spear, like a spinning bullet or football, will go farther and harder than a floating one.

"Hok," he almost wheedled, "let me cut the throat of this ill-mannered stranger."

Romm stooped swiftly for yet another javelin, but Hok lifted his broad hand. "He is my guest, Zhik." And, to Romm, "I will throw a second time. Watch."

He took up his shaft, studied it and the ground and the far upward jut of that string-sped throw of his rival. In his heart he knew that such a feat was beyond his own simple skill. Then a plan came to suggest itself, and he almost smiled in his beard, but forebore. He placed himself, gathered his strength, and threw. Compared to Romm's peerless attempt, his javelin seemed barely to rise above treetop height. And it came down almost exactly between the marks made by his own first attempt and Romm's.

"Two ten-tens and seventy-eight!" called out the marker from afar. There was aghast silence, broken only by Romm's laugh.

"Your second is less than your first," he said to Hok, and to the watchers: "Ho, people! This chief of yours has a weak arm and a dim eye. Would you not rather follow a true javelin-master like me?"

It was offered as a joke, but one or two received the suggestion seriously. There were men who were jealous of Hok. They smiled back at Romm, and whispered together. Zhik glared that way, and once again he half-drew his dagger.

Hok watched Romm pick up and wind his third javelin. The fellow's hope seemed suddenly clear to him. He would beat Hok in this contest, but make capital of it slowly. He would gather some admirers—malcontents and young hero-worshippers—and wait his time. Some day, when Hok was absent or ill, he might try to seize power... Romm was gazing again at the group of women. His close-set eyes frankly admired Oloana, who turned away as before. Then Romm spoke to Hok:

"Your throws are beneath my best striving," he sneered, and with careless ease spun away his javelin. High it went, but not so high as before, and it fell to drill itself into the snow just on the near side of the third marker-branch. "Two ten-tens and ninety-eight!" cried the marker.

Romm shrugged, thrust his throwing cord into his bag, and turned his back as though scorning to see the final attempt of his rival. And now, for the first time, Hok showed care in choosing a javelin.

He picked up and discarded three before he found one that pleased him—a straight and flawless shaft, a light, narrow head. He tried its balance and spring carefully. Then he planted his feet with precision, poised himself twice and finally, with all the strength and skill of his huge wise body, made his final cast.

Away hummed the javelin, and in its wake rose the roar of Hok's people. For it was such a cast as Hok had never made, as no other man could have made without such a device as Romm possessed. It was coming down now—even with Romm's third try—no, beyond! And the marker was pacing off, and shouting his result:

"Three ten-tens and nine paces!"

The winter air seemed to smoke and quiver with the prolonged howling of Hok's people. Even those who had been ready to side with Romm were dancing and whooping. It was long moments before the din abated and Hok could hear the harsh accusation of Romm, voiced through set teeth:

"It was not fair! You tricked me—made your second throw weak, so that I would not do my best the third time!"

But it was Hok's turn to exult. His big white teeth glittered in the sun-brightness of his beard. "Call it a trick, if you will. I matched my heart's trickery against the trickery of your buckskin thong. Twice out of three times I out-threw you."

"It was false! Cowardly!" Romm raged. His half-built fabric of sedition against Hok was crumbled to nothing, and he lost all caution and control. "I will—"

His fist flew out, and Hok twitched up a great shoulder to ward the blow from his jaw. His smile grew broader.

"You have struck at me," he said, as silence fell all around them. "I owe you no further debt of hospitality or protection. And if this is to be a contest of strength—"

With the swiftness of a lashing snake, he hurled his own boulder-like fist into the center of Romm's angry visage, and the trickster somersaulted twice backward before he lay still and stunned, his eyes closed and blood on his nose and mouth.

The silence remained. Hok stooped for Romm's bison-wool mantle, then walked to the side of his motionless adversary and spread it over him. He lifted Romm's javelins and broke them, one and then the other, across his lifted knee, and dropped the pieces on the snow-crust. Finally he rummaged in Romm's belt-bag and secured the buck-skin thong whereby such amazing feats of javelin-throwing had been achieved.

"And now," he addressed the onlookers, "return to your work or other occupation. When this man wakens, he should know that he is not to see us any more. But if he tries to come back among us, let the children throw stones at him."

However, Romm made no such attempt. Later in the day, as Zhik subsequently reported to Hok, Zhik watched him rise and tramp glumly away. Zhik followed Romm stealthily, for the brother of Hok was not one to give up the project of killing someone he disliked; he wanted the roan-head to get well out of the hunting lands and therefore away from any lingering impulse in Hok to spare him. Later Zhik would overtake the fellow, goad him into drawing axe or dagger, and fight it out to a grim finish.

But just at sunset, the thing became impracticable. For Zhik, rounding a thicket, saw a half dozen Gnorrls come trotting from the north to meet Romm. And they did not attack him—they hailed him with gestures of clumsy respect, they came close and fell on their faces before him, even as scouts of the tribe had seen them grovel before the red sun at rising. Finally they went away together—Romm and the Gnorrls—as friends and allies.

All this Zhik reported to Hok, who digested and rationalized it:

"Romm, then, has joined the beast-men. He has become their chief, and they worship him; perhaps his red hair makes them think he is from the sun." Hok spat. "A man joining the Gnorrls! It is more disgusting than Gnorrls alone."

"And he saved your life only to discredit you before the men of our camp," contributed Zhik. "Thus we others would be more easily beaten. I still want to come within knife-stroke of him."

"Such a chance may still come," smiled Hok. "Romm plays some long game with us—something beyond killing us for the sake of his Gnorrl friends. But so far he has found the playing rough. In time to come it may be rougher still."

As usual, he spoke with chieftainly confidence; but his big, brave heart was full of wonder and meditation.

Chapter III
The New Weapon

On the third day after his contest with Romm, Hok sat by a small tallow-lamp* in the rear of his cave, the place where he retired for meditation and experimentation. The wise Oloana, knowing her husband's preoccupied mood so well, warned all to leave him alone.

He was examining the cord he had taken from Romm's belt-bag, twisting and twining and pulling it. Earlier he had tried to use it as Romm had, with very indifferent success—it would take long practice to learn the art. But the principle of shaft-spinning was manifest to him, and he determined to achieve or improve upon it.

"What that boastful wanderer could do, Hok can do better," he told himself with utmost confidence. "He was not so strong as I, but the cord strengthened him. It is like the throwing stick of the Gnorrls, who can send a stone farther than it can be thrown by hand—they split a stick, push the stone in, and whirl it as though with an arm twice lengthened."**

The thought of a stick as a throwing device impelled him to poke among the weapon materials in a nearby corner. He fetched forth a long, straight piece of hickory that he had cut months ago to make a javelin shaft. It was nearly as long as himself, two fingers thick at the mid-point where the balance would be, and the two ends tapered somewhat by long and judicious scraping with rough flint. He tested it by careful bending—it had springy strength, and in the hands of a Gnorrl it would make an ideal stick for stone-throwing. He looked from it to the cord, and back again.

---

* Such lamps, made of soapstone, are often found among Paleolithic remains.

** Neanderthal man certainly used such a device, as examination of his flint tools shows, sometimes even shaping a stone to fit in a cleft stick for throwing. See Osborn, *Men of the Old Stone Age*.

"Romm uses a cord, the Gnorrls use wood, to make their casts long," he muttered. "I, who wish to outdo them both, might use wood and cord as well. How?"

He tied a noose in the cord and drew it tight over one end of the shaft. Lodging the butt of the hickory in a crack of the rocky floor, he pulled at the cord. The tough wood bent slowly and unwillingly. Hok pondered, then nodded to himself. A stone—yes, or a javelin—fastened somehow to this cord, would be whipped strongly forward at will. He carried the device outdoors and to the meadow behind the settlement where, unobserved, he could test and judge.

Driving him on with his experiments was the submerged, only half-conscious fear of what Zhik had told him—of Romm and the Gnorrls. Hok hardly knew he was looking for a weapon. He only knew he was working on something.

His experiments with stones and wooden splinters were clumsy, but they gave him something to think about. When after repeated tuggings, he broke Romm's cord, he returned to his cave for another, longer and thicker. This he knotted to one end of the stick, pulling at it in various manners.

The power was there, he knew, but he was still at a loss as to how it could be used. Finally, partially by chance and partially by half-formed inspiration, he drew the wood into an arc and made another noose in the cord with which to catch and hold the free end.

He now had a tense figure of wood and buckskin, that would hold its shape even when he laid it by itself upon the snow. Turning the thing over, he tested its tough elasticity by drawing upon the cord. The bent bar of hickory was like a flexed muscle, ready to strike or shove.

But still he was perplexed. He had started with a cord like Romm's, a stick like the Gnorrl throwing-tool, and had evolved something vastly different from either. As he frowned and pondered, movement rustled at his elbow. A small, firm hand came into view, with a round rod of wood. With this it plucked at the tight-drawn cord. A humming sound responded, like that of bees.

"It sings," came the voice of Ptao, Hok's small son. Serious blue eyes regarded the strange engine from under a shock of straw-yellow hair. Again Ptao plucked the taut cord with the haft of his toy spear, drawing it back and bending the bow a trifle. The strength of the hickory was too much for his young muscles, and it almost snapped the stick out of his hand.

At once Hok built upon his new ideas with still another.

"Let me see that little spear, my son," he said, and the lad trustfully handed over his toy. Hok had whittled it days ago from a shoot of ash, too small for a real javelin, and it was a faithful model of real weapons. The point had been made as sharp as a wasp-sting, and hardened judiciously in the fire.

Hok used the butt as Ptao had done, to evoke musical humming from the tight-drawn string. He pushed harder with it, carrying the string backward and bending the hickory length into a deeper arc. Then suddenly he let go, and with a whispering *thung* and a whack the toy flew some feet away. Ptao, light on his little moccasined feet sped in pursuit and brought the thing back to his father. Another try—another. And then Hok felt that he knew what might be done to make the work a success.

Drawing his flint knife, he scraped a notch in the butt of Ptao's little spear. This notch he used to catch the center of the cord, and clipped it there between the great fingers of his right hand. His left hand caught the wooden arc at the point where the balance would be on a javelin, and the forward end of the spear fell across and above his clenched fist. He held it in place with his forefinger, took a firm stance as though to throw. Then he lifted the device—and loosed.

With a great explosive whoop, the cord snapped taut again. It drove Ptao's spear forward and away—away, away, as a swallow hurtles to escape a falcon. Hok, his left hand still clutching the machine of wood and buckskin, stared after the shaft, his lips parting in his beard with amazement.

"It speeds!" he gasped. "It speeds—straight, and more swiftly and far than any javelin—"

"Father!" cried Ptao, alarmed and disappointed. "My spear—look, it is lost, out of sight over there in that thicket!"

Hok's free hand dropped on Ptao's tousled head. "Do not grieve, my son. Tonight, I will cut you another and better little spear—yes, and some more, to throw with this new weapon—"

He broke off, gazing once more along the path of the missile.

"*Boh!*" he cried, in imitation of the sound his engine had made at the moment it straightened and threw the missile; and a new word came, along with a new weapon and a new force, into the world of men.*

The next morning Hok went hunting, alone. He shot at everything he saw, from rabbits to snow-bogged elk, missing again and again and losing several of his new-made arrows; but his skill improved with the hours, and he brought back a doe and some grouse. After that he practiced daily. He learned that the little darts he made would split if launched against a hard target like a tree or stone—a misfortune for a good arrow was as difficult to fashion as a bowstave; but he improved his workmanship, and fumbled in Oloana's sewing-kit for some gay red feather-fluff to tie upon the shafts and make them easier to find after shooting.

Thus Hok grew proficient with the new weapon he called a bow, but he laid it away, with his arrows tipped with skewer-like splinters of bone. The wood was too weak, the buckskin cord tended to stretch. He would return later, when he had more time, to fashion a better bow. There was work to be done now.

The spring was foreshadowed by thaws and rains. The first crocus blossoms, white and yellow and purple, thrust their hardy faces out of drifts, and Oloana twined them in her black cloud of hair, looking forward to lilies and violets.

---

* The word "bow" comes to us through Old English and before that through early German and Sanskrit, from some unthinkably old root; undoubtedly it is onomatopoeia—formed in imitation of the sound of a bow drawn and loosed, exactly as described here.

BATTLE IN THE DAWN

Willow scrub burst into little furry tufts, then into catkins. The snow-patches dwindled and the game herds fattened on tender grass, while the skeletal trees clothed themselves in leaves once more. The lad Ptao, diligently practicing with the new spear his father had made for him, brought down a north-winging raven, and the hunters foretold for him a career as a great hunter. It became warm, bright, one could travel in clout and moccasins without winter's cumbersome fur mantles and leg-swathings.

Then the awful day dawned.

Chapter IV
The Triumph of the Beast-Men

Hok had guessed that the Gnorrls would try something—one or two of their people had been killed by his hunters during the cold weather, and that meant attempts at revenge. The mystifying factor was Romm, wise and wicked and spiteful, who would incite and direct them. Hok kept a pair of scouts on the plains north of his settlement, and one morning those scouts came home in a breathless scamper. Sure enough, Gnorrls were coming—many of them, and very purposefully.

Hok gave orders swiftly. The Gnorrls always lived and moved in larger groups than true men,* but their organization was clumsy. They made a line, continuous but open. That line began to move forward at a steady lumbering trot. When it had moved well out, there formed and set out a second line, and then a third. Behind the third wave more Gnorrls bunched into clumps, as though to act as a reserve, rushing to whatever point the battle would develop.

"See!" growled Zhik. "Did I deceive you? More Gnorrls than we thought possible—and better armed—and wiser led! Hok, it is in my mind that this may be our last fight!"

Hok was thinking the same thought, and he resolutely put it from him. From the armful of javelins spread at his feet, he caught up one and set himself for the throw.

"Ready, all!" he thundered for his warriors to hear. "When they come within range, I will throw—do the same, each of you! Let this be a fight for the Gnorrls to remember all of their days!"

---

* The Neanderthal brain was extremely developed at the rear, where many psychologists say that social impulse has its basis; and it is certain that they lived in great hordes, while both Hok's people and more recent savages tend to gather in small communities.

From the valley came cadenced howls and jabbers—the Gnorrls, too, were receiving orders from their war-chiefs. One such chief pushed ahead of the line, and Hok, watching him draw into range, whipped forward the first javelin of the fight. It struck his quarry full in the midriff. The Gnorrl chieftain fell, but his followers tramped unhesitatingly forward over the ground spattered with his blood.

Hok's men went into action the next moment. Every one of them was strong of arm, deadly of aim—few, if any, of that rain of javelins went wide of the mark. The Gnorrls fell like leaves in a gale. But there were more Gnorrls than javelins, and they did not falter in their advance. The gaps in the front were filled from the lines and groups behind.

"Back to the rocks!" yelled Hok, and followed his men there. They had placed other sheafs of javelins ready behind the ramparts, and began to hurl these. The range was point-blank now, the oncoming mass of Gnorrls so close that the defenders could see the glaring eyes and snarling fangs of their foemen. Hok's party was doing deadly execution—for a moment, Hok dared hope that even this mighty mass of enmity could be broken, driven back.

Fleetingly, he thought of his bow, but it was too imperfect and there was only one. There was only this chance—

But, even as the hope dawned, Zhik was tugging at his elbow.

"They are behind us!"

Hok turned, and saw. Another great cloud of Gnorrls, in open order, was bearing down from the left, moving to flank them and hem them in. Hok swore agonizedly.

"Retreat!" he thundered at the top of his lungs. "Throw all your javelins—quickly—and get out of here!"

He was almost too late. The charge from the front had come up to the barrier of rocks. For the moment, retreat was out of the question—men must fight, and desperately, with axe and club and stabbing-spear, to win free. Moments, precious moments that might score the difference between life and death, were eaten up in that hand-to-hand struggle.

Then Hok's force rolled back, leaving half a dozen dead behind—yes, and wounded too, pain-wracked hunters to be clubbed and trampled by the Gnorrls. The reserve party of youths was trying to stem the flanking movement, and very unsuccessfully; for those Gnorrls had spears, and could throw them. They replied to the volleys of the young warriors, and several Gnorrl casts found their mark. With throaty war-cries, the attackers hurled their lumpy bodies into the fray.

They met Hok as he and his first line of defense found time to turn and run back. Before he could do otherwise, Hok grappled a grizzle-pelted Gnorrl in the forefront of the flanking horde.

The beast-man's ungainly, lump-thewed arms clamped about him, and Hok knew a moment of revulsion comparable to that which rises upon touching a snake . . . the very disgust gave him strength to tear the creature from him, slam it to earth and split the ridged skull with a downward sweep of his axe.

Smoking blood and brains spurted forth to drench him. He was up and chivying his demoralized followers into a faster flight.

They distanced the pursuit for a time, then slowed up as Hok made a stand while Zhik and two other swift runners raced ahead to break up the camp—against such a whole generation of battling Gnorrls as this, not even the home stronghold could stand.

Again the people of the riverside retreated, but perforce more slowly. They had to fight the foremost Gnorrls now and turn them back, so that the women could gain a start to southward, carrying the youngest children and leading those who could toddle.

It was a day to remember, all through the lives of those who survived it—a day to remember in nightmare visions.

Mercifully, the Gnorrls broke their early disciplined ranks, in their eagerness to overtake and kill. Thus, turning to defend the fleeing women and children, Hok's surviving warriors had only the swift-running vanguard of the enemy to meet—they were not too crushingly outnumbered. Thundering his wild war-cry, Hok actually ran to meet a leader of the Gnorrls, caught upon the halt of his stabbing-spear the terrific downward smash of a flint-headed club.

The blow broke his own weapon in two, but he flailed with the ragged end of the wood at the Gnorrl's face, made it yelp and give back; then, stooping quickly, he caught up the fallen piece with the spear-head and drove it like a dagger between the thick ribs of the thing's chest. For the sake of defiance, and to put heart into his own fellows, he sprang upon the floundering body and roared anew his challenge and triumph. But the moment was brief—the Gnorrl next closest threw its javelin, which swished past Hok's elbow and pierced the warrior just behind him.

Another flurry of hand-to-hand combat, with death on both sides. Zhik, white-lipped and fire-eyed, grappled a Gnorrl chieftain like a giant hairy frog, and the powerful monster tripped him and fell upon him. Hok ran in and brained the Gnorrl as it wrestled uppermost, then caught his brother's hand and jerked him to his feet. After that, the great press of pursuing Gnorrls caught up, and again the men must run, to catch up with their women, form and defend again.

By late afternoon they were far south of their camp. In the evening they came to a stream, a tributary of their own river, swollen by spring rains into a churning muddy flood.

None of the surviving tribesmen, faint with running and fighting and horror, wanted to attempt that crossing. But Hok, glancing back to where the leading Gnorrls were closing in once more, forced them to it.

He hurled in some of the big children himself, poking them, along with the butt of his axe until, crying in terror, they struck out for the opposite shore. Their mothers followed perforce, and then the rest of the women. Hok swam across, encouraging and harrying, lending a hand here and there to weak paddlers who might go under or be swept away by the freshet; then, even though his mighty thews were agonizedly tired, he made his way back to fight the rearguard action on the other bank. It was the last clash of the day, and the bloodiest. Gnorrls died. So did men; and only a handful of survivors were able to slip away, when darkness came and none could throw spears or clubs or stones after them as they strove in the water.

The Gnorrls, poor swimmers, made their campfires on the brink of the stream. Hok marshalled the remnant of his people and took them far away, until darkness was so thick that they could not see to walk or guess the way. Then, by the light of a little fire under the lee of a hill, he counted noses.

There were not many to count. Of his thirty warriors, eight still answered to their names—every one a peerless fighter even against Gnorrls, every one wounded in several places. But now, Zhik was the only one whose eye shone fearlessly. The fifteen boys who had sallied forth with hopes of glory that morning were now but nine, and not a one of them but wept in forgetfulness of any ambition to be a warrior. Barp and Unn, Hok's young brothers, were both dead, cut down in the attempt to turn back the flanking party of the Gnorrls at the first encounter. Of the women, most had escaped—only a few sick and old had been cut off at the camp—and a good number of the children.

Hok's heavy heart lifted a little as his son Ptao came wearily to him and smiled a filial welcome. And Oloana, too, was there, having killed four Gnorrls with her own hand. Now she brought green leaves to patch the dozen cuts and slashes upon her husband's face and body, wounds he was now aware of for the first time.

Before dawn, Hok had this stricken troop on the move southward. That day they saw the last of the hunting grounds they had so gloriously wrested from the Gnorrls years ago—driven, beaten, half obliterated, they were returning to the forests below, where game was scarce and rival hunters many. It was a doleful homecoming.

And the scouts on the rearward watch reported that the Gnorrls had not stopped following them.

Chapter V
Two Against the Gnorrls

Eight days had passed, and the ninth was darkening into the night. Five chiefs of the southern forest clans sat around the council fire Hok had made in a pine-circled clearing, and soberly disagreed with him; for in their eyes he was no longer Hok the Mighty, ruler and champion of the folk who held those good northern huntings—he was a beaten fighter, with his following cut to pieces, and in his retreat he had brought the Gnorrls south, further south than any living man had ever known them to come.

"The watchers say that they are as many as autumn leaves in a gale," said Zorr, the father of Oloana, squatting opposite Hok at the head of his young warriors. "It is best, perhaps, that we parley with them."

"Parley!" repeated Hok, as one who does not believe his ears. "As well parley with wolves, with boars, as with the Gnorrl. You all know that."

"But this man Romm is their chief," said a fellow named Kemba, scratching himself. "He can be reasoned with. As a matter of fact, Hok," and Kemba's voice took on a cunning note, "I think it is your blood he is after, not ours. What do the other chiefs think?"

All applauded save Zorr, who was not anxious to desert his son-in-law. Hok, still stiff with weariness and wounds, rose and glared around, his nostrils expanded like a horse's. He hefted his war-axe of flint, on the blade and handle of which the blood of a dozen Gnorrls had dried.

"I say, fight to the death," he snapped. "Who says the same?"

"I!" barked Zhik, and rose to stand beside his brother. A few more rose, in the rearward quarters where the subordinate warriors sat. Hok counted them, and they were his own veterans, fresh from the awful conflict and still scabbed over with wounds, but ready for all that to follow him into more games with death. One or two of the southern fighters rose with them, but none of the chiefs. Kemba sneered at Hok; he would not have dared to sneer a season ago.

"You have our leave to head back to the north and fight," he said. "After all, it is your quarrel, not ours. We have never had to fight the Gnorrls."

"Because I stood between you and them!" Hok almost roared. "Kemba, if this were an ordinary matter, I would kill you for the way you talk. But there is not time or strength among us for a battle, save with the Gnorrls." He put out an appealing hand toward Zorr. "Hark you, father of my wife! I am not afraid to die—but what will become of Oloana? What of Ptao, the son of your daughter? Romm and his Gnorrls will not spare them."

Zorr's grizzled black beard quivered, but he shook his head slowly. "There must be a vote of the chiefs, and we must both bide by that vote," he reminded heavily.

"Listen to me," said Hok. "I have a new weapon. It is a thing of strong wood and buckskin, and with it I can hurl small javelins a great distance. With this weapon—if all our warriors learn to use it—we can drive back the cursed Gnorrls—"

"Would it take long to learn to use this—ah—strange weapon of which you speak?" a crafty-looking old man asked.

"Not long. Perhaps ten days. But until then we would have to fight them off with the weapons we now have."

The crafty-faced one smiled. "In ten days perhaps none here would be alive," he said. "It would be wiser to parley. I will not listen to madness."

"Listen, this once!" Hok roared then. "Listen, before voting—I offer myself as a single warrior against the Gnorrls."

Even the crafty-faced one fell silent after that, only exchanging sharp glances with the other chiefs squatting about the council fire.

Then as the silence lengthened and still no one spoke, Hok stood up with a grim smile. "Agreed then," he said and stalked off to get ready for the dawn.

Just before first light, as he was gliding swiftly through the gray-lit forest north of the encampment, Hok's keen eyes found the track that could only have been made by a Gnorrl. So they had come this far, even among the trees, to spy him out.

Leaning close to the ground, his quick ear caught a noise—pit-pat, pit-pat. Two feet approached, near at hand and behind; another human being moved on his trail. Even as he listened the noise ceased, as though the pursuer listened for him in turn.

Hok dodged sharply around some bushes. With a sudden flex and jerk, he strung his huge bow, and upon the string notched an arrow. If this was the Gnorrl who had made the track, its pursuit of him would be short and tragic. His eyes found an opening among the bushes, and to this he drew his shaft, tense and ready to drive murderously home.

A body, stealthy and active, moved into his line of vision. Hok's fingers trembled on the verge of releasing the cord, then he suddenly relaxed his archer's stance and sprang through the bushes with a whoop.

"Oloana!" he cried; and his wife faced him, startled but radiant.

Her fine, strong body was clad in leopard fur, in her girdle she carried a short axe and dagger. Her hand bore one javelin while a second swung in a shoulder loop. On her feet were stout traveling moccasins, and the pouch at her side bulged as with provisions for a journey.

"I have overtaken you," she said breathlessly. "Which way do we go?"

Hok's tawny head shook emphatically. "You must return to the camp," he told her. "I face the Gnorrls alone."

"I am coming with you," she replied, as definitely as he.

"I forbid it." His bearded face was stern. "Your place is with the tribe, or what is left of it—"

"You made over the command to Zhik," she reminded him.

"Ptao is there—you should remain with him—"

"Ptao is a well-grown boy. You were not many years older than he when you became a chief. And you left him, too, in Zhik's care. I heard."

He tried yet again: "If I die, Oloana—what if I die?"

She gestured the words out of his mouth. "If you die, Hok, am I to remain alive? Be a wood-carrier for my father, or—perhaps—marry for softness' sake, a man who is but the quarter of your shadow? I am your wife. I do not intend to be your widow. If you die, then I shall die, too."

And now Hok fell silent, letting her finish her argument.

"You are one pair of eyes, one pair of hands, against all those Gnorrls," she summed up. "Let me be your helper—watch in the other direction, strike a blow to defend your back. If one fighter has a chance to conquer, two might have a double chance. You are the chief—I am the chieftainess!"

Determination had come back into Hok's heart, and now joy followed it and swelled through him. He laughed aloud, and caught Oloana in his arms, hugging her with a sudden fierceness that squeezed the last gasp of breath out of her. Then he motioned toward the open country.

"Come then, woman. Hai! The Gnorrls do not know what misfortune is marching upon them!"

Chapter VI
The Deceit of Romm

They camped that night on the stream that had saved their people from complete ruin, and it took them all the next day to re-traverse the ground they had lost in a single afternoon of running battle. Hok had a thought that made him grimace wryly—those Gnorrls made one travel fast!

Four times during the hours of light they lay flat in brushy clumps or among high heather while patrols—not mere groups, but patrols of Gnorrls moved by, in one direction or the other. Hok, who could appreciate organized reconnaissance, saw at once that this must be an important piece of Romm's work. The scouting Gnorrls travelled in half-dozens, with one active fellow moving well in front and two more some paces to the right and left as flankers. The leader and a subordinate held the central position, chattering orders, and at the rear point moved a "get-away" Gnorrl who could scuttle back and warn his comrades if the rest were surprised and struck down. Gazing at these bands, Hok's eye gleamed hardly and his fingers plucked longingly at the string of his bow; but he sent no arrows. He was not seeking the blood of a Gnorrl, but of Romm.

In the evening they camped, fireless, in a thicket not far below their old fort-village. At sundown they heard distant howling and jabbering, from many hairy throats—the Gnorrls were worshipping the sun as it set. But when the last red ray had faded on the horizon, the clamor rose even higher. Why? Then Hok remembered that the beast-men had been seen bowing before Romm, the roan-headed. Romm would find such adoration glorious, but Hok could not think of it without spitting.

Anyway, that crude, harsh litany told him what he wanted. The main body was close at hand, while the observers and raiding groups were all to the south, combing the open country between here and the forest. Perhaps he had come just in time—the Gnorrls would be on the point of a concerted move toward the forest and the final defense position of his own people. Two days' march would take them there—but meanwhile, they would expect no enemies this close to the heart of their main body.

His early plan took even more definite form. He whispered to Oloana:

"No wild beasts will threaten, with so many Gnorrls about—and no Gnorrl will move abroad in the dark. I will leave you here. Sleep lightly, with your hand upon your javelin. If I do not return before sunrise, go back southward."

Her hand found his in the night, her mouth kissed the side of his face. Then he moved stealthily out of the thicket, and along the way northward. The voices of the Gnorrls were guide enough.

He carried his strung bow in his left hand, with arrow notched and kept in place by his forefinger. At his right hip, within quick snatch of his free hand, hung both his axe and his dagger. His moccasins made no noise on the earth, for Hok was night-born and did not need to grope his way.*

A little shred of new moon rose, showing him his river, the bluffs and, as he drew near, great sleeping encampments of the enemy. He pressed close to the river to avoid these and so come undiscovered to the waterside shelf that gave narrow ingress to the hidden beach where his clan had once lived happily.

Toward the outward approach of that shelf he made his way, but paused. The wind blew downstream, and toward him. His distended nostrils caught the musky odor of Gnorrl—alive and close at hand. A sentinel bode there, proof enough that something of importance lay beyond. The something of importance would be Romm, and the Gnorrl chiefs who would make up his retinue and command-staff.

Hok came close to the rocks, pressed his big, supple body against them, and gingerly peered around the corner with one eye. There was light enough to see the guard—a big young Gnorrl, standing up to block the way, but quite evidently sleepy. The creature leaned its burly shagginess against the side of the runway, and supported itself with the butt of its javelin—weariness brought stupidity, Hok knew.

The lone adventurer drew back, unstrung his bow, pouched his arrow, and slung them both behind him. Instead he took his stabbing-spear in both hands, and again moved close to the entrance of the runway. The Gnorrl was within leaping reach.

Hok peered, gauged positions, distances, and above all the exact spot where the brute's wide, chinless jaw merged into the bull-neck. Then, with the smooth swiftness of a huge cat, he sprang from shelter and forward, his spear darting ahead of him and thrusting home, with all of his weight and force behind it.

The dull eyes of the Gnorrl opened, the slab-lipped mouth gaped; but then the flint point found its mark—the hairy protuberance in the center of the broad gullet, which has come to be called the Adam's apple. The spearhead

---

* The almost universal superstition that night-born persons can move surely at night seems to have some foundation in fact.

split that lump of cartilage and killed the warning cry before it could be voiced.

Driven on by Hok's grim charge, the spear drove through windpipe, muscle, the bone and marrow of the spine at the back. Down flopped the slackening bulk of the sentry, and Hok, planting his moccasin-sole on the shaggy breast, wrenched his spear free. A lunging kick sent the carcass from the edge of the runway and into the quiet fast flow of the river.

Again Hok paused, listened and sniffed. No other guard waited at the far end of the passage, and he continued along it. Beyond, the light was better and he could see the sandy space where once had been gathered his people's homes and possessions.

But the huts were torn down now, lying in ruins. The level sand, once as clean and smooth as the cave-wives could make it, was foul with the remains of cooking-fires, heaps and scatterings of spoiled food, kindling, and all other untidiness of the Gnorrls. It was strewn, too, with sleeping figures, who sprawled and snored grumblingly—the chief individuals of the great Gnorrl invasion that lay bivouacked on the nearby plains.

As he hoped, none had been astir save the guard he had dealt with just now. And there was but one fire—up above his head, just within the wide mouth of the grotto he once had inhabited.

Delicate-footed as a stalking wildcat for all his size and weight, Hok picked his way among the sleepers. One of them he had to step across, at the foot of the slanting pathway to the grotto, and even as he bestrode this figure it moved and moaned as in a dream. Hok froze tensely, his blood-drenched spearhead dangling within a hand's breadth of the open mouth; but then the Gnorrl subsided into deeper slumber, and Hok passed on. Like a blond shadow he stole up to the floor-level of the grotto and gazed in.

The fire was small but bright, made with pine knots; and before it sat a single figure, back toward him. Hok saw a shock of hair the color of a sky at sunset, protruding above a wolf-skin robe that seemed to be drawn across humped shoulders to fend off the night's chill.

Romm!

Here was the settlement of old scores, the defeat of the Gnorrls, literally within stabbing distance of him. Romm, living, had brought about this dire invasion, this threat to the very life of the human race; Romm, dead, would mean the crumbling of the top-heavy Gnorrl army, its return to a mere unpleasant and solvable problem. Hok's hands tightened on his spear-shaft, and he moved forward, upon the floor of the grotto. A rush, a stab—and away up the path to the top of the bluff, a dash through the sleeping hosts, and back to Oloana in triumph!

His left moccasin took a long stride forward, and with a smooth gliding shove he put the keen flint into the wolfskin, just where a spine should run between the shoulder blades. The seated form seemed to give his weapon no more resistance than an empty bladder, and it fell forward with his shove, into the fire. The red hair blazed up, into rank smoke. Hok clenched his teeth to keep from voicing an exultant cry of victory . . .

Then, between his own shoulders, a cold, sharp point set itself.

"Do not move, Hok," said a quiet, jeering voice he knew. "Being thought a god, I made that dummy so that my worshippers would think I never slept; wakening yonder in the shadows, I saw you attack what you thought was Romm. But Romm lives; and if you so much as breathe deeply, this knife will slide into your heart like a snake."

Chapter VII
The Fire and the Arrow

Hok's first reaction, even before astonishment, was of chagrin—in his instant of success, he had been trapped like a big rabbit. That moment of self-denunciation kept him from moving, from whirling and trying to grapple Romm; and the same moment gave Romm himself the opportunity to make sure of his captive.

The roan-head must have held the knife in one hand and a noose of cord in the other. That noose now dropped over Hok's shoulders, jerked tight, and pinioned him. A half-hitch snapped around Hok's ankle, and he found himself thrown violently. Then Romm knelt upon his chest, the knife at his throat, while he finished the binding as to elbows, wrists and knees.

"You may sit up now," Romm granted at length, and Hok did so, glaring. Romm was quietly exultant, his eyes dancing in their close-set sockets, his teeth grinning like a red squirrel's. The renegade ruler of the Gnorrls examined Hok's weapons—the spear, the axe, the knife and finally the bow. "What is this thing?" he demanded.

"You pass yourself for a god among these beast-things," growled Hok. "A god should not ask for information."

Romm chuckled in his maddening way, rose to his feet and turned the unstrung stave this way and that. He studied the notch, narrowed his eyes in an effort to gauge purposes, and finally tried to pull the string into place. Romm's lank arms, though sinewy, did not approach the strength needed to bend that stiff bar of yew. At length he tossed it into a corner. He had not bothered to pry into the otter-skin pouch which Hok still wore, filled with arrows.

"It looks like a fishing pole, badly made," he said. "Well, Hok, you fished for me, but it is you who have been hooked and landed." From the fire he dragged the remains of the dummy he had made to simulate himself—winter leggings stuffed with dried grass, a cross of sticks to support the draped mantle in lifelike manner, and a gourd to which had been stuck, with balsam, tufts pulled from his own thick thatch.

"I made it to deceive the willing fools you call Gnorrls," he laughed, "and it did more—it deceived even the wide and brave Hok, and so saved my life."

"Why do you not kill me?" challenged Hok.

"That will come later. Tomorrow the Gnorrls must see you, bound and helpless. They will marvel more greatly at my power—thinking that my wisdom and magic snatched you, the one man they fear, from your hiding in the forest. And among us we will invent for you a death for all to see, and in which a great proportion may share."

"Be sure of my death when you see me dead," warned Hok in the deeps of his chest, and Romm laughed the longer.

"You are bound, helpless, while I am content to wait for my revenge," he said, "and there is no reason for us to sleep the rest of this night. Let us talk—about me as a god and you as a doomed man."

The joyful commotion of the wakening Gnorrls offended the sunrise and the blue spring sky; for at dawn Romm had summoned their chiefs and shown them his prisoner, the giant they called the Slayer From Afar.

Hok's reputation and fierce skill had kept his people from being obliterated on the retreat short days ago; only the thought of him had dampened the enthusiasm of the marchers for a bold entry and showdown under the shadows of the trees. And now they had him.

Because Romm was at his side as he was pushed and dragged up the high trail to the meadow where once he had won a certain javelin-throwing, the Gnorrls did not at once fall on him and tear him to pieces. But Hok knew that death was staring him between the eyes, and that this time the stare would not falter.

Well, he thought with fierce philosophy, these foul beasts who dared walk upright in grotesque semblance of man should see how a chief died. Meanwhile, his death here and now would stiffen the defense to the south—the vote of the chiefs had promised that. If Oloana could know that he was lost, and slip back to safety . . .

As if reading part of the thought, Romm spoke her name. "Do not be concerned for Oloana, your wife," he said, and smiled. "I myself shall comfort her for your loss."

Hok growled wordlessly, like a wolf, and it pleased Romm. "Yes, not all your people will die. I would be lonesome as one man, even though a god among the Gnorrls. The warriors will fall in battle, as they would wish. Such children as we capture can be reared and taught to obey me. And the women—a few—especially Oloana."

Bound as he was, Hok sprang at him. It took the abhorrent hard hands of seven Gnorrls to hold him from knocking Romm down with the impact of his straining body, and for a moment the godly arrogance of the roan-head was tremblingly near a break. Only when Hok was thrust safely back did Romm find the note of mockery again. "Nothing you can do will save yourself, Hok—nor Oloana."

By that time Hok had gained his self-control back. His heart was white-hot within him, like a stone in the midst of a pit-fire; but there was clarity of thought within him also, the determination to foresee and find and use the chance that must exist, however slim, for a turning of the tables.

They had come to the middle of the meadow. Rich green grass showed through the higher patches of winter-killed weeds and cane, and to north and south ran thicket-like belts of brush. Where Hok was halted, with uncountable Gnorrls swarming close in great hairy droves and knots, some of the horde were planting a great upright pole. Around about the beast-people blackened the level space for two javelin-flights in every direction, and the bright air grew heavy with the foul scent of them.

Hok's guards pushed his back against the pole. Others bound him fast with two turns of rawhide thong. One Gnorrl brought its knobby arms full of wood, which it arranged at Hok's feet.

Romm leaned on a staff—it was Hok's unstrung bow, that had so mystified him the night before. "You see the death I have planned?" he queried. "Slow fire—to roast, not burn . . . the Gnorrls believe that what they eat will give them its peculiar virtue. And so, when you are roasted, these Gnorrls will eat you!"

He had stepped close, and the last words he flung out with his nose close to Hok's. The bound man gazed in disgust at Romm; and deliberately, as one who reckons with the results of his action, he spat in the renegade's face.

Every Gnorrl roared furiously, the whole of them as with one earth-shaking voice. There was a rush from all sides, but Romm flung up his arms and barked a single commanding syllable. The beast-men gave back grumpily, and Romm wiped the spittle from his flushed face. Then his toothy grin returned. Slowly he shook his head.

"It will not work," he said, in a voice like water under ice. "My friends here almost did as you hoped—tore you to pieces quickly and mercifully. But no. You will roast."

Hok let his gaze wander past Romm. He was bound so that his face turned south, toward the thicket where he had left Oloana. Many broad, brutal faces, with blue lips and chinless jaws and shaggy bodies, ranged before him to watch his miserable death. Beyond them was the green and brown of the meadow grass, more distant clumps and . . . yes . . . Oloana. That was her head, thrusting craftily out of some willows . . .

With a glowing coal of dead wood, Romm was igniting the fuel heaped at Hok's feet. Smoke rose, then a licking tongue of flame that scorched the captive's shank, mounted higher and singed the lion's skin he wore. The end was upon him . . . and Oloana was in the open, moving behind the backs of the intent Gnorrls, well within fair javelin range.

"Oloana!" Hok roared suddenly and at the top of his great lungs. "Throw a javelin—kill me! Then run!"

And she threw it. The shaft sang and shone in the air, came coasting over the heads of the Gnorrls, past the bending back of Romm, and struck—not Hok, but the stake to which he was tied, just beside his flank.

On the instant, Romm straightened and whirled. He, and every chattering Gnorrl saw Oloana, poising her other javelin.

Pointing, the roan-head bellowed orders to his Gnorrls. It was as though Hok could understand perfectly; he was urging his followers to rush after the woman he coveted, capture her and bring her unhurt to him. Like a stampeding herd of cattle, the Gnorrl pack dashed past and away from the bound man at the burning stake, and in his eagerness for Oloana, Romm ran with them.

Even before they had left him, Hok was alone, forgotten in the chase. He stiffened himself against the bite of the rising flame, and the wedged javelin-point rasped his ribs. Into his mind came inspired hope.

Writhing hard to the other side he drew the rawhide that held him as taut as he could. A strand of it fell across the sharp edge of the javelin's head. The burning fire quickened his struggles and jerks. Rasped and stretched, the cord frayed, then parted. Another floundering heave, and Hok fell free, still bound as to hands and feet, but away from the fire.

His wrists he lifted to his mouth, tearing with his strong teeth at the confining leather. A thought's space more and that, too, parted. Then he was freeing his feet and knees, and stood erect.

Oloana had thrown her second javelin at Romm, and had missed—the shaft quivered in the earth, not a dozen paces from where Hok stood, and Romm raged in the midst of his great yelling cloud of Gnorrls. Hok saw his wife running beyond—not fast enough. She might distance the clumsy beast-folk, but not Romm.

He still felt fire; the otter-skin quiver, which had gone to the stake behind his hip, was ablaze, together with the arrows it held. He tore the thing from him, dropped it. Within reach of his hand lay his bow—Romm had laid it down to kindle the fire.

No time to lose; Hok's brain did a lurid sum in addition. Oloana fled, the Gnorrls pursued, and he had the bow and flaming arrows. Could he?—Snatching up the yew staff, he bent and strung it. From the smouldering quiver he whipped a straight arrow, that sprouted fire like a blossom. With a quick drawing pluck, he pulled the shaft to its burning head, and sped it away—neither at Oloana nor at the Gnorrls, but at the ground between them.

It sang up through the air, then down. It dived into a shaggy bunch of reedy grass, killed by this winter but still standing, just as Oloana cleared that very spot. And the grass tore up in flames, bounding high and fierce.

The foremost Gnorrls cowered back. To them it was as if that fire had leaped magically from earth's heart.

Then, as if in beneficent alliance with Hok in his lone fight against myriads, breeze rose from the south and hurled the greatening fire in a charging sheet upon the army of the Gnorrls.

Chapter VIII
The Death of a God

Hok had only half hoped for such a result of his shot; but, seeing the leap and rush of the fire, he saw and knew the chance that had come to him. He caught up other arrows, still burning, and sent them skimming away, to kindle other blazes in a line with the first. Before the Gnorrls could recover their initial panic and divide to dash around the first small grass-fire after Oloana, he had made a burning fence between her and them—a fence that rose high and hot from several different points, and moved menacingly upon the shaggy host.

The Gnorrls retreated, and so did Romm. Hok, cut off from his wife by both Gnorrls and fire, ran, too—faster than any. He gained the top of a rise where the grass grew shorter, and felt that he had time to pause. He looked back.

At a good four ten-tens of paces, Romm had halted his hosts. They stood in their tracks, clumped around him, although the rising conflagration pressed close behind them. Why did Romm do this suicidal thing? . . . but as Hok asked himself that, the answer became clear. The renegade was kneeling, to twirl something between his hands—a fire-stick! That was it, Romm was making fire, with a hard wood spindle on a soft slab—fire in front of him, when at his back was a blaze like a forest of glowing heat!

Hok's mystified scowl faded, for he knew Romm's intention. The same wind that brought burning death upon the Gnorrls from the south would carry this new fire ahead of them, giving them a burned-off refuge.* Hok leaped up and down upon his knoll, and bawled at the top of his lungs:

"Romm! I am free—free! I am going to kill you!"

---

* Frontiersman often saved themselves from prairie fires thus.

Not until that moment had Romm realized that his prisoner was escaping. He straightened quickly, yelled a reply that Hok could not catch, then seized a javelin and rapidly wound it with his cord. With an explosive jerk he sped the weapon at Hok—it fell many paces short, and Hok laughed his loudest. Romm made a gesture of helpless disgust, then dropped to his knees and resumed his fire-making.

Hok had one arrow left. The fire had gone out on its bone-shod tip. Putting it to the string, he planted his feet, clamped the arrow-butt between his grasping fingers, and drew with all his strength. For a moment he paused with bow at full bend, gauging air currents, elevations, direction. He dared not miss . . . he let the arrow fly.

Romm never knew what death soared down out of the heavens. The darting shaft pierced him, where his neck joined his shoulder, and drove on downward into his lungs. His throat filled with blood, he writhed upward from his knees to his feet, flourished his arms in frantic agony, and slammed down upon his face. He never moved again.

Hok, gazing, heard the voices of the Gnorrls. They jabbered in a way he recognized—it was the worship-clamor. The ugly monsters still stood where Romm had halted them, though the fire had come almost to their shoulders. Their arms extended toward him, Hok. Their guttural cries were addressed to him.

They were worshipping Hok, as they had worshipped Romm. The enemy who had slain their red god was greater—they turned to him now, with their prayers and terrors. They pleaded for deliverance from the fire.

But Hok yelled again, to curse them. As if invoked by his curse, the fire suddenly whipped to greater and swifter banners of heat. It charged in among the Gnorrls, scorching and singeing. The things screamed in a way to deafen all the world, and began to run.

The whole meadow, with its reed-tussocks and bush-clumps, was flaming around them.

Hok ran, too, far in advance of them. He did not turn back to see the destruction of his enemies. Changing direction, he came to the bluffs above the river, and sprang far out. The water hurried up to meet him, received him and closed over his head. He drove deep down into its troubled depths, but up he came in a moment, swimming hard with his free hand and trailing the bow behind him.

The current carried him quickly past the old beach where his folk had once camped and which lately had been the sleeping-ground of the Gnorrl chief. It was ablaze now, all the refuse and grass-bedding and trash having caught fire from sparks above. Below it the river widened and the current slowed; on the shore, the grass showed untouched by flame. Hok fought his way to the shallows, then to the waterside. Oloana came running to meet him.

"You are safe," she panted. "Yes—and you still have that thing you call a bow."

"It must dry carefully," replied Hok, "for it has stood our good friend this day. Tomorrow I shall cut new arrows for it."

That night they made their beds on the sand of the fire-purged beach. Nothing but ashes remained of the enemy camp, and the day of heat had cleared the air of Gnorrl-scent. Far away to the north, the dark sky was lurid with the still-marching flames.

"How many Gnorrls came alive out of that business?" wondered Oloana.

"Few, very few." answered Hok. "There are, of course, scouting parties south of here. We will avoid them on the way back, and lead warriors to surprise and swallow them. I doubt if the Gnorrls will have the numbers or courage to look us in the face for many years. And then we will have our bows."

"And we have our home again," rejoiced Oloana, like the good housewife she was. "A few hours will rebuild the huts—and people from the south will strengthen our numbers more than ever—"

She broke off and gazed anxiously at her husband. "Hok!" she cried. "What is the matter?"

For he, chief and champion and conqueror, sat with his bearded face in his big hands. He shed the first tears his eyes had known since childhood. His body shook with great, racking sobs.

"Oh, the young men of our people who have died because Romm would be worshipped by the beast-people!" he mourned brokenly. "Oh, my two young brothers, Barp and Unn—and the brothers of all the rest, brave men, good men, who live no more! How can all the hunters of all the southern forests ever fill their places?"

Hok and the Gift of Heaven

Foreword

Their names still clash in our ears, the great swords of old—Arthur's Excalibur, Roland's Durandal, Siegfried's Gram. They make lurid light across the centuries, whether in David's hand, or in D'Artagnan's, or Custer's. The last of them is not yet sheathed or sated.

A mighty warrior and artificer was he who first fashioned and wielded such a blade. The Bible calls him Tubal Cain, the Greeks named him Vulcan. Actually he was Hok, who lived by battle but had no taste for battle's sake, who never tortured a weak foe or feared a strong one; who glimpsed not only the promised strength of cold, sharp iron, but the woe as well.

In those days of man's first youth, hardly anything happened that was not of consequence. The complex brain, the eloquent tongue, the skillful hand, made this two-legged animal ruler of his world. He knew a ruler's joys, sorrows and cares. Not least of the things which embody joy, sorrow and care is the sword, born in fire, baptized in blood, mirroring the light and dealing the darkness. Nor has its horror and fascination vanished from the Earth we know.

Chapter I

The gift seemed first to be a threat, an assault, hurled from the very cope of the dawn sky in a swaddling of fire to land between two parties of stone-axe warriors intent on bloody battle.

That battle was coming as a logical sequence of the sudden self-importance of Djoma the Fisher, chief of a tribe that dwelt and seined at the seashore. He felt himself the invincible leader of a terrible community of fighting men. Vaingloriously he sent a messenger over wooded hills to the north and east, to inform a certain smaller settlement there that he wanted at once, in tribute, every specimen it owned of that powerful new weapon its chief had invented and called the bow.

But the settlement in question was of the warlike Flint People, and its chief was Hok the Mighty, who respected nothing save the worship of the Shining One and feared nothing save being bored. Sitting above his village of mud-and-wattle huts, on the threshold of the cave he had won in combat from overwhelming masses of the fierce sub-human Gnorrls, he grinned in his sun-colored beard and heard out the blustering demand of the envoy. Then he gave the boys of the village leave to drive the stranger away with sticks and stones. In due time the fellow limped home to the seaside, and Djoma led every fighting man he had—more than a hundred—to take the bows by force.

Warned by his scouting hunters to the southwest, Hok marshaled sixty of his own stark fighters on a rise of ground where the invaders must pass. Djoma, marching by night with intent to surprise the Flint People around their breakfast fires, came just at the first gray flush of autumn dawn upon a ready skirmish line of warriors, brawny and bearded, clad in skins of lion, wolf and bear, ready to shoot with the bow or strike with the axe.

In front of these defenders strode Hok himself, taller and broader than any man on the field. The skin of a cave-lion was slung around his powerful loins, moccasins of bull-hide shod his feet. The wings of a hawk were bound to his temples, and he bore in one hand a bow with arrow ready on string, in the other a war-axe with a blade of black flint a full span wide. This latter he tossed high in the air like a baton, catching it deftly as it descended.

"Hai, you strangers, you eaters of fish!" he thundered his defiance. "What do you seek here?"

"We seek those things you call bows," replied Djoma, quickly and to the point. He, too, came forward from his horde, and he showed almost, if not quite, as tall as Hok. Sunlight on the water had long ago burnt him as brown as a field stone, and his black beard spread in a sooty cascade over his broad, bare chest. He carried a stabbing-spear, with a shaft as thick as his wrist and longer than his body. "I sent a man to get them, but—"

"Ho! Ho!" laughed Hok. "Does that man's back still tingle from the drubbing our little sons gave him? We surrender none of our things when proud strangers command them. Come and take them if you can, Djoma the Fisher. I think it is something else you will get, less to your liking than bows."

Djoma roared to his swarthy following, which roared back and charged. At once Hok gave an order of his own, and the Flint People lifted their bows. A blizzard of arrows met the onslaught full and fair, striking down men on all hands. The charge wavered, while the defenders quickly set new shafts to their strings. Another deadly volley might have turned Djoma's threatening advance into a rout.

But then there fell from heaven a fiery thing that for the instant made all the dimness of heaven as bright as noontide—fell hard and heavy upon the rise of ground which Hok's men held and up which Djoma was trying to charge. It struck where an outcropping of a certain soft black stone showed.

As the prodigy rocketed down to earth, the two opposing throngs, defending bowmen and rushing Fishers, gave a concerted yell of amazed terror and flung themselves flat on the earth. Only Hok, in the forefront of his party and nearest of all to the place where the thing struck, remained on his feet and gazed. The earth reeled under him, like a treetop in a gale. Next instant, an upflung lump of the soft black stone struck him hard in the face, so that he seemed to whirl away into an emptiness as black as the stone itself.

When his senses crept back into him, the sun was up and bright, and he was alone. Apparently the battle had rolled away from him—he saw only dead, both of his own folk and of the Fishers. It was hot, too. The heat was what had awakened him. It seemed that the earth was afire nearby, and a morning wind had sprung up, enlivening the blaze and straining it toward him.

Blinking and snorting, Hok got to his feet. His head ached from the chance blow that had stunned him, but he had been stunned before, and like the later Athenians always treated headaches with contempt. He gazed about him, wondering again which way the battle had gone. Beside him lay his own bow and axe—his own side must have triumphed, else surely he would have been killed and plundered as he lay helpless. Thus allaying any anxiety, he turned back to the strange fire.

It filled the rift in the slope where the outcropping of black stone had been, now torn open as if by the blow of a mighty axe. The breeze, blowing into the opening, fanned the flame to an intense pallid heat. Hok came as close as the scorching air would allow, peering. He could see the thing that had fallen from the sky, in the very midst of the furnace. It was a round, glowing lump, bigger than his head.

"The Shining One hurled it," he remembered in his heart, "for it came from the sky, his home. Was he displeased with me, or was it a warning? . . . Had he truly wished to, he could have killed me like a fly."

Hok stooped and picked up a piece of the outflung black stone. Tentatively he tossed it at the glowing lump in the hottest heart of the fire. It seemed to him that the black stone vanished at once.

"Hai! The thing eats black stones," he mused. Some paces downhill from the fire showed another outcropping. Going there, Hok pried out great brittle chunks of the stuff and filled his arms with them. They blackened his chest and ribs, but he bore his burden to the fire and threw it in.

"If you are a living thing, from the Shining One, Hok is your friend," he announced. "I will bring you all you wish of the black stone."

He did what he could to fulfill this promise. Again and again he brought as much as he could carry, ripping out great dusty boulders of the material with his huge hands, later by prying at it with the stout handle of his axe. High he piled the dark heap, shutting away the flames. It made a cairn as high as his chest, and wider across than he could have spanned in three strides. "That should satisfy the thing," he decided.

But he was wrong. There was a crackling and a steaming. Between the bigger lumps darted tongues of the inner fire. As Hok gazed, fascinated and wondering, the whole heap suddenly burst into roaring holocaust. He was forced to retreat before it.

"The black stones burn!" he cried. "Yes, and more hotly than wood!"*

So small a thing as a battle with invaders was now driven from his mind. The Shining One had thrown down a marvel to him, and it behooved him to see it out. See it out Hok did, while the sun climbed higher and higher, and the blaze shot up higher than a tall tree, died down. Hok was able to approach again. At length there came a rain, a spatter that was brisk but not heavy. The fire, burning itself out, perished. He walked close, his moccasins squelching in the damp.

"Where is the gift of heaven?" he asked the smouldering ashes. With reverent insistence, he poked among them with the butt of his axe.

Something gleamed up, like water, but hard—like ice, but warm. Grunting in his new amazement, Hok scooped the ashes away to either side.

The meteor that had fallen and set so great a fire was reduced by its own works to a jagged piece of fused clinker. But from the heart of it had issued

---

* No formal history can trace the first use of coal, which must have been accidental as in the present example. The early great civilizations knew nothing of coal, but European barbarians before the Roman conquest seem to have used it since prehistoric times.

something long and lean and straight, like a sleeping snake. The thing was still hot as Hok touched it, and he had to drag it forth in a fold of his lion's skin—it was as broad as his three fingers, and well longer than his arm, tapering to a point and harder than any flint he had ever known. Yet, hard as it was, it had a springy temper to it that no stone had ever displayed.* Holding the broad end in wrappings of skin, Hok hefted it.

"The gift of heaven!" he called it again. "This is a weapon, then. But how to use it?"

The rain had abated. Hok bore his find away toward his village, studying it intently with the eye of a master workman.

It already had the beginnings of an edge to either side of it, sharper than his sharpest chipped stone, and its point was finer and leaner than any dagger he knew. As with flints, Hok tried to improve the thing by chipping with a small, heavy hammer-stone. The substance rang to a tone he had never heard before, but showed no breakage or other great effect. He learned to rub and whet, and this made the edge keener. So Hok labored as he strolled on toward home, and as he came thither in the late afternoon he had finished the blade to his liking—with a keen point, a slicing edge, and at the broad end a grip for his hand wound tightly with rawhide thongs slit from his lion's skin.

He grinned and chuckled over the thing. First he would show it to Oloana, his comely wife, who always shared his triumphs and enthusiasms—her midnight eyes would glow like stars at the sight of this new thing. And he would let Ptao, his bright-haired little son, try to lift the thing's long weight....

"Hok! Hok!"

His brother Zhik, sub-chief under him, was running toward him from the direction of the village. "You live!" he panted.

"Of course I live," said Hok, laying his sword across his arm for easier carrying. "How went the fight after I was knocked over? Did you kill many of the Fishers before they ran?"

"Before—they ran?" Zhik repeated, and shook his tawny head. "But they did not run, Hok—we did."

Hok straightened up and glared, his teeth showing. "Ran? We? How was that, Zhik?"

His brother spread helpless hands. "It was that thing that fell and struck you down. Because it fell toward us—"

Hok clutched Zhik's arm to calm him. "What happened? Speak clearly, and briefly."

The words came out in a tumble. "We were frightened. The Fishers yelled to each other that the spirits fought on their side, and came at us. They drove us before them. You were thought to be dead, and nobody touched you, since heaven itself had claimed your life—"

"But I am alive," Hok assured him again. "Well, and after you ran from them?"

---

* Meteoric iron generally has from 4 to 10 per cent of nickel, with traces of cobalt, copper, tin and carbon—an alloy that is a makeshift steel, not at all unsuitable for making weapons.

"We ran, thinking the Shining One hated us. But Oloana, when we told her at the village, insisted on going to find your body." Zhik shook his head ruefully. "We tried to make her stay, but she would go—she and Ptao, your son."

Hok suddenly grew chill, as though new and cold rain had fallen upon him. He sensed worse news to come. "Why have I not met them, then?" he asked.

Zhik grimaced wretchedly over what he must say. "The—the Fishers had followed us for some distance, picking up some bows dropped by our wounded. And they came upon Oloana and Ptao, carrying them back toward their village by the sea."

The glare in Hok's blue eyes grew paler and hotter. His big right hand closed upon the hide-wrapped hilt of the sword that was cradled on his left arm. "They captured Oloana and Ptao?" he repeated. "And no man tried to stop them—not even you, my brother?"

"We thought it was the will of the Shining One, grown angry. We did not know that you were alive—" Zhik broke off, and put his hand on his brother's shoulder. "Come to the village. Eat and rest. We will rally the warriors that are left. When they see that you live, they will follow—"

"There is not time. Go back, and say that I have followed Djoma and his skulking Fishers." Hok suddenly lifted the sword. It caught the glow of the sun in blinding flashes. He flourished it above his blond head bound with the hawk wings.

"The Shining One gave me this," he cried, "and gave me also a deed to do, worthy of such a weapon—I want no help from the others. This sharp Widow-maker will cut me a way through the Fishers, and gain back what I have lost! Good-by, Zhik!"

He spun around and set off at a run, his eyes searching the plain for the tracks of his enemies.

Chapter II

Shang, the great cave-bear,* had scented food earlier that day—tender meat, human meat—and had followed it hungrily up wind. The first chill of autumn, that had turned the leaf-thickets brown and yellow and crimson, had been felt by Shang. He had been eating nuts, adding layers to the store of fat that covered his powerful frame against the long winter sleep in his cavern, and the flesh of man would prove a welcome variant. But there had been too many men, all armed and close together. Shang had watched them from a distance, his big brown body hidden in bushes—dark, bearded males, with among them one woman and one boy, these bound and guarded. Shang's mouth watered for the boy in particular, but he dared not charge the whole throng. Men had a way of fighting as an aggregation. And so he let the horde go by, dolefully and grumpily watching.

It was only a little later that he smelled man again, then sighted him. A straggler? No, for this was of another sort—big and blond and ruddy, this one, and his eyes were on the tracks of the previous party. Shang, wise in animal divination, recognized that he was a stern fighter and a brave one. But Shang did not fear one human being, even as big and resolute-seeming a one as this. He waited until the solitary marcher came within six bounds of the hiding place in the bushes; then, with a deafening cry that was half cough, half roar, he charged.

Hok took one glance at the apparition—a shaggy dun monster almost as large as a bison bull, with an open red mouth that could have engulfed his head at a single snap—and quickly sprang aside. As Shang blundered past

---

* The cave-bear, *Ursus spelaus,* was a larger and heavier creature than his modern cousin, and was a contemporary and enemy of stone-age man. The cave-drawings of Aurignacian and Magdalenean times include many representations of the cave-bear, and at least one cave-bear skeleton shows marks of a fierce attack with stone weapons.

and wheeled for another rush, Hok swarmed up the nearest tree, a thriving young beech, and came to rest in the main fork.

Howling and snarling, Shang reared his bulk to a height half again that of a tall man, and with claws like daggers he ripped and tore at the bark of the tree. But he could not climb after Hok, as a smaller and more active bear might, and the fork was well out of his reach.* Slavering hungrily, he circled the tree and flourished those immense armed paws.

Hok gazed at him, then away toward the west and south. In that direction led the trail of Djoma and the Fisher war party—and Oloana and Ptao. He himself was safe from the ravening beast, but only as long as he remained stranded. What would happen meanwhile? Leaning down, he addressed the big cave-bear:

"Hai, Shang, who would eat me—what if I come down to dispute the matter with you?" He twiddled the sword that had never left his hand. "I am but one man against your paws and teeth, but the Shining One has given me a fang to match yours. Hai!" he ejaculated again. "I will wait no longer. Prepare to fight for your dinner, Shang."

He paused only to slash away a thick branch of the tree and trim its foliage. The heavy, sharp sword clove the wood as though it were a grass-stalk. Hok grunted his approval, and suddenly tumbled himself out of his perch, landing upright on his moccasined feet, sword and branch lifted in his hands.

"Come, Shang, and eat Hok! He has proved a tough morsel for hungrier beasts than you."

As though he understood the challenge, Shang heaved himself upright on his rear legs again. Monstrous, grossly manlike, he lumbered forward to strike this impudent human thing to earth. Hok laughed, as always in the face of deadly peril. His right hand advanced the sword.

Shang dabbed at the shiny thing the man was holding out. In times past he had encountered weapons, and had knocked their wooden hafts to splinters with sweeps of his paws before descending upon the unarmed wielder. But he barely touched the iron, then snatched back his big forefoot with a howl of pain. The edge, whetted assiduously by Hok, had laid open Shang's calloused palm to the bone.

"You taste the Widow-maker, Shang," Hok taunted him. "Come, try with that other paw."

Shang was not one to give up for one wound. He tramped closer, both arms lifted, his mouth open and steaming. Hok gazed for a long, meditative moment, down that gaping throat. Then he suddenly sprang to meet the huge beast.

His left hand thrust with the branch, jagged butt foremost. It went between the open jaws, stabbing the gullet cruelly. A strangled yell rose from Shang's deep chest, and both paws struck at the stout billet of beechwood. Hok, safe for the moment from blow or hug, struck with what he held in his right hand.

---

* Remains of *Ursus spelaus* show that, for all the size of the animal, the phalanges bearing the claws were weak, denoting a loss of climbing ability from long dwelling in caves.

The gleaming gray blade, swift as a serpent's tongue, pierced Shang's broad belly. As it went home, Hok ripped upward with all his strength, drew his weapon clear and sprang backward as far as he could. Shang, still erect, stared and gestured stupidly. Then he toppled forward, with an abrupt thud that shook the earth.

Hok waved the sword, now running blood to its hilt.

"The gift of heaven is a great marvel and magic," he exulted. "What spear or axe could have slain Shang so swiftly?"

From his head he stripped the hawk wings and tossed them on the subsiding body of the bear. If Zhik rallied the warriors and led them after him, they would come upon this evidence of Widow-maker's deadliness, would see by the hawk wings that Hok was the single-handed slayer. It would give them heart after their defeat.

Meanwhile, Hok took up once more the trail of Djoma's band.

"Woman," said Djoma haughtily, "there is no need for you to look back. You will not see that country again."

Oloana, bound and dishevelled in the midst of the marching Fishers, faced him with an air fully as haughty as his own. So did the lad Ptao, who trudged at her side with arms trussed but with frost-yellow head flung desperately high.

"Hok the Mighty is my husband," said Oloana with murderous dignity. "He will follow and take revenge. Even now he may be on your heels."

At that word it was Djoma who glanced back, suddenly and with furtive excitement, as though Oloana had conjured up a great honey-haired menace. But the back trail, through thickets and over knolls, was empty of any hostile figure. Recapturing his boldness, Djoma sought to wither her:

"I say again that Hok was stricken dead, by the fire-ball sent by his own angry god. He alone dared stand up before it, and in punishment he was slain."

"We passed the place of the battle," reminded Oloana. "I saw other dead, and on the ground lay Hok's bow and his axe, but not his body. He lives and follows. Prepare your skull for smashing, because he will not spare you."

"If he was gone, the angry Shining One carried him away," insisted Djoma. "In any case, my god is stronger than yours—he is the Sea-Father. Did he not give me victory? Did he not send rain at the moment I captured you, to show that you were his gift to me? Let Hok come, if he still lives. I will shed his blood with this spear." He flourished the weapon boldly, and his men, hearing the vaunt, yelled approval.

"My father will pluck you to pieces like a little roast sparrow," spoke up the proud young voice of Ptao. "When I am grown—"

"And when, cub, will you be grown?" jeered one of the men who marched as a guard beside him. "We will take you to our place by the sea, and there we will eat you."

"I would sicken your narrow stomach," snapped the boy. "Eat fish, and leave strong meat alone."

One or two of the captors laughed at this repartee, and the guardsman growled. The march continued in silence.

The young son of Djoma, a towering youth with a downy black beard that grew in two points, came close to his father. "I am old enough to marry," he ventured. "Let me have this woman we took from the enemy. See, she has dark hair, like our own people. And she is strong and brave and good to look upon. To judge from that sharp-tongued son of hers, she would give fine warriors to make the tribe mighty."

"Speak of this another time, Caggo," bade Djoma gruffly. His own eyes were bright as he studied Oloana sidelong. She strode free and proud, for all her plight. Djoma was remembering that he, too, was without a mate since Caggo's mother had been snapped up by a shark while swimming a year ago. If Oloana had been the mate of one mighty chief, what more fitting than that he take her for himself? . . . "Such things as concern captive women are to be decided by council of the elders," he elaborated. "Wait until we get home."

Caggo nodded acceptance, but contrived to walk near the prisoner, admiring her frankly. She spat once between his tramping feet, and took no other notice of him.

"We have heard little of you Fishers, for we never troubled ourselves about your country or possessions," she told Djoma balefully. "But now Hok will give you his attention, and you will not find it welcome. I think that stealing me will be the worst day's work you have ever done."

"We will see, we will see," said Djoma darkly, but once again he glanced hurriedly backward. His eyes dilated with sudden panic. Was that a human figure, that thing showing itself briefly among bushes far behind? If so, what did it bear that gleamed like sun on the sea? He looked hard, but saw nothing else. The thing had ducked from sight, if indeed he had really seen something. Djoma cursed himself roundly for letting his nervousness create visions. Perhaps some beast of prey, coming to the deserted battlefield, had dragged away the corpse of the Flint People's chief, because it was the largest there. In any case, Hok was dead. He, Djoma, had seen the fellow fall. And Djoma must remember in the meanwhile his own position as a leader. There must be no appearance of fear.

Yet the feeling could not be rationalized away. That night the band camped by a grass-collared spring, and ate in serious silence its ration of sundried fish. Oloana and Ptao, tied by the feet to a sapling, refused with disgust offerings of such food,* and talked loftily to each other of the vengeance to be taken upon the impudent raiders who had dared use them thus.

But as night fell, Djoma looked once more along the back trail that was now too dim to be seen, and gave an order. Some of his warriors unslung the foot-lashings of the prisoners and herded them well away from the camp, binding them again under some low brown bushes. Djoma camped there also, with

---

* Most inland savages, unfamiliar with fish, are suspicious of it. Both the Apaches and Zulus repudiated it as poison.

Caggo and one or two others. They spent the night without a fire—dangerous to do in strange country, but Djoma felt somehow that camping with a fire would be more dangerous still.

There were yells in the night. At dawn, Djoma returned to the main bivouac and learned that at dead of night something had struck down two of his sentries and raged through the camp, killing a third man and injuring five more before it was driven away. Nobody was sure who—or what—the attacker was. The wounds it had dealt were strange enough; deep, clean slashes, terrible to see, and one almost delicate stab.

Djoma ordered a forced march home.

Chapter III

Thus Hok, following on their heels, was not able to raid a second night camp, for Djoma marched all that night. He and his men were back in familiar country by now, and made better progress than their lone pursuer, who furthermore had a close call with a black leopard in a little glen between two of the wooded hills. By the next dawn, Hok was far behind in his chase. He wiped Widow-maker clean of leopard blood with a handful of coarse ferns, and studied the trail.

"Here among the warriors marched Oloana," he decided, picking out certain narrow footmarks. "Yes, and here went Ptao beside her—not faltering, but striding out like a warrior. O Shining One!" and he raised his anxious face to the rising orb on the eastern rim. "Keep my wife and son alive until I come at their captors with Widow-maker, your gift. Keep that chief of the Fishers alive, also—let nothing befall him save at my hand."

He trotted ahead on his grim lone hunt.

In the early afternoon of this third day, he came out from among heights, hills and thickets upon a rocky stretch of plain. Beyond was a ridge of gray granite, with a gnarled oak tree growing at its foot, the leaves turning tawny with autumn's first frosts. The multitude of footmarks, so easy to trace across the soil of forest or meadow, was all but lost on this hard surface. Hok went more than half by guess, up the ridge to the backbone of rock at the top.

It was hot underfoot, with a heat more than that of the autumn sun. Hok paused, looking this way and that. Beyond was more timber, but sparse-grown and stunted by the wind that blew from the sea—he could see that, too, on the horizon, a chill gray gleam like the light reflected from Widow-maker. To his right rose a shimmer in the air, as from a great fire. Hok scowled.

"Have men camped here?" he asked himself, looked again, and crossed the rocks to investigate. The footing grew hotter to his moccasins, but he did not see the cause until he was almost upon it—a deep pit, round and as wide across, perhaps, as a man is tall. That pit was filled with fire, blue and orange, with no discernible bottom or source of fuel supply. Hok came as close as he could, gazing down.

"The Lair of Fire," he said aloud. "I have heard of this place from traveler guests at my cave. It has always been thus, though nobody knows where the fire gets its fuel—fire cannot burn rocks and earth.* It is a strange matter." He peered into the Lair of Fire, again. "It is a good omen that my path should cross here, for fire is of the Shining One, who watches over me at this place."

Silently the blue-yellow flames fluttered, and one of them rose momentarily, pale and lean as the blade of Widow-maker.

"The fire makes me a sign—a sign concerning my weapon," Hok decided. "What is it that you wish to say, fire?"

There was a rose-tinted swirl in the blue heart of the glow, and several flames sprang up, seeming to pen like begging fingers toward him. Hok drew away.

"You want your gift again," he said accusingly. "No, fire. Widow-maker is a gift from the Shining One, not a loan. I need the gift to win back what the Fisher chief dared to steal from me."

The pit glowed redly, as if with sudden anger, and Hok made hasty departure. Going down the other side of the ridge, his feet gratefully found cooler earth. But his mind remained troubled.

Why had there been a sign at the Lair of Fire that he must give up his sword? Did the Shining One repent of his generosity? Was Hok to be warned from the adventure he had undertaken? The big man scowled and wagged his golden head, as though to banish the disturbing mystery from his thoughts. He picked up the trail of Djoma once more, and made speed upon it.

Night had fallen, nippy and moonless, upon a broad bay of the ocean where Djoma and his followers had their habitation. To seaward flickered a multitude of red lights, the supper-fires of the village, seeming to float on the surface of the quiet water. On shore, just above high tide mark, burned a single blaze of driftwood, with a greenish tinge to it because of the crusting of salt on the sticks. Nearby a dugout canoe had been dragged up. Within the circle of light squatted two black-haired sentries, each with his spear thrust into the sand beside him. After the manner of sentries since time's beginning, they grumbled at extra duty.

"How can this pursuer, if he is but one man as it seems, be a threat to our entire people?" demanded one. "I think that Djoma is too easily frightened."

"Do not let him hear you say so," counseled his companion, "or he will prove his courage by dashing out your brains with his axe. I saw that sun-haired giant at work the night he raided our camp, and he is a fierce one. Perhaps Djoma is right to leave a guard on shore here, where he must come if he is to attack

---

* The Lair of Fire was a well of natural gas, set ablaze by lightning or other cause, such a phenomenon as exists in many volcanic regions throughout the world.

our village. Yet I wish it was another than I who sat here with you." The warrior stretched and yawned. "I am weary from much marching and fighting."

The first speaker sat up more alertly, his ears seeming to prick. "What was that?" he demanded sharply. "It sounded like a scraping or crawling upon the beach, just there beyond the firelight." And he pointed.

The other laughed. "You hear strange things because you are young and nervous. When you are my age, and have stood many night watches, you will be calm and brave. That noise was a snake, or a nesting bird."

The younger man had forgotten his criticism of Djoma. "If the stranger comes—" he began.

"We will both stay awake," his comrade comforted him. "The light of our fire will shine on that strange weapon as he comes. We will both yell, and charge him from either side. Help will come to us at once, many men in canoes from the village."

The plan recommended itself to the nervous one. "We might kill him before any came," he suggested. "Then Djoma would praise us, perhaps make us sub-chiefs.... Listen! I heard the noise again."

His more sober companion had heard it likewise. They both rose swiftly, seizing their spears.

"It came from directly landward of our fire," whispered the less agitated warrior. "Let us move forward a little distance apart, so that we can come up on any stranger from both sides. Then, if he attacks one of us, the other can stab him in the back."

"Well said," muttered the youth approvingly. They advanced with stealthy strides, weapons poised. Again the cooler head of the two was struck with an idea. He snapped his fingers for attention, then pointed with his spear toward a great tussock of broad-leafed vegetation that thrust up from the sand, the only nearby cover that might shelter a man. The two tightened their grips on their weapons, and charged.

As one they hurled themselves upon the tussock, as one they plunged their points into its heart—just an instant too late.

For Hok, within that shelter, had divined their purpose. He had leaped back and up, just as the spears crossed in the tangle of leaves and drove deep into the sand on which he had been crouching. Next moment he shot out his two long arms in opposite directions, fastening a hand on each of the swarthy throats of his would-be slayers.

Two hairy mouths fell open to scream for help, but Hok's quick grip had been sure and tight. No wind could come from panting lungs to give those mouths voice. Letting go of their spears, the two men strove frantically to tear away the giant fingers that strangled them. But Hok, strongest man of his time and country, laughed harshly, while his double clutch tightened as mercilessly and progressively as rawhide lashings in a hot, dry sun.

"You wanted to find me," he taunted his two victims. "You found me. Ah, you have eaten too many fish, and your mouths gape. You are dying like fish drawn out of the water... your flappings grow weak, weak... they cease."

He released the two limp-grown forms, and they collapsed in one heap at his feet. Hok spurned them, but they were both finished. He chuckled again, without mirth, and rubbed his terrible hands together. Walking forward to the fire and beyond it, he stared at the lights of the village across the water.

"I have disposed of the two warders, and without warning from this place none will expect me out there. What sort of place is Djoma's village—an island?"

Beside him was drawn up the canoe, hollowed by fire from a single log, but Hok did not know how to use such a device. He tested the lashings that moored Widow-maker to the girdle at his waist, then waded quickly into the sea-water. With powerful, silent strokes he swam toward the place where his wife and son were held prisoner.

As he approached through the water, the fire-lights seemed to rise from before him to hang above him—they were kindled at a height. Now he drew close enough to see that an angular blackness, more solid than the mere gloom-color of the night, rose from the quiet waves. The island must be rocky. He paddled in noiselessly to where there would be a shore.

But there was no shore.

Chapter IV

Hok was puzzled, his blue eyes narrowing in the dark. Was he swimming into a sea-cave? Turning over on his back, he groped to right and left with his hands. The cave, if it was such, must be very wide. He let himself float to one side, and collided with wood, apparently a tree-trunk growing out of the water at this point. Puzzled and cautious, he drew himself up and climbed it. For more than his own height he clambered above water level, holding on to old broken branch-stubs. Lifting his hand, he felt wood above him—solid wood, a seeming roof of it. If this was indeed a cave, then the cave was made of tree-stuffs instead of rockstuffs, with water for floor. Hok slid carefully down again, and swam a little way back the way he had come.

He began to skirt the village, trying to see what it stood on, if not an island. All he could make out at first was a cliff-like overhang that shut away the light of fire and stars. Then, around to one side, he came to where a hut stood at the very edge of things, with a fire at its doorway. People lounged there, talking. Hok lay low in the brine, and by the firelight made out the mystery in part.

The seeming riddle was that this island-thing was truly made of wood—made by man, by Djoma and his tribe, probably started long before them by their fathers. Up from the harbor bed projected tree-trunks, on the forked tops of which had been laid rafterlike poles. These in turn supported close-laid crosspieces of wood, each the half of a split log with the flat side up. All this was bound by broad lashings of rawhide, dried until it was as old and hard as flint itself. Upon this platform stood huts, of mud-daubed wickerwork with thatch roofs, just as the huts of Hok's own tribe stood on solid earth.

It behooved Hok to learn more about this strange construction. He dipped under water and swam down to the base of one upright log. It had no roots in the sea-bottom, but had been driven there somehow, and was made solid by the heaping of big stones around it. Lashings to cross-bars, which were lashed in turn to other uprights, made it still more strongly set in place. Hok swam on around the village of the Fishers. He saw that it was of the same fashioning throughout—hundreds of big trunks, each painfully hewn on shore with stone axes, then floated out and planted on end in a predecided position, and finally the complex fabric of the platform woven and lashed and built upon the top of this artificial water-forest. He shook his drenched head in wonder. Such a work represented colossal effort and ingenuity. It must have taken years—lifetimes, perhaps. Finished, it gave the Fishers a fortress almost unvanquishable, where they could live securely, protected in the midst of the waters that also furnished their scaly food.*

At a corner near the shore was a low-set section of platform, its edges sloping down almost to water level. All around this were tied up the scores of dugout canoes that belonged to Djoma's people. But on this platform was another sentry party, four or five men this time, gathered around a fire that had a hearth of flat stones set in clay. They would discover Hok if he clambered out, probably would kill him before he could gain his feet and defend himself. He must win foothold in the village at another point.

Even as he came to this realization, something made a swishing sweep through the water at him.

He kicked sidewise only in the nick of time. A shark, thrice his length, slid past like a javelin within arm's reach of him, then brought itself round with frightening grace to make another ravenous charge.

Hok dipped his right arm down under water, seizing the hilt of Widow-maker. With a jerk he broke the sword loose from its lashings at his waist. The shark was upon him again, and he saved himself from a crippling bite by putting his left palm on its ugly snub nose, letting himself be carried backward through the water. At the same time he brought up Widow-maker's point, in the knowing way he had already learned. It grated on the coarse sandy hide, and he gave a vigorous shove. A moment later the shark's throat was pierced and Hok threw himself strongly sidewise, dragging on the hilt and opening the wound into a terrible gash.

The shark gave a convulsive leap clear of the water, almost disarming Hok as he dragged Widow-maker clear. It fell back with a mighty splash, and writhed past him, so that its coarse hard hide rasped skin from his shoulder. Hok swam swiftly away, for the commotion had attracted the attention of the sentries on the boat-platform.

With yells and cries the men caught brands from their fire and held them aloft, shedding light over the sea. Hok, coming under the shelter of the higher platform well beyond, saw the waves he had just quitted being churned into awful turmoil.

---

* Such stilt-supported communities were one of the most elaborate triumphs of prehistoric man's inventive genius, arguing considerable industry and cooperative planning. The most interesting remains have been discovered in old lake beds of Switzerland. Probably others existed at the seashore of the Stone Age and were washed away. Venice and the Aztec capital of Tenochtitlan were elaborations of the water-town idea, and the savages of New Guinea still build such towns.

BATTLE IN THE DAWN

The wounded shark was being set upon by its comrades—a whole school of them. The harbor must have been well swarmed by the ravenous creatures, drawn to the village of Djoma by the mass of refuse thrown from its platform daily, and it was a wonder that Hok had not been molested before. Even now, some of the sharks that had gathered to the smell of gushing blood turned off to pursue him. With Widow-maker held crosswise in his teeth, Hok swiftly climbed one of the uprights that supported the platform, clinging to it just beneath the cross-logs, while sharks drew silently into a press below him. Immediately overhead there was a thundering, shaking rush—the struggle of the great creatures near the boat-platform was drawing a fascinated throng of Fishers to see and exclaim.

Hok stayed where he was, with enemy warriors and their families racing above him and hungry sharks snapping just beneath his moccasin-soles, until the platform above him vibrated no longer. Then he caught hold of a horizontal pole, drew himself up and swung his weight upon the broad floor that supported the village. Quickly he crept between two of the deserted huts, glancing in all directions to make certain that he had been unobserved. This part of the village, at least, was completely deserted. Hok moved stealthily inward among the press of dwellings, toward a large central one which must be the habitation of Djoma. This was really a combination building, made up of several huts joined with tunnel-like passages to make a structure of several rooms that would house the chief, his family and dependents. Here, at least, remained someone—a guard, gazing wistfully in the direction of the torchlight and turmoil. He plainly stayed where he was under orders, to watch over something of value within.

Hok felt that he was close to the thing he had sought. Slipping around the side of the house as noiselessly and grimly as a huge blond ghost, he clove the man's skull with Widow-maker. Leaping across the body as it fell, he entered the place where Djoma lived.

A few coals of fire burned upon a broad hearth of stones set in clay, and he stirred them up with his sword-point. At once he beheld one of the treasures the warrior had been left to protect—the captured bows that Djoma had gleaned from the field of that unlucky battle three days ago. They were bound into a great sheaf, a good load for a strong man. Hok dragged them out, found a place in the platform where a split log was poorly fastened. He cut the stout lashings and pried the slab loose, then pushed the bundle of weapons through and heard it splash beneath. No Fisher would ever use those captured bows nor learn from studying them how to make similar ones—the tide would wash them out to sea. But this was only the smaller item of Hok's double quest.

Where were Djoma's captives?

He entered the hut again, peering around in the half-gloom. "Oloana!" he called softly. "Where are you?"

"Hok!" came back a glad cry, and with a leap he was across the floor, hewing with Widow-maker at a woven door that blocked off one of the sections of the multiple hut. The tough withes that had made the basket-like obstruction fell to pieces before his onslaught, and from the dark hole thus exposed Oloana and Ptao rushed out. He caught one in each arm, and all three hugged, muttered and chuckled in their joy of reunion.

"I knew my father would come," Ptao found breath to say. "I told them that—both Djoma and Caggo. They laughed, but I knew from their eyes that they were afraid."

"Djoma and Caggo," repeated Hok. "Djoma is the chief of these Fisher-folk, I believe, but who is Caggo?"

"The son of Djoma," Oloana informed him. "He has spoken of taking me as his wife. I scratched his face once, and he keeps away, but he swears to tame me."

"I will find occasion to speak to Caggo," promised Hok, "but first, to get you free of this place, which smells of rotten fish."

"That you will never do," growled a voice behind them.

Chapter V

Intent on freeing his loved ones, Hok for once had relaxed that stern sense of vigilance that every hunter and warrior must have and employ if he will prosper. The Fishers had returned from the diversion made by the sharks, had overheard Hok in the hut, and now they swarmed within the doorway and on the platform outside and around—warriors to the front, armed and fierce. In the fore of the throng stood Caggo, towering up to Hok's height and extending almost as broad across the chest and shoulders. With one foot he kicked up the fire, making light for all to see. His right hand lifted an axe of obsidian, black and broad. Just behind him, with a spear similarly poised, scowled Djoma.

"You did come, Hok," said Djoma in a voice as bitter-cold as the drip from a crag of ice. "I thought you dead, slain by your own god. Well, it proves that your god is weaker even than I thought. I will do a better job than he."

Hok moved so that his body sheltered Oloana and Ptao. His grip tightened on the thong-bound hilt of Widow-maker.

"The Shining One gave me this weapon," he cried, and the declaration rang like a blow of the sword itself. "Widow-maker has drunk the blood of many Fishers. He will drink more, whenever you move to attack."

"Huh!" snorted Caggo. "I do not fear that shiny thing, which looks more like an icicle than any club or spear. You seek to frighten us by lies, Hok. I myself will cut you down, and that woman of yours will see that I am greater than you and worth having."

He dared to grin impudently at Oloana, who stood behind Hok, and Hok went mad.

"A-hai!"

Widow-maker sang in the air, and Caggo did not dodge quickly enough. The edge took him on the jowl. Away flew his shaggy dark head, like a flung clod. Only the grin remained—the grin and the double-pointed beard—for all the rest had been smitten cleanly from Caggo's body by that terrible slash. And while all the Fishers stared in frozen horror, the grin seemed to relax and grow wry as if, even without a head, Caggo knew that oblivion had come upon him. The lifted axe sank down in the lifeless hand, the knees bent and buckled, the decapitated body sank down and collapsed.

Hok broke that stunned silence with a joyous yell of battle, and charged into the thick of the Fishers. Thrust, slash, hack—three of them were down in the space of as many breaths. The others shrank and scrambled away. Had they not been cramped inside the narrow door those nearest him might have pressed back and created a rout of the whole party. But the stout walls of mud and wicker hemmed them in with him, and they must fight. All around him they waved their weapons.

"Do not kill!" thundered the voice of Djoma, who had himself retreated into a corner before Hok's rush. "Take him alive—drag him down, bind him!"

It was easier said than done, but a horrified youth chanced to run blindly upon Hok's point. Widow-maker wedged between two ribs, and before Hok could wrench the iron clear, the others rushed from all sides. They swarmed over Hok like ants. He stumbled and fell, then struggled up with a powerful effort, shaking himself free and striking in all directions. Oloana screamed a warning, but too late—Djoma, running up from behind, struck once with the clubbed haft of his spear. Hok felt a thick blackness swallow up his senses.

He awoke to the impact of many water-drops—he was outside, and it was raining. Many voices murmured around him. Opening his eyes, he saw that dawn was coming among the clouds.

"See, he wakens, he lives," cackled a wrinkled old woman with cruel features. "I thought him dead, he lay still so long."

"Had he died I would have been sorry," responded the voice of Djoma. "Look up, Hok. You are my captive. To show his favor, the Sea-Father sends rain. It is his sign, veiling the weak face of your Shining One."

The prisoner sat up. He was bound with many tight-drawn straps around legs, arms and body—straps of fish skin. The swarthy folk who had captured him had canoed him ashore from their water-girt village, and had laid him upon a great rock on the beach. Beside him was Oloana, also bound, and little Ptao. They had both been staring anxiously, and as Hok showed that he was alive and undamaged, they had the heart to smile. He smiled back, with an expression full of love and encouragement.

Djoma did not like such evidence of cheer among his captives, for he cleared his throat snarlingly to attract their attention. The light rain flowed down his beard in silvery drops.

"You killed my son, Hok," he said coldly.

"I meant to," replied Hok, his muscles surging against his bonds. "If I were free, and had Widow-maker, I would kill you as well."

"But you are not free," taunted Djoma. "As for the thing you call Widow-maker, it is here." He held out the sword, still bloody from the death-blows Hok had dealt with it. As he spoke, lightning crackled across the sky, and thunder roared.

"Ah," said Hok, "your Sea-Father is not the only one who sends signs. There was a javelin of fire waved by the Shining One."

"But the rain drowned it at once," flung back Djoma. "My god is far stronger than yours."

"Hear him, Shining One," muttered Hok tensely. "Set me free, that I may drive his lies down his throat."

Djoma laughed at the prayer. "Your worship will do you no good, Hok. I have won."

Hok again strove to break the fish-skin cords. They creaked, but held. "Set me free," he challenged, while the rain beat on his head and shoulders. "My bare hands against whatever weapons you choose—even against Widow-maker. We will see then who is the stronger. I dare you to do battle with me!"

It was a bold defiance, and had its effect upon the listening Fishers who stood grouped all around. They muttered together, perhaps hoping that the test would be made—a fight between chiefs was always well worth watching. But Djoma, whose theological arguments had been so good, had yet another answer ready.

"You shall die without the chance to fight, Hok. Bound as you are, you shall be thrown from the platform of my village where the water is deepest and the sharks are thickest. What they leave of you will bait fish for us. But first," and his black-bright eyes turned toward Ptao, "there is something you must watch."

Hok, too, gazed at Ptao through the downpour, and the fear he would not confess for himself could not be hid as he wondered how the boy was threatened. Djoma noted, and chuckled his triumph.

"You struck down Caggo, my son. So, Hok, I will strike down yours."

For a moment Hok thought that blackness would overwhelm him again. Mightily he strove to gain his feet, but they were bound at the ankles and would not gain a grip on the rock. A great crackling bolt of lightning quivered in the sky, and the rain fell more heavily and coldly. Djoma put forth his free hand, caught Ptao by the shoulder and jerked him erect upon the rock.

"Djoma," Hok choked out, "before all your folk I name you the blackest and lowest of cowards. To kill a boy, a little boy—and bound, at that!"

"Do not speak to him, father," came the steady young voice of Ptao. He gazed fearlessly up into the grinning hairy face of Djoma. "He is less than a snake with a poisoned fang. I am not afraid to die, for my fear would make him happy."

"That is a brave cub," said a watching warrior, with honest admiration.

"So shall he not be allowed to grow up," snapped Djoma. "Look well, Hok. I shall kill him with your weapon that killed Caggo."

Slowly, with full sense of the drama in the situation, the chief of the Fishers lifted the sword high in air, so that its point rose heavenward in the rain.

Hok suddenly cried out, in deep agony of spirit, a last prayer:

"Shining One! Save Ptao and strike down this enemy—let me win us free, and never again shall your weapon be used to stab or strike! I swear this, by the fire you gave my people in the long ago—"

"Useless!" howled Djoma, with a wild ringing laugh. The sword quivered before falling.

Thunder broke open the sky, and down jabbed one more bolt of lightning. The uplifted Widow-maker caught that lightning, glowed as with white heat.

Djoma, his laugh of mockery all unfinished, whirled over and down like a dead leaf. On his face he lay without a tremor. A purple-black wale streaked his body, from the fork of his right hand that had held the stolen sword, down across his shoulder and back, to the heel of his right foot that had stood in a pool of water.

At the same moment, Hok rolled violently from the rock where he had lain, and whipped himself erect. The final summoning of his strength had broken those strained cords of fish skin.

A scooping grab, and he had the sword that had guided down a death of fire upon Djoma. It swung around his head like a crystallized flame.

"Hai! I am Hok—I kill!"

But he could kill only the slowest of the Fishers. For, in deadly terror, they ran before him like deer, diving into the water or scrambling aboard canoes to escape. Within seconds he stood alone on the beach, astride of the body of Djoma, panting and glaring. He now had time to realize that the rain had ceased suddenly and that the sun, his god, shone in the blue morning sky.

"Hok! Hok!" cried Oloana tremulously from where she lay bound. "Cast us free, and let us be gone."

He hurried to her side. The edge of Widow-maker served to sever the bonds that held his wife and son. The three departed unchallenged from the beach where Djoma lay dead, and to which the Fishers dared not return.

Chapter VI

It was noon when they came again to the Lair of Fire. All three were eating ravenously, for Hok had not tasted food since before the first battle with Djoma, and neither Oloana nor Ptao had been able to stomach the unfamiliar provisions of fish offered them. On their march home they had picked handfuls of berries, acorns and rose hips to stay their hunger. But Hok ceased munching as he came to the granite ridge and looked beyond to where flames rose stealthily from their pit, as though to peer at him. His face grew grave and intent, as when he thought deep thoughts.

"I do not like this place," said Oloana. "It is too warm underfoot."

"Wait here," rejoined Hok briefly, and approached the Lair of Fire alone. He walked gingerly but as became a chief, carrying Widow-maker with him. His wife and son watched with curious eyes.

At the brink of the flame-pit, Hok took his stand. His nostrils drank the pungent, half-smothering odor of the rising gases. He began to speak:

"You asked me for Widow-maker once, and I refused. I thought then that only Widow-maker would win back Oloana and Ptao. I was wrong to think it, for Widow-maker was almost turned against us. Only my prayer and promise caused the Shining One to fight on my side, throwing fire down to destroy the chief of the Fishers and to prove that their god, the Sea-Father, is weak and of little account."

He paused. There was a whispering noise far beneath in the glowing depths, as though the creature that breathed out the fire was agreeing with him.

"You, being of flame, are kin to the Shining One," continued Hok formally. "I vowed to him that Widow-maker would not be used again after we were set free. I now keep that vow. You asked for it once. Here it is."

His hand yearned to keep its grip on the good sword that had served him so famously, but he forced himself to cast it in. The bright gray blade seemed to float on the surface of the fire for a moment, as though the uprush of gas supported it. Then it was gone from view, gulped away into the abyss. Up shot a tongue of flame, seeming to make acknowledgment of the returned gift.

"It was not a gift to me—only a loan," said Hok, and retraced his steps to where the woman and boy waited for him.

Leading the way down the other side of the rocky rise, he paused once more under the gnarled oak tree that grew there. His big hands fastened upon a low-growing bough, and with a sudden exertion of his strength he ripped it loose. Stripping away the twigs, he tested the balance of this rough club, and nodded approval.

"It will serve to fight off any dangers that may rise on our way home," he announced.

Ptao's blue eyes, already bright with the dawning enthusiasm for the hunt and the wartrail, appraised the makeshift weapon. "Why did you not keep the bright thing you call Widow-maker?" he asked. "It was splendid to fight with. No axe or spear or club was ever so deadly."

"I know it, my son," nodded Hok, "but I had spoken a word of promise to do as I did. And words of promise, you know, must be kept."

"True," agreed Oloana, glad of a chance to impress a lesson in ethics upon her youngster.

The boy nodded his bright head in imitation of his father. "Yet," he continued, "it was mighty in your hand, and it would have been mighty in mine, too, when I was grown and had become chief after you."

Hok smiled at that, in understanding and comradeship.

"You speak wisdom, son of mine. In my hand and in yours, Widow-maker would be a good thing. Yet, after we are both gone, who knows? A man like Djoma, or worse than Djoma, might make the good thing bad. It is best that the gift of heaven go back whence it came."

They resumed their homeward march. And so, for the time being, the dawn of the Iron Age was delayed.

Hok Visits the Land of Legends

Chapter I

Only Hok could have done it—only Hok the Mighty, strongest and wisest and bravest of the Flint Folk whose chief he was. For Gragru the mammoth was in those days the noblest of all beasts hunted by man—to bring one down was an enterprise for the combined hunter-strength of a tribe. Save for Hok, no man would even think of killing Gragru single-handed.

But Hok had so thought. And for Hok, to think was to do. When winter's heaviest snow had choked the meadows and woods that Hok's people had won by battle from the half-beastly Gnorrls, he put his plan into action.

Not that food was scarce. A late flight of geese had dropped floundering on the frozen river before the village of mud huts, and Hok's sturdy young son Ptao had led the other children to seize them. Hok's brother Zhik had traced a herd of elk to their stamped-out clearing in a willow thicket, and was planning a raid thither. But Hok's big blond head teemed with great thoughts; his blue eyes seemed to gaze on far distances of the spirit. Already he thought of such game as trivial.

On a cloudy gray day, not too cold, he spoke from his cave-door. "I go on a lone hunt," he told the tribe. "It will be several days, perhaps, before I return. In my absence, Zhik is your chief." Then he gave his handsome wife Oloana a rib-buckling hug, and told young Ptao to grow in his absence. He departed along the river trail, heading south for mammoth country.

His big, tall body was dressed in fur from throat to toe. His long shanks wore tight-wound wolf-skin leggings, fur inside. His moccasins, of twofold bison leather, had tops reaching almost to the knees, and were plentifully tallowed against wet. His body was wrapped in the pelt of a cave-lion, arms fitting inside the neatly skinned forelegs, mane muffling his neck and chest. Foxfur gloves protected his hands. All openings and laps were drawn snug by leather laces. Only his great head, with golden clouds of hair and beard, was defiantly bare to winter.

BATTLE IN THE DAWN

Leaving the village, Hok paused to strap his feet into rough snowshoes.* The Flint Folk had developed such things by watching how nature made broad the feet of hare, ptarmigan and lynx to glide on top of the snow. Hok's weapons were a big bow of yew, a quiver of arrows, a big keen axe of blue flint. At his side hung a sizeable deerskin pouch, full of hunter's gear and provisions.

Away he tramped, his blue eyes scanning the horizon. Far off was a black bison, snow-swamped, with wolves closing in. Nearer, gaunt ravens sawed over a frost-killed deer. Winter was the hungry season—eat or be eaten was its byword. Hok's people would eat plentifully of Gragru's carcass . . . Hok journeyed west and south, to where he had once noted a grove of pine and juniper.

It was all of a morning and part of the afternoon before Hok reached the grove. He smiled over nearby mammoth tracks, large enough for him to curl up in. The prey had been there. It would return. He began preparations.

He set up headquarters in the center of the grove, scooping out a den in the snow and laying branches above it for a roof. His bow and arrows he hung to a big pine trunk, away from damp.

Then, axe in hand, he sought out a springy red cedar, felled it and trimmed away the branches. Dragging it to his camp, Hok laboriously hewed and whittled it into a great bow-stave, twice as long as himself and thicker at the midpoint than his brawny calf, with the two ends properly tapered.

Bending the bow was a task even for Hok. From his bag he took a great coil of rawhide rope, several strands thick. With a length of this he lashed the bow horizontally to the big pine. To each end he fastened a second line, making this fast to a tree behind. After that, he toiled to bend one arm, then the other, using all his braced strength and weight and shortening each lashing. The stout cedar bent little by little into a considerable curve.

Next Hok affixed his bowstring of rawhide, first soaking it in slush. When it was as tight as he could make it, he lighted a row of fires near it. As the string dried and shrank in the heat, the bow bent still more.

Meanwhile, Hok was cutting an arrow to fit that bow, a pine sapling thrice the length of his leg. From his pouch he produced a flint point longer than his foot, flaked to a narrow, sharp apex. This he lashed into the split tip, and with his axe chopped a notch in the opposite butt. The finished arrow he laid across his big bow.

"My weapon is ready to draw for killing," he said with satisfaction, and put himself to new toil. A lashing of rope held the arrow notched on the string, and Hok carried the end of this new lashing backward, around a stump directly to the rear. With braced feet, swelling muscles, panting chest, he heaved and slaved and outdid himself until the bow was drawn to the fullest and his pull-rope hitched firmly to the anchorage. He stepped back and proudly surveyed the finished work. "Good!" he approved himself.

---

* Professor Katherine E. Dopp and others have pointed out the absolute necessity for the invention of snowshoes by Stone Age hunters of Hok's time.

He had made and drawn a bow for such a giant as his old mother had spoken of, long ago in his childhood. The big pine to which the bow was bound stood for the archer's rigid gripping hand.

The back-stretched rope from the arrow's notch was the drawing hand. All that was needed would be a target in front of it.

And Hok arranged for that. He cut young, green juniper boughs and made two heaps, three strides apart, so that the arrow pointed midway between them. Then he hacked away branches and bushes that might interfere with the shaft's flight. It was evening by now. He built up his fire behind the drawn bow, toasted a bit of meat from his pouch, and finally slept.

At dawn he woke. Snow was falling. Hok rose and gazed along the little lane in front of the arrow.

There came the prey he hoped for.

Gragru the mammoth, tremendous beyond imagination, marched with heavy dignity to the enticing breakfast Hok had set him. A hillock of red-black hair, more than twice Hok's height at the shoulder,* he sprouted great spiral tusks of creamy ivory, each a weight for several men. His head, a hairy boulder, had a high cranium and small, wise eyes. His long, clever trunk sniffed at one stack of juniper, and began to convey it to his mouth.**

Hok drew his keen dagger of reindeer horn. The mammoth gobbled on, finished the first stack, then swung across to the second.

Hok squinted a last time along the arrow. It aimed at the exact point he had hoped—the hair-thatched flank of the beast. Hok set his knife to the draw-rope—sliced the strands—

Huong! With a whoop of freed strength, the bow hurled its shaft. A heavy thud rang back, and Gragru trumpeted in startled pain.

"You are my meat!" yelled Hok. Gragru wheeled and charged the voice. Hok caught his bow and arrows from their hanging place, gathered the snowshoes under his arm, and danced nimbly aside. "I shot you!" he cried again. "I, Hok!"

Blundering through the brush, Gragru looked right and left for his enemy; but Hok had sagely trotted around behind him. A savage exploration of the thicket, to no avail—then Gragru sought the open again. His blood streamed from wounds on either side where the pine-shaft transfixed him, but he still stood steady on his great treestump feet.

Hok came to the fringe of the junipers. "You shall not escape!" he yelled at the mammoth. "Hok will eat you!"

This time Gragru did not charge. He knew that death had smitten through hair and hide and bone, to the center of his lungs. No time left for combat or revenge—time only for one thing, the thing that every mammoth must do in his last hour.

---

* This was a specimen of the Imperial Mammoth, which stood some 14 feet high. Partial remains of such a giant can be seen at the American Museum of Natural History in New York City.

** Examination of the stomachs of frozen mammoth remains has enabled scientists to decide on juniper as a favorite article of their winter diet.

He turned and struggled away southward through the snow.

Hok watched. He remembered the stories of his fathers.

"Gragru seeks the dying place of the mammoth, the tomb of his people, that no man has ever seen or found.* I shall follow him to that place—learn the secret and mystery of where the mammoth goest to die!"

Quickly he bound on his snowshoes, gained the top of the drifts, and forged away after Gragru, now a diminishing brown blotch in the middle distance.

---

* A similar legend is told about modern elephants and their "graveyard"—it is a fact that bodies of naturally dead elephants are seldom seen. The great beds of mammoth fossils in Russia, from which as much as 100,000 pounds of ivory was gleaned annually in pre-Soviet times, may bear out Hok's belief.

Chapter II
Where Gragru Died

Even the elephant, degenerate modern nephew of Gragru's race, can outrun a good horse on a sprint or a day's march; and the beast Hok now followed was among the largest and most enduring of his kind. Despite the wound, the shaft in his body, and the deep snow, Gragru ploughed ahead faster than Hok's best pace.

The tall chieftain, however, had a plain trail to follow—a deep rut in the snow, with splotches and spatters of blood. "Gragru shall not escape," he promised himself, and mended his stride. The rising wind, bearing more snowflakes, blew at his wide shoulder and helped him along. Ahead was a ravine, its central watercourse many men's height deep under old snows. Gragru sagely churned along one slope, into country more than a day's journey from Hok's village. Hok had hunted there only a few times.

They travelled thus, hunter and hunted, all morning and all afternoon. Evening came, and Hok did not pause for a campfire, but gnawed a strip of dried meat as he marched. His longest pause was to melt snow between his ungloved hands for drink. Then on into the dusk. The clouds broke a little, and the light of a half-moon showed him the trail of Gragru.

With the coming of night he heard the howl of winter-famished wolves behind. They were hunting him, of course.* The safety of a tree, or at least

---

* Hok's people were contemporary with *Cyon alpinis fossils*, a species of wolf larger and stronger, and probably fiercer, than modern types. Such hunting animals must have had to pursue and drag down the powerful game of the age, and would not have shrunk too much from combat with man. At least once among the remarkable artworks of Stone Age man is included a painting of a wolf—a lifelike polychrome on the wall of the cavern at Font-de-Gaume, once the home and art studio of a community of the magnificent Cro-Magnons, Hok's race.

a rock-face to defend his back, was the dictate of discretion; but Hok very seldom was discreet. He paused only long enough to cut a straight shoot of ash, rather longer than himself. Then, resuming his journey, he whittled it to a point with his deerhorn knife. This improvised stabbing spear he carried in his right hand, point backward.

The howling chorus of the wolves came nearer, stronger. It rose to a fiendish din as they sighted Hok. He judged that there were five or six, lean and savage. Without slacking his pace, he kept a watch from the tail of his eye. As they drew close to his heels, several gray forms slackened pace cautiously. Not so the leader—he dashed full upon Hok and sprang.

Hok had waited for that. Back darted his reversed spear. The tough ash pike met the wolf's breast in midair, the very force of the leap helped to impale the brute. There rose one wild scream of agony, and Hok let go of the weapon, tramping along. Behind rose a greedy hubbub—as he had foreseen, the other wolves had stopped and were devouring their fallen leader.

"The bravest often die like that," philosophized Hok, lengthening his stride to make up for lost time.

The long ravine came to a head in a frozen lake. Across this, to the south, brush-clad hills. Gragru's wallowing trail showed how hard he found those hills to climb, and Hok made up some of the distance he had lost on the levels. As the moon sank before morning, Hok caught up. Gragru had paused to rest, a great hunched hillock in a shaggy pelt. Hok yelled in triumph and Gragru, galvanizing into motion, slogged away southward as before.

Another day—second of pursuit, third of absence from home. Even Hok's magnificently trained legs must begin to suffer from so much snowshoeing; even Gragru's teeming reservoir of strength must run lower from pain and labor. Given a chance to idle and nurse himself, he could let the air clot and congeal the wounds, but the shaft still stuck through him, working and shifting to begin fresh bleedings. The trail now led through impeding thickets, and after a brief spurt by Gragru, Hok had a new advantage, that of using the mammoth's lane through the heavy drift-choked growth. By afternoon more snow fell, almost a blizzard. Lest he lose the trail entirely, Hok tramped in Gragru's very tracks instead of on the firmer drifts beside.

"He weakens," Hok told himself, eyeing new blood blotches. "At this point he rested on his knees. Yonder he fell on his side. Brave beast, to get up again! Will he reach the dying place?"

Full of admiration for Gragru, Hok half-wished the animal would triumph, but he did not slow down. Hok was weary, but warm from his exertions and far from faltering.

Night again. During the darkness Hok again kept up a dogged march. Up ahead somewhere, Gragru was forced to make a halt of it. His wound was doing its grim best to heal. Once or twice the mammoth's trunk reached back and investigated that lodged shaft. But there was too much wisdom in that high crag of a skull to permit tugging out of the painful thing—that would mean bleeding to death on the spot. Once again, as the deepest dark heralded the dawn, Hok drew nigh to his massive quarry. Once again Gragru stirred to motion, breaking trail for the third day of the chase.

The mighty stumpy feet were shaking and stumbling by now. Gragru fell again and again. He rose with difficulty after each fall, groaning and puffing but stubborn. A fresh hunter might have caught up—but Hok, however much he would not admit it, was himself close to the end of endurance. His deep chest panted like a bullfrog's. He breathed through his mouth, and the moisture made icicles in his golden beard. Frost tried to bite his face, and he rubbed it away with snow. Only his conscious wisdom kept him from tossing aside his furs as too much weight. By noon he made his first rest-stop. Knowing better than to sit down and grow stiff, he leaned his back to a boulder and gulped air into his laboring lungs. After he had paused thus, and eaten a mouthful of meat, he was no more than able to resume the pursuit, at a stubborn walk.

"Gragru," he addressed the fugitive up ahead, "you are strong and brave. Any man but Hok would say you had conquered. But I have not given up."

The afternoon's journey led over a great flat plain, rimmed afar by white wrapped mountains and bearing no trees or watercourses that showed above the snow. Almost on its far side was a gentle slope to a ridge, with a peculiar length of shadow behind. Hok saw Gragru ahead of him. The mammoth could barely crawl through the drifts, sagging and trembling with weakness. Hok drew on his own last reserves of strength, stirred his aching feet to swifter snowshoeing. He actually gained.

Narrower grew the distance between them. Hok drew the axe from his belt, balanced it in his gloved right hand. Coming close, he told himself, he would hack the tendon of Gragru's hind leg, bring him down to stay. After that, get close enough to wrench out the piercing shaft, so that a final loss of blood would finish the beast. Then—but Hok could wish only for a camp, a fire, sleep.

He toiled close. Closer. Gragru was only fifty paces ahead, tottering to that ridge of the slope. At its top he made a slow, clumsy half-turn. His head quivered between his big tussocked shoulders, his ears and trunk hung limply. His eyes, red and pained, fixed upon Hok's like the eyes of a warrior who sees death upon him. Hok lifted his axe in salute.

"Gragru, I am honored by this adventure," he wheezed. "Eating your heart will give me strength and wit and courage beyond all I have known. You will live again in me. Now, to make an end."

He kicked off the snowshoes, so as to run more swiftly at Gragru's sagging hindquarters. But, before he moved, Gragru acted on his own part. He stretched his trunk backward to the shaft in his wound.

Hok relaxed, smiling. "What, you would die of your own will? So be it! I yield you the honor of killing Gragru!"

The mammoth's trunk surged with all the strength it had left. Fastening on the head of the lance, it drew, dragged, pulled the shaft clear through and away. A flip of the trunk, and the red-caked weapon flew out of sight beyond the ridge. Then, blood fountaining forth on both sides, Gragru dragged himself after the shaft. He seemed to collapse beyond the ridge.

"He is mine," muttered Hok into the icicles on his beard, and lifted his axe. He ran in pursuit. So swift was he that he did not see what was on the other side of the ridge until too late.

There was no other side, really. Ground shelved straight down from that highest snowclad point, into a vast, deep valley. There was a drop of eight or ten paces, then the beginning of a steep muddy slope. Hok felt a beating-up of damp warmth, like the rush of air from a cave heated with many fires. He saw thick, distant greenery below him, with a blue mist over it as of rainclouds seen from a mountain top. All this in one moment.

Then his moccasins slid from under him on the brink, and he fell hard.

Striking the top of the slope all sprawling, he rolled over and then slid like an otter on a riverbank. Perhaps something struck his head. Perhaps he only closed his eyes as he slid.

In any case, Hok dropped into sleep as into warm water. He never even felt himself strike a solid obstruction and halt his downward slide.

Chapter III
The Jungle Beneath the Snow

Hok stretched, yawned, opened his eyes. "Where have I fallen?" he inquired of the world, and looked about to answer his own question. He had plumped into a great bushy thicket of evergreen scrub, and had lain there as comfortably as in a hammock. By chance or instinct, he still clutched his big flint axe. Above him was the steep slope, and above that the perpendicular cliff with a crowning of snow. But all about him was a springlike warmth, with no snow at all—only dampness.

Hok wriggled out of his branch, examining himself. His tumble had covered his garments with muck. "Pah!" he condemned the mess, and used his gloves to wipe his face, hair and weapons. A look at the sky told him it was morning—he had slept away his fourth night from home.

Then he gazed downward. The valley seemed to throb and steam. He made out rich leafage and tall tree-summits far below. One or two bright birds flitted in the mists. Hok grimaced.

"Summer must sleep through the cold like a cave-bear," he decided. "I will go down and look for Gragru's body."

There were shoots and shrubs and hummocks for him to catch with hands and feet, or he would have gone sliding again. The deeper he journeyed, the warmer it became. Now and then he hacked a big slash on a larger tree, to keep his upward trail again. Those trees, he observed, were often summer trees, lusher and greener than any he had ever seen.

"Is this the Ancient Land of safe and easy life?"* he mused.

---

* Johannes V. Jensen, Danish poet and scholar, predicates his celebrated "Long Journey" saga on the race-old myth of a warm Lost Country—the memory among Ice-Age men of the tropical surroundings among which the earliest human beings developed, and which were banished by the glaciers.

BATTLE IN THE DAWN

He threw off leggings and gloves and the muddy lionskin cloak, tying these into a bundle to carry. Further descent into even more tropical temperature, and he hung the superfluous garments in a forked branch of a ferny thicket. "I will get them when I return," he decided, and went on down, clad only in clout and moccasins. Bow, quiver and pouch he slung from his shoulders. The deerhorn dagger rode in his leather girdle. His big axe he kept ready in his right hand for what might challenge him.

The first challenger came, not up from the valley, but down from the misty air. Hok saw gray-green pinions, four times wider than his own armspread, and borne between them something like an evil dream of a stork. The wings rustled as they flapped—he saw, as they settled upon him, that they were unfeathered membranes like a bat's—and two scaly rear talons slashed at him.*

"*Khaa!*" cried Hok, revolted, and set himself for defense. He parried the rush with his axe. The side, not the edge, of the flint struck that monster's chest, blocking it off. Down darted the long lean neck, and the sharp-toothed beak fastened in Hok's hair. A moment later the clutching lizardly feet closed on the axe-haft. Hok found himself carried shakily aloft.

There was a struggle for the axe. The thing could barely sustain Hok's weight clear of the ground, and it tried to kill, not capture. A long tail belabored him like a club, hideous hand-like claws on the wing-elbows scratched and scrabbled at his chest and throat. Hok, dangling in midair, found himself able to voice a savage laugh.

"*Ahai!* You think to eat Hok, you nightmare? Others have found him a tough morsel!" Quitting hold of the axe with one hand, he whipped the dagger from his belt. Thrusting upward, he pierced the scaly throat to the bone.

The jaws let go his hair, and emitted a startled screech. Snaky-smelling blood drenched Hok, and the two fell. The wings, though out of control, partially broke the tumble, and Hok had the wit and strength to turn his enemy under and fall upon it. They struck the slope some paces lower than where the fight began. Hok pinned the still struggling nightmare with his foot, and cleft it almost in two with his axe. Then he stepped clear, nose wrinkled in disgust.

"*Khaa!*" he snorted again, mopping away the ill-scented gore with handfuls of fern. "I'd have doubly died if that bird-snake had eaten me. Are there others?"

His question was answered on the instant. Dry flappings, shrill screams—Hok sheltered in it thicket, and watched a dozen more birdsnakes swoop down to rend and devour their slain brother. It was a sight to turn the stomach of a Gnorrl. Hok slipped away down slope.

Now he came to a gentler incline and larger trees. He journeyed on without mishap for the rest of the morning. Hungry, he ate several strange fruits from vine and tree at which he saw birds pecking. Once, too, a strange thing

---

* The race of pterodactyls, of which this specimen was a survivor, had wingspreads as wide as twenty-five feet, with beaks four feet long.

like a tiny tailed man* scolded him in a harsh high voice and flung down a big husk-fibered nut. Hok dodged the missile, split it and enjoyed both the white flesh and the milky juice. "Thanks, little brother!" he cried up at the impish nut-thrower.

When noon was past, Hok had come to where he could spy the floor of the valley.

With difficulty he spied it, for it was dusky dark. From it rose fumes, mist-clouds, earthy odors. It was a swamp, from which sprouted upward the tallest and biggest trees Hok had ever seen. They grew thickly, interlaced with the root-ends and butts of vines and creepers, hummocked around with dank clumps of fungi, rimmed with filthy pools. Swarms of biting insects rose, and Hok retreated, cursing.

"I see nothing of Gragru down there," he said. "I'll go sidewise."

Nicking a tree to mark the turnoff, he travelled directly along the slope. Nor had he far to go before he saw Gragru.

Here was the place where mammoths were entombed. Above, extending up the valley's slope, was a tunnel through trees and thickets, kept open by so many falling, rolling masses of dead or dying mammoth-meat. At the bottom of the chute rose a stinking stack of remains. Hok could not have counted them—there must be thousands of desiccated and rotted carcasses, the bones gray and the curling tusks white. On top lay the freshest of these, Gragru his quarry. And beside it was one that had beaten Hok to the kill.

"First bird-snakes," grumbled Hok. "Now elephant-pigs."

For the thing was bigger than an elephant and grosser than a hog. Its monstrous bulk, clad in scant-bristled hide of slate gray, stooped above the carcass. Its shallow, broad-snouted skull bent down, and powerful fangs tore the hairy hide from Gragru's flesh, exposing the tender meat. That head lifted as Hok came into view, a head larger than that of a hippopotamus. Two small hooded eyes, cold and pale as a lizard's, stared. The mouth sucked and chewed bloody shreds, and Hok saw down-protruding tusks, sharp as daggers. Upon the undeveloped brow, the swell of the muzzle, and the tip of the snout were hornlike knobs—three pairs of them.**

Fixing Hok with that lizardlike stare, the big brute set its elephantine forefeet upon Gragru's bulk and hitched itself nearer. Its bloody, fang-fringed jaws seemed to grin in anticipation of different meat.

"Thing," Hok addressed the monster, "you came unbidden to eat my prey. You yourself shall be my meat, to replace that which I killed."

---

* In Europe, where Hok lived, no remains of native monkeys or apes more recent than Pliocene times have been discovered; but, as the paleontologist Osborn reminds us, the tree-dwelling habits of such beasts might have made the remains difficult to keep whole.

** *Dinoceras ingens*, one of the largest and ugliest of the Dinocerata, flourished in Eocene times and may have lived later. It partook of the natures of rhinoceros and swine, and its teeth suggest it ate both animal and vegetable food. Its many head-bumps may have been primitive horns. Specimens have been found that were twelve feet long and eight feet tall at the shoulders.

He lifted his bow, which was ready strung, and reached over his shoulder for an arrow. Just then the elephant-pig moved toward him.

For all its unwieldy bulk, it came at antelope speed, that great toothed maw open to seize and rend. Hok swiftly drew his long arrow to the head and sent it full at the long protruding tongue. The monster stopped dead, emitting a shrill gargling squeal, and lifted one horn-toed foot to paw at the wound. Hok retired into a bushy thicket, setting another arrow to string.

That thicket would have shielded him from the charge of a buffalo or lion; but the bulk of the present enemy was to a buffalo or lion as a fox to rabbits. It charged among the brush, breaking off stout stems like reeds. Hok, lighter, had difficulty getting aside from its first blind rush. He gained the open, and so did the elephant-pig. It spied him, wheeled to charge again.

He discharged a second arrow, full at one of those dead eyes. The six-knobbed head twitched at that moment, and the shaft skewered a nostril instead. Again a horrid yell of angry pain. Hok sprang away from under its very feet as it tried to run him down, found himself heading into the swampy bottom. There was a great cylindrical mass among the trees, a trunk which even this hideous monster could not tear down. Hok ran to it, seeking to climb the rough lappings of bark.

"You cannot climb quickly enough," said a voice from within the tree. "Come inside, where I can look at you."

Chapter IV
The Man Inside the Tree

It is often like that, even with a hunter as wise and sharp-eyed as Hok. Not until the voice spoke to him in the language of men,* was he aware that near him in the great trunk was a gaping hole, big enough for him to slide through, and full of blackness.

The tree itself was not a tree. For trees are straight upward shoots of vegetable growth—this seemed a high-built close-packed spiral, as if someone had coiled a rope, or a worm had made a great casting. Between two woody curves, one upon the other, showed the shoulder-wide hole.

"Make haste," bade the voice inside.

Hok saw that the elephant-pig, after a momentary questing to spy and smell him out, was ponderously wheeling to charge. He waited for no third invitation, but dived into the space, head first. A struggle and a kick, and he was inside, among comforting dimness that bespoke solid protection all around. A moment later the huge beast struck outside, with a force that shook every fiber of the strange stout growth within which Hok had taken refuge.

"He cannot break through to us," assured the voice, very near. "This vine is stronger even than Rmanth, the slayer."

---

* The old legend, mentioned in the Book of Genesis and elsewhere, that once all men were of one speech may well be founded on fact—witness similarities of certain key words among races so far scattered as Welsh, Persian, and Mandan Indian. Even in the Stone Age there seems to have been commerce and alliance, which means that men must have understood each other. Languages were simple then. Only with widely divergent races, as the beastlike Gnorrls or Neanderthal men, would there be a definitely separate tongue, hard to pronounce and harder to understand because of differences in jaw structure, brain, and mode of life.

Hok made out a dark shape, slender and quiet. "Vine?" he echoed. "But this is a tree, a dead hollow tree."

"The tree that once stood here is not only dead, but gone," he was quietly informed. "If there were light, you would see."

Momentary silence, while Hok pondered this statement. Outside the elephant-pig, which seemed to be named Rmanth, sniffed at the orifice like a jackal at a rat-burrow.

"You don't sound like a mocker," was Hok's final judgment aloud. "And it is true that this is a strange growth around us. As for light, why not build a fire?"

"Fire?" repeated the other uncertainly. "What is that?"

Hok could not but chuckle. "You do not know? Fire lights and warms you."

"For warmth, it is never cold here. And for light—I do not like too much."

"There is need of light in this darkness," decided Hok weightily. "If you truly do not know fire, I can show better than I can tell."

He groped with his hands on the floor of the cavern into which he had come. It seemed earthy, with much rubbish. He found some bits of punky wood, then larger pieces, and cleared a hearth-space. From his pouch he brought needful things—a flat chip of pine, one edge notched; a straight, pointed stick of hard wood; a tuft of dry moss.

"Thus," lectured Hok, "is fire made."

Working in the dark, he twirled the stick between his palms. Its point, in the notch of the chip, rubbed and heated. Within moments Hok smelled scorching, then smoke. A faint glow peeped through the gloom. Lifting away the chip, Hok held his moss-tinder to the little coal of glowing wood-meal. The rising blaze he fed with splinters, then larger pieces. The fire rose. "There!" cried Hok, and had time and illumination to look up.

His first glance showed him the refuge—a circular cavity, twice a man's height in diameter, and walled snugly with those close-packed woody spirals. High above the space extended, with what looked like a gleaming white star at some distant apex. The floor was of well-trampled loam and mold, littered with ancient wood chips. His second glance showed him his companion.

Here was a body slimmer and shorter than the average man of the Flint People. The shoulders sloped, the muscles were stringy rather than swelling, there were no hips or calves. Around the slender waist was a clout rudely woven of plant fiber, its girdle supporting a queerly made little axe and what seemed to be a knife. The feet, outthrust toward Hok, looked like hands—the great toe was set well back, and plainly could take independent grasp. On the chest—quite deep in proportion to the slimness—and on the outer arms and legs grew long, sparse hair of red-brown color. Hok could not see the face, for the man crouched and buried his head in his long arms.

"Don't," came his muffled plea. "Don't . . ."

"It will not hurt," Hok replied, puzzled.

"I cannot look, it burns my eyes. Once the forest was eaten by such stuff that struck down from heaven—"

"Lightning," guessed Hok. "Oh, yes, fire can be terrible when big. But we keep it small, feeding it only sparingly. Then it is good. See, I do not fear. I promise it will not hurt you."

His tone reassured the man, who finally looked up, albeit apprehensively. Hok studied his face.

Long loose lips, a nose both small and flattish, and no chin at all beneath a scraggle of brown beard. From the wide mouth protruded teeth—Hok saw businesslike canines above and below, capable of inflicting a terrible bite. This much was plainly of animal fashion, unpleasantly Gnorrlish. But neither the fangs nor the shallow jaw could detract from the manifest intelligence of the upper face.

For here were large dark eyes, set very well under smooth brows. The forehead, though not high, was fairly broad and smooth, and the cranium looked as if it might house intelligence and good temper.

"Don't be afraid," persisted Hok. "You were friendly enough to call me into this shelter. I am grateful, and I will show it."

Rmanth, the monster outside, sniffed and scraped at the entrance. He seemed baffled. Hok leaned against the wall. "What is your name?" he asked.

The other peered timidly. Hok saw the size and brilliance of those eyes, and guessed that this man could see, at least somewhat in the dark. "Soko," came the reply. "And you?"

"Hok the Mighty." That was spoken with honest pride. "I came here from snowy country up above. I had wounded a mammoth, and followed him down here."

"Mammoths always come here," Soko told him. "Rmanth and his people before him—for he is the last of a mighty race—ate their flesh and flourished. If we dare descend the trees, Rmanth kills and eats us, too. In the high branches—the Stymphs!"

"Stymphs?" echoed Hok. "What are those?"

Soko had his turn at being surprised at such ignorance. "They fly like birds, but are bigger and hungrier—with teeth in their long jaws—man cannot prevail against them—"

"Oh, the bird-snakes! One attacked me as I came down. I knifed it, and descended before its friends came."

"You were climbing downward," Soko reminded. "There was cover below. But if you leave the cover to climb upward, you will be slain in the open, by many Stymphs. Not even Rmanth ventures above the thickets."

"As to your elephant-pig, Rmanth," continued Hok, "he has tasted my arrows."

That was another new word for Soko, and Hok passed his bow and quiver across for examination. "One shaft I feathered in his tongue," he continued, "and another in his nostril."

"But you were forced to take shelter here. Meanwhile, those wounds will make him the thirstier for your blood. He will never forget your appearance or smell. If you venture out, he will follow you to the finish. Between him and the Stymphs above, what chance have you?"

"What chance have I?" repeated Hok, his voice ringing. "Chance for combat! For adventure! For victory!" He laughed for joy, anticipating these things. "I'm glad I came—these dangers are worth traveling far to meet . . . but tell me of another wonder. This tree, which is not a tree, but shelters us in its heart—"

"Oh, simple enough," rejoined Soko. He was beginning to enjoy the comradeship by the glowing fire. Sitting opposite Hok, his slender hands clasped around his knobby knees, he smiled. "A true tree grew here once, tall and strong. At its root sprang up a vine, which coiled tightly around like a snake. In time the vine grew to the very top. Its hugging coils, and its sap-drinking suckers, slew the tree, which rotted and died in the grip. But the vine held the shape to which it had grown, and when we tree-folk dug out the rotten wood, little by little, it made a safe tube by which we could descend to the valley's floor."*

"That must have taken much labor," observed Hok.

"And much time. My father's father barely remembered when it was begun, that digging."

"You speak as if you live up above here," said Hok.

"We do," Soko told him. "Come, kill the fire lest it burn the forest, and I will take you to the home of my people."

He rose and began climbing upward.

---

* Several types of big tropical vine, both in Africa and South America, create this curious growth-pattern by killing the trees they climb and remaining erect in the same place.

Chapter V
The World in the Branches

Hok quickly stamped out the fire. Its dying light showed him a sort of rough ladder—pegs and stubs of hard wood, wedged into the spaces between the coils of that amazing vine. Soko was swarming well above ground level already. Slinging his weapons to girdle and shoulder-thongs, Hok followed.

Hok had always been a bold and active climber, able to outdistance any of his tribefellows, in trees or up cliffs. But Soko kept ahead of him, like a squirrel ahead of a bear. The tree-man fairly scampered up the ladder-way.

"This is another way in which Soko's people are different from the Gnorrls,"* muttered Hok.

The climbing-sticks had been meant for bodies of Soko's modest weight, and once or twice they creaked dangerously beneath the heavier Hok. He obviated the danger of a fall by keeping each hand and foot on a different hold, dividing the strain four ways. Meanwhile, the light above grew stronger, waxing and waning as Soko's nimble body cut this way and that across its beam. Finally, noise and bustle, and a new voice:

"Soko! You went down to see what was happening with Rmanth. What—"

"A man," Soko answered. "A strange man, like none you ever saw."

Hok took that as a compliment. He was considered something of a unique specimen, even among his own kind.

"He is master of the Hot Hunger," Soko went on, and Hok guessed that he meant fire. "He has killed one Stymph, he says, and has hurt Rmanth."

A chatter of several agitated voices above. Then, "Will he kill us?"

---

* The Neanderthal men were of massive, clumsy build—obviously poor climbers.

"I think not," said Soko, and drew himself through some sort of gap above. "Come on out, Hok," he called back. "My friends are eager to see you."

Hok came to the opening in turn. It was narrow for his big body, and he had difficulty in wriggling through. Standing on some crossed and interwoven boughs, he looked at Soko's people.

All the way up, he had thought of Soko as fragile and small; now he realized, as often before, that fragility and smallness are but comparative. Soko, who was a head shorter than himself and slim in proportion, would be considered sturdy and tall among the tree-folk—almost a giant. He was the biggest of all who were present. Hok smiled to himself. While he had been pegging Soko as a timid lurker in a hollow, these dwellers of the branches must have thrilled to the courage of their strong brother, venturing so close to the mucky domain of the ravenous Rmanth.

As Hok came fully into view, the gathering—there may have been twenty or thirty of Soko's kind, men, women and children—fell back on all sides with little gasps and squeaks of fearful amazement. With difficulty the chief of the Flint People refrained from most unmannerly laughter. If Soko was a strapping champion among them, Hok must seem a vast horror, strangely shaped, colored and equipped. He smiled his kindliest, and sat down among the woven branches.

"Soko speaks truth," he announced. "I have no desire to fight or kill anyone who comes in peace."

They still stood off from him, balancing among the leafage. He was aware that they moved so swiftly and surely because they got a grip on the branches with their feet. He was able, also, to make a quick, interested study of the world they lived in. Though Soko had led him upward in a climb of more than twenty times a man's height, the upper bole in the vine spiral was by no means the top of the forest. Leafage shut away the sky above, the swampy ground below. Here, in the middle branches of the close-set mighty trees, appeared something of a lofty floor—the boughs and connecting vines, naturally woven and matted together into a vast bridge or platform, swaying but strong. Layers of leaf-mold, mixed with blown dust, moss and the rotted meal of dead wood, over-spread parts of this fabric. The aerial earthiness bore patches of grass and weeds, bright-flowering plants, as richly as though it were based upon the rock instead of the winds. Birds picked at seeds. Hok heard the hum of bees around trumpet-shaped blooms. It was a great wonder.*

"I wondered how you tree-men possibly live off the ground," he said with honest admiration. "Now I wonder how you can live anywhere else but here." A deep-chested sigh. "Of such fair places our old men tell us, in the legends of the Ancient Land."

That friendly speech brought the tree-dwellers closer to this big stranger. A half-grown lad was boldest, coming straight to Hok and fingering his leather moccasins. Hok's first thought was how swiftly young Ptao, at home by the

---

* This description is no fancy. The author himself, and many others, have seen such sky-gardens among the branches of modern rainforests in West Africa.

frozen river, could thrash and conquer such a youth—the second was a hope that Ptao would be forebearing and gentle to so harmless a specimen. The others gathered around reassured. They began asking questions. It was strange to all that a human being could kill large beasts for food and fur, and the men were particularly fascinated by Hok's flint weapons.

"We have our own stories of old times, when our fathers made stone things," volunteered Soko. "Now we satisfy ourselves with what bones we can raid from that great pile of mammoths, when Rmanth is not there gorging himself." He produced his own dagger, smaller than Hok's reindeer-horn weapon, but well worked from a bone fragment. "After all, we need not fight monsters, like you."

"If you did fight like me, all together, and with wisdom and courage, Rmanth would not have you treed," said Hok bluntly. "Perhaps I can help you with him. But first, tell me more of yourselves. You think it strange that I wear skins. What are these weavings you wear?"

"The forest taught us," said Soko sententiously. "As the branches weave and grow together, so we cross and twine little tough strings and threads drawn from leaves and grasses. They give us covering, and places to carry possessions. Is it so marvelous? Birds do as much with their nests."

"Nests?" repeated Hok. "And how do you people nest?"

"Like the birds—in woven beds of branches, lined with soft leaves and fiber. A roof overhead, of course, to shed the rain." Soko pointed to a little cluster of such shelters, not far away in an adjoining tree.*

"You do nothing but sleep and play?"

"We gather up fruits and nuts," spoke up another of the tree-men. "That takes time and work, for a man who has gathered much must feed his friends who may have gathered little."

"It is so with my people, when one hunter kills much meat and others return empty handed," nodded Hok. "What else, then?"

"A great labor is the mending of this floor," replied Soko, patting with his foot the woven platform. "Branches rot and break. We look for such places, through which our children might fall at play, and weave in new strong pieces, or tie and lace across with stout vines."

Once again Hok glanced upward. "And what is there?"

A shudder all around. "Stymphs," muttered Soko, in a soft voice, as if he feared to summon a flock of the bird-snakes.

"Ugly things," said Hok. "I may do something about them, too. But I am hungry just now—"

Before he could finish, the whole community dashed away like so many squirrels through the boughs, to bring back fistfuls of nuts, pawpaws and grapes. Hok accepted all he could possibly eat, and thanked his new friends heartily.

"I did not mean that you must feed me," he told them. "You should wait for me to finish my talk. But since you bring these fruits, I will make my meal of them. You may take my provision."

---

* The great apes make such nests, roofs and all.

From his pouch he rummaged the remainder of his dried meat. It was one more new thing to the tree people, who nibbled and discussed and argued over it. Flesh they had occasionally—small climbers, fledgling birds, even insects—but nothing of larger game, and both cooking and drying of food was beyond their understanding. Hok chuckled over their naivete.

"A promise!" he cried. "I'll give you Rmanth himself for a feast, and I shall roast him on a fire, that which you call the Hot Hunger. But let Soko sit here by me. I want to hear of how you came to this place to live."

Soko perched on a tangle of vines. "Who can tell that? It was so long ago. Cold weather drove us from the upper world," and he pointed northward. "Those who stayed behind were slain by it. Our old men tell tales and sing songs of how the remnants of the fleeing tribe blundered in here and gave themselves up as trapped."

"Why did the ice not follow you in?" asked Hok.

"Ask that of the gods, who drove it to right and left of our valley. In any case, we were sheltered here, though there were many fierce creatures. But the cold was fiercer—we could not face it—and here we stay."*

"Treed by Rmanth and harried by those Stymph bird-snakes," summed up Hok. "You are happy, but you could make yourselves much happier by some good planning and fighting. Who is your chief?"

"I am their chief," growled someone behind him, "and you had better explain—quickly—why you seek to make my people dissatisfied."

---

* The Piltdown Race seems to have flourished in the Third Interglacial Epoch, a warm age when even northern Europe was as pleasant and temperate as Italy. Such African-Asiatic fauna as hippopotami and tigers flourished side by side with these forerunners of human beings. When the Fourth Glaciation brought ice and snow to cover Europe, the robust Neanderthals and the later, greater true men of Hok's race could survive and adapt themselves; but a less rugged prehuman type like the Piltdown must flee or perish.

Chapter VI
A Chief Passes Sentence

There was a sudden gasping and cowering among all the tree-folk, even as concerned the relatively sturdy Soko. Hok turned toward the speaker, expecting to come face to face with a fearsome challenger.

Around the spiral vine-column a little grizzled form was making its way. This tree-man was old and ill-favored, with almost pure, white whiskers on his chinless jaw. He wheezed and snorted, as though the exertion were too much for him. Perhaps this was due to his weight, for he was the fattest Hok had yet seen among those dwellers of the trees. His belly protruded like a wallet, his jowls hung like dewlaps. But there was nothing old or infirm about the power in his big, close-set brilliant eyes.

Gaining the side of the nearest tree-man to him, this oldster put out a confident hand and snatched away a sizeable slice of the dried meat Hok had distributed. Though the victim of this plunder was an active young man, he did not resist or even question, but drew diffidently away. The old man took a bite—his teeth, too, were young-seeming and rather larger and sharper than ordinary—and grunted approval. Then his eyes fastened on Hok's in a calculated stare of hostility.

But Hok had met the gaze of the world's fiercest beasts and men, and his were not the first eyes to falter. The old tree-chief finally glanced away. Hok smiled in good-humored contempt.

"Well?" challenged the oldster at last. "Do you know how to act before your betters?"

Hok was puzzled. The simple truth was that Hok had never recognized anyone as his better from his youth upwards.

Years before, when a big boy not yet fully mature, the slaying of his father by Gnorrls had made him chief of his clan. His young manhood had barely come to him before he had driven those same beastly Gnorrls from their rich hunting-empire of meadows and woods, and founded in their stead an alliance of several tribes, with himself as head chief. The mighty nation of Tlanis was sunken under the sea because of him. The Fishers in their seaside pile-villages had changed their worship from water-god to sun-god out of sadly learned respect for Hok. If ever he had been subordinate, even only the second greatest individual in any gathering, he had had plenty of time to forget it.

Just now he spat idly, through a gap in the woven branches.

"Show me my betters," he requested with an air of patience. "I know none, on two legs or four."

"I am Krol!" squeaked the other, and smote his gray-tufted chest with his fat fist. "Be afraid, you hulking yellow-haired stranger!"

"Men of the trees," Hok addressed those who listened, "is it your custom to keep fools to make game for you? This man has white hair, he should be quiet and dignified. He is a bad example to the young."

It was plainly blasphemy. Soko and the others drew further away from Hok, as though they feared to be involved in some terrible fate about to overwhelm him. The chief who called himself Krol fumbled in his girdle of twisted fiber, and drew forth an axe of mammoth ivory set in a hardwood handle. Whirling it around his head, he cast it at Hok.

Hok lifted a big knowing hand, with such assurance that the movement seemed languid. The axe drove straight at his face, but he picked it out of the air as a frog's tongue picks a flying insect. Without pausing he whirled it in his own turn and sent it sailing back. It struck with a sharp *chock*, deep into a big branch just above Krol's head.

"Try again," bade Hok, as though he were instructing a child in how to throw axes.

Krol's big fangs gnashed, and foam sprang out in flecks upon his lips and beard. He waved his fists at his people.

"On him!" he screamed "Seize him, beat, him, bind fast his arms!"

Hok rose from where he sat, bracing himself erect. He looked with solemnity upon the half-dozen or so biggest men who moved to obey.

"Come at me, and you will think Rmanth himself has climbed up among you," he warned. "I do not like to be handled."

Krol yelped a further order, backing it by a threat. The men rushed unwillingly.

Hok laughed, like an athlete playing with children. Indeed, the tree-men were childlike in comparison with him. He pushed the first two in the face with his palms, upsetting them and almost dropping them through the branchy fabric. A third attacker he caught and lifted overhead, wedging him in a fork of the boughs. The others retreated fearfully before such effortless strength. Hok laughed again, watching.

But he should have watched Krol as well. The plump old despot had stolen close unobserved. In one hand he clutched a big fiber husked nut, of the milky kind Hok had enjoyed earlier in the day. A swinging buffet on the skull, and

Hok staggered, partially stunned. At once the tree-men rushed back, and before Hok could clear his brain and fight them off, he was swamped. They looped his wrists, ankles and body with quickly-plucked vine tendrils tough and limber as leather straps.

Krol found time to take some fruit from a child, and husk it with his teeth. "Now, stranger," he sniggered, "you will learn that I am chief here."

Hok had recovered from that stroke. He did not waste strength or dignity by striving against his stout bonds.

"A chief who plays tricks and lets other men do the fighting," he replied. "A chief who strikes his enemies foully, from behind."

Krol had repossessed his ivory axe. He lifted it angrily, as though to smite it into Hok's skull. But then he lowered it, and grinned nastily.

"I heard you blustering when I came up," he said. "Something about fighting. What do you think to fight?"

"I spoke of Rmanth, the elephant-pig," replied Hok. "Yes, and the Stymphs. Your people fear them. I do not."

"Mmmm!" Krol glanced downward, then up. "They are only little pests to mighty warriors like you, huh? You do not fear them? Hok—that is your name, I think you said—I will do you a favor. You shall have closer acquaintanceship with the Stymphs."

Mention of the dread bird-snakes made the tree-folk shiver, and Krol sneered at them with a row of grinning fangs.

"You cowards!" he scolded. "You disgrace me before this boastful stranger. Yet you know that Stymphs must eat, if they are to live and let us alone. Hoist this prey up to them."

"Bound and helpless?" demanded Hok. "That is part of your own cowardice, Krol. You shall howl for it."

"But you shall howl first, and loudest," promised Krol. "You biggest men, come and carry him up. Yes, high!"

That last was to quicken the unwilling limbs of his fellows, who seemed to like Hok and not to like the prospect of mounting into the upper branches.

Thus driven to obedience, four of the biggest men nimbly wove more vines around the captive, fashioning a sort of hammock to hold him and his weapons. Soko, stopping to tie a knot, gazed intently into Hok's face. One of Soko's big bright eyes closed for a moment—the ancient and universal wink of alliance, warning, and promise.

The four scrambled up and up, bearing Hok among them. Now the sky came into view, dullish and damp but warm. Apparently the valley was always wreathed, at least partially, in light mists. Into a tall treetop the big captive was hoisted, and made fast there like a dangling cocoon. Krol panted fatly as he clambered alongside. The others departed at his nod. Soko, passing Hok, jostled the big bound wrists. Hok felt something pressed against his palm, and closed his fingers upon it.

The hilt of Soko's bone knife! With difficulty he fought back a smile of triumph...

Then he was alone in the treetop with Krol.

"Look up, you scoffer," bade Krol. "In the mists—do you see anything?"

"Very dimly, I make out flying shapes," replied Hok quietly. "Two—three—no, many."

"They can see you, and plainly," Krol informed him. "Like my people, the Stymphs have ability to see far on dull days, or dark holes, or even at night. They have cunning sense of smell, too. Probably they scent some prey close at hand now, and wonder if I have hung something up for them."

"You hang food for the Stymphs?" demanded Hok.

"Yes, such men as displease me—don't stare and wonder. I am chief of my tribe. I must keep an alliance with other powers."

Krol squinted upward, where the Stymphs hovered in the mist-wreaths. Opening his wide mouth, he emitted a piercing cry, half howl and half whistle. The bird-snakes began to flap as if in response.

"They know my voice; they will come," announced Korl. With the evilest of grins, he swung down to the safety of the foliage below.

No sooner was he gone than Hok began to ply that bone knife Soko had smuggled to him. It was difficult work, but he pressed the well-sharpened edge strongly against the vine loops around his wrist. They separated partially, enough to allow him to strain and snap them. Even as the boldest Stymph lowered clear of the mists and began to angle downward, Hok won his arms free. A few mighty hacks, and he cleared away the rest of his hammocky bonds.

The tree-folk had bound his unfamiliar weapons in with him. Drawing himself astride of a big horizontal branch, Hok strung the big bow and tweaked an arrow out of his quiver.

"I have a feeling," he said aloud to this strange land at large, "that I was sent here—by gods or spirits or by chance—to face and destroy these Stymphs."*

---

* Readers who know the mythology of ancient Greece will already have seen some connection between the surviving pterodactyls called Stymphs and the Stymphalides, described as "great birds" who ate men. The ancient Greeks said that Stymphalides had plumage of metal, which sounds very much like reptilian scaliness. Hercules, the Grecian memory of Hok, is credited with destroying these monsters as one of his twelve heaven-assigned labors.

Chapter VII
The Stymphs

So confident was Hok of his ability to deal with the situation that he actually waited, arrow on string, for a closer mark. After all, he had killed one such bird-snake with a single quick thrust of his dagger. Why should he fear many, when he had arrows, an axe, and two knives? A big Stymph tilted in the mist and slid down as if it were an otter on a mud-bank. Its long triangular head, like the nightmare of a stork, drooped low on the snaky neck. Its jag-toothed bill opened.

Hok let it come so close that his flaring nostrils caught the reptilian odor; then, drawing his shaft to its barbed head of sandstone, he loosed full at the scaly beast. Hok's bow was the strongest among all men of his time, and a close-delivered arrow from it struck with all the impact of a war-club. The flint point tore through the body, flesh, scales and bone, and protruded behind. The swoop of the Stymph was arrested as though it had blundered against a rock in midair. It whirled head over lizard tail, then fell flooping and screeching toward the great mass of foliage.

"Ahai!" Hok voiced his war-shout, and thundered mocking laughter at the other Stymphs. "Thus Hok serves those who face him. Send me another of your champions!"

Several of the abominations had flown a little way after their falling friend. But, before they could get their cannibal beaks into the stricken body, it had lost itself among the branches, and they came up again to center on the more exposed meat in the treetop. Two advanced at once, and from widely separate angles.

Hok had notched another arrow, and sped it into the chest of one. Before he could seize a third shaft, the other Stymph was upon him. Its talons made a clutch, scraping long furrows in his shoulder. He cursed it, and struck a mighty whipping blow with his bow-stave that staggered it in mid-flight.

Clutching the supporting branch with his legs, he tore his axe from its lashing at his girdle, and got it up just in time to meet the recovering drive of the brute. Badly gashed across the narrow, evil face, the Stymph reeled downward, trying in vain to get control of its wings and rise again.

More Stymphs circled this third victim of Hok, and tore several bloody mouthfuls from it. A loud clamor rose over Hok's head—the smell of gore was maddening the flock. Slipping his right hand through the thong on his axe handle, he looked up.

The sky was filling with Stymphs. Though never a man to recognize danger with much respect, Hok was forced to recognize it now. Where he had thought to meet a dozen or score of the monsters, here they were mustered in numbers like a flock of swallows—his system of counting, based on tens and tens of tens, would not permit him to be sure of their strength, even if he had time.

For they had dropped all over him, all of them at once.

A toothy jaw closed on his left elbow. Before it could bite to the bone, he whipped his axe across and smashed the shallow skull with the flat of the blade. Back-handing, he brought the axe round to smite and knock down another attacker. Axe and bow-stave swept right and left, and every blow found and felled a Stymph. The stricken ones were attacked and rended by their ravenous fellows, which made a hurly-burly of confusion and perhaps saved Hok from instant annihilation by the pack. As it was, he knew that the Stymphs were far too many for him.

The end of this furious struggle in the open top of the jungle came with an abrupt climax that Hok never liked to remember afterward. He had ducked low on his limb to avoid the sweeping rush of a big Stymph, and for a moment loosened the straddle-clutch of his legs. At the same moment another of the creatures dropped heavily upon his shoulders, sinking its claws into his flesh. Its weight dislodged him. Hok lost all holds, and fell hurtling into the leafy depths below. His right hand quitted its hold on the big axe, which remained fast to his wrist by the looped thong. Reaching up and back as he fell, he seized the Stymph by its snaky throat and with a single powerful jerk freed it from its grasp upon his ribs and brought it under him. Its striving wings were slowing the fall somewhat, though it could not rise with his weight. A moment afterward, the two of them crashed into the mass of twigs and leaves, hit an out-thrust bough heavily.

The Stymph, underneath, took most of that shock. Its ribs must have been shattered. At the instant of impact, Hok had presence of mind to quit his grip upon its neck, and managed to fling his arm around the branch. He clung there, feet kicking in space while the Stymph fell shrieking into the middle branches.

Again he was momentarily safe. He looked up. The Stymphs, where they were visible through sprays of greenery, were questing and circling to find him, like fish-hawks above the water's surface.

"Ahai! Here I am, you bird-snakes!" he roared his challenge, and climbed along the branch to a broader fork, where he could stand erect without holding on. And here he found shelter, even from those ravenous beaks and claws.

A great parasitic growth, allied to giant dodder or perhaps mistletoe, made a great golden-leafed mat above him, circular in form and wider across than the height of two tall men. It could be seen through, but its tough tendrils and shoots could hold back heavier attacks than the Stymph swarm might manage.

"Come on and fight!" he taunted again. "I have killed many of you, and still I live! Ahai, I am Hok the Mighty, whose sport it is to kill Stymphs and worse things than Stymphs!"

The flattened, darkling brains of the Stymphs understood the tone, if not the words of that defiance. They began to drop down on winnowing scaly wings, peering and questing for him. "Here, just below!" he cried to guide them. Then he slung his bow behind him, and poised his axe, spitting between hand and haft for a better grip.

They settled quickly toward him, wriggling and forcing their way through the upper layers of small twigs. He laughed once again, and one of the Stymphs spied him through the tangled matting. It alighted, clutching the strands with its talons, and with a single lancing stroke of its tight-shut beak drove through a weak spot in the shield. Hok stared into its great cold eyes, and shifted his position to avoid its snap.

"Meet Hok, meet death," he said to it, and chopped off that ugly head with his axe. The body flopped and wriggled beyond his jumble of defending vegetation, and three of the other Stymphs came down all together to feast upon it.

That was what Hok wanted. "So many guests come to dine with Hok?" he jibed. "Then the host must provide more meat."

He laid his longest arrow across the bow-stave. For a moment the three fluttering birdsnakes huddled close together above the prey, almost within touch of him. Setting the head of his arrow to an opening among the whorls and tangles, he loosed it at just the right moment.

A triple shrillness of pained screaming beat up, and Hok was spattered with rank-smelling blood. Skewered together like bits of venison on a toasting-stick, the three Stymphs foundered, somersaulted and fell, still held in an agony of conjunction by Hok's arrow. For the first time, unhurt Stymphs drew back as in fear. Hok made bold to show himself, climbing up on top of his protecting mat.

"Do you go?" he demanded. "Am I as unappetizing as all that?"

They came yet again, and he dodged nimbly back into safety. More arrows—he had a dozen left. These he produced, thrusting them through broad leaves around him so as to be more quickly seized and sped. Then, as the Stymphs blundered heavily against his shield of natural wicker-work, he began to kill them.

Close-packed as they were, and within touch of him, he could not miss. By twos and threes his arrows fetched them down. Even the small reptile-minds of the flying monsters could not but register danger. Survivors began to flop upward, struggle into the open air above the branches, retreat into the mist. Hok hurled imprecations and insults after them, and once more mounted the mat to kill wounded wretches with his axe, and to drag his arrows from the mass of bodies.

Well-mannered as always, he took time to thank the curious tangled growth that had been his bulwark. "My gratitude to you, who made me a shield from behind which I won this victory," he addressed it. "You were sent from the Shining One, whom I worship. He knew I needed help, down here in the mists beyond the reach of his rays. My children shall never forget this kindness."*

From below came an awkward scrambling, and Krol, the chief of the tree-folk, mounted upward into view.

"Greetings," Hok chuckled at him. "See what sport I have made with your friends.

Krol might have feared the huge blood-smeared chief of the Flint People, had he not been so concerned with the retreat of the Stymphs overhead.

"They will go," he chattered. "They will never come back, because they fear you. If I had known—"

"If you had known, you would not have hung me up for them to eat," Hok finished for him. "As it is, I have driven off your ugly allies, by fear of which you ruled your people. That fear will be gone hereafter. So, I think, will you."

Hok swung down to a branch above Krol and feinted a brain-dashing blow with his axe. Then he laughed as the tree-chief let go all holds, dropping six times his own length through emptiness. He caught a branch below.

"You and I are enemies!" he snarled upward, "Though you have beaten my Stymphs, there remain other things—even Rmanths! I shall see you dead, and your body rended by the tusks of Rmanth, Hok the Meddler!"

And then, though Hok began climbing swiftly downward, old Krol was swifter and surer. They both descended through thickening layers of foliage, to the woven living-place of the tree people.

---

* The surviving myth tells how Hercules (Hok) was sheltered from the Stymphalides by the buckler of Pallas Athene, so that he was able to win victory at leisure.

Chapter VIII
The Dethroning of Krol

By the time the slower-climbing Hok had come down to that mighty hammocklike footing, Krol had had precious minutes to gather his followers and howl orders and accusations into their ears.

"Ah, here he comes to mock us, the overgrown invader!" Krol yelled, and shook a furious finger toward the approaching Hok. "He has slain the Stymphs who protected us!"

"I have slain the Stymphs, who feasted on any tree-man daring to climb as high as the open air above the forest," rejoined Hok, with a lofty manner as of one setting Krol's statement right. "I have helped you, not injured you."

Krol glared with a fury that seemed to hurl a rain of sparks upon Hok. "You biggest men," he addressed the other tree-folk out of the side of his broad, loose mouth, "seize him and bind him a second time."

Hok set his shoulder-blades to the main stem of a tree. He looked at the tree-men. They seemed a trifle embarrassed, like boys stealing from a larger. Soko, the biggest among them, was plainly the most uneasy as well. Hok decided to profit by their indecision.

"You caught me once because I was playful among you," he said. "Hok never makes the same mistake twice. Standing thus, I cannot be knocked down from behind. Meanwhile," and he quickly strung his bow, notching an arrow. "I shall not only strike my attackers, I shall strike them dead."

"Obey me!" blustered Krol, and one of the men lifted a heavy milknut to throw. Hok shot the missile neatly out of the hand that held it.

"No throwing," he warned. "Charge me if you will, but make it a fight at close quarters. Those who survive will have a fine tale to tell forever." He glanced sideways, to a gap in the matting. "But the first man to come within my reach I shall cast down there. Krol, is your other ally, Rmanth, hungry?"

The half-formed attack stood still, despite Krol's now hysterical commands to rush Hok. When the old tree-chief had paused, panting for breath, Hok addressed the gathering once again:

"You cannot hope to fight me, you slender ones. The Stymphs, who have held you frightened for so long, fell dead before me like flies in the frost. Of us two—Hok or Krol—who is the greatest?"

"Hok is the greatest," announced Soko suddenly.

It was plain that none had dared suggest rebellion against Krol since the beginning of time. Krol was as taken aback as other hearers. Soko turned toward Krol, and the old chief actually shrank back.

"He admits killing the Stymphs; he admits it!" jabbered Krol, flapping a nervous paw at Hok. "If they are gone, how shall strangers be kept out of this land of ours?"

Hok guessed that this was an ancient and accepted argument. The tree-folk naturally feared invasion, must have been taught to think of the Stymphs as their guardians against such a danger. He snorted with scornful amusement.

"The old liar speaks of this land of yours," he repeated. "How is it your land, men of the trees, when you can neither tread its soil nor look into its sky—when bird-snakes prey on you above, and an elephant-pig prowls below, so that you must dwell forever in this middle-part like tree-frogs?" He paused, and judged that his question had struck pretty close to where those folk did their thinking. "I have been your benefactor," he summed up. "The open air is now yours, for Krol says the Stymphs have fled from it. The next step is—"

"To kill Rmanth?" suggested someone, a bolder spirit among the hearers.

"The next step," finished Hok, "is to get rid of that tyrant, Krol."

Krol had drawn back into a sort of tangle of branches and vines, which would serve as a partial screen against any rush. He snarled, and hefted his ivory-bladed axe in one hand.

"You speak truth, Hok," put in Soko, more boldly than before. "Go ahead and kill Krol."

But Hok shook his golden shock-head. "No. I could have done that minutes ago, with a quick arrow, or a flick of my axe. But I have left him for you yourselves to destroy. He is your calamity, your shame. He should be your victim."

Krol made play with his axe. "I will hew you all into little shreds!" he threatened in a high, choked voice. Soko was the first to see how frightened the old despot was. He addressed his fellows:

"Men of my people, if I kill Krol, will I be your chief?" he asked. "Such is custom."

Several made gestures of assent, and Soko was satisfied.

"Then I challenge him now." With no wait for further ceremony, Soko put out one lean, knowing hand and borrowed a weapon from the woven girdle of a neighbor. It was a sort of pick, a heavy, sharp piece of bone lashed crosswise in the cleft of a long, springy rod. He approached Krol's position.

"Come and be killed," Soko bade his chief, in a sort of chant. "Come and be killed. Come and—"

Krol came, for he was evidently not too afraid of anything like an even battle. Hok, a giant and a stranger, had terrified him. The repudiation of the whole tribe had unmanned him. But if Soko alone was a challenger, Krol intended to take care of his end.

There was still pith in his pudgy old arm as he swung the ivory axe at Soko. The younger warrior parried the blow within a span's distance of his face, missed a return stroke with the pick. A moment later they were fencing furiously and quite skillfully, skipping to and fro on the shaky footing. Hok, who had a fighting man's appreciation of duelling tactics, watched with interest.

"Well battled!" he voiced his applause. "Strike lower, Soko, his guard is high! Protect your head! Don't stumble or—Hai! Now he is yours!"

Indeed, it seemed so. Krol had feinted Soko into a downward sweep with the pick, and had slipped away from the danger. With Soko momentarily off balance, Krol struck with his axe; but a quick upward jerk of Soko's weapon-butt struck his wrist, numbing it. The axe fell among the trampled leaf-mold on the branchy mat. Krol was left unarmed before Soko.

Now despair made the challenged chief truly dangerous. Krol sprang before Soko could land a last and fatal stroke. He threw his arms around Soko's body, and sank his sharp fangs into Soko's flesh at juncture of neck and shoulder. The two scrambled, fell, and rolled over and over, perilously close to a terrible fall. The chattering onlookers danced and gesticulated in pleased excitement.

Hok, whose own teeth were far too even for use as weapons, was about to remark that biting seemed grossly unfair, when the issue was decided. Soko tore loose from the grip of Krol's jaws and turned the old man underneath. Krol doubled a leg and strove to rip Soko's abdomen open with the nails of his strong, flexible toes, but a moment later Soko had hooked his own thumbs into Krol's mouth corners. He forced his enemy's head back and back, until the neck was on the point of breaking. With a coughing whine, Krol let go all holds, jerked himself free, and next moment ran for his life.

At once the spectators gave a fierce shout, and joined the chase. Hok, following over the swaying mass of boughs, could hear a hundred execrations being hurled at once. Apparently every man and woman, and most of the children, among the tree-folk had a heavy score to settle with the fierce old fraud who had ruled them. Soko, leading the pack, almost caught up with Krol. But Krol avoided his grasp, and disappeared into something.

Hok came up, pushing in among the yelling tree-men. He saw a new curiosity—Krol's fortress.

It was made like the nest of a mud-wasp, a great egg-shaped structure of clay among the heavier branches of a tall tree. Apparently Krol had spent considerable time and thought on his refuge, against just such an emergency as this. Hok judged that within was a basketry plaiting of close branches, with the clay built and worked on the outside thickly and smoothly. The whole rondure was twice Krol's height from top to bottom, and almost the same distance through. It was strongly lodged among several stout forks, and had but one orifice. This was a dark doorway, just large enough for Krol to slip through and perhaps a bit too narrow for shoulders the width of Soko's.

"Krol's nest is well made," Hok pronounced, with frank admiration. "My own tribesmen sometimes make their huts like this, of branches with an outer layer of earth. Why are not all your homes so built?"

The yelling had died down. Soko, his big eyes watching the doorway to the mud-nest, made reply:

"Only Krol could fetch clay. We dare not go to the valley's floor after it."

"No," rejoined a grumble from inside. "Nor do you dare go after—*water!*"

That reminder plainly frightened every hearer. They drew back from the den of Krol, looked at each other and at Soko.

"What does he mean?" demanded Hok. "Water does he say? When it comes to that, where do you get water?"

Soko pointed to the opening. "He gets it. Krol." Soko's throat, still torn and chewed from the battle, worked and gulped. "We should have thought of that. Without Krol, we can get nothing to drink."

One or two of his hearers made moaning sounds and licked their mouths, as if already dry and thirsty. Hok questioned Soko further. It developed that the tree-folk had big dry gourd-vessels, fashioned from the fruit of lofty vines, and these they let down on cords of fiber. Krol, the single individual who would venture to the ground level, scooped up water from a stream there, and the others would draw it up for their own use. Hok nodded, praising in his heart the wisdom of Krol.

"It is yet another way in which he kept his rule over you." he commented. "Yet Krol must die some day. How would you drink then?"

"When I die, you all die," pronounced Krol from his fastness. "I declare you all in danger. Without me to guide your gourds into that stream, thirst will claim you one by one."

Silence. Then a wretched little man attempted a different question:

"What is your will, mighty Krol?"

Krol kept majestic silence for a moment. Finally:

"You will all swear to obey my rules and my thoughts, even unspoken wishes. You will range far to pluck all the fruits I like, and bring them to me. You will yield Soko up as a victim—"

"Wait, you tree people!" burst out Hok in disgust. "I see you wavering! Do you truly mean to let that murderer destroy Soko, who is the best man among you?"

Nobody answered. Hok saw them stare sickly. Krol went on:

"I had not finished. Soko as a victim, I say. And also this troublesome stranger, Hok. Their blood will increase my walls."

Chapter IX
The Hot Hunger Obliges

For a moment Hok had an overpowering sense of having guessed wrong. He had spoken the truth when he announced that the killing of Krol was the tree-men's responsibility, not his. Violent death was no novelty in his life, and he inflicted enough of it on large, strong foes to be hesitant about attacking weak, unworthy ones. Too, he had no wish to take on the rule of Krol's people as an additional chore. If Soko, who seemed a fair chieftainly type, did the killing, then Soko would confirm himself as leader. Hok could depart from this Ancient Land with a clear conscience.

But just now his half-languid forbearance was shunting him into another nasty situation. Three or four of the men were murmuring together, and there was a stealthy movement of the clan's whole fighting strength in the direction of Soko. At once Hok pushed forward at and among them. Quick flicks of his open hands scattered them like shavings in the wind.

"Fools!" he scolded them. "Weak of wit! You deserve no better than a life roasting in these trees. Soko and I have brought you to the edge of freedom, and you cannot take advantage!"

"That is good talk," seconded Soko, with considerable stoutness. "Krol has fled before me. Since he will not fight, I am chief. Let any one man among you come and strive with me if he thinks otherwise."

The half-formed uprising was quelled. One or two men fidgeted. Said one: "But who will fetch us water?"

"Who but Krol?" chimed in the old rascal from behind his mud walls. "I make no more offers until you come to me with thirsty throats, begging."

The speaker glanced sidelong at Hok. He half-whispered: "Krol wants the blood of Soko and the stranger—"

"He shall have blood enough, and to spare, if you even think of fighting," Hok cut him off roughly. "Krol spoke of using it for the thickness of his walls. What did he mean?"

Soko pointed to the den. "He mixes earth with blood, and it turns into stone."

Hok came toward the big egg of clay, and saw that Soko spoke the truth. The texture of that fortress was more than simple dried mud. Hok prodded it with his finger, then a dagger-point, finally swung his axe against it. He made no more than a dent. Even his strength and weapons could not strip that husk from Krol.*

"Hai, the old coward has built strongly," he granted. "Well, the front door is open. Shall I fetch him out?"

Soko nodded eagerly, and Hok cut a long straight shoot from a nearby branch. This he poked in through the entrance hole. It encountered softness, and Hok grinned at the howl that came back. Then the end of the stick was seized inside, and he grinned more widely.

"Do you think to match pulls with Hok?" he queried. "A single twitch, and you come out among us."

Suiting action to word, he gave his end a sharp tug. Krol let go, and Hok almost fell over backward as the stick came into view.

But upon it was something that made the tree-folk scream with one voice of horror, while Hok himself felt a cold chill of dismay.

Krol had clung to the end of the stick only long enough to attach a peculiar and unpleasant weapon of his own—a small, frantic snake banded in black and orange. This creature came spiralling along the pole toward Hok, plainly angry and looking for trouble. Hok dropped the pole, grabbing for his bow. Fallen upon the woven floor, the snake turned from him to Soko, who was nearest at the moment. Soko scrambled away, bellowing in fear.

But then Hok had sent an arrow at it, and spiked it to a lichen-covered stub of bough that thrust into view from the platform. The ugly little creature lashed to and fro like a worm on a fishhook. Its flat head, heavily jowled with poison sacs, struck again and again at the shaft that pierced it.

"*Wagh!*" cried Hok, and spat in disgust. "The touch of that fang is death. Does Krol live with such friends?"

"Snakes do not bite Krol," volunteered Soko, returning shakily.

I do not blame them," rejoined Hok. "Well, he seems prepared for any assault. Siege is the alternative."

"I am thirsty," piped up a child behind its watching mother. Hok ordered a search for milknuts, and half the tribe went swinging away through the boughs to bring them. Soko lingered at Hok's elbow.

"Hok! Only the death of Krol will save us. There are some in the tribe who will slay us if we sleep, if we relax watch even—"

---

* Blood and earth, mixed into a primitive cement, dates back to long before the dawn of history. It is fairly universal among the simple races of the world, and is used to make durable hut-floors in both Africa and South America. The blending calls for considerable judgment and labor; the author has seen samples, and has tried to imitate them for himself, but with only indifferent success.

"And your blood will plaster my walls afresh," promised Krol, overhearing.

Hok made another close inspection of Krol's defenses, keeping sharp lookout lest Krol turn more snakes upon him. He hacked experimentally at several of the branches that supported the structure, but they were tough and thick, and would take days to sever. After a moment, inspiration came to him. He began to prune at nearby twigs and sticks, paying especial attention to dry, dead wood. Soon he had cleared most of the small branches from around the den, and stacked his cuttings carefully to one side.

"What will you do to force him out?" asked Soko.

"It is not I who will force him out," replied Hok cryptically. "It is my friend, the Hot Hunger."

"The Hot Hunger!" repeated Krol, and his voice sounded hollow.

As the nut-gatherers returned, Hok gave them another errand, the collection of small faggots of dry branches. They obeyed readily, for Krol voiced no more threats, and Soko was acting the part of a chief. As the little stores of fuel came in, Hok began to peg and tie them to the outside of the scaly den. Finally, while all watched in round-eyed wonder, he fished forth his fire-making apparatus.

Upon a thick carpet of green leaves he kindled the smallest of fires. All but Soko, who had seen fire-building once before, whimpered and drew away. Hok was all the more glad, for he wanted no crowding and bough-shaking to set the tree tops ablaze. Having found and kindled a torch to his liking, he stamped out the rest of the fire with his moccasin heel and returned to the fuel-festooned den of Krol.

He ignited the broken, splintery end of a twig. It flared up, and other pieces of wood likewise. Hok nodded approval of his work.

"See, it will soon be night," he announced. "Will someone bring me a little food? I shall watch here."

"Watch what?" asked one of the tree-folk.

"Krol's embarrassment. Where are some of those milknuts?"

Twilight was coming on, with dusk to follow. Most of the tree-men led their families to distant nests, peering back in worried wonder. Soko remained with Hok.

"You are going to burn Krol," guessed Soko, but Hok shook his head in the firelight, and pegged more sticks to the blood-mingled clay.

"Help me to spread thick, moist leaves to catch any fire that falls, Soko. No, Krol will not wait long enough to be burned. But eventually he will come forth to face us."

From within the den came a strange sound, half wheeze and half snarl.

"You are a devil, Hok," Krol was mumbling. "It grows hot in here."

Soko was encouraged. "Come and be killed," he set up his chant of challenge. "Come and be killed. Come and be killed."

Krol wheeze-snarled again, and fell silent. Hok fed his fire judiciously. The blood-clay cement was scorching hot to his fingertips. Dusk swiftly became night.

"Hok, listen," ventured Krol after a time. "You and I are reasonable men. Perhaps I was wrong to make an enemy of you. You are wrong to remain an enemy of mine. I have it in mind that you and I could do great things. Your strength, with my wits—"

"This talk is not for bargaining, but to throw us off guard," Hok remarked sagely to Soko.

Soko peered into the dark opening of the den. "Come and be killed," he invited Krol.

Krol wheezed again. This time with a sort of sob as obligato.

"Your hearts are as hard as ivory," he accused shakily. "I am old and feeble. The things I did may have been mistakes, but I was trying to help my people. Now I must die horribly, of the Hot Hunger, because a big yellow-haired stranger has no mercy."

Hok lashed a handful of fresh fuel together with a green vine and tied it to a peg he had worked into the clay, setting this new wood afire.

"I judge that Krol is at his most dangerous now," he told Soko. "Beware of those who seek to make you sorrow for them. Tears bedim the eyes."

"Come and be killed," repeated Soko.

He had come quite close to the opening, and Krol made his last bid for victory and safety.

He dived forth, swift and deadly as the little coral snake he had attempted to use against Hok. The impact of his pudgy old body was enough to bowl over the unready Soko.

Winding his legs and one arm around the body of his younger rival, he plied with his free hand a long bone dagger.

Hok, on the other side of the fiery den, hurried around just in time to see two grappled bodies roll over, and then fall through a gap in the broad mat. Two yells beat up through the night—Soko's voice raised in startled pain, Krol's in fierce triumph. Then, as Hok reached the gap, there was only one voice:

"There, Soko, hang like a beetle on a thorn! You shall have time to think of my power before you die! I, Krol, depart for Rmanth, my only friend, whom I shall feed fat with the corpses of my rebellious people!"

Chapter X
Hok Accepts a Challenge

In the complete darkness, climbing might have been a dire danger; but the fire that still burned around the abandoned fortress of Krol shed light below. Hok was able to find footing among the branches, and to descend with something of speed.

At a distance of some twenty paces below the matted mid-floor of the jungle, he found Soko. His friend seemed to dangle half across a swaying branch-tip, struggling vaguely with ineffectual flaps of arms and legs. Of Krol there was no glimpse or sound.

"Soko, you still live!" cried Hok. "Come with me, we will hunt for Krol together!"

"But I cannot come," wheezed Soko, pain in his voice.

A sudden up-blazing of the fire overhead gave them more light, and Hok saw the plight that Soko was in. Evidently Krol and Soko had fallen upon the branch, Soko underneath. As earlier in the day with Hok and the Stymph, so in this case the lower figure in the impact had been momentarily stunned. Krol, above, had taken that moment to strike downward with the big bone dagger, pouring all his strength into the effort.

That dagger had pierced Soko's body on the left side, coming out beyond and driving deep into the wood of the branch. As Krol himself had put it, Soko was like a beetle on a thorn. "I cannot come," he moaned again, making shift to cling to the branch with both hands, to ease the drag on his wound.

Hok balanced himself on the bough, and began to work his way out toward the unhappy tree-man. There was no nearby branch by which to hold on or to share Hok's weight. The single outward shoot swayed and crackled beneath him. He drew back to safer footing.

"I must find another way to him," muttered Hok, tugging his golden beard. Then he thought of such a way, and began to climb upward again.

"Don't leave me," pleaded Soko wretchedly.

"Courage," Hok replied, and searched among branches for what he needed. He found it almost at once—a clumsy mass of vines, strong and pliable as leather thongs. Quickly he cut several of the sturdiest strands, knotting them together. Then he located a stronger branch which extended above the one where Soko was imprisoned. He slid out along it, and made fast one end of his improvised line.

"I am in pain," Soko gasped, his voice weak and trembling.

"Courage!" Hok exhorted him again. He hung axe, bow, quiver and pouch on a stout stub of the base branch. Then he swung down by the knotted vines, descending hand under hand toward Soko.

He came to a point level with the unfortunate prisoner of the wedged dagger, and almost within reach. By shifting his weight he made the cord swing, and was able to hook a knee over the lower bough. Then, holding on by a hand just above a knot in the vines, he put out his other hand to the knife that transfixed Soko.

Even as he touched it, Soko gave a shudder and went limp. He had fainted.

Hok was more glad than otherwise, and forthwith tugged on the tight-stuck weapon with all his strength. It left its lodgment in the wood, and came easily out of Soko's flesh. With nothing to hold him to his lodgment, Soko dropped into emptiness.

Hok made a quick pincer-like clutch with his legs. He caught Soko between his knees, as in a wrestling hold. His single hand hold on the vine was almost stripped away, but he grimly made it support the double weight. The bone dagger he set between his teeth. Then, still holding the senseless Soko by pressure of his knees, he overhanded himself upward again. He achieved a seat on the larger branch, and laid Soko securely upon a broad base of several spreading shoots.

Soko bled, but not too profusely. Krol had struck hastily for all his vicious intent, and the knife had pierced the muscles of chest and armpit, just grazing the ribs without hurting a single vital organ. Hok quickly gathered handfuls of leaves, laying them upon the double wound and letting the blood glue them fast for a bandage. In the midst of these ministrations, Soko's wide eyes opened again.

"You saved me, Hok," he said in a voice full of gratitude. "That makes twice or three times. Krol—"

"He still lives," rejoined Hok grimly, repossessing himself of his weapons. "Perhaps he steals upon us even now."

Soko's brilliant eyes quested here and there in the night. "I think not," he said. "I have command of myself again. Shall we go upward?"

His wound was troublesome and he climbed stiffly, but he was back to the side of the dying fire well before Hok. "I thirst," he complained.

"Because you have lost blood," Hok told him, and took a fiery stick to light the inside of Krol's abandoned den. Among the great quantity of possessions he saw several gourds. One of these proved to be full of water, warm but good. He gave it to the thankful Soko.

Soko drank, and passed the gourd to Hok. "How can we kill Krol now, my friend?" he asked. "Because we must kill him. You understand that."

Hok nodded, drinking in turn. "You shall do it without my help, so as to be chief according to custom. My task will be to destroy Rmanth, and roast him for your people. I made such a promise."

"Promise?" repeated Soko. "Who can keep a promise like that?"

"I have never broken a promise in my life, Soko. Here, help me put out this fire, lest some coals destroy the jungle. And tell me how we shall find Rmanth."

Soko could not do so. His only ventures to the ground had been by way of the vine-spiral tube in which Hok had first found him. He reiterated that Krol, and Krol alone, possessed the courage and knowledge to face Rmanth and come away unhurt.

"Well, then, where do you let down gourds for water?"

"Near the hollow tube. Why?"

"Tomorrow all the tree-dwellers shall have fresh water. That is another of Hok's promises. Will you watch while I sleep, Soko? Later waken me, and sleep yourself."

Soko agreed, and Hok stretched out wearily upon ferny leafage. He closed his eyes and drifted off into immediate slumber.

Sleeping, he dreamed.

He thought he saw a marshalling of his old enemies. He himself was apparently arrayed singly against a baleful mob. In the forefront was Kimri, the black-bearded giant from whom he had won the lovely Oloana. There was also Cos, a paunchy, nasty-eyed fellow who had ruled the walled town of Tlanis until Hok adventured thither and changed all that. Over the head of Cos looked Romm, who once made the bad guess that renegading among the Gnorrls would give him victory over Hok's Flint Folk. Djoma the Fisher slunk pretty well to the back, for he was never over-enthusiastic about fighting Hok man to man. It was a delightful throng of menaces.

"I will have the pleasure of slaying you all a second time," Hok greeted them, and rushed. One hand swung his axe, the other jabbed and fenced with a javelin. In his dream, those second killings seemed much easier than had the first. The ancient enemies fell before him like stalks of wild rice before a swamp-buffalo. He mustered the breath in his deep chest to thunder a cry of triumph, when—

They seemed to fade away, and at the same time to mould and compact themselves into yet another form. This one was hairy, pudgy, grizzled, but active. Bestial lips writhed and fluttered, wide eyes that could see in the dark glared.

"So, you big yellow-haired hulk!" choked a voice he knew, beside itself with rage. "I find you unprepared, I kill you *thus!*"

Hok threw himself forward, under the stroke of some half-seen weapon. His hands struck soft flesh, and he heard the threatening words shrill away into a shriek.

Then the dream became reality.

Dawn had come. Soko, wounded and weary, had dozed off during his watch, and Krol had returned to take his vengeance.

Only Hok's sense of danger, shaking him back to wakefulness, had given him the moment of action needed before a blow fell. Krol had poised a big club, a piece of thorn-wood stout enough to break the skull of a horse. This weapon now swished emptily in air, as Hok grappled and held helpless the gray old sinner.

"Soko! Soko!" called Hok loudly.

Soko looked up, washing the sleep from his own eyes. "Eh?" he yawned, then he too was aware of the danger. He sprang up.

"Soko," said Hok, "I swore that you would kill this man and become chieftain in his place. Do so now. Do not let him escape once more."

Soko drew a dagger. Hok let go of Krol.

The deposed ruler of the tree-men made a last effort to break for safety, but Hok blocked his retreat. Then Soko caught Krol by his long hair. The dagger he held—it was the same big bone blade that had spiked Soko to the branch last night—darted into the center of Krol's chest. Blood bubbled out. The old despot collapsed, dying.

The wakening tree-people were hurrying from all sides to stare and question. Hok clapped Soko's unwounded shoulder.

"Obey your new chief," he urged the gathering. "Be afraid of him, follow him, respect him. He is your leader and your father."

Krol looked up, blood on his wide mouth. "What about the water?" he sneered, and with a coughing gobble he died.

There was silence, and Soko, in the first moment of his power, could only look to Hok for guidance.

"People of the trees," said Hok, "I have been challenged. Krol was bad and deserved death. But he spoke the truth when he reminded us that water was not at hand while Rmanth roamed below. In other words, Rmanth must be destroyed. I promised that, did I not?" He balanced his axe in one hand, and nodded to Soko. "Come, Chief. We will arrange the matter."

Soko followed him, trying not to seem too laggardly. Hok raised his voice: "Go to the usual place, you others, and let down your gourds. Water shall be yours, now and forever after.

He and Soko came to the tube that gave sheltered descent to the round level. Hok entered it first, swinging downward by the rough ladder-rungs. Soko for once did not climb faster than he. Hok came to the floor of the cavity, and without hesitation wriggled through the lower opening into the outer air, standing upon the damp earth of the valley bottom. Soko had to be called twice before he followed.

"Look around for that stream of water," directed Hok. "There, isn't that it, showing through the stems below us? Come on, Soko. You are a chief now."

At that word, Soko drew himself up. "Yes, I am a chief," he said sturdily. "I will do what a chief should do, even though Rmanth eats me."

"You shall eat Rmanth instead," Hok said confidently. "But first, the water."

They came to the edge of the stream. Gourds dangled down from above, on lengthy vine strings. Hok and Soko guided them into the water, and tugged for them to be drawn up. Glad cries beat down from the upper branches, as the hoisters felt the comforting weight of the containers.

"The voices will bring Rmanth," Soko said dully.

Hok glanced over his shoulder. "He is already here. Leave him to me. Go on and fill gourds."

He turned from Soko and walked back among the trees, toward the gray bulk with its six knobby horns and hungry tusks.

"I have a feeling that this was planned for both of us," Hok addressed the elephant-pig. "Come then. We will race, play and fight, and it shall end when one of us is dead."

Chapter XI
The Termination of Rmanth

Several accounts have descended to us of how Hok raced, played and fought that day.* But names have been changed, some facts have been altered for the sake of ritual or romance. In any case, Hok himself talked little about the business, for such was not his way. The only narrators were the tree-folk, who did not see much of what happened. Which makes the present story valuable as new light on an old, old truth.

Hok saw that Rmanth was at least six times more angry than when they had met last. The arrow in his tongue had evidently broken off or worked its way out, though pink-tinted foam flecked Rmanth's great protruding tusks. The arrow in his nostril still remained, and his ugly snout was swollen and sore. His eyes remained cold and cunning, but as Hok came near they lighted with a pale glow of recognition.

"You know me, then," Hok said. "What have we to say and do to each other?"

---

* The myth that will rise quickest to the reader's memory is the one concerning Hercules and his conquest of the mighty wild boar of Eurymanthis. It is odd, or not so odd, that Greek myths tell the same story in several forms. Thus Theseus, who may be another memory of Hercules or Hok, destroys such a giant swine in his youthful journey to his father's court. Meleager hunts and kills the Calydonian boar. And one of the Tuscan heroes of Latin legend, named in "The Lays of Ancient Rome" as an adversary of Horatius, won his fame by killing a boar "that wasted fields and slaughtered men."

Such super-swine are described as unthinkably huge and strong, clumsy but swift, with fierce and voracious natures that made them a menace to whole communities and districts. Not even the European wild boar, wicked fighter though it is, could approximate such character and performance. It becomes increasingly sure that Ramanth, the boar of Eurymanthis, and those others, trace back to tales of the now extinct Dinoceras.

Rmanth replied by action, a bolting direct charge.

Tree-thickets sprouted between the two, but Rmanth clove and ploughed among them like a bull among reeds. His explosion into attack was so sudden, so unwarned, so swift, that Hok's sideward leap saved him barely in time. As it was, the bristly flank of the beast touched him lightly as it drove by. Rmanth, missing that first opportunity to finish this maddening enemy, turned as nimbly as a wild horse, head writhed around on the huge shoulders and horrid fangs gaping for a crushing bite.

Hok hurriedly conquered an instinctive urge to spring clear—such a spring would only have mixed him up in the brush, and Rmanth's second pounce would have captured him. The part of wisdom was to come close, and Hok did so. He placed one hand against Rmanth's great quivering haunch, the other hand grasping his bow-stave. As the big brute spun to snap at him, Hok followed the haunches around. Rmanth could not get quite close enough to seize him. As the two of them circled, Hok saw a way into the open, and took it at once. He slipped around and behind a big tree. Rmanth, charging violently after, smote that tree heavily. Hok laughed, then headed toward the slope which he had traveled the day before.

Rmanth's thick head must have buzzed from that impact against the tree. He stood swaying his muzzle experimentally, planting his forefeet widely. Hok had done all his maneuverings with an arrow laid ready across his bow, held in place with his left forefinger. Now he had time to draw it fully and send it singing at Rmanth's face.

As before, he aimed at the eye. This time his aim was not spoiled. The shaft drove deep into one cold, wicked orb, and Rmanth rose suddenly to his massive hind-quarters, an upright colossus, pawing the air and voicing a horrible cry of pain. Such a cry has been imagined only once by modern man and the imaginer was both a scholar and a master of fantasy.* Hok clinched forever his right to his reputation of stoutheartedness. He laughed a second time.

"An arrow in your other eye, and you'll be at my mercy!" said he, reaching over his shoulder for another shaft in his quiver.

But there was not another shaft in his quiver.

The battlings with the Stymphs, his knocking of the milknut from an assailant's hand, the hurried destruction of Krol's gaudy snake had used up his store of shafts. If Rmanth was half-blinded, Hok was wholly without missiles. He felt a cold wave of dismay for a moment, but only for a moment.

"Perhaps I was not fair to think of hacking and prodding a helpless enemy to death," he reflected. "This makes a more even battle of it. At any rate, Rmanth has forgotten that Soko will be filling the water gourds. Let me play with him further. Here he comes!"

And here he came, in another of his mighty bursts of power, swift and resistless as an updriving avalanche.

---

* " . . . something between bellowing and whistling, with a kind of sneeze in the middle . . . and when you've once heard it you'll be *quite* content." —Lewis Carroll, in *Through the Looking Glass*.

Hok dared wait longer this time, for Rmanth must charge up the hill. He had quickly returned his bow to its shoulder loop, and now took a stout grip on his axe. As the gasping form-fringed maw, from which lolled that inflamed tongue, was almost upon him, he sprang aside as before and chopped at the remaining good eye of Rmanth. Missing, he struck the gray hide of the cheek. His heavy flint rebounded like a hailstone from a hut-roof. Hok turned and ran, leaping from side to side to confuse his enemy, and paused near the great sloping trail down which dying mammoths were wont to slide themselves. A carrion stench assailed his nostrils, and he remembered his original quarrel with Rmanth.

"You ate my prey," he accused the lumbering hulk, which turned stubbornly to pursue him further. "Gragru I trapped, wounded, and chased. He was mine. He recognized my victory, but you lolled below here and gorged yourself on my hunting. You owe me meat, Rmanth, and I intend to collect the debt."

His voice, as usual, maddened the elephant-pig. When Hok began to scale the slope backward, Rmanth breasted the climb with great driving digs of his massive feet and legs.

But now the advantage was with Hok. Lighter, neater-footed, he could move faster on the ascent than could this mighty murderer. Indeed, he could probably gain the snow-lipped plain above and escape entirely. But he did not forget his promise to Soko's people. Victory, not flight, was what he must achieve.

"Come near, Rmanth," he invited, moving backward and upward. "I want a fair chance at you."

Rmanth complied, surging up the slanting trail with a sudden new muster of energy. Hok braced himself and smote with his axe at Rmanth's nose. Right between the two forward horns his blade struck, and again Rmanth yelled in furious pain. But the blow only bruised that heavy hide, did not lay it fully open.

Rmanth faltered, and Hok retreated once more.

"This nightmare cannot be wounded," he reflected aloud. "At least not in the side or head or muzzle, like an honest beast. What then? The neck, as with a bull?"*

But there was no way to get to Rmanth's neck. He did not charge with head down, like a stag or bison or rhinoceros, but with nose up and mouth open, like a beast of prey. Hok wished that he had a spear, stout and long. It might serve his turn. But he had only the axe, and it must not fail him. He continued his retirement, along the trail he remembered from his previous descent.

So for some time, and for considerable rise in altitude. Then, suddenly, Rmanth was not crowding Hok any longer. Hok paused and grimaced his defiance.

---

* The sturdiest of animals can be dealt with by attacking the spine through the mane of the neck. Most familiar of such attacks is probably the sword-thrust of the matador in a Spanish bullfight. The bull is induced to lower his head, bringing into reach a vulnerable spot the size of one's open palm at juncture of neck and shoulders. Elephant and rhinoceros also can be killed by a proper stab there, since the spinal cord is close to the surface, for all the thick, hard hide. Scientists think that the down-pointing front teeth of the sabre-tooth tiger—extinct, or very rare, in Hok's time—were designed by nature for just such a mode of killing.

"Tired?" he jeered. "Or afraid?"

Plainly it was the latter, but Rmanth's fear was not for Hok. He turned his one good eye this way and that, looking up into the sky that at this point was not very misty. He sniffed, and wrinkled a very ugly gray lip that reminded Hok of Krol.

Then Hok remembered. "Oh, yes, the Stymphs. Krol told me that you did not venture far enough from the shelter of the trees for them to reach you. But think no more about them, Rmanth. I killed most of them. Those who lived have flown away. Perhaps the snow will destroy them—they seem to think it a kinder neighbor than Hok."

He moved boldly into an open space on the slope. Rmanth snorted and wheezed, seeming to wait for sure doom to overtake the audacious human. Then he squinted skyward again, was plainly reassured and finally followed Hok upward.

"Well done, elephant-pig!" Hok applauded. "This is between you and me. No Stymph will cheat the conqueror."

More ascent, man and beast toiling into less tropical belts. Hok found himself backing into a ferny thicket. It was here that—yes, wadded into a fork was his bundle of winter clothing.

As he found it, it seemed that he found also a plan, left here like the clothes against his need. He felt like shouting out one of his laughs, but smothered it lest Rmanth be placed on guard. Instead he seized and shook out the big lion skin that was his main protection against blizzards. Its shaggy expanse was blond and bright, like his own hair.

"See, Rmanth," he roared, "I run no more! Catch this!"

He flung the pelt right into Rmanth's face.

Next moment those mighty fangs had closed upon the fur. The horrid head bore its prize to earth, holding it there as if to worry it. His neck was stooped, the thick skin stretched taut.

Hok hurled himself forward in a charge.

Before Rmanth was aware that the hide in his jaws was empty, Hok had sprung and planted a moccasin upon his nose, between those forward horns. Rmanth emitted a whistling grunt and tossed upward, as a bull tosses. Hok felt himself flipped into the air, and for a moment he soared over the neck-nape, the very position he hoped for.

Down slammed his axe, even as he hurtled. It struck hard, square, and true across the spine of Rmanth, back of the shallow skull. Hok's arms tingled with the back-snap of that effort, and his body was flung sidewise by it.

But Rmanth was down, stunned or smashed. He floundered to his knees. Hok ran to him, dagger out. A thrust, a powerful dragging slash, and the thick hide was torn open. Once more the axe rose and fell. The exposed spinal vertebrae broke beneath the impact with a sound like a tree splitting on a frosty night.

Rmanth relaxed, and abruptly rolled down the slope, as dead mammoths were wont to roll. Hok saved his last breath, forbearing to shout his usual signal of victory. Snatching up his crumpled lion-skin cloak, he dashed swiftly downward in pursuit of that big lump of flesh he had killed.

Chapter XII
The Feast and the Farewell

Those men, women and children who had been Soko's tree-people sat at last on the solid soil, stockaded about with the mighty trees of the jungle, and roofed over with the impenetrable mat of foliage, vines and mould that had once been their floor and footing. They sat in a circle near the brink of the stream, and in the circle's center was a cheerful cooking-fire of Hok's making. The air was heavy with the smell of roast meat.

There had been enough of Rmanth for all, and more than enough. Once Hok had found Soko and shown him the carcass, it had been possible, though not easy, to coax the other men down to ground level. And it had taken all the muscle of the tribe, tugging wearily on tough vine-strands, to drag Rmanth to the waterside. After that, it was an additional labor, with much blunting of bone knives, to flay away his great armor of hide. But when the great wealth of red meat was exposed, and Hok had instructed the most apt of the tribe in the cooking thereof—ah, after that it was a fulfillment of the most ancient dreams about paradise and plenty.

Three or four tribesmen were toasting last delectable morsels on green twigs in the outlying beds of coals. More of them lolled and even slept in heavy surfeit, assured that no great trampling foe would overtake and destroy them. The children, whom no amount of gorging could quiet down, were skipping and chattering in the immemorial game of tag. To one side sat Soko, on a boulder that was caught between gnarled roots, and his pose was that of a benevolent ruler.

A comely young woman of his people was applying a fresh dressing of astringent herbs and leaves to the wound Krol had made the night before. Grandly Soko affected not to notice the twinges of pain or the attractions of the attendant. He spoke with becoming gravity to Hok, who lounged near with his back against a tree, his big flint axe cuddled crosswise on his lap.

"There is much more meat than my people will ever finish," Soko observed.

"Build fires of green wood, that will make thick smoke," Hok directed. "In that smoke hang thin slices of the meat that is left. It will be dried and preserved so as to keep for a long time, and make other meals for your tribe."

Soko eyed Hok's bow, which leaned against the tree beside him. "That dart-caster of yours is a wonderful weapon," he observed. "I have drawn two shafts, still good, from Rmanth's body. If I can make a bow like it—"

"Take this one," said Hok generously, and passed it over. "I have many more, as good or better, in my own home village. Study the kind of wood used, how it is shaped and rigged, and copy it carefully. Your men can hunt more meat. A jungle like this must have deer and pig and perhaps cattle. Since your people have tasted roasted flesh, they will want more on which to increase their strength."

"We will keep coals from that cooking fire," said Soko.

"Do more than that," Hok urged. "You have seen my fire-sticks and how I used them. Make some for yourself, that the fire may be brought to you when you need it." He peered around him. "See, Soko, there are outcroppings of hard rock near and far. I see granite, a bit of jasper, and here and there good flints. Use those to make tools and weapons instead of bone or ivory."

The dressing of Soko's wound was completed. Soko dismissed the young woman with a lordly gesture, but watched her appreciatively as she demurely departed. Then he turned back to his guest. His smile took from his face the strange beast-look that clung to the wide loose lips and chinless jaw.

"Hok," he said, "we shall never forget these wonders you have done for us, and which you have taught us to do for ourselves. In future times, when you deign to come again—"

"But I shall not come again," Hok told him.

Soko looked surprised and hurt. Hok continued:

"You and I are friends, Soko. It is our nature to be friendly, unless someone proves himself an enemy. But your people and my people are too different. There would be arguments and difficulties between them, and then fights and trouble. When I leave here, it will be forever. I shall not tell at once what I have seen. What I tell later will be only part of the truth. Because I think you and your kind will be better off untroubled and unknown in this valley."

Soko nodded slowly, his eyes thoughtful. "I had been counting on your help from time to time," he confessed. "Perhaps experience will help me, though. What shall we do here after you are gone?"

"Be full of mystery," said Hok sententiously. "The Stymphs seem to have flown away, but their reputation will linger over your home. I judge that game does not prowl near, and only the mammoth knows the valley—to dive into it and die. If ever a hunter of my sort comes near, it will be the veriest accident.

"Thus you will have the chance to make your people strong and wise. They have regained the full right to walk on the ground and breathe air under open skies, which right was denied by Krol. In times to come, I venture to say, you shall issue forth as a race to be great in the outer world. Meanwhile, stay secret. Your secrecy is safe with me."*

He rose, and so did Soko. They shook hands.

"You depart now, at only the beginning of things?" Soko suggested.

"The adventure and the battle, at least, are at an end," Hok reminded him. "I am tormented by a sickness of the mind, Soko, which some call curiosity. It feeds on strife, travel and adventure. And so I go home to the northward, to find if my people do not know of such things to comfort me. Goodbye, Soko. I wish you joy of your Ancient Land."

He picked up his furs and his axe, and strode away toward the trail up the slope. Behind him he heard Soko's people lifting a happy noise that was probably their method of singing.

---

* Again referring to the Greek myths, there is the tale of how Hercules came close to the garden of the Hesperides, a fruitful paradise guarded by dragons. Now we know the source of that story.

Additional Materials

The Love of Oloana

This rare short story, written in 1935 and technically the first of Manly Wade Wellman's tales of Hok the Mighty, never found a market in the pulp magazines of its day, although it did show up in a revised form as a chapter in the novella "Battle in the Dawn." Planet Stories is proud to present the first mass-market publication of the original work.

It was one of the smallest pools of that dense, semi-tropic forest of the Ancient World, a dark jewel over which boughs and vines laced into a green, arched ceiling. The girl turned over lazily on its ripply surface, swam three strong, slow strokes to the brink, and waded out.

Her tanned, glistening body might intrigue even a modern eye. Richly, delectably curved at shoulders, breasts and thighs, she was formed for deep warmth of love. Formed, too, for the ideal motherhood of a race—a strong race that might some day conquer even the mammoth and the sabre-tooth tiger and emerge from the darkness of the Stone Age into mastery of the whole wild planet. First she donned her single garment of soft fur, that fell below like a short skirt from waist to mid-thigh, while above it looped over one round shoulder to hide half the generous swell of her breasts. Next she slipped her slender feet into sandals of deer-hide. On one round arm she fastened a sort of bracelet, made of small shells strung together. Finally she fumbled in a belt-pouch, brought out a saw-tooth comb crudely carved from horn, and, leaning against a half-rotten stump, began to untangle her great, damp clouds of blue-black hair.

Oloana, girl of the Stone Age, feared nothing. The fierce huntsmen of her tribe had long ago driven the beasts of prey from this part of their forest. As for human menaces, who would dare molest the daughter of the head chief and the beloved of the most celebrated warrior? Who would dare so much as look at her, for all her smouldering beauty?

Yet someone was looking. He lounged apelike in a tree-fork overhead, lithe and lean and cord-muscled as the leopard whose pelt he had taken for a loincloth. Unlike Oloana's dark kinsmen, he boasted a shock of lion-tawny hair, cut shoulder length and bound at the brows by a snakeskin fillet. His face, plucked clean of beard according to custom of his own far-off people, was not tanned but freckled. The scar of some bygone adventure seamed his rugged young cheek, adding sternness to his good looks. He wore moccasins instead of sandals, and the sharp-ground stone heads of his axe and javelin were of a make unknown in that forest. He was Hok—Hok the Mighty—an adventurer from the open country to the north, now drinking in the fairest sight on all his travels.

His blue fighter's eyes sparkled with delight as they lingered on the charms of the dark girl. His wide mouth spread wider in an admiring grin. His big hands trembled, as if eager to clutch and hold. Was there ever such a girl? No, not among all the tribes he had visited. He wanted her. And to want, with Hok the Mighty, was to take.

He twitched the javelin free from its leather loop at his shoulder. Noiselessly, he rose erect on his perch, drew back his arm in a lithe gesture, and cast the shaft.

It yelped in the air, then thudded into the stump. Oloana screamed in sudden terror and tried to spring away. No! The stone head of the javelin, driving deep into the wood, had pinned fast her scanty skirt. Even as she struggled a triumphant laugh rang above her. A long-limbed demon with blazing eyes fell out of the branch-filled sky and seized her.

"Mine!" he cried, in a language similar to her own.

She screamed again and struck at him. Her fist rang on a chest as hard as wood. He laughed the louder, drew her close and plucked away the tight-wedged javelin as easily as a man of today would gather a flower. Still struggling, and shouting in fear and anger, she felt herself tossed lightly onto his broad shoulder. And then he ran.

For another, deeper shout answered Oloana, and then more shouts. Her people—the dark forest men—had heard and were coming. Hope thrilled the girl as she fought to get free. But Hok only chuckled and fled the faster.

Louder came the pursuing cries. Racing men were visible now through the thickets and trees behind—yelling, black-bearded, fierce.

"No arrows!" bellowed one great voice, the voice of Oloana's chieftain father. "You might kill her. Catch him!"

"We have him!" bawled another—Kimri, the giant who was to marry Oloana. "He's running toward the ravine!"

It was true—a narrow, ancient crack had cut deeply into the forest floor, and there the thief must come to a halt. Oloana ceased her cries. In half a dozen seconds her ravisher would be brought to bay, struck down, and herself rescued. Even as she exulted in the thought, she heard his sharp exclamation of surprise as the ravine, a good thirty feet across and fifty feet deep, came into sight.

But he did not slacken his pace. Once more she screamed, screamed her loudest, as Hok raced to the very brink of the chasm and sprang out over it.

For one horror-stricken moment she gazed down at the rock-torn current far below. But they did not fall. A shock—her despoiler's free hand had made a lightning clutch upon a dangling vine. Their weight carried them floating onward, upward, while the far bank rushed to meet them. His feet found the brink, he let go the vine and he tottered there for a moment while she gazed backward into the depths with wide eyes. Then he found solid footing and turned for a moment to shout mockeries.

The black-beards lined the other side, cursing and raving. Several aimed arrows or spears. Hok laughed and swung Oloana's squirming body in front of him.

"No arrows!" commanded the chief again, his thundering voice full of anxiety. "Cross after him."

"No man dares the leap," taunted Hok.

"I will follow!" screamed Kimri, towering among his fellows, hoarse with rage. "I will follow and take her back."

"Follow, then," laughed Hok, and plunged anew into the depths of the forest.

For hours his tireless lope ate up the miles. Oloana had ceased to struggle, for struggling was useless. She knew now that she was in strange country—her own part of the forest was left far behind. Just when she wondered if her captor would ever grow weary, he halted abruptly and lowered her from his shoulder, setting her feet on the earth but still holding her by the wrist. She found herself in a little clearing among birch trees, with a murmuring trickle of water crossing it and, to one side, a low, rocky mound with a cave in it.

"We stay here tonight," said Hok in a voice of authority.

Her eyes cast fire of hatred at him, and her full, golden-brown breasts rose and fell with each tempestuous breath as she probed her mind for insults fierce enough.

"You dared steal me!" she gritted at him.

He made a careless gesture with his free hand. "You are a woman," he said, as if that explained everything. "I am a man. My name is Hok."

"A man?" she repeated in biting scorn. "A man, with no beard?"

"The men of my tribe pluck out their beards with clam-shell tweezers," he explained.

"Your face is the face of a boy. Kimri will follow us. He will crush your skull like a toadstool."

"Let him try," said Hok. "Come into the cave."

"I won't!"

He lifted her lightly from her feet and carried her in.

She screamed once more, though she knew help was far away. Her flying fists glanced from his chest and face like hailstones from a cliffside. He laid her gently on the rocky floor, easily pinning her struggling body with one hand. The other hand slid caressingly over her cheek, down to her shoulder, then further to imprison one of her trembling breasts. She tried to strike it away from her body; she might as well have tried to uproot an oak tree.

"You are beautiful," he said softly. "What is your name?"

She did not answer, but fought as fiercely and futilely as ever. His imprisoning arm slid around her and drew her close to him, pressing her thighs, belly and bosom against his hard flesh. He slipped the strap of her garment from her shoulder and began to peel the fur casing from her body like a rind from some delicious fruit.

In desperation she bit his shoulder until the blood came. He did not cry out, did not flinch even. She knew then that she was beaten.

Deep night found a blazing fire at the mouth of the cave. Lying across the opening, Hok was grilling bits of slaughtered bird on the end of a stick. He drew the meat from the flame, studied it with the practiced eye of a skilful bachelor cook, then offered the choicest morsel to Oloana.

"Eat," he urged.

She gazed at him from where she crouched in the farthest corner. Her big, tear-filled eyes gleamed in the firelight.

"You will not let me go?" she pleaded.

He laughed and shook his tawny head. "You are mine. I am tired of my own people, and I do not want to live alone. You are the only woman I ever wanted. We can be father and mother of a new tribe."

"A new tribe?" she murmured, and began to creep toward him.

"Yes. You have not told me your name yet."

"Oloana," she breathed, and came to his very side.

"Oloana." He savored the word. "It is beautiful. Will you—"

Out flew her hand. Next moment she had caught his javelin from where it leaned beside him at the cave-mouth, whirled it and plunged it straight toward her own heart. Hok's fist darted like the head of a snake. Deflected, the sharp point of the weapon slid off across the polished globe of one breast, leaving a jagged thread of blood. A moment later he had disarmed her and clutched her close.

"You might have killed yourself," he scolded.

She burst into new tears. "I will kill myself," she wailed. "I hate you. I hate your love. As soon as you let go of me I will kill myself."

He tore from his shoulder the strap in which he slung his javelin. Pulling her wrists together, he bound them deftly. Still she glared through her tears.

"My feet are free to run away!" she cried, and, springing up, darted from the cave and leaped across the fire. But before she had run half a dozen steps he had overtaken her and dragged her back.

"There are tigers in this part of the forest," he warned her. "They would eat you."

"Let them," she cried passionately. "I hate you!"

Back in the cave again, he took the thong that served him for a belt and bound her ankles also. She lay helpless but tameless, her face dark with rage and dislike.

He held a bit of savory meat to her lips, but she turned her head away.

"You will not eat?" he queried, but she did not answer.

Hok twined his corded arms around his updrawn knees and gazed at her in perplexity.

"I wanted you," he said, a little querulously. "I thought you would want me, too."

She spat at him for reply, then rolled over and closed her eyes.

"Sleep, then," he conceded. "I will sleep, too—upon my weapons."

In the morning he woke to find Oloana propping herself up on her bound hands to stare at him with unforgiving eyes.

"Let me untie you," he offered at once.

"I'll kill myself," she replied, her voice as bitter at the night before.

"Don't kill yourself, Oloana." He moved quickly to her side and gathered her into his arms. She made no move, either of resistance or surrender, only lay quiescent and hated him with her gaze.

"Can't you love me?" he half-pleaded. His immense hands, powerful enough to rend the tines from a deer's antlers, quested over her smooth, soft body. She quivered at their touch. Was it a throb of delight, awakened in spite of her professed hate of him? Or was it a cringe of fearful loathing? Hok, simple hunter that he was, had no way of knowing. He released her and let her sink back to the floor.

"You must be thirsty," he suggested. "I'll bring you water."

Walking out into the clearing, he stooped to pick a half-dried gourd from a spreading vine. Deftly breaking it in half, he cleansed the withered pulp from one cup-like piece and filled it at the brook. Carrying it back, he offered it to Oloana. She said nothing and when he held it to her mouth she jerked her head away as before, spilling the water on her face and breast.

"You do no eat or drink, Oloana," he said. "You will die."

"Let me die, then," she snapped.

He made no reply, but considered her for a long time. Finally he rumpled his hair in perplexity and went to sit outside. Things were not going as he had hoped. Oloana had been the incarnation of his primitive dreams when first he had seen her. And in his arms last night she had thrilled him even beyond those dreams—the more so because she had fought him and he had been the stronger. But now what?

She was not submitting. She was not even enduring. She would fight always, revile him always. Given a chance, she would kill herself—and Hok did not want that.

What would it be like, life with a sullen, hateful woman, a woman who must always go tied for fear she would run away, must be guarded lest she turn his spear on herself? And could even the closest guarding prevent her? Hok suddenly saw a vision—Oloana no longer vibrant with glorious life but still and voiceless, her eyes suddenly empty of light and hate, her brown skin gone dull, and blood flowing from where, through her heart, was thrust his javelin. He dashed the back of his hand across his brow to drive out the picture. So vivid had it been that he whirled and stared into the gloom. She lay there, still bound, still resentful.

"I hate you," she flung at him.

He strode in, stooped and drew her to her feet. His hands caught the leather that bound her wrists, his muscles suddenly swelled and cracked, his breath came in a single explosive pant. Then the cord broke. Bending, he hooked his great fingers under the thong around her ankles. A heave and tug and that, too, tore apart.

"I shall run," she warned him.

"Run, then, Oloana," he replied.

She drew herself up, statue-still in amazement.

"I thought I had you," he tried to explain. "I carried you here and tied you up. But I do not have you." The words died in his throat and his forehead crinkled at the paradox. "You hate me, Oloana. Go."

"You do not want me now?" she challenged him.

His hands grasped her shoulders, then slid to her flanks, gripping her soft flesh so strongly that she almost whimpered. Their eyes were close to each other. His blazing stars fastened upon her sulky mouth, as full and red as some jungle fruit. How sweet that fruit would taste, he suddenly thought. His face darted down at hers, their lips crushed together for a whirling moment. Clumsy, savage, unpredicted, it was perhaps the first kiss in the history of the human race.

Then, still more abruptly, he spun on nimble feet and fairly raced out of the cave, out of the clearing, into the unknown, untracked forest, with a heart in which he seemed to carry the heat of Oloana's breath, the heat of her fruit-red lips.

But he did not run far. Somehow it had been easier to run the day before, for all his struggling burden of loveliness. Hok lagged. His troubled eyes sought the ground. His feet took him where they wished.

The day and the miles wore away, like rock under falling water. Twice or thrice he gathered a handful of berries to eat and found them like dust in his mouth. He drank at tinkling springs, then spewed out the water as if it were brackish. Once he saw a wild pig rooting in a thicket, and he felt for his javelin. Then he remembered that he had left it in the cave. He had left Oloana there, too. His brows drew together in troubled sorrow. He could get another javelin; but he could never get another Oloana.

It was early evening. He walked slowly down a game-lane. Then something huge and swarthy flashed from behind a tree and flung itself upon him.

On the instant Hok was fighting for his life. One glimpse he caught of that distorted, black-bearded face before they grappled—Kimri, the baffled giant who had sworn to follow him and take Oloana back. Hok's leopard-lithe arms whipped around his adversary's huge body, crushing like twin pythons. Hok's tawny head bored with deadly force into the great black beard, driving Kimri's jaw and forcing it upward and back. The dark man of the forest was the biggest of the two but not the best—a moment later Hok curved his heel back of the other's and threw his whole might forward. Down they went with a crash, Kimri underneath, while Hok's clutching fingers drove through the tangles of beard and closed on the bull-like throat beneath.

"You came to find Oloana," he snarled, swelling with the first joy he had known that day. "You find—death!"

Kimri had only breath for one strangled yell. His writhing face purpled as he tore at the garrotting grip and his great body squirmed and floundered in an effort to dislodge the man on top. Hok laughed grimly, his teeth stripped to the gum in a triumphant fighting grin as he burrowed his thumbs deeper into the flesh of Kimri's neck.

But a flurry of feet drummed up behind Hok. Two steely hands hooked under his chin from the rear. He bit a finger to the bone, heard his new assailant howl, and next moment was yanked bodily backward and away from the half-dead Kimri. As he tumbled he whirled cat-like, got his feet under him and rose to face a second black-beard. At the same moment something shot forward to prick his chest over the heart—a foot-long dagger of bone, sharp as a needle.

"Move!" dared the newcomer. Hok saw that it was Oloana's father, chief of the forest men. "Move—and die!"

Kimri also struggled up, gasping and holding a hand to his bruised throat. He caught up his fallen axe and raised it aloft to cleave Hok's skull.

"No!" barked the father of Oloana. "The rope!"

At the voice of authority Kimri gained control of himself and whipped from his girdle a coil of rawhide line. Quickly he flung a loop of it over Hok's shoulders, jerked it tight, then ran the rest of it round and round, pinioning the prisoner's arms to his body. In half a minute Hok was as helpless as Oloana had been a few hours ago.

"Now," said the chief, "where is Oloana?"

Hok shook his head.

"Speak!" snarled Kimri, and struck Hok's mouth with his horny palm. Blood sprang to the bruised lips, but Hok grinned.

"A woman's blow," he mocked. "Untie me and I will take the hand from your body like a berry from a bush."

"Where is Oloana?" repeated the chief.

"I do not know. I set her free."

"You lie!" raged Kimri. "Tell us where you have hidden her."

"I have not hidden her. She must be halfway home by now."

"Tell us," Kimri insisted, "or we will kill you."

"You will kill me anyway," said Hok.

Foam flecked Kimri's beard, and he flourished his axe again. But once more the chief intervened.

"It is nearly night," he told his companion. "We will camp. He can think until morning. Then," and he grinned significantly at Hok, "if he still is silent, I will do tricks with the hot coals."

They herded him through the trees for nearly a mile. In a grove at the edge of a brush-faced bluff they came to a halt, shoved their prisoner violently down at the foot of a big tree and tethered him between two gnarled roots with the free end of the rawhide. Then Kimri kindled a fire with rubbing sticks. Over its blaze the chief set slices of venison to broil.

Dark came. The two captors ate and talked in low tones. Several times they glanced toward Hok, but said nothing to him. Finally both stretched and yawned. Kimri came to the big tree, examined the knots that bound Hok, and finally gave him a hearty kick.

"Tomorrow you will talk," he prophesied balefully, and returned to the fire. The two forest men built it up with great billets of hard wood that would burn for a long time. Then they lay down and fell into the quick, healthy slumber of wild things.

Hok did not sleep. He tried his bonds, cautiously at first and then with all his magnificent strength, but the rope was of sound rawhide and passed many times around his body. Not even he could burst it.

He must lie there, then, and think. Think of Oloana and her beauty, and of how he had failed to win her. With the dawn his enemies would wake and question him again. The chief had hinted of fire-torture. And he, Hok, could truly tell them nothing. He could only bear the pain, give them scornful smiles and curses. If lucky, he might taunt them into finishing him quickly. He hoped so.

He dozed for a time, then started awake. What was that? He felt, rather than heard, the stealthy approach of two furtive feet. The flickering fire suddenly cast a bright tongue skyward, and he saw the newcomer—a woman, crowned with clouds of midnight hair, dressed in scanty fur that could not hide the rich beauty of her body. He knew that body. How could he forget? Oloana had tracked him down.

She bent to look at Kimri, at her father. Another tongue of flame rose, and by its light she saw Hok. She tiptoed toward him. Her right hand lifted—his javelin.

Kneeling, she slid her other hand across his chest to where his great heart beat beneath two crossed strands of rawhide. Hok looked into her eyes and smiled. If she but knew that she was cheating her father and Kimri—if she knew how they would rage when they found him quickly slain and beyond torture! The leveled point came down, down. He braced himself as it pricked his skin. Then—

The rawhide relaxed its hold on him. A strand parted, another and another, before the keen flint edge of the javelin head. Wondering, he stood up, free and chafing his cramped wrists and forearms. She cautioned him to silence with finger on lips. Together they stole toward the edge of the bluff.

Oloana, going first, brushed against twigs that crackled.

Next instant Kimri's awakening roar smote their ears. Hok whirled to meet the rushing giant, while Oloana sped like a deer down the steep slope. A charge and a grasp, and the two who wanted Oloana were straining and heaving in each other's arms. A moment later they tripped, fell, and went spinning over and over down the declivity.

At the bottom they flew sprawling apart, rose and circled watchfully. Kimri's hand sought the haft of his dagger. "Come on and fight," Hok dared him.

But even as Kimri gathered himself to spring he started, stiffened, the wrath on his hairy face gave way to blank surprise. A moment later he pitched forward and lay still. Oloana, behind him, wrenched her javelin out of his back. She looked apologetically at Hok.

"You were the strongest, I know," she pleaded. "I only wanted to help."

From the top of the bluff sounded her father's yells for Kimri. Hok put out his hand for the javelin.

"No," she said, holding it out of his reach. "He is my father. Let us run away."

In a far thicket Hok coaxed a fire from rubbing-sticks. Together they lounged in its warm light, their backs to a boulder.

"Oloana," he now found time to ask, "why did you follow me? I thought—"

"Yes," she nodded happily, "I, too, thought I hated you. But before you left me, free and alone, you—" She paused, seeking words.

"What did I do?" he prompted.

"This!" Her round arms twined around his neck. Her lips pressed his. It was, probably, the second kiss in history.

"You liked it?" he started to ask, but the words were smothered by the third kiss. Gathering her half-naked loveliness close to him, he joyfully stopped talking.

The Day of the Conquerors

While following novella by Wellman does not feature Hok the Mighty as a character, the protagonist's people belong to the same tribe as Hok—the Flint Folk—thereby placing the story the same continuity as the rest of the tales in this collection. "The Day of the Conquerors" appears here for the first time since its original publication in the January 1940 issue of Thrilling Wonder Stories.

Prologue

How do we know that this world cannot be visited from beyond space? How do we know that it has not happened already, far back in the darkest hour before history's dawn?

The Chinese tell of an antiquity when a giant and flaming dagger—the very pattern of a giant space ship—dropped from heaven and disgorged conquerors. The Greeks once worshipped a father of gods who hurled thunderbolts like javelins. There are a myriad of tales concerning enchanted strongholds, grotesque scoundrels who owned flying carpets and magic missiles, winged dragons and strangely powerful Jinni, and living monsters of stone, brass or iron.

But there is another side of the picture. There are the glad memories of heroes and princes who invaded these unvanquishable fortresses, outwitted these bizarre enemies, learned their deadly secrets and turned them against their wielders, with the result that man lives and prospers unthreatened today, free to make his own magic by science—science that has raised him to the throne . . . and may yet, through misuse, hurl him into the pit.

Are these old legends real evidence? Did they begin with the day of dread when strangers came from a far world to settle and conquer this one, routing and almost destroying the human race in its youth—only to be checked and defeated by some paladin of daring wisdom who we remember as Ulysses, St. George, or Jack the Giant Killer?

Maybe . . . .

Chapter I
The Pioneers

The ship that dropped down out of the sky was a gray-gleaming torpedo of metal, driven and guided by rocket blasts. The dozen who made up its crew were of the System's most advanced race, and themselves the leaders of that race. Their star-spanning craft bore witness to that leadership. They had sailed from their own world, the world that was fourth from the sun, the red planet. Now, with diminishing speed they were approaching the planet that circled just to sunward of them.

The Martians were a frail-looking lot, a fact consistent with creatures of a light-gravity planet like theirs. Their bodies were narrow and soft, and their arms and legs of a sticklike length and slenderness. But their eyes were bright, and their craniums swelled impressively above their skull-thin faces with sharp, toothless mouths and long snipe-noses. Their color was a dark red, like baked clay, and they wore close-fitting garments of metallic weave.

While the commander steered, the others gathered about a great telescopic vision screen, studying the new green world to which they were voyaging.

"It has much water, three times as much as land," computed one. "Vegetation, large and small, covers everything. Life is rich here."

The others thrilled to the report. Their own planet was dying, a globe almost empty of air and water. Their hunger, their thirst, had driven them to hunt a new home for their race. Here might be that new home.

"Look for animals," spoke the commander from his steering levers.

They did so, questing here and there with the point of vision. At last, focusing by means of many dials and gauges, they could see one creature of the new planet. It was massive, mighty, its body covered with shaggy wool and supported upon four pillar-like limbs. Its mouth sprouted two great white teeth, and between those natural spears the nose sprouted into a wriggling arm or tentacle.

They looked upon the mammoth, which observers of today know only by its fossil bones. Interest and apprehension mingled in their minds. Ages before, the last wild creature had died on Mars, where every square foot of habitable ground, every breath of oxygen, every mouthful of food or water was needed for the dominant race.

"A mighty beast," said the observers to each other. "Cunning, too—see how big its skull is, and how it uses that twisting member like a hand. It might be dangerous."

"Not to us," pronounced the commander arbitrarily. "We have the power to defeat it—and use it for our own purpose."

The group around the vision screen sought another viewpoint, focused upon another scene of life. Several beasts could be seen this time—a lithe, tawny mother at the dark door of a cavern, cradling two cubs between her forepaws and licking them affectionately, while a male, thickly maned on throat and shoulders, stood guard over them. It was a family of cave-lions such as once roamed young Earth, carnivora beside which modern lions would seem small and timid.

"There is real ferocity," commented one watcher. "See how Nature has made that thing of muscles and fangs and claws. It could strike as swiftly as lightning, almost—and as fatally."

"A natural machine of combat," agreed his companions.

"Yet our artificial machines have outdone Nature," spoke up the leader dryly. "Do not fear any blood-drinking brutes. We can do with them what we wish."

They turned their peering view-mechanism elsewhere, studying birds that flew. This latter fact reassured them that their own flying machines could travel in this heavy atmosphere. They noted monkeys playing among bright green foliage, herds of antelope, a lumbering cave-bear, a giant snake.

At last they came to the landfall, in the center of a gently cupped green valley. Leaving his controls, the commander moved to a gauge and quickly checked its figures.

"The air is good, full of oxygen," he reported. "Open the hatch and we will emerge."

No sooner had they quit the zone of the ship's artificial gravity than they gasped and staggered—the new world exerted almost thrice the pull they had known at home. But the more bracing, oxygen-rich air helped them to make the required effort, to overcome this unaccustomed environmental feature.

They proceeded routinely to make a fortress. One Martian, with an atomic blast-control, walked heavily in a wide circle around the ship, turning the nozzle of his mechanism against the ground. It churned up the earth into a great red-brown bank, which he shaped by skilful manipulation of the blast-control, and drew into existence as swiftly as he walked. Displacement of atoms, within planned limits, made such earth-sculpturing quick and sure.

Meanwhile others, exerting their stringy muscles against the threefold gravity, were joining together parts of a flying machine, with a closed central gondola in which a pilot could sit forward and two observers aft. It had planes jutting to either side, a rocket engine for propulsion, and a destroying flame-ray at the front.

Three were told to board the machine and go off exploring. The other worked to finish the earthen rampart, and to raise shelters inside it. The shelters took longer and finer work with the blast-control, but the commander would not rest until they were finished.

"From the looks of this sky, and the samples of the atmosphere, we may have storms," he pointed out. "They could do us more harm than any strange beast, or combination of beasts on this planet."

He had picked up a length of stick, to help support his heaviness in the new gravity. He walked to where one of the adventurers, the youngest, was bringing out and assembling with a wrench certain strange bits of machinery. As this work progressed, it took a form like that of the Martians but heavier—a body, two legs, two arms, a cylindrical head that bore a foggy-lensed lamp instead of a face. It was a robot.

"Vwil," said the commander, "you are meditative."

The young Martian addressed as Vwil lubricated the joints of the completely assembled robot, then pressed a switch in its body. The metal image came to life, moving stiffly but surely, like a Martian in armor. Vwil handed it the wrench and pointed silently to the interior of the spaceship. It moved away understandingly, brought out armfuls of new parts, and began building them into other robots.

Meanwhile, Vwil faced his chief. His features, though thin, were fine-cut and responsive, and lacked the hard determination of the other's.

"I was wondering," he said, "if there were not creatures like us on this planet."

The commander's harsh mouth screwed into something like a smile, and he shook his head.

"No Vwil. Nothing so close to your romantic dreams. We have observed no cities, no machines—"

"Are cities and machines everything?" broke in Vwil, no so courteously as he should. "I see this world as a great garden, full of good things, as our own was in the beginning. Perhaps there are fellow beings, not as wise as we, but good and kindly—"

The commander interrupted. "Sentimentality is not good, Vwil. We outmoded it many generations back, and it does not fit your otherwise fine scientific character. Least of all is their place for it here. We are overcrowded and underfed at home—we are here to explore and establish a colony, not to dream."

He paused a moment musing.

"Yet you give me a thought. There may be animals here who approximate us—walking upright on two legs, with deft forelimbs like hands, and a considerable braincase at the top. If so, they may prove most useful." He scrutinized the robot, which was working on yet another replica of itself. "More useful even than those things of metal and motor."

"You would enslave such unhappy beings?" suggested Vwil.

The other sneered.

"Do not torture yourself with dreams of how unscrupulous I am, until we know that there is such an animal—a two-legged entity, similar to us in shape, and of good potential intelligence."

Vwil patently wished there would be nothing of the sort, for the commander's attitude was of one who planned ruthless miracles.

The two did not know it, but even as they conversed, a tall biped, shaped like the Martians, but along more powerful lines, was skirting a waterside not far beyond their horizon.

Chapter II
The Defier of the Gods

He was blue-eyed that specimen, and his shaggy hair was black. Despite his great length of limb and body, he was broad only where it counted most, in shoulders and hands. The bright sun he worshipped as a god had tanned all of him save where buckskin girdled his loins and sandals shod his feet. His face—broad-browed, square-jawed, straight-nosed, ready to smile—was clean of beard, as befitted a young bachelor of his people. His name was Naku, and he belonged to the Flint Folk—the tribe of hunters and fishers who dwelt in a village of wattle-and-daub huts under a lakeside bluff, and shipped beautiful tools and weapons from stone.

His name meant Lone Hunt. It signified that from boyhood he had preferred to play and adventure by himself rather than with the shrill naked rabble of other children. Now, as a young man, he still liked solitude. Neither sullen nor timid, he was yet reserved and meditative.

He might have become a priest, but the Flint Folk had begun to turn away from the sun-worship to which they were bred, and Naku scorned the new cult of the Thunderer—the more so because two years before, that surly deity had sent a storm and sunk the canoe in which his father and mother had been paddling on the lake.

Naku was a mighty stalker of game and shooter of arrows, the swiftest runner and the fourth best wrestler in the village. Secretly he hated the Thunderer for killing his parents, and often dreamed of vengeance.

Just now, following a deer-track along the lake's margin, he reviewed in his mind all he had heard of the angry, bloodthirsty Thunderer. The fat lame priest, Ipsar, said it was like a great eagle, but larger and more deadly. Only Ipsar had seen it, and Ipsar preached terrifyingly about its powers and anger. But he, Naku, would never worship—might even find a way to make war against—

BATTLE IN THE DAWN

What Was That Shadow That Fell Upon Him?

Even as the great bulk blotted the sun from him, Naku dived sidewise from the beach into a reedy thicket, like a frog into water. His hunter's instinct told him that the thing lived, flew like a bird—but was far bigger than any bird or beast he had known. From his place of hiding he glanced up, at great motionless wings, a gleaming body, and a quivering tail-like stream of smoke. The creature had a voice, too, a rhythmic rumble like the deep song of a locust. This much Naku noticed before the thing whipped out of sight beyond the horizon, as swiftly as it had come.

"Whoo!" said Naku, and came into the open. He had seen the Thunderer, heard it. Old Ipsar had foretold something of that sort for unbelievers—the fierce god would appear and strike them dead. Musing thus, Naku felt relieved. It had come for him, but had failed to strike or seize him. His dash to cover must have baffled it.

A new doubt rose. If the Thunderer could fail, it might not be a god after all. No, only a dangerous monster, like the dragons of old, of which grandsires told children, the beasts that had fought and frightened the ancestors of the Flint Folk.

Such a thing would be fought against, perhaps killed. Naku looked to the arrows in his otter-skin quiver. He set one to his bowstring and moved forward, warily but steadily. Forgetting the deer he hunted, he left the lake shore and struck through the forest in the direction taken by the flying thing. He moved swiftly, cunningly, between trunks of maple, beech and oak. After trotting many bow-shots of distance, he came to the edge of the woods at the brow of a hill. Beyond was a valley he knew, shaped like one of the clay saucers which the Flint Folk knew how to model. From behind a spray of willow shoots, Naku peered out.

He frowned. Did he know this saucer-valley, after all? Surely it had been only a green round dip, with a pond at the bottom. Whence had come those strange lumps and ridges of red-brown stuff, like clay gigantically molded and baked? It was—yes—it was a village, a fortress made here of earthy materials. Within an uneven curved compass of walls or dikes rose the round and conical tops of buildings. And lights flashed from the hidden inner court of the enclosure, and smokes ascended, smokes colored brown, slate-blue, blood-red, black. Naku sniffed. Those smokes were unpleasant pungency.

Meanwhile, just outside the walls, the great flying mechanism that Naku fancied was the Thunderer had come to rest.

He peered and appraised. The big bird must live here, and indeed it was doing a most domestic thing—laying eggs. He saw objects issue from within it, two of them. But not eggs. These moved, they were alive. Baby birds? No. Animals? None that Naku knew. Men? Well they might be men.

They were shaped something like himself, but were gaunt, scrawny, like rude figures scratched on a board or bone with single marks for limbs. Their heads were long and puffy, like very ripe gourds, and had no hair. Their skins were colored a deeper, warmer red than the walls they approached, and their eyes were large and round and green with snipe-noses and thin mouths.

213

Except for those heads, and their spidery hands, the creatures were sheathed in tight, shiny clothing.

As Naku watched, the new mysteries moved toward the red-brown wall. A round opening appeared, like a cave-mouth from which a stone is rolled away. They went in, and the hole closed. For the first time, a man of Earth had seen an automatic door-panel in use. Only the giant flying thing, grounded and silent, remained outside.

All these things were strange, without precedent in Naku's experience, but he did not let his wonder paralyze him.

"It is more and more like the strange tales of the grandfathers," he told himself, "tales of beasts that speak, of dead warriors' ghosts that come at night to foretell the future, and other things. This is like such a story," Naku decided sagely, "but instead of hearing it told, I see it happening. Men who see such things become great and strong if they can profit by what they see."

Thus heartened by his own reasoning, he studied the situation cagily.

"The Thunderer has built a home here," he concluded. "He is an enemy—and, I think, not a god. I shall kill him."

Stepping into the open, he aimed his arrow. With a sudden skillful flexing of all the proper muscles, he drew that arrow to the head and released it. The flint-tipped shaft yelped in air, flew across the valley like a little flying serpent, and struck its mark fair in the gleaming flank.

The monster seemed to speak, with a voice such as Lone Hunt had never heard—like the ringing of a water-drop in a pool, but unthinkably louder. Naku's people knew nothing of metal. Naku was having new experiences indeed. He felt a thrill of exultation, for the echoing ring of the plates must be the cry of a wounded creature.

Setting a new arrow to string, he watched. A great hold had appeared in the forward part of the body, and something moved there. Lone Hunt sped his second arrow straight for and into that hole, and the movement checked abruptly. A new sound drifted forth—a wailing sigh, as from a severed throat. Lone Hunt grinned. He was conquering the Thunderer.

But, at the new cry, the hole reappeared in the wall. Out scrambled two of the twig-thin creatures, perhaps the same pair that he had seen before. They hurried to the forward orifice, and hauled into view a companion. That companion lay still and limp and from its high skull jutted Naku's arrow. The two living things examined the corpse and the shaft. Even at that distance, they seemed agitated.

Naku flourished his arms.

"Hai! Hai!" he yelled defiantly. "I killed him, I—I—I! The Thunderer blew storm and frowned my father and mother. I, Naku, take vengeance."

The creatures turned toward him. One was handling something that gleamed and twinkled, a short rod the length of Naku's forearm and as thick as his two fingers. From this bright object suddenly belched a greater brightness—a flash of lightning, surely, that leaped clear across the intervening space at Naku.

But he had expected some sort of assault, a charge or a hurled missile. He fell flat on his face, and just behind him and above him he heard a crackle of fire. The trees kindled to that beam of light, which cut through the space just occupied by Naku's own torso.

The hunter cursed, scrambled well to one side, rose behind a bit of scrub and launched yet a third arrow. It struck the skinny chest of the ray-wielder, and he collapsed across the body of his dead friend. The light switched off. The surviving stranger bundled himself frantically into the forward opening of the Thunderer, and the shiny shell closed up. Naku felt himself master of the field—the Thunderer struck dead, and two of its mysterious children—

Wait! The Thunderer was not dead! It rose from the ground, swooped toward him!

Naku did not fear greatly. He thought that he could spring into the woods, where that immense soaring mass could hardly follow him.

But the Thunderer, too, wielded the lightning; it flung a burning white flash at him. Naku, retreating among the trees, felt them spring into fire around him. He himself was saved because he shrank behind a big gnarled oak—the other side of it blazed up in the moment he stayed. Springing sidewise, he ran and ran. Chance brought him to a creek which flowed lakeward. His mind struck the saving equation for him—the enemy fought with fire, and he, Naku, would protect himself with water.

In he splashed, and none too soon. He swam down the muddy bottom, and heard dully a great swishing gasp—the ray of hot light was drawn along the surface of the water, turning it to steam. The creek heated unpleasantly in that brief moment before the ray left it. Naku swam as far as he could on the bed of the stream, came to a wide pool, and cautiously peeped out.

He could see the flying monster high up, hovering in place and probing the forest with its ray, as a boy stirs grass with a stick to find a hiding lizard. Flames darted above the treetops everywhere, and this was no place for a man whose bow had been ruined by water, anyway. Naku swam swiftly but silently with the current, came to shore a long bowshot ahead, and ran back the way he had come.

He paused once more on the shore of the lake, near the spot where he had first seen the Thunderer in the sky. Glancing back, he found that his enemy had flown away, but the forest roared with the fire it had kindled to destroy him.

Naku, the swiftest racer of his tribe, outdid himself in the flight for home.

When the flying machine returned to the Martian camp, there was a grim council.

"Two killed out of twelve, and by one primitive animal with the crudest weapons," summed up the commander bleakly. "And he got away." His gaunt, hard features seemed turned to carved wood. "I am not pleased."

"We did not know of attack," protested the one who had flown after the raider. "Anyway, I set the forest afire. He will not survive that."

"I am afraid that he has already escaped, and warned others," replied the commander.

Vwil spoke up. His face was calmer, gentler, than the others. "Perhaps, if he understood that we meant friendship—" he began.

"Do not speak for everyone, Vwil," snubbed the commander. "This is war. If the creature escaped, he will bring others of his kind. We will prepare for that."

He turned toward the knot of new-assembled robots, fixing his eyes upon them. He did not speak or gesture, but their delicate receiving mechanisms understood and obeyed his thought-impulses—they came toward him, a full score of silent metal men, each with a glowing face-lamp that gave off pulsations of white light. At his unspoken will they moved quickly to the spaceship in the center of the stockade, and entered. They emerged with a variety of weapons.

"I still hope—" began Vwil timidly.

"It makes no difference what you hope," the commander snapped. "If we are to be safe here, we must be masters. These savages are intelligent, brave, warlike. We must teach them a lesson, in terms they understand."

The others nodded agreement—all save Vwil. He was deep in thought.

Chapter III
Battle

At home, on the sandy, hut-studded level between lake and bluff, Naku was talking more loudly and passionately than any had ever heard him. First he thrust himself upon Rrau, the war chief, and began to fling earnest words at him. Others, curious, came around, and what they heard caused them to beckon still others. As the men of the tribe poured from their huts and thickened into a big audience, Naku ceased his talking to Rrau alone. A great log lay at hand, and he sprang upon it, raising his voice so that all might hear.

"Men of the Flint!" he addressed them. "I come from seeing marvels. The Thunderer nests near here, it hurls fire upon the forest and threatens to kill us all! With it come strange creatures, like ugly dreams of skinny men, who attack good warriors, but who can themselves be killed!" He paused, and an amazed murmur went up. "I have seen the monster, and have shot arrows at the men-things it spawns—I have killed two!"

The murmur died. All gazed aghast at the comrade who had dared face and defy the Thunderer. Those nearest him moved away, and Naku saw and laughed.

"You are afraid that I will be struck with the Thunderer's lightnings? You do not want to share that death? But I was threatened and escaped. It hurled fire—and missed! Men of Flint, my friends and brothers, this Thunderer is no god. He is only a dangerous and evil monster, and must be killed."

He glanced shrewdly around. Here and there he saw a bright face among the dark ones, a face suddenly touched with hope. Others of the Flint Folk disliked the Thunderer worship, yearned like himself for the return of service to the warm, beneficent Shining One, the sun. One such face was that of Rrau, the war chief. If the brave and popular leader should join his voice to Naku's. . . . But here came hobbling a fat excited figure—Ipsar, the priest who led the new cult of the Thunderer.

Ipsar was the only man of the village whose life was so soft and easy that he could grow fleshy. He wore a great red beard, like the lightning itself, braided into two plaits. His body was clad in a deerskin skirt and jerkin, and painted over with mystic jagged symbols. Around his neck were looped great chains of bright pebbles and shells, and other chains bound his fat arms and legs.

Upon his head rested a strange cap or helmet, a curved and spiraled thing that gave off faint flashes of rainbow-tinted brilliance. Ages before it had been the shell of a nautilus-like sea creature and had become a fossil, turning to stone. Found by some Oceanside loiterer, it had been prized, and in some way—a tedious succession of tradings, journeyings, thefts, war-plunderings—it had come the far distance from the sea, through the hands of a dozen peoples, into possession of the Flint Folk. Unique, glorious, and full of mystery, it was the sacred headdress of the priest. Some of the inner spirals and partitions had been cut away, so that the thing fitted Ipsar's head snugly.

"Liar!" screamed the red-bearded man at Naku. "You speak sacrilege. If the Thunderer hurled fire at you—"

"I say that fire has been hurled. Look."

The young man pointed to where, in the forest far along the lake's margin, rose brilliant banners of flame and clouds of smoke. "But it missed me. The Thunderer, I saw again, is no god. If he is, let him strike me!"

Everyone waited. Naku shook his fist into the sky.

"I defy the Thunderer, I challenge him to fight me. See, nothing happens! If it hears, it is afraid!"

He gazed at the press of men around him, and farther at the timid, shifting fringe of women and children. He felt that his people half believed. Then another figure sprang to the log at his side. It was Rrau, as lean and gray and fierce as a wolf. The chief glared and his beard bristled.

"Naku speaks the truth!" he trumpeted like a mad mammoth. "I have never believed in the Thunderer, but when others of you turned after Ipsar's preachings I kept still. I am a man of war, not of words, and I thought to let the matter be proven before I took one side or the other. I say now, that it is proven!" He turned to Naku. "This man I know of old, and his father before him. He does not lie. What he says has happened. If he defies the Thunderer, so do I!"

At such an uncompromising statement from so important a figure in the community, a ragged cheer went up. Even those who had worshipped the Thunderer at Ipsar's cunning behest did so through fear—fear has always won more respect and service than beneficence. The old cult of the Shining One had been less exciting, but more kindly. If the fierce new deity could be overthrown, the Flint Folk would be thankfully pleased. One or two of the fiercest set up a shout.

"War! War!"

"Fools!" snarled Ipsar, but his voice was drowned in the swelling outcry. Rrau sprang down to earth and spoke to a brawny fellow near him.

BATTLE IN THE DAWN

"Seize that priest and hold him prisoner. His words, not Naku's, are lies. We will go and see this Thunderer. If he seeks to do us harm—well, our arrows of flint are sure, our axes and spears of stone are sharp."

But Ipsar went skipping and hirpling away, swift for all his infirmity. He looked funny, and the simple Flint Folk laughed. That laughter spelt the sudden end of his influence, of his soft living, and of the power of fear he wielded. Almost at once he was forgotten. Even the man to whom Rrau had spoken turned from pursuit, anxious to be one of the adventurers who would march against the Thunderer.

Rrau counted the fighting men present. There were a good sixty, more than two thirds of the able-bodied men of his tribe. He weighted the number against what Naku had told him of the Thunderer's fortress.

"These are enough," he pronounced. "There must be more of us than of those Thunder Folk, and Naku says that they are weak and thin to the seeming. Also we will sneak upon them without their knowledge. When the others return from hunting, let them stay here and keep watch." He lifted his voice to bellow orders: "All warriors, go to your huts, take your best weapons! Follow me! Naku, lead the way!"

More cheering and enthusiastic hubbub. The party formed quickly, a column of twos, with Rrau and Naku walking together at the head. The women exhorted their males shrilly, and the men laughed back that they would return with the wing-feathers of the deposed god with which to sweep the hearths of their huts. At Rrau's gesture, the column moved out.

The noise and laughter died out quickly, but not the determination. Naku led his companions in a wide curve to avoid the section of forest that still smoldered, and Rrau kept watchful scouts far to right and left of the main body. At length the expedition came to the trees at the brink of the cuplike valley. Rrau and Naku, moving cautiously forward, peered out and down.

"The fortress looks larger than you described it," said Rrau at once.

"It has grown since I was here," replied Naku, wondering how, in less than half a day, the strange Thunder Folk had made great curving redoubts that swelled their lair to almost twice its original size. He and Rrau studied the light reflections and rising threads of smoke that showed inside, speculating vainly on what they might be. They had no conceptions of furnaces, refiners or forges.

There was a busy sound in the air, a blend of clanking metal, churning wheels, dragging of weights. The Thunder Folk—those invaders from a far world—were tightening their grip upon the empire they hoped to conquer.

"Look!" said Naku suddenly.

"From another part of the forest's edge, beyond the section which had burned, darted a human figure. It was heavy-set and ran unsteadily down the slope toward the walled spaces in the bottom. The sunlight glowed upon a flying red beard. Ipsar, the priest was hurrying toward the lair of his god, the Thunderer.

Naku fitted arrow to bow, but the priest was too far away and moving too fast for a sure shot.

"He goes to warn the monster," he muttered to Rrau. "He is afraid for it. He knows that it is not all-powerful."

"That is well," responded the chief. "We shall destroy him along with his Thunderer."

At that moment, the circular door in the rampart opened. Something poked itself out—a gleaming something, at which all the hidden Flint Folk stared. It drew itself into view, a joined object that moved and postured, and seemed to have a form grotesquely human.

"Is that one of the Thunder Folk?" the chief asked Naku.

"No, it is something new. It looks stronger, and it has no face—only that round light in the front of its head."

The robot moved to meet Ipsar. A second robot emerged. Behind them lurked one of the stick-limbed Martians, a baton-like ray-thrower in his red hands.

Ipsar sensed danger, and howled for mercy, throwing up his fat arms. The robots moved to either side of him, towering high above his head. They clutched his shoulders with the lobster-claw appendages that served them for hands. Ipsar winced, but when they drew him toward the door he went willingly enough.

"Let us begin the fight," said Rrau, and Naku, stepping into the open, drew and aimed his arrow.

He intended it for Ipsar, who patently meant to betray his people to the enemy, but just then one of the metal giants interposed its cylindrical body, and against it Naku sped his shaft. True to the mark sang his shaft, and bounced away. Loud rang the impact, the same sort of vibrating noise that Naku had evoked when he first shot at the flying machine he called the Thunderer.

But the robot was not hurt. It only turned itself in the direction from which the arrow had come, seeming to glare upward at the forest-edge with its foggy light that was like a single eye in its blank, hard head. The other dragged Ipsar into the stronghold.

"Shoot, all of you!" growled Rrau at the other men.

"They, too, sprang into the open, a skirmish line of ready warriors. At almost the same breath of time, their arrows were launched, a sudden storm of flint, converging on that dull-shining figure that stopped to face them.

The air rang with the multiple impact, but the arrows glanced away like hail form the side of a cliff. The thing did not even reel. Instead it took a slow step toward them.

Another robot came forth from the fortress and another and another. They ranged themselves beside the first. Then more appeared, a dozen, twenty. Some carried the metal rods that threw flaming rays. Others had long blades, with keen edges. One or two bore sheafs of shackles.

Again a volley of arrows, straight to the targets, but absolutely ineffectual.

"They must have shields of some kind—or magic," muttered Rrau. Again he raised his voice: "Do not fear, men of the Flint! Take axes and spears—they are fewer than we—charge at them!"

BATTLE IN THE DAWN

He himself sprang forward and led the rush, his mighty axe whirling overhead—a keen, heavy blade of stone set in a tough shaft of dark wood. Rrau could strike heavily and accurately enough to split the skull of a bison, and if these shining things were men—even men with some sort of armor, like a tortoise or crocodile—he would show them who was master. Inspired by his example, the other Flint Folk whooped and charged.

The robots did not move, either to retreat or to resist. They only stood in a row, each posing a weapon. It was not until Rrau, twenty paces in advance of his charging tribesmen, was almost upon them that a robot stepped forth, lifting the ray-rod in its clawlike hands.

"Hai-yah!"

Rrau thundered his warcry, sprang high into the air and for the moment was on a level with his tall opponent. With both sinewy arms he swung his axe in a great whistling arc, full upon the top of the metal lump that did duty for the robot's head.

Thunk! It drove home, a blow that would have severed a tree-trunk or smashed a granite boulder—but the robot barely buckled. The flint edge crumbled, the metal head wagged and only a slight dent showed.

Then came the response. The machine-man leveled the weapon it held. Forth gushed a streak of white fire. Rrau, chief and champion of his people, at whose name enemies trembled and sought to hide, was suddenly nothing—nothing but a fluff of smoke, a settling scatter of ashes. He had been rayed out of existence.

As if by signal, the other robots came into the fight. With a knowing sweep of their rays, they blasted and burned the oncoming horde of fighting men. Warriors were blasted to smoke atoms, before they could cry out with pain. The survivors paused, wavering. And then the robots moved upon them with deliberate intent, swinging their blades and plying their rays.

The Flint Folk knew fear, a fear of which no mortal need be ashamed. They turned and ran, all save one—Naku, who had run abreast of Rrau but at a distance, and was now cut off by the counter-charge of the robots. The machine-men had fixed their attention on the main body and seemed to ignore this isolated figure, but he could not reach the shelter of the trees.

Turning, he fled along the curve of the great wall. One robot was aware of the sudden movement. It detached itself from the detail and clanked in swift pursuit.

Within the Martian ramparts, the commander was grimly jubilant. "See, they run!" he cried, gazing into the vision-screen that had been set up in his hut-like shelter at the center of the enclosure, just beside the parked spaceship. "They cannot hurt our robots, and cannot stand against our weapons. We have completely wiped out those who were too slow or too stupid to flee. The extermination of the survivors will be easy."

"Could they not be spared?" offered Vwil, and his superior made a gesture of disgust.

"Sentiment again—it has no place in science or conquest. Yet the study of captives of this race might be interesting. The single specimen who came to us of his own accord is, I think, unusual. For one thing, his brain refuses to receive the command-impulses of my own mind, as have those of the other animals we have snared."

He jerked his high-skulled head toward a quarter of the settlement where, in a row of pens, were imprisoned some antelopes, two bison, and three disconsolate mammoths, as well as some other beasts.

"If he was controllable, he might become a useful slave, a supplement to these expensive and limited robots."

The two gazed to where sat the pudgy form of Ipsar, the renegade priest. He was shackled and disconsolate, his read beard out of its plaits, and a robot stood near to guard him. On his head still rested the fossil nautilus-shell that did duty for ceremonial helmet. None of the Martians had seen fit to remove it.

"His face looks evil," observed Vwil. "The fact that he came submissively to us, while the others fought, shows that he is a traitor to his own kind. Therefore—"

"Therefore," the commander finished for him, "he may help us with our conquest. But your arguments have given me a new idea, Vwil. Not long before the battle, I sent a flying detail to capture some more of these bipeds. We may not kill off the race. Not all of it, anyway."

Chapter IV
Captured

Naku, the fleet of foot, sped around a curve of the wall, out of sight of both his routed companions and the robots. There he paused, panted and listened.

Clunk, clunk, clunk, came a rhythmic muffled ring. Two feet—feet of that strange gleaming stuff that vibrated when struck. One of the strange monsters was pursuing him.

For a moment Naku felt a grip of unreasoning panic, then his wits came to his rescue. One monster pursued him, only one. Perhaps the others knew nothing of him. If he broke into the open, he would be sighted and overhauled. But just now the odds were even, and perhaps, with luck—

He pressed his body close against the wall, and his right hand poised a spear with a flint tip.

The robot came into view along his back trail, and it held in one claw a curved blade, in the other a pair of shackles joined by a linked chain. Death or capture for Naku! And its round glowing face-lamp turned upon him. Abruptly it bore down.

Naku threw his spear, instantly and with deadly accuracy, full at that disc of light. It was a direct hit, with all of the rugged strength of his muscles behind it. And, as he had been inspired to guess, that disc was the one vulnerable spot.

The pane of clouded glass, that to Naku looked like ice, splintered away. The flint head of the spear crashed into the lighting mechanism behind, obliterated it and lodged among the ruins. The robot stopped its advance, staggered, and dropped the shackle. Clumsily it clawed away the shaft, then stood, baffled and disconsolate, its arms outflung as though to grope. It acted like a man suddenly gone blind.

"Ho, you are wounded!" Naku taunted it. "I struck you—I, Naku, the enemy of your father, the Thunderer."

But it could still hear, or at least it had some sense that approximated hearing. At the sound of his bantering voice, it groped quickly toward him. If those great toothed pincers could close upon his body, he would be lost. He had no weapon left save the flaked poniard at his girdle, and he did not want to come close enough to use that. Therefore he retreated before it, and it heard the soft shuffle of his sandals. It tried again to close in. Naku, still fearful of being caught in the open, stayed close to the wall, falling back and watching his blinded pursuer.

He saw that its limb-joints and the juncture of its neck at the top of the body cylinder gleamed with an oily blackness. Naku did not understand mechanical lubrication but he knew about the use of bear-fat, dried out and used to dress wounds or sunburn. Once or twice, in wrestling games, certain of his fellows had craftily greased themselves to foil a grip. Naku, still breaking ground before the uncanny metal thing's blundering, began to put two and two together.

The black oil at the joints was to make for easy, slippery motion. If it were clogged, the thing might be overcome. He remembered a counter-stratagem he had once played on an unethically oiled wrestler. Stooping quickly, he clutched both big hands full of gritty earth. Then he straightened up and stood his ground.

"Hai!" he addressed his adversary. "Come close now, if you dare!"

It charged at the sound of his voice. It towered above him by the height of his own head, and seemed of tremendous weight. Naku pluckily met its rush, however, and with desperate precision hurled his two handfuls of grit, one upon each shoulder joint. Then he sprang aside.

The effect was all that he could wish. The monster blundered past him, but the lubrication of the metal shoulders was clogged at once, and the arms could barely move. They made harsh rattling sounds, and seemed to lose control of themselves. Standing still, the robot cocked his grotesque blind head, as though to listen for his movement.

"Here I am!" shouted Naku beside it, and again sprang aside. As it turned and stepped in the direction of his voice, he placed both hands against its flank and gave a mighty push. It stumbled, crashed hard against the wall, lost balance and fell. The blade it held went spinning away.

At once Naku sprang in, scooping and hurling earth with the savage swiftness of a fire-fighter. He heaped grit upon the joints of hips, knees, elbows, neck. The metal body ceased its struggles, whirred and grated inside, slackened off. Naku felt a high thrill of victory. He stepped close to examine his fallen foeman. Was it dead, or only shamming?

At that moment, a whirr sounded from the heavens, and something dropped down—that flying thing, the Thunderer. Naku dropped his own body, like one stricken, and shielded himself behind the bulk of the robot, peeping warily over its torso with one eye.

The machine settled itself, before the section where the door would be, but far enough out to be within the line of his vision, and out came two of the scrawny men, with a robot. The robot held the end of a chain to which, like a dog on a tether, was fastened a fourth figure.

A human being, like Naku himself—no, not like him. It was a young woman, a girl.

Naku lifted his head by the breadth of a finger, to see more clearly. She was a prisoner, it was plain to see, for her wrists were securely shackled. He could not tell from what tribe she came, but guessed that it lay well to the north. She had the blonde hair of the northerners, lots of it in disordered clouds about her face. A handsome thing she was, too—slender in her brief tunic and kirtle of deerskin, straight and proud and shapely.

Her captors led her out of sight.

Naku pondered this new thing he had observed. Apparently the Thunder Folk did not mean to kill indiscriminately, after all. The girl, though securely bound and guarded, did not appear harmed in the least. And the heavy, shiny hulk he had conquered with his hurled heaps of dirt had carried not only a weapon, but a shackle with which to bind him. Naku smiled to himself yet again, in self-applause at his new triumph.

"Three I have overcome," he thought. "One died of an arrow in the very heart of the Thunderer—a second before the opening of their lair—and now this one, a strange giant and the biggest of the three. There will be a fourth victim, and a fifth. I will conquer them all. I, Lone Hunt, am stronger and greater than these Thunder People!"

It was a proud thought and, even in those far-off young days, pride often went before a fall.

In the midst of his musings, Naku was aware that he was being approached stealthily from behind. He sprang up and spun around his hand to his dagger-hilt.

Two creatures had evidently issued from another door, farther along the wall, and now stole upon him—a big gleaming robot, and a gaunt, heavy-trudging Martian with a dark red face. The Martian, in advance of his metal servitor, leveled a small shining rod that had a round opening in the end pointing toward Naku.

The simple warrior had seen the rays in action all too closely, and he knew what such a device might be. He could neither fight nor fly. All that was left for him was to die bravely, he felt, and that he determined to do.

"Throw your fire at me, coward," he challenged. "I have killed more than one of your brothers. I am not afraid to die. I laugh at you."

And he did so, merrily. The skull-lean, snipe-nose face of the Martian smiled in answer, neither fiercely or mockingly. The tube, pointing at Naku, gestured at him has though to bid him turn and walk.

Naku shook his head.

"Not I," he demurred. "If you want to burn me, do it now—not sneakingly from behind." And he planted his big feet, glaring at what he felt certain was his destruction.

The creature sighed as though in regret, and touched a little projection on the rod. Fire gushed forth—not white, but pale blue. It enveloped Naku like a splash of water. He felt no pain, only languor. His senses were slipping. His knees sagged, his eyes closed, and he felt himself gently collapse.

The Martian commander came from his headquarters just as Vwil entered the fortress. Behind Vwil clumped a robot, carrying in its arms a limp human form.

"Did you venture out?" said the commander.

"Yes. I was at the power-caster, and the gauges showed that one receiving set had ceased to take energy. I guessed that it must be a damaged robot, and reconnoitered. I found that this native had overcome and wrecked one of the robots. I disabled him with the sleep-ray—"

"Why did you not kill him, since he had harmed us?" broke in the other. "Oh but I forgot that laughable softness of your spirit. Well, perhaps you did rightly. If he was adroit enough to defeat a robot, he may have a nervous system complex and sensitive—worth my experimentation. Have him put in the new pen with those others of his kind."

Chapter V
Conference with the Invaders

When Naku awoke, he felt sunshine in his face, earth against his sprawling back, and a pillow, soft but firm, under his head. He opened his eyes, and looked into a most admirable face.

It was a woman's face—young, oval, firm-jawed, straight-nosed, blue-eyed. It was flanked by two braids of sun-colored hair that caught gleaming lights. A low voice questioned him anxiously.

"Are you badly hurt?"

Naku sat up, flexed his arms and stirred his legs.

"No," he decided. "I remember being struck down by blue fire. What has happened?" He turned to face the girl on whose lap he had been pillowed. "Who are you?"

"My name is Arla. We are prisoners of these—I do not know what they are called, but they are very evil."

Ordinarily Naku, reserved from boyhood, would be wary and shy before a stranger girl, but this one had done her best to help him. He studied her closely, and remembered seeing her before—this was the captive who had been brought in the Thunderer, the flying thing. He smiled at her thankfully, and looked around.

They were in a cage, with a flat roof of hard-packed earth, such as the Martians know how to fashion with their control-devices, and walled with perpendicular bars of metal. Part of these bars made up a door, fastened with a complicated lock. Against the door, at the far end of the enclosure, sat Ipsar, still dressed in his garish garments of priesthood, but very rumpled and disconsolate. He met Naku's eyes, and growled:

"Be careful of that woman. She is a wasp."

"He says that because he felt my sting," Arla informed Naku. "I do not seek the caresses of fat strangers."

227

Naku, studying the priest, saw that one of his eyes was badly bruised, as from the impact of hard little knuckles, and grinned. Then his face went serious again.

"We three must be friends and help each other," he pronounced. "These Thunder Folk have killed many men of my people, and hold us captive. How can we get away from them?"

"We cannot get away," said Ipsar sourly. "The power of the Thunderer is too great. He flies, he strikes fire—"

Arla shrugged her pretty shoulders in contempt.

"I know about this thing he calls Thunderer," she said. "It is no living bird, but a thing made and operated by men—or, rather, by these manlike devils you call the Thunder Folk. The thing is hollow inside, with doors, like a hut; but it is a hut that can fly."

"Can it be?" cried Naku, trying to comprehend.

"I have been inside and have seen. One of the Thunder Folk sits among strange sticks and round whirling things, and by handling them makes it go fast or slow, up or down. It swooped upon me as I fetched water just outside our village to the north. I was made stupid by fear, and those inside seized me. I rode in the thing with them, and used my eyes."

Naku digested this.

"How can a thing not alive be made to fly or moth otherwise?" he demanded.

"Can not a man make an arrow fly in the direction he chooses, by the power of his bow and the aim of his eye?" returned Arla. "Can a noose of rope not draw tight, as though it were a hand? This flying thing operates in the same way, but more wonderfully."

The idea sank in, and Naku had a contribution of his own.

"The big, strong things that walk and fight, and seem to be men," he said, " the ones made of shiny hard stuff and bearing round foggy lights in their faces—they, too, must be strange fashionings. They are—tools!"

"Even if so," argued Ipsar, "they are too deep a matter for us to understand. We must submit to the power of the Thunderer."

"The Thunderer, I say, is only a tool, a utensil that flies at the will of its owner," snapped Arla.

"I think that she speaks truth," seconded Naku. "If it is a deep matter to handle or to operate it, maybe I still can learn, as a child learns to shoot with the bow or to make a noose."

The argument was interrupted by a clatter at the door behind Ipsar. Startled, the priest slid sidewise, and the section of bars swung back. There stood a Martian, supporting himself on a stick against Earth's sore pull of gravity. He beckoned to Naku with a hand that, though claw-thin, was plainly human, of flesh and bone.

"He wants you," spoke Ipsar. "Obey him—go."

Naku shook his head, and felt for his dagger. It had been taken from him.

"I will not obey," he said sturdily. To the Martian he snarled: "Come in and try to take me. I will break your scrawny back across my knee."

BATTLE IN THE DAWN

The Martian only smiled—Naku saw that this was the one who had overwhelmed him with the blue ray. Then the Martian turned and fixed his brilliant green eyes upon an attendant robot. He did not speak nor make a gesture, but the metal monster understood. It entered the cage with heavy steps, seized Naku and carried him out, struggling and kicking like a naughty child.

As it bore him away, his angry eyes had a glimpse of the interior of the fortified place, and it was as if he were in another world. The ground underfoot was paved in geometric design. Strange shelters of tile and metal stood here and there with, in the center of them, the great gray-gleaming fish that was the spaceship.

Here and there stood or sat Martians, but none of them moved more than necessary against the drag of Earth. Most of the work—smelting, digging, building, with a variety of incomprehensible machines—was in charge of robots. All the horizon that might be familiar to Naku, the green slopes of the valley and the forest above and beyond, was shut away by the high red ramparts.

Naku's captor carried him straight to the spaceship and in. At once Naku felt a strange lightness, as though he could float. The gravity screen of the vessel was set to the pull of Mars. Inside a cubical compartment, the robot thrust him into a chair, strapped his wrists to the arms and his ankles to the forelegs. Then it stumped out. The Martian who smiled seated himself opposite Naku, before a flat-topped piece of furniture studded with push-buttons, levers and gauges.

The Martian pressed a lever. Another of those strange light-rays, with which the invaders seemed to do so much of their working and fighting, gushed out—a soft cloud of orange radiance. It smote Naku full in the face, but did not blind or irk him. He felt all fuzzy inside his skull for an instant, then more awake than ever before. The Martian's smile grew broader, more understanding. For the first time, his lips moved and he spoke.

And Naku could understand him.

"Do not be afraid," he was saying, "and do not be mistrustful. This ray frequency makes our thoughts communicable one to the other. My name is Vwil, and I come from another world, another star."

"Then go back to that other star," said Naku at once. "We do not want you here."

A rueful smile from Vwil, as though he would like Lone Hunt to be friendly.

"Our world is poor, starving." Vwil argued. "We have flown here in hopes of finding a place that will support life for ourselves, our comrades, and our children to come. Your world is larger than ours. It is rich, with much vegetation and water and air. There is room here for both your people and mine."

"I cannot live as neighbor of the Thunderer," snapped Naku. "I have killed some of your people—two of the thin, red-faced ones like you, and one of the big shiny ones with a round light for a face."

He stared at Vwil, and his young eyes were as hard and sharp as war-axes.

"If I was free this moment, I would kill you."

"It is you who want to fight, not I," Vwil replied with a sigh. "What is your name?" Naku told him, and Vwil continued: "You started the fight, Naku. Yet I think we can be friends. This ray of light makes it possible for us to talk. Can we not touch hands and be helpful to each other?"

Naku wagged his head in fierce negation.

"I used to know this valley," he said. "It was peaceful, silent, green. Deer ate grass, and birds flew over it. Now you have built this fort and killed the grass. You swallow the very ground. Only the Thunderer spreads its wings—and the Thunderer is not alive, but a tool, a flying house," he added, remembering what the girl Arla had told him. "You have fought my people once, and beaten them. But there are others, Vwil the Invader. Many others, more than you can count—tribes and nations of fighting warriors!"

His chest swelled, as for the first time in his life he considered all mankind as a single battling unit.

"You may beat others, but those who live will learn your secrets to use against you. Even I, a young man and a prisoner, have learned much in little time. And in the end—"

"Wait!" came a new, cold voice.

Vwil rose from where he sat, and his attitude was respectful. A second Martian came and took the seat Vwil had quitted. His face was hard and full of ruthless wisdom.

"I have heard your soft words, Vwil," said the newcomer. "I disapprove. As commander, I will finish this interview. You may go."

Vwil departed from the chamber, but once he looked back. His brilliant eyes caught Naku's, who saw that they were full of pleading. Then the Martian commander addressed the captive:

"Let me tell you the truth of your situation and that of your people. You have boasted to that weakling, Vwil, of your triumph—two of us, and one of our robots, have fallen before you. Let me bolster your conceit further, and inform you that these are all our losses—inflicted by your hand alone. The rest of your race has not done us one bit of harm. And you, being a prisoner here—"

"I will escape," Naku promised him.

The commander smiled, not like Vwil, but as fiercely as a hungry wolf. His skull-face was a mass of crinkles, as hard and set as dried leather.

"I think not. Our first specimen of your race, the fat one with red hair on his chin, disappointed my experiments. He could neither be made to understand our speech, nor to receive the impulses of my will. You, under this ray, are more receptive."

So they had tried their tricks on Ipsar and without success! Naku wondered about it. Was he not stronger of will, quicker of mind, than the pudgy priest? What shield then, had Ipsar against the science of these invaders. If he, Naku, could get such a shield—

"Naku," the Martian chief was saying, his eyes fixing the young man's, "do you hear my words?"

"Of course I hear them," replied Naku.

"Do you obey me?"

"Obey you?" repeated Naku wrathfully, and met the blazing eyes opposite. He was ready to fight against his bonds, to burst them and leap at the contemptuous thing who presumed to set himself up as master . . . but a new thought came. He was a captive. These were wiser, stronger beings. They must know best. Naku felt no surprise that his attitude changed so suddenly, under the green gaze of the spider-man with the lean red face.

"I obey you," said Naku humbly.

"You know," continued the inexorable voice, "that we, being desperate for life, are justified in coming from our poor world to your rich one—that it is our place to rule and yours to serve."

Of course that was the truth, Naku realized. Just as man could conquer and exploit the animals, so could these Thunder Folk, being wiser and stronger, conquer and exploit man. It was a law of nature, said Naku to himself—he should be grateful that he was allowed to live. So completely had Naku's attitude changed under the suggestive power of the Martian.

"It is your place to rule," Naku repeated, "and mine to serve."

"Good." The commander rose, came to him, and unfastened his bonds with a deft flip of the buckles. Naku rose respectfully.

"I have hopes of your kind," announced the commander. "Be good servants, recognize—prosper, even—under our rule. Now return to your cage."

Submissively, Naku did so.

"And so," the Martian commander finished his report to Vwil, "I succeeded. The exertion of my will-power, while the ray was turned on, conquered the creature's primitive individuality on the instant. Henceforth he will understand and obey us. When one of us meets his eye and speaks his will, the creature will carry out the order. These natives who call themselves 'men' are slaves ready to our hand—physically strong and adroit, cheaper than robots, intelligent enough to receive thought-impulses and obey, but not to overthrow."

"That is interesting," said Vwil. "I am sorry that I cannot report so encouragingly on my own labor."

"Your own labor," repeated his chief. "What have you been doing?"

Vwil held out a chart, on which he had noted various chemical figures.

"It is the question of fuel. We have not enough to return to Mars."

"We can manufacture more when the time is ripe," snapped the commander. He was irritated once more with Vwil. This enigmatically gentle scientist, so brilliant and yet so weak from the Martian standpoint, was always a challenge. Just now the commander had recited his triumph over Lone Hunt, not as a leader informing a subordinate, but as a subordinate seeking the commendation of a leader. And Vwil, unimpressed, had only admitted his own failure in another field.

"This planet, however rich, lacks certain necessary elements," Vwil was saying. "Also, the explosive power of metals seemed subdued. I fear that we cannot manufacture proper fuel—we are stranded."

"Let it be so," growled the commander. Suddenly he felt more ruthless and determined than ever. "We shall make ourselves lords of this world. The men whom we capture shall serve us in a closer capacity than as slaves or robots." His eyes glittered a brighter green. "Listen, Vwil, to what I plan."

"Yes?"

"Our brains are great, but our bodies weak. These natives, less developed of mind than we, have yet strong bodies, well adapted to the particular life-struggle here. The inference is obvious."

"Perhaps," said Vwil. "Yet I do not approve—"

"Once more, I remind you that I command. We shall transplant our brains to their bodies. We will become immortal, even—as a body grows old, we can shift the Martian brain in it to a new, young body. Always we shall take the finest physiques for ourselves, and the rest of the human race shall serve as slaves. When more of our people come—"

"Will more come?"

"We cannot return, as you have shown," said the commander. "Unless we do return, reporting this planet as unfit for habitation, others will follow to see what has become of us. We, the pioneers, will also be chiefs and heroes of the new colony of Mars."

His voice rose exultantly, his lean face was suffused with a darker red. It was as though he saw the enslavement and exploitation of all humanity achieved, the complete control of Mother Earth in the bony hands of his own invading race.

"Let the flying detail go and seek for more good specimens," he rasped. "Let them bring only the finest, killing all others. Meanwhile, we must experiment. Who is our dullest brain, the one with whom we can experiment the most cheaply? Bring him to the surgery, also that fat fool among the prisoners, and make ready for an operation."

Chapter VI
The Shell Cap

A day and a night had passed since Naku had been returned to the cage from his interview with Vwil and the Martian leader. Away from the influence of the Martian, he could once again think for himself. With the dawn, the flying machine—Naku no longer thought of it as the living Thunderer, but as what Arla had pronounced it, a complicated tool—came winging back from another expedition. It had swooped at night upon a camped hunting party, killed two men and captured a third. As robots led this hunter to the prison, Arla sprang up from where she lay asleep on soft sand.

"Lumbo!" she cried, in a voice that betrayed both happy surprise and concerned question. The young man in the grip of the robots was a blond-haired, blue-eyed specimen like herself, and his face—it was as handsome as her own, but with masculine strength of contour—lighted up in recognition. He was thrust in, and Arla seized him in a welcoming embrace.

"They have not hurt you?" she demanded in tender concern.

Naku watched, with feelings he did not bother to diagnose, since they were strangely glum. He had known Arla only a few hours, and up to now had not had the time to consider whether she was desirable or not, until this stranger suddenly claimed her affectionate attention. He must be her husband or lover—and Naku suddenly disliked the idea.

He turned over in his mind thought of a sudden plan to provoke a quarrel with the blond youth. It would lead to a fight, with Arla as prize of victory. Naku gauged the other's volume of muscle, his quickness of reaction. Probably here was a good fighter, but Naku felt himself to be both stronger and fiercer. . . .

The robots who had brought the man called Lumbo had also roused fat Ipsar from slumber and dragged him out. Ipsar struggled and protested, and the seashell cap fell from his tossing head and lay just inside the barred door as it slammed behind him. Arla turned toward Naku, her blue eyes filled with golden joy-light.

"Naku," she said, "this is my brother, Lumbo—the son of my father and mother. He was surprised and captured by these Thunder Folk, but now he is here, with you and me. The three of us are wise and strong. We will find a way to escape."

Her brother! Naku's dark, square-jawed face glowed with a joy to match Arla's own. His welcoming hand caught Lumbo's and squeezed it until the other winced.

"I am glad to see you," said Naku honestly. "Glad that you are Arla's brother."

Arla bowed her head shyly—she, at least, understood the inference. Lumbo rejoined courteously, and added: "Arla is right. We three should win out of this trap. Tell me what you know of our captors."

The trio of young people sat on the sand, Lumbo in the center. Arla and Naku alternated in setting forth both observation and theory. At the end, Lumbo summed up:

"We are unarmed, and caught like fish in a net. But," he added weightily, "from what I have seen and from what you tell me, I have it in mind that we are also like netted fish in that those who caught us must work clumsily with us, like fishermen wading and swimming in water. I mean that these stranger people, whom Naku calls the Thunder Folk, do not feel natural upon our world. Light weights are heavy to them, and the air is thick to their breathing. We, who are used to these things, have the advantage by at least that much."

He paused to let the idea sink in, and picked up the shell-cap that Ipsar had dropped.

"What is this thing?" he asked. "Does it belong to the Thunder Folk?"

"It was the cap worn by Ipsar," Naku replied. "He wore it to show that he was a priest." Taking it from Lumbo's hands, Naku set it upon his own shaggy black hair to demonstrate. The thing fitted snugly, and weighed little. The three prisoners continued their talk, and Naku forgot that he wore the shell.

Meal time came, and it was Vwil who brought food in his own spidery hands—metal bowls, in which were contained sliced roast meats and several kinds of fruit. He spoke in friendly fashion to Naku, but his purring words were unintelligible. Naku shook his shell-capped head, and both he and Vwil stared uncomprehendingly. They had understood each other well the day before, in the spaceship. What was wrong now.

Naku, perplexed, lifted a hand to rumple his hair. That hand twitched back the shell cap, and at once he knew what Vwil was saying in the language of the Martians:

"Answer me, Naku. I am still ready to be your friend to help you if I can. Do not pretend to be deaf."

"I am not deaf," grumbled Naku, and Vwil also understood. "It seems that—"

He was about to say that the knowledge of Vwil's language had seemed to escape him for a moment, but on impulse he broke off. Dropping his hand from his head, he let the shell settle back into place. At once he was unable to comprehend Vwil's words, but the Martian's manner suggested a friendly farewell. Left alone, the three began to eat, and Naku had something amazing to relate.

"I could understand him, and he could understand me, only when I pushed back this shell cap," Naku informed the others. "When I have it on my head, he speaks strange words."

"We did not understand him at any time," contributed the girl Arla, sinking her white teeth into a big yellow plum.

That was an additional item to consider, pondered Naku. He remembered the orange ray, and how Vwil apparently used it to establish communication with him. Arla and Lumbo, who had never felt that ray, could not understand. The consideration extended itself; they would never understand the Martians until the ray was played upon them.

Naku remembered something else. The Martian commander had spoken of Ipsar, had said: "He could neither be made to understand our speech, nor to receive the impulses of our will." Naku took the shell from his head and gazed at it. Yes, Ipsar had worn that shell until his recent struggle with the robots. Naku, wearing it, had shut away the understanding of Vwil's words, as a wall might shut away light—even the light of the orange ray. What did it portend?

Forgetting to eat, Naku groped for a decision. Again he studied the shell. It was of unthinkable age, enameled with the stony lime of petrification, and it hid his thoughts from the Martians. Naku, like all his people, believed that the heart, not the brain, was the seat of the reason and the emotions, and so the idea of an insulated brain-case was not easy to grasp. But the facts were before him and he decided to accept them.

He considered, too, that the ray-induced ability to understand the Martians also bent one's will to those strange and forbidding creatures. The commander had said so, and had demonstrated it. But he, Naku, had the shell-cap. Without it, he could understand the Martians, benefit by what they said. Wearing it, he could withstand their wills. Naku began to think that here was a chance for escape—even victory.

Lumbo was haranguing his sister on that very subject.

"Without beating these Thunder Folk, destroying them, it makes no difference how far we run from them. What they say and do shows that they intend to rule the world, and us. We must fight—win."

So they all talked. Naku kept the shell cap on his head lest a Martian, passing, overhear and understand him and report that the captives plotted. He also stared through the bars at the garrison, their buildings and equipment, and at the walls that seemed ever to grow and embrace more territory. Soon these walls would enclose the whole valley, encroach on the forest. Would the fortress eventually overflow all the world?

In the midst of this, figures approached. All three looked up. Two robots came, and the Martian commander, and Ipsar the priest.

But Ipsar no longer went in a prisoning grip—he walked beside the commander, who leaned for support on the fat shoulder. Ipsar's cranium was swathed in white bandages, and seemed to have swelled beneath them. He spoke and the voice was Ipsar's, but the words—they were in the language of the Martians!

Wondering, only half guessing, Naku whipped off the insulating cap. At once he made out the words, and they were addressed to himself:

"You with the black hair, prepare to go with this party." With his own plump hand, Ipsar unfastened the barred doorway. "Come forward, I tell you."

"Come out," seconded the commander, catching Naku's eyes, and Naku obediently emerged. "What do you hold in your hand, that stony thing like a bowl?"

Ipsar closed the gates upon the staring Arla and Lumbo, and came close to Naku.

"Yes," he said curiously, "what is that?"

His query saved Naku, saved mankind, saved the world. For the young man, held by the will of the commander, would have replied truthfully and fully concerning the cap's power to shut off thought-impulses. But Ipsar's evident ignorance of the object he had worn so long and constantly made Naku turn toward him.

"Do you know what it is? You, as priest, had it always on your head."

"Did I? And Ipsar took the cap, lifting it to his bandaged pate. But the swathings and the enlargement made it impossible to fit the shell in place.

"I will wear it no more," he announced. "Here, prisoner, it is yours."

Contemptuously he slapped it upon Naku's head, and at once the next speech of the commander slid into unintelligible purrings and snortings. Naku could not understand them—and could not feel the impulse to obey in his heart.

When he did not act upon whatever order was given him, the commander fiercely repeated it, and pointed toward the center of the fortress, where the spaceship still lodged. Ipsar, on the other side of Naku, was also speaking in the Martian tongue, but, like the commander, was only astonished and not suspicious at all at the captive's lagging. Sure of their psychic control over Naku, neither appealed to the robots.

Naku made up his mind at once. He took a step toward the ship, and the robots also turned away, leading the party toward it. At once Naku went into action.

A backhanded flip of his big left fist sent the commander spinning head over heels like a straw figure. Whirling without an instant's pause, Naku struck with both hands at Ipsar. His left sank into the priest's flabby belly and, as Ipsar doubled over, Naku's right landed flush on his bearded mouth.

Down went Ipsar, and from behind the bars of the cage both Arla and Lumbo cheered loudly. Naku did not wait to acknowledge the applause. Already the robots turned toward him. One held a ray-throwing rod.

Springing across the floundering form of Ipsar, Naku fled for his life in among the buildings of the Martian settlement.

Chapter VII
In the Mammoth Pen

Two buildings, square storehouses, were set so closely together that Naku had to squeeze between them. But he hesitated only a moment to do it, not caring that bits of skin were scraped from the points of his broad shoulder. Behind the houses was an alley, and into this the two robots were already dashing from either end. Because Naku seemed trapped between them, and also to avoid injuring its companion, the robot with the ray-device did not use it.

But Naku saw a wall or paling, of the red tile-like substance that the controlled atomic machines, made out of plain earth. He charged at it and dived over, head first, though it was as tall as he. Landing on hands and knees beyond, he waited a breathless moment. The robots could not follow him, and he heard them clanking away to cut him off beyond. Like a fox he doubled, hurling himself back across the wall and into the alley. Up this he tore, just behind the robot with the ray-rod.

There was an open street at the end of the alley, and across this he made a dash. Shouts greeted his appearance—full half a dozen armed Martians had gathered at the call of their leader, and moved to bring him to bay against a wall. But Naku was an outdoor man, thrice as strong and active as the most vigorous Martian, and the wall had inequalities enough to give him hand- and footholds. He swarmed up like a monkey. A flame-ray struck just where he had been as he mounted, turning the red of the wall to cindery black. Then he was over the coping.

He had hoped to land in open country, but this part of the wall, once the outer rampart, had been passed by the encroaching works of the Martians. Beyond it was a higher wall, and the space between was full of sheds, shelters, and stacks of metal and other materials. It contained, too, a great pen or cage

237

of metal bars with a flat earthen slab for roof—a structure similar to that in which he had been held, but larger and more coarsely made. He could thrust himself between those bars; and, with the noise of pursuit greatening behind him, that is what he did.

He raced to the cage, squeezed in, without more than glancing at the great brown-black lumps that seemed to pulsate inside. Anything, he told himself, was less terrible and more practicable to deal with than Martians or their robot-slaves—and, even when he saw that the tenants of this enclosure were mammoths, he did not emerge again. For the Martians, four of them, accompanied by armed robots, were coming into view, through ports in the wall. Naku flung himself at full length into a heap of grassy forage which the Martians had sagely given to the captive beasts.

Here he lay still.

There were three mammoths, male, female, and calf—great shaggy mountains of flesh, more than twice a tall man's height at the blocky shoulders. Their woolly skulls were high-domed, the index of cunning brains that were mirrored in their tiny, questing eyes. Their legs were like living tree-trunks, covered with hair like thick, coarse moss. And their trunks, as pliable as anacondas and clever as hands, now began to swing and writhe. They squealed and muttered to each other. The sudden appearance of their chief enemy, man, alarmed and infuriated them.

They moved, all three as one, toward the heap of grass into which Naku was burrowing. He felt, rather than saw, their great hillocky bodies above him. He heard the rumbling intake of their breath, the rustle of the trunks that began to squirm about him.

The Martians, toward which he dared not lift his face, were patrolling near the cage, shouting to each other and to the robots. A mammoth's trunk groped along the calf of Naku's leg, paused on his bare back, and tweaked his flesh painfully. Naku stoically refused to twitch or gasp. The largest mammoth, changing position, set a massive foot within arm's length of Naku's head, and also explored with its trunk. The top of the member found the shell that covered Naku's cranium, prodded it tentatively, and dislodged it.

At once Naku could comprehend the speech of the Martians. Even in the midst of peril from the mammoths, he listened carefully. The commander was doing all of the talking:

"We may have underestimated these beings that call themselves human. At first the black-haired specimen seemed completely under control, but in some way it wore off. Well, he must have gone over our wall. Go, two of you, on a flying detail. If you catch him, bomb or ray him. He knows too much to be allowed life."

Naku exulted in his hiding. The wise, harsh chief of the enemy was mistaken about him—and afraid of him, eager for his death. Naku swore that in this last case he would disappoint the commander; and then he felt the trunk-tip of the largest mammoth combing his hair. The big beast was snarling to itself, shifting ponderously on its feet, trying to guess what lay so still among the heaped grass, smelling of man but not moving. And the Martians heard.

"Those animals we captured are nervous," one of them said to the commander. "Let us see what they do."

The commander approved, and the party came near. The big mammoth, seeing his captors approach, moved grumpily forward to the bars. A foot swept across Naku's prostrate back, barely a palm's breadth above it, then another. The fugitive, daring to glance up, saw that he now lay under the hair-thicketed belly.

Sensible of his mortal peril, yet he knew that he was for the moment hidden as under a shadowy roof. The Martians were conversing just outside the bars.

"Fix the thing's eyes with yours," the commander was telling one. "See if you can read its mind—impossible you think? There is something wrong here, but the animal's brain is too primitive to communicate its impressions to ours."

"That is true," agreed the Martian addressed. "Probably these beasts saw the escaped human run near their cage, and climb over the outer wall."

"Probably," said the commander. "If I could but fix that black-haired one's eyes with mine again, I might subdue his will. But time is too short for experimenting. I am weary of walking on this thrice-gravitied planet. Let them bring that other male, the one with the yellow hair, to the operating room."

They moved away. Naku slipped stealthily from under the mammoth's belly, around its massive hindquarters and into the back of the cage. The big beasts stood together, watching the departure of the Martians. Naku found a space between the rear-hindmost bars and the adjacent partition, a place where he could lie and be safe both from the blundering ill-will of the mammoths and the discovery of the Martians.

He reckoned up the evidence in what he had just heard. The commander of the enemy had said something about wishing to look him in the eye. In such a gaze, then, must lie the power to enslave one's will. Naku decided never to look another Martian in the eye, especially when he did not wear the shell cap. Then he looked for the shell cap—it still lay among the cut grass at the front of the mammoth's cage. And, hearing the ill-tempered squeals and snorts from the three giants, Naku dared not go back just now for it.

He continued his diagnosis of the Martians' conversation. Lacking Naku, the commander ordered that "the other male, the one with yellow hair" be brought out. That would be Lumbo. What was to happen to Naku's new friend?

His meditations were interrupted by a low menacing growl, at his very ear. He whirled over in terror. Nothing was there but the wall. From behind it came another growl. Naku guessed at once that a cave-lion, perhaps several, were penned up next to the mammoths, and that they smelled him where he lay.

"Lions and mammoths," he thought. "These Thunder Folk hold them safe in traps now, and have nothing to fear. But suppose that they, and whatever other animals are captured, should be let loose?" He smiled tightly, and his eyes shone at the thought.

But he remained where he was, perforce, while the sun passed zenith and slid down, down, to the horizon and beneath it. He heard bustlings in the open and, once, the takeoff of the flying machine. The enemy sought him afar—not here.

When dark came, he slipped from his hiding.

The Martian camp was lighted here and there by flares of a dozen colors and intensities—the gleam of rays that delved, built or modified things according to the will of their operators. But there were plenty of shadows, and Naku, subtle hunter and woodsman that he was, knew how to take advantage of them, hide in their hearts, pick his course from one to another. Even in the face of passing Martians and robots—there seemed to be more of these latter than before, as though the invaders built new ones of materials prepared in the cap—Naku retraced his steps across the inner wall, up the alley and between the storage sheds until he was again in sight of the cage where he had been held prisoner.

He gazed long and critically through the gloom, and saw only one figure inside—a slender, dejected figure, that of the girl Arla. He approached cautiously and lay in a blot of darkness.

"Arla!" he called softly. "It is Naku, escaped from the Thunder Folk. I am hungry and thirsty. Is there anything left from your evening meal?"

She turned toward him, made a sign with her hand to show that she understood, and came close to where he had crept up against the bars. First she handed out a bowl of water, which he drained gratefully; then a platter of meat and cooked herbs. Naku began to eat ravenously, but he saw that she trembled and heard her sob to herself.

"You are crying," he said. "Why? They have taken away your brother Lumbo, is that it?"

"Yes," she replied brokenly. "He fought the shiny things that look like men but are only walking, wrestling tools—two of them dragged him away. Naku," she addressed him earnestly, "you must leave here, or awful things will happen to you too."

Naku emphatically shook his head.

"No Arla. Up until now, I have outfought and outwitted these powerful Thunder Folk. I shall do so still. I shall not leave here until you are free also."

"But they will catch you and do terrible things. I am afraid that my poor brother—"

"Did they take him to that great round shiny house in the middle?" Naku meant the spaceship. "Listen Arla. I will go and spy on them. I will save your brother."

He said it as he if he already saw a way to succeed, and his confident words put an end to her sobs. She put out a hand between the bars. It was a slim hand but strong, and it clutched Naku's own broad one and seemed to draw strength from him. Naku squeezed her fingers encouragingly.

"Be brave, Arla," he begged. "I will not desert you. I am Naku—wiser and stronger and braver than the Thunder Folk—and I like you." Again she seemed to believe, to win hope from his own confidence. As for Naku, he warmed to her still more.

"Arla," he said, "you are from a stranger people, whose customs I do no know. Do you know what a kiss is?"

"A kiss?" she repeated. "Oh, you mean—like this?"

Their heads came close together, and their mouths touched through the bars. "You must go now," she whispered.

"I will go, but to find and save Lumbo," he replied, and crept away.

Still taking advantage of sheltering patches of shadow, he approached the spaceship. Its ports were mostly open, and one of them gave off light. Naku came to it, and found it above his head. But nearby was a great block of wood from which the Martians had cut lumps for their building. Naku dragged it close, stood upon it, and peeped into a chamber of the craft—the chamber which the Martians used as a surgical operating room.

Chapter VIII
Naku Finds Allies

Naku could see plainly all that happened in that room.

Upon two raised metal slabs lay two prone figures. The nearest of these was Lumbo, the brother of Arla, fastened down by bands at wrist and ankle, around the middle and the neck. He lay still and pale, but not dead—even though his blond head was cleft apart and a Martian fumbled inside his skull with twiglike fingers. Upon him played a green light, one of those myriad rays with which the Martians accomplished their wonders.

On the other slab sprawled a Martian, the commander himself. But it could not be, Naku mused wonderingly—for near him stood two of his subordinates, and they were plainly doing him harm! One, plying a gleaming instrument like a knife, but with a tip that whirred like a dragonfly's wing, was making a hole in his brow. The other held the top of his chief's huge cranium and, as the one with the knife cut it away, lifted loose the skull-cap like a bowl.

"Hurry," said the one who stood by the unconscious Lumbo, "we are at the moment for which we have labored these many hours. Spray the brain with the life-ray."

A companion did so, using a nozzle that gushed green light.

"Now, then, into this other cranium."

From the cut-away skull of the Martian commander, deft hands drew a crinkled gray lump, like a huge nutmeat. Naku saw it for a brief instant as it was carefully slid into the cleft in Lumbo's head. The operators exclaimed in triumph, and turned on the green light more strongly. It seemed to heal, to some degree, Lumbo's wound, though his brow bulged with the extra volume of brain it now contained. After a moment, he stirred, stretched, and spoke:

"Unfasten these shackles, someone."

As Naku stared and wondered, the operator hurriedly did so. Lumbo, so lately their prisoner, sat up on the edge of his slab and pointed to the silent form of their commander.

"Throw that carrion away," he directed, and a robot lugged it out through a panel-way.

"I feel splendid," went on Lumbo, stretching luxuriously. "I can understand how the primitive natives of this planet can set so much store by physical health. And my intellect, I am sure, is not impaired by so much as an atom's force."

The Martians agreed sycophantically, and one began to bandage the half-healed cranium. Naku was torn between utter amazement and utter delight. In some way, his friend Lumbo had established command over these enemies. Perhaps it was because he had not died of that fearful wound in the head—they might think he was a mighty magician. But then, they had seemed to work hard to cure him. Naku scowled. His own head ached with the labor of trying to understand.

Another figure entered. It was Ipsar. Lumbo, as the bandage was swaddled around his brow, addressed the priest:

"The operation was a success. It will follow with others, as swiftly as I obtain prime specimens of the human race to replace our own bodies. But I have orders for you."

"Yes," nodded Ipsar respectfully.

"It is possible—probable, even—that we can pass on our mental powers and other characteristics to human progeny; the children, that is, of these new bodies of ours and females of the human race."

"Yes," repeated Ipsar.

"We have one female prisoner. I give her to you for a mate. And now leave me—I have had little enough rest since I arrived."

He stretched out on the slab, and closed his eyes. A robot moved forward, as if on guard. The other departed.

To Naku there were many mysteries. The fact that Lumbo's body was now governed by the Martian chief's brain he could not grasp. The things spoken by that brain though Lumbo's mouth registered only vaguely, smacking to Naku of some strange occult viewpoint. But one thing was certain—Lumbo had told Ipsar that he might have the captive Arla for a mate.

Naku stepped down from his block of wood. He could understand that thing least of all. Did Lumbo think to bribe Ipsar into an alliance? Was he not powerful enough already, in whatever strange way he had taken to seize control of the Martian party? Or was it that he valued his sister lightly, and cared little whom she might marry? Brothers were sometimes like that—but Naku was no brother of Arla. He had other hopes about her.

He saw fat Ipsar, tramping across to the cage, and followed quickly and silently, keeping yet again to the shadows. The priest deftly unfastened the gate and entered. After a moment Naku heard Arla cry out in fear:

"No, let go of me!"

"Little fool," Ipsar was replying angrily, "you will be far better off than most females—they will become like a race of robots. You, as my mate, will have the advantage of—"

"I cannot understand your talk," Arla gasped. "Let go!"

Naku charged the door, sprang into the cage. Ipsar held Arla by her wrists, but with a single clutch and heave Naku tore the two apart from each other. Then he smote Ipsar in the center of the face and sent him staggering back into a corner.

"Arla is mine," Naku growled at him. "Do not move toward her, or I will kill you."

Ipsar did not move toward Arla. He was tugging something from a loop in his girdle—something that gleamed, even in the dimness of the cage. Naku had seen too many ray-rods in the past day or so to mistake this one. He made a quick, overwhelming lunge. Down went Ipsar again, giving one hoarse howl for assistance. Then Naku's right hand clamped over his mouth, and Naku's left hand imprisoned his weapon arm.

"Run!" Naku bade Arla. "The door is open—run and hide!"

She needed no second bidding—she was gone. Naku wrung Ipsar's fat wrist until the ray-rod fell from his hand, then switched his left grip to the throat.

"Traitor!" he growled at the priest. "You turn against your own people to help these devils from another star," and his fingers, digging through the frill of red beard, sank into Ipsar's windpipe. Naku rose to his feet, dragging Ipsar with him. He bent the pudgy form across his knee, bent it back, back—he heard the snap of the spine. Ipsar went limp.

Dropping the body, Naku turned to follow Arla into the open, but there was a sudden malevolent clanking, and a robot towered in the doorway. Its face-lamp glowed as it peered in. Its claws held a ray-rod.

In desperation, Naku snatched up a ray-rod of his own—the fallen weapon of Ipsar. He pointed the lens-end toward the figure of metal. His hand found a yielding stud upon the rod's smooth surface and he pressed it as he had seen the Martians and robots do.

Out gushed a finger-narrow stream of flame, straight at the center of the robot's torso. There was a sudden clangor, a red-hot glow of the creature's metal and then it fell noisily. Naku, releasing the switch, saw his weapon's ray subside. He ran, jumped across the prostrate robot, and was free.

Arla was nowhere in sight. Like himself, she would know how to take advantage of the shadows. But there was a commotion all through the fortress. Robots were moving hither and thither, singly and in little groups, with Martians slumping around in command.

"I have made too much noise," Naku told himself savagely.

Once again he fled for the only quarter of the camp he knew anything about—between the storehouses, up the alley and to the old rampart wall that was now an inner fence. Up this he swarmed, and a searching Martian saw his silhouette against the night sky, yelled and pointed. There was a rush of feet, both metal and living, as robots and their masters converged in pursuit.

Naku slid down on the other side of the wall, glaring wildly to left and right. He saw once more the pen where the mammoths were confined, the same that had given him such precarious asylum earlier in the day. Again he was inspired.

"Hai, mammoths!" he shouted, rushing up. "Great hairy ones, mountains of meat—prepare to come out and fight for your lives!"

The three mighty things cocked their great fanlike ears, as though they understood. Naku came close and turned his ray-rod against the fastenings of the big barred door.

His pursuers were in sight now, and yelled to each other in triumph. But they did not ray him at once, for he stood among their shelters and possessions, and a flash of heat might destroy other things beside this troublesome human savage. Meanwhile Naku had destroyed the big locked catch, and with all his strength dragged the door back on its hinges.

The largest mammoth, disgruntled at the commotion in front of him, rolled out immediately. The Martians saw that he was free, cried out in alarm, and drew back together in a little group. The mammoth hoisted its trunk, trumpeted, and hurled its great bulk forward.

The other two scrambled heavily to follow their leader.

Naku, crouching low to let the rush go by, sped on to the next cage.

"Ho, you lions in there!" he cried, in fierce gaiety. "You, too, shall be let out to battle!"

The big cats hissed at his shouts, which they could not understand. But when he rayed the lock from their door and dragged it open, they understood that. Out they came, in a tawny torrent, and dashed in sudden rage for the place of greatest noise and commotion.

Vwil, roused from his laboratory work in a shed near the spaceship, ran out into the night to investigate the growing commotion. His meager muscles made it a slow journey to the quarter where the captured animals were kept, and already the mammoths were out and had rushed the party that searched for Naku.

Two Martians and six robots made up that party. Though they had ray-rods, they forbore to use them for a moment, fearing to injure valuable property. After that, it was too late. The biggest beast trod on a robot as on a beetle, smashing it to a welter of case-fragments and wheels and wires, then caught another in his trunk and hurled it far over a shed.

The other robots stood their ground, threatening with their weapons. But the two Martians, able to know fear and caution, retreated into a squat building that housed a half-assembled atomic motor. The two smaller mammoths began systematically to tear it to pieces with their trunks.

"Get into the open!" Vwil yelled to his companions. "Use your rays!" Suiting action to word, he turned his own ray-rod on the biggest mammoth, the full force of the leaping heat-flash striking it broadside in the region of the heart. The monster screamed once, then fell abruptly silent. The flame had torn clear through its huge bulk, killing it instantly. It collapsed, gushing smoke that gave off a disgusting burnt odor, almost overwhelming the robots.

Heartened, the cowering pair in the motor-shed peeped out and leveled their rays. The smallest mammoth, less angry and perhaps more intelligent than his fellows, backed up as by instinct of danger, but the other took the full impact of both discharges in the head, and keeled over heavily upon the hardened pavement. At that moment the fight seemed won.

But other forms were maneuvering in the open space, lithe and menacing forms. The lions were loose. Somewhere farther along sounded the truculent bellow of wakened bison.

Chapter IX
The Battle of the Beasts

Naku, hurrying down the row of cages, rayed open door after door. All the brute inmates thankfully emerged—the mammoths and lions were quickly joined in freedom by a bull bison, half a dozen frantic deer, three great apes of a species that ordinarily Naku would avoid, and a vast and grumpy cave-bear. As he freed each, Naku ducked around the corner of the pen, and the beasts gravitated toward the commotion in the center of the open.

Turning from the bear's prison, last of the cages, Naku came face to face with a robot. He lifted the ray-rod, which he regarded by now as a familiar weapon, and pressed the switch; but it gave forth no flame. Its charge was exhausted. The robot took a clanking stride forward, its talons extended to seize Naku.

At that moment something rose behind it, even bulkier and more terrible than itself. The released cave-bear had come erect upon its rear legs, and was as much taller than the robot as the robot was taller than Naku. Two sturdy, shaggy forepaws extended and encircled the round metal torso.

Naku retreated, but over his shoulder he watched the struggle with fascination. The robot tried to jerk free, but the fleshy arms of the bear were too strong for its mechanical lurchings. It reached back a claw, clutched and tweaked a furry shoulder. The bear roared, swung a paw, as a man strikes a fly with a flat palm. The metal skull of the robot, which could turn the most desperate blow of a war-axe, collapsed under the weight of that buffet. The bear shoved the tottering hulk aside and moved toward the thick of the fight.

Naku gained the inner wall and mounted it. Once again he looked back—the animals were being destroyed by freely-used rays, but these same rays had set a dozen fires among inflammable dumps and stores. Even the hardened earth seemed to collapse and reek before the glowing spears of pure heat.

"This place may burn to nothing," Naku told himself. "I must find Arla—yes, and Lumbo. I promised to rescue Lumbo."

He ran back toward the spaceship, not taking so much trouble to stay in the shadows, for he saw neither Martians nor robots. They must have gathered to deal with the loosed animals in the cage-quarter. Once he dared call out for Arla, but there was no response. Perhaps, he considered, she might have won clear from the fortress, would be waiting outside. After he had found Lumbo and helped him to safety, Naku would look for her, find her. That would be pleasant.

He came to the great round hull of the ship, moved cautiously along its side, and located a door. It was shut, but not locked. After a moment he solved the trick of its fastening, pushed it back and entered. Inside, he found himself once more light and springy, as though two-thirds of his weight had been taken away. He was able to move silently down a metal-faced corridor. A table stood against one bulkhead, with a ray-rod upon it. He picked up the weapon, and advanced more confidently.

Coming to the entrance of a compartment, he saw a Martian inside, seated before a complicated mass of machinery-wheels, bobbing levers, electrodes that gave off rhythmic bands of sparks. From the various terminals rose pulsating rays in all colors of the rainbow. The Martian kept it in operation by constant pressing and shifting of an intricate system of keys, buttons and switches.

"Thunder Creature," Naku addressed the operator, "stop that work."

The Martian turned upon his seat. He looked at the leveled ray-rod, and was afraid.

"You are the human prisoner who escaped," he said shakily to Naku. "Be careful of that thing you hold. It might cause damage—you do not know its power—"

"But I do know its power," Naku assured him. "With another thing like it I have killed some of your brothers, and have burned open the doors of all the prisons in which you held beasts. What is that tangle of stuff you work with, making to move and light up? It is a tool, I think, like the flying house and the man-shapes with lamps in their heads."

The Martian, helpless but plucky, was silent.

"Tell me, or I will burn it with this weapon," Naku insisted. "No, do not stop to make a lie in your heart. And do not try to catch my eyes, I will not look at them." The ray-rod in his hands threatened the machinery.

"Do not destroy it," begged the Martian. "This is the basic-power machine—the broadcaster of energy to all our affairs. If it were damaged, the flying machine could not lift from the ground, the robots could not move, the very ray-rods could not be charged when exhausted—"

"It seems," broke in Naku, "that without this thing running and dancing and shining like that, you would be weak and easily conquered. Is that not so? Well, I shall wreck it."

He sent a gush of heat-ray into the heart of the mechanism. It grated, emitted a puff of oily vapor, and halted abruptly, its lights dimming.

The Martian gave a wail of dismay, and sprang wildly at him. Naku laughed fiercely, and swung the ray-rod like a club. His assailant went over like a reed in a hurricane, and lay still.

Abruptly, there rose new pandemonium outside, yells of mortal terror from Martian throats. Their lights had gone out, their machines had ceased running. Even their robot slaves, powered by the energy waves from the machine Naku had wrecked, were suddenly stilled. Only the ray-rods, each charged temporarily, remained potent against the heterogeneous swarm of brutes they fought. The Martians began to retreat toward their ship.

It was dark in there, too, but Naku was wise in night movements. He groped along the wall to another opening, from which came a gentle filtering of light. It was a chamber with an open port, and the flickering fires among the cages in the middle distance gave a little glow there—enough for Naku to see a stiff-frozen robot in a corner, a pair of slabs, a shelf of surgical instruments and other materials, and the outstretched form of Lumbo.

He went to the side of Arla's brother and nudged him.

"Lumbo," he called softly. "It is I, Naku, come to save you. Wake up, Lumbo!" The blond youth stirred, sighed and awoke. Naku could not see his face in the dimness, but Lumbo evidently recognized him. A gusty snarl came from his mouth, and he sprang without warning upon Naku. A moment later the two were sprawling on the floor, Lumbo above, striking heavily at his would-be rescuer.

"I will kill you, black-hair," he panted between blows.

Naku blocked the worst of the punches with his crossed arms, then, recovering from his half-paralysis of surprise, shot his hands upward and pinned Lumbo's either biceps. With a sudden exertion of all his strength, he whirled the attacker sidewise and off of him. Rolling as he did so, he came up on top, pinning Lumbo against the cold metal floor.

"You are dreaming, Lumbo!" he cried. "I am no enemy, but Naku—we were captives together, and planned to escape and overthrow the Thunder Folk!" As Lumbo struggled, Naku tightened his grip. "Lie still," he warned. "I am stronger than you. If you force me to fight you—"

At those words, Lumbo relaxed.

"You are Naku," he said slowly, as though to inform himself. "Yes—yes, of course I remember. Let me up. We are friends, escaping together."

They rose and went out side by side, Lumbo's hand on Naku's shoulder. Naku decided that the other was still sick, perhaps a bit delirious. His head was heavily bandaged, and Naku remembered the strange behavior of Ipsar after such an experience. But there were other things to consider.

In the open, Naku displayed his ray-rod. "See," he addressed his friend. "This is a weapon of our enemies. It makes fire—so." And he spurted out flame, into the door of a shed. At once the place blazed up.

"You know how to operate it!" gasped Lumbo, and Naku did not take time to dream that Lumbo's surprise was other than that of joy. He was setting other fires.

"We will burn their whole camp," he announced. "Look, where the strongest fires are. I have let go the animals, and they fight the Thunder Folk."

"Then let us go that way," said Lumbo at once, and started off swiftly, dragging Naku along.

Together they climbed the inner wall that Naku was getting to know well. Behind them the fires Naku had set were growing brighter. The battlefield they now saw was strewn with dead bodies—the beasts of Earth, the men of Mars, the fallen, empty robots—but no living thing stirred.

Lumbo bent over some of the corpses. "Most of my—most of the garrison must be dead," he pronounced. "The expedition is a failure."

"The animals are all slain, too," added Naku. He hurried to the pen where the mammoths had been kept. Its wooden joinings were afire, and the earthen roof flaking to bits. He could plainly see the interior.

With a cry of pleasure, he rushed in and snatched up something round and white, that had miraculously escaped the trampling feet of the mammoths. Then he hurried back to Lumbo.

"Look," he said. "This shell, that Ipsar wore, helped me to do what I have done. When I wore it, the language of the Thunder Folk was lost to me, and the will-power they exerted over me was brought to nothing."

"Is that true?" demanded Lumbo sharply. With a forefinger he tapped the shell experimentally. "Hmmmm," he said as though to himself. "It is not impossible—no. Made by nature as an absolutely tight vessel, with no single orifice—then transmuted by ages into inert stone, of the finest insulating elements—it could prove practicable, though we never guessed it—"

Naku did not know what the other was mumbling about.

"I wore it thus," went on Naku, and donned it.

Lumbo was talking on—but in the purring language of the Martians.

Naku stared, felt a coldness of fear about his heart, and lifted the thing from his head. Immediately he understood again.

"Do not put it on a second time," Lumbo commanded him earnestly, and fixed Naku's eyes with his. "Give it to me."

Submissively Naku handed the shell over, and Lumbo hurled it down. With a powerful kick he smashed it. His eyes held Naku's.

"You will obey me," he said.

"I will obey you," agreed Naku, "but what—what—"

"You cannot comprehend, of course. Let me say it simply. You call me by the name of your friend, Lumbo. This is his body—but the mind is that of another. Yes, the mind of the chief of your foeman. Without that petrified shell that deflected the will-impulses from your head, you can understand me. I hold you as my slave, my robot, my tool."

Naku stared, stood silent. "I will obey you," he said again.

"This place burns," spoke the Martian commander through the lips of Lumbo. "The ray-blasts are fiercer than the fires you know. The flame they began will destroy even tiles, even metals. But we will get away. I shall survive, with you for my slave, until more of my people—in spaceships—"

Neither he nor Naku heard the stealthy feet that had come up behind him. But now Lumbo's eyes, still holding Naku's, bulged almost from his head. His mouth fell open, but speech died in it.

His body drew up stiffly, his hands flung themselves out.

Through the center of his naked breast something came into view, like a serpent rising from a pool.

It was blood-dyed, keen, the point of one of the great blades with which some of the robots had been armed.

Lumbo crumpled down upon his face. And his slayer, who drew forth the weapon, was Arla.

Chapter X
Vwil's Farewell

Naku, himself again, gazed at the girl with new wonder. Then he sprang around Lumbo's body, and caught her in his arms. And she wept as though her heart was smashed within her.

"I killed him, my brother—no, not my brother!"

"No, he was not your brother," agreed Naku, "but how did you know?"

"He spoke with the tongue of the Thunder Folk. I could not understand, but I knew that the enemy had gone into him. His heart was no longer Lumbo's heart. Oh, Naku, have I done well?"

"You have done well," said Naku, and comforted her. His eyes darted here and there. The fires were feeding everywhere, greater and wider and brighter. He drew her away from them, toward an unburnt quarter. As their flames followed, he led her farther and farther. They retreated toward the center, where lay the spaceship.

Arla recovered herself, and gazed about dauntlessly. Grief could harrow her, but not danger.

"This place burns, and all its devils with it," she ventured.

"And we too," replied Naku.

"But we have won," was her almost joyous rejoinder. "Our death will be a good one. Every one of the Thunder Folk gone—"

"No, not all!" exclaimed Naku, and sprang forward, ready to do battle with his fists, his only weapons. A gaunt, high-skulled figure hurried heavily toward them, a surviving Martian. But one claw-hand was lifted in truce.

"Is it you, Naku?" panted the anxious voice of Vwil. "Come, I can save you."

"How?" demanded Naku. "The fire is all around us—but wait, your chief said, when he spoke from my friend's body, that there was a way. Lead, but no treachery."

The three hurried to the spaceship and into it. Down a corridor Vwil led the way, then down another. They came to a central chamber, stacked high with cylindrical drums.

"This is all the fuel that is left," panted Vwil. "Bring it." He hoisted a container, Naku seized three, and Arla two more. They hurried down yet another passageway, and arrived at the far side of the ship. Here Vwil flung upward a great slide that revealed the open, and began to roll forth a little fish-shaped car, similar to the space ship itself in form but on a much smaller scale. It ran upon a little landing gear, and with Naku's muscular help, Vwil got it into the clear.

"It is a life-rocket, not dependent on the energy-broadcast machinery," he explained. "It will carry us away. Go back, Naku, for the rest of the rocket fuel, while I pour this into the tanks."

Naku obeyed, making several trips. At last Vwil motioned them into the tiny compartment that did service as cabin and control-chamber, and devoted himself to the controls. There was a roar, a shudder of the vessel.

It was so. Vwil flew them high into the night air, then made a landing at the rim of the valley. They came out again, and looked down at the flaming structures that were once the stronghold of Earth's invaders and would-be conquerors.

"Will you slay this one, too?" whispered Arla to Naku as they emerged, but he shook his head.

"Vwil is kind. He alone seemed to be a friend when I was a prisoner. And he has now saved our lives, when he could have left us in the midst of that fire."

Vwil, too, came into the open.

"I have checked the equipment," he announced. "Emergency rations, water enough, and the fuel, though it would hardly stir the big ship, will carry this little one all the way home."

"Home to your star?" demanded Naku. "Is that where you go?"

"Where else?" smiled Vwil. "This world has hardly been hospitable."

"But you will bring back others to fight and kill us."

Vwil shook his domed head.

"No. I go to make a report to my people that your world is uninhabitable."

Naku looked his incomprehension, and Vwil elaborated:

"My commander used to say harsh things about my soft weakness. He scorned me for being merciful. Perhaps he was right—but he is dead, and I alone am left. My judgment must suffice. And I want nothing else to do with you men."

"We fight hard," agreed Naku.

"I am not even sure that we would win a permanent victory over you," went on Vwil. "You might be defeated temporarily, then rally and wipe us out. And we of my world are not seeking to die; we are seeking to live."

Naku felt a sudden burst of warm generosity.

"Vwil," he said, "your kindness counts for something. Perhaps we can live in peace, if we make every effort—"

"No, my friend," broke in Vwil. "You are wrong. You and I might live as neighbors and comrades. But my people are greedy, and yours are stubborn. There could be only war between them. It is better that we keep our ways separate."

He put out his hand, and Naku took it and shook it. Arla, who had understood none of Vwil's talk, did the same.

"And now I will enter my craft," finished Vwil. "I will give you time to get well away from the blast of the rockets. Good-by."

Vwil got into the life-rocket and closed the door. Naku and Arla walked briskly away, far along the rim of the valley. As they did so, they heard the roar of the takeoff behind them, and turned to see. But Vwil was no more than a comet in the upper sky, seeming to slide away between the stars.

The two had time to look at each other and smile. It seemed to them that nothing would ever be exciting again, except each other.

"Rrau, the war chief of my people, is dead," said Naku. "Ipsar, the priest, is dead. I am young, but probably I shall rule what is left of us."

"Do your men take more than one wife?" asked Arla, and Naku shook his head. "One man takes one woman. Come with me, Arla. We shall reach home by morning, and I shall send a messenger to your tribe, with news and offers of friendship. After these dangers, men may learn to live at peace."

Vwil, afar in his lonely little ship, glanced back once. A rearward port showed him the globe of Earth, already falling thousands of miles behind.

"It is a beautiful place, and rich," he sighed to himself, "but I may be forgiven for lying to my people about it. No riches are worth pain and cruelty. We need more room, more food, more water—we shall find some other planet, deserted and wanted by no one. It will be strange if we Martians cannot make of such a place what we want it to be."

Author's Note

During the past summer, as Mars came closer and closer to Earth, I thought (most science fiction fans undoubtedly had the same fancy) of the possibility of a Martian invasion. Far from thinking such a thing impossible, I wondered why ancient advanced Mars hadn't jumped us up before. Then I wondered if, indeed, there had been an invasion—unsuccessful.

I turned over in my mind many legends, some of the oldest known to man. I believe that in every fairy tale, myth, or legend there is a kernel of truth—and some of them spoke pretty loudly of strange enemies coming down from heaven and being defeated. There I had it. And The Day of the Conquerors *is, by comparison, a realistic treatment of the evidence of those myths and legends.*

Some may challenge the quickness with which my savage stone-age men learn to use weapons and tools of the Martians; but savages are ever quick to learn, as pioneers in Africa, the South Seas, and our own Old West could tell. And Upper Paleolithic men, such as the Cro-Magnon race, had amazing brain equipment— taller brows and bigger skull capacities than we, their degenerate children!

I could not resist the introduction of a sympathetic invader—call it wishful thinking if you like. I have said before, and will say again, that should there prove to be intelligent life on other worlds, it will behoove us in the future to understand and befriend, not suspect, and fight, such creatures. Of course, we can't get along even with brother human beings, so I may be asking too much.

Manly Wade Wellman
January, 1940

Untitled Hok Fragment

This collection closes with the unfinished opening of a story by Manly Wade Wellman that purportedly would have spun the tale of Hok the Mighty's hunt for the mysterious white mammoth. Legend has it that the typed manuscript page of the fragment was found beside Wellman's typewriter after his death, with a blank page bearing the numeral "2" freshly inserted in the spool. Unfortunately, readers will never know what the author had in store for his mighty Stone Age hero in the tale, but one can be assured it would have been an adventure like none other.

In those days Hok the Mighty was chief of the Flint People, where they lived in their line of caves taken from the fierce, half-human Gnorrls. Mighty he was called, for that was what he was, tall, huge-muscled, tawny-haired and tawny-bearded. His loincloth was a leopard's pelt, his cloak the fur of a black-maned lion. He could wrestle down the next strongest man in the tribe, could throw a javelin farther and truer than anyone. He killed lions and cave bears with a single blow apiece of his great axe of blue stone. He hunted down bison and deer, and fetched back loads of meat as much as two ordinary men could lift.

At dawn he would climb the highest rock above the caves and sing, deep-voiced, to the rising sun that made his hair and beard sparkle. All listened and joined in on Hok's song. The men respected him, would have feared him if he hadn't been so good-tempered. The women smiled their admiration, but Hok smiled back only on Oloana, his lovely wife with hair like the night without stars. He was Hok the Mighty, unchallenged in the world he knew until there came into it the subtle man named Plorr and the giant creature named Guargu, that was as blinding white as snow and seemed impossible for even Hok to kill.

BATTLE IN THE DAWN

Plorr came among them one spring day when Hok and two others hunted and killed a red deer among the grass scattered with flowers. Plorr was dressed in a fitted loincloth and cape of white-tanned doeskin, and on his feet he wore shaggy shoes instead of the moccasins the Flint People had. He was tall and bonily thin, his sharp face was scraped clean of beard, and his long hair was braided behind his neck. In his right hand he carried a javelin. He put up an open hand in the peace sign, and he smiled crookedly at Hok.

"Are you the chief here?" he asked, in a language like theirs.

Hok smiled back. "If I'm not the chief, you can tell me about yourself until the chief gets here. We don't see many strangers. What's your name, and what do you want?"

"I'm Plorr."

(fragment ends)

From Amazing Stories, *May 1940.*

An Autobiography
by Manly Wade Wellman

I cannot guarantee this account of my own life will be either comprehensive or interesting. It could be, but then it would be confessional rather than autobiographical. About me, as about most human beings, the best stories go untold.

Every individual, says the philosopher, is an omnibus in which rides the great and varied company of his ancestors. Let us stop and examine the passengers my own personality conveys. They are English, Scotch, Gascon French, German Swiss . . . a proud lot, expert searchers for trouble, often mistaken but never in doubt. I count among them one good artist, two good novelists, three good doctors, several Confederate officers, and one Yankee cavalryman; an Episcopal bishop, and many sinners; a Napoleonic guardsman, who was on retreat from Moscow and saw his emperor plain, asking for roast potatoes. Before these, in pre-colonial days, I count Jacobites and Whigs, Lancastrians and Yorkists, Saxons and Normans—my ancestors fought so much among themselves that I wonder how they ever managed to collaborate in the enterprise that eventually introduced me.

And, of course, far back behind and before all these, there once strode and swaggered a big, bearded hunter, clad in skins and wielding flint axe and spear—my Stone Age forebear, who I hope was a gentleman and a fair fighter. For all he did not know how to read or write or hold a teacup, I do know that he still stirs appreciatively in the aforesaid ancestral omnibus whenever I set down on paper how Hok the Mighty (my idealization of that far-gone father) invades new wonders, or spits between hand and haft to get a firmer grip of his weapon. . . .

And I am the descendant of these. Do they approve of me, I wonder? Despite my family's pre-Revolutionary roots in America, it fell out that I was born abroad—deep in the interior of Angola, Portugal's West African colony, where my parents sojourned a good thirty years ago. There I was reared, in a way to enchant any child—the country may not be the most beautiful on Earth, but I never saw its equal. The people were magnificent, and left me with the love for good savages that must creep out when I write about Hok's tribe. I grew up to boyhood speaking Umbundu better than English—perhaps I don't speak English well as yet.

But to America I came, lest I become a sort of savage myself (I wish I had!); to school in Washington, Kansas, Utah, Minnesota, New York; to work in many interesting and toilsome fields, in more states than those. I like soldiering least, and film reviewing best. Between times I wrote, and having done my most successful work in fantasy and science fiction, in which I allied fields, I have produced and published something like two hundred stories.

As I stand today, I am mountainous in size, dark in complexion, unkempt in appearance, retiring in disposition. I live on the side of a New Jersey hill, a furlong from the road, and I wish I were even more withdrawn than that. With me live the following individuals, all enduring and understanding comrades: my wife, who also writes fantasy as Frances Garfield; my son, Wade; and my Persian cat, Michael. Hobbies? I have few—no busy writer has time for much except writing. But I once boxed and wrestled, I still take time for hiking, fencing and badminton in season.

Widely influential even decades after his death, MANLY WADE WELLMAN *(1903-1986) was an American author of everything from science fiction and fantasy to young adult fiction, detective mysteries, and nonfiction works of history and Americana, even contributing early on to Will Eisner's classic comic* The Spirit. *Today, Wellman is best known for the unique voice and brooding, evocative landscapes of his fantasy and horror stories set in the Appalachian Mountains, their plots drawing on the native folklore of the region and often starring his iconic character Silver John (as featured in the collection* Who Fears the Devil? The Complete Tales of Silver John, *Planet Stories, 2010). Along with John, Wellman's most popular characters remain occult detective Judge Pursivant and playboy-adventurer John Thunstone. Wellman's work has won multiple Locus Awards and World Fantasy Awards (including one for lifetime achievement), a British Fantasy Award, and the Edgar Allan Poe Award from the Mystery Writers of America, and been nominated for numerous others, including a Hugo Award, five more World Fantasy Awards, and a Pulitzer Prize.*

Collect all of these exciting Planet Stories adventures!

THE WALRUS AND THE WARWOLF
BY HUGH COOK
INTRODUCTION BY CHINA MIÉVILLE

Sixteen-year-old Drake Duoay loves nothing more than wine, women, and getting into trouble. But when he's abducted by pirates and pursued by a new religion bent solely on his destruction, only the love of a red-skinned priestess will see him through the insectile terror of the Swarms.

ISBN: 978-1-60125-214-2

WHO FEARS THE DEVIL?
BY MANLY WADE WELLMAN
INTRODUCTION BY MIKE RESNICK

In the back woods of Appalachia, folk-singer and monster-hunter Silver John comes face to face with the ghosts and demons of rural Americana in this classic collection of eerie stories from Pulitzer Prize-nominee Manly Wade Wellman.

ISBN: 978-1-60125-188-6

THE SECRET OF SINHARAT
BY LEIGH BRACKETT
INTRODUCTION BY MICHAEL MOORCOCK

In the Martian Drylands, a criminal conspiracy leads wild man Eric John Stark to a secret that could shake the Red Planet to its core. In a bonus novel, *People of the Talisman*, Stark ventures to the polar ice cap of Mars to return a stolen talisman to an oppressed people.

ISBN: 978-1-60125-047-6

THE GINGER STAR
BY LEIGH BRACKETT
INTRODUCTION BY BEN BOVA

Eric John Stark journeys to the dying world of Skaith in search of his kidnapped foster father, only to find himself the subject of a revolutionary prophecy. In completing his mission, will he be forced to fulfill the prophecy as well?

ISBN: 978-1-60125-084-1

THE HOUNDS OF SKAITH
BY LEIGH BRACKETT
INTRODUCTION BY F. PAUL WILSON

Eric John Stark has destroyed the Citadel of the Lords Protector, but the war for Skaith's freedom is just beginning. Together with his foster father Simon Ashton, Stark will have to unite some of the strangest and most bloodthirsty peoples the galaxy has ever seen if he ever wants to return home.

ISBN: 978-1-60125-135-0

THE REAVERS OF SKAITH
BY LEIGH BRACKETT
INTRODUCTION BY GEORGE LUCAS

Betrayed and left to die on a savage planet, Eric John Stark and his foster-father Simon Ashton must ally with cannibals and feral warriors to topple an empire and bring an enslaved civilization to the stars. But in fulfilling the prophecy, will Stark sacrifice that which he values most?

ISBN: 978-1-60125-084-1

Pick your favorites or subscribe today at paizo.com/planetstories

City of the Beast
by Michael Moorcock
introduction by Kim Mohan

Moorcock's Eternal Champion returns as Michael Kane, an American physicist and expert duelist whose strange experiments catapult him through space and time to a Mars of the distant past—and into the arms of the gorgeous princess Shizala. But can he defeat the Blue Giants of the Argzoon in time to win her hand?

ISBN: 978-1-60125-044-5

Lord of the Spiders
by Michael Moorcock
introduction by Roy Thomas

Michael Kane returns to the Red Planet, only to find himself far from his destination and caught in the midst of a civil war between giants! Will his wits and sword keep him alive long enough to find his true love once more?

ISBN: 978-1-60125-082-7

Masters of the Pit
by Michael Moorcock
introduction by Samuel R. Delany

A new peril threatens physicist Michael Kane's adopted Martian homeland—a plague spread by zealots more machine than human. Now Kane will need to cross oceans, battle hideous mutants and barbarians, and perhaps even sacrifice his adopted kingdom in his attempt to prevail against an enemy that cannot be killed!

ISBN: 978-1-60125-104-6

Northwest of Earth
by C. L. Moore
introduction by C. J. Cherryh

Ray-gun-blasting, Earth-born mercenary and adventurer Northwest Smith dodges and weaves his way through the solar system, cutting shady deals with aliens and magicians alike, always one step ahead of the law.

ISBN: 978-1-60125-081-0

Black God's Kiss
by C. L. Moore
introduction by Suzy McKee Charnas

The first female sword and sorcery protagonist takes up her greatsword and challenges gods and monsters in the groundbreaking stories that inspired a generation of female authors. Of particular interest to fans of Robert E. Howard and H. P. Lovecraft.

ISBN: 978-1-60125-045-2

The Anubis Murders
by Gary Gygax
introduction by Erik Mona

Someone is murdering the world's most powerful sorcerers, and the trail of blood leads straight to Anubis, the solemn god known as the Master of Jackals. Can Magister Setne Inhetep, personal philosopher-wizard to the Pharaoh, reach the distant kingdom of Avillonia and put an end to the Anubis Murders, or will he be claimed as the latest victim?

ISBN: 978-1-60125-042-1

Collect all of these exciting Planet Stories adventures!

THE SWORDSMAN OF MARS
BY OTIS ADELBERT KLINE
INTRODUCTION BY MICHAEL MOORCOCK

Harry Thorne, outcast scion of a wealthy East Coast family, swaps bodies with a Martian in order to hunt down another Earthman before he corrupts an empire. Trapped between two beautiful women, will Harry end up a slave, or claim his destiny as a swordsman of Mars?

ISBN: 978-1-60125-105-3

THE OUTLAWS OF MARS
BY OTIS ADELBERT KLINE
INTRODUCTION BY JOE R. LANSDALE

Transported through space by powers beyond his understanding, Earthman Jerry Morgan lands on the Red Planet only to find himself sentenced to death for a crime he didn't commit. Hunted by both sides of a vicious civil war and spurned by the beautiful princess he loves, Jerry soon finds he must lead a revolution to dethrone his Martian overlords—or die trying!

ISBN: 978-1-60125-151-0

ROBOTS HAVE NO TAILS
BY HENRY KUTTNER
INTRODUCTION BY F. PAUL WILSON

Heckled by an uncooperative robot, a binge-drinking inventor must solve the mystery of his own machines before his dodgy financing and reckless lifestyle get the better of him.

ISBN: 978-1-60125-153-4

ELAK OF ATLANTIS
BY HENRY KUTTNER
INTRODUCTION BY JOE R. LANSDALE

A dashing swordsman with a mysterious past battles his way across ancient Atlantis in the stories that helped found the sword and sorcery genre. Also includes two rare tales featuring Prince Raynor of Imperial Gobi!

ISBN: 978-1-60125-046-9

THE DARK WORLD
BY HENRY KUTTNER
INTRODUCTION BY PIERS ANTHONY

Sucked through a portal into an alternate dimension, Edward Bond finds himself trapped in the body of the evil wizard Ganelon. Will Bond-as-Ganelon free the Dark World from its oppressors—or take on the mantle of its greatest villain?

ISBN: 978-1-60125-136-7

THE SHIP OF ISHTAR
BY A. MERRITT
INTRODUCTION BY TIM POWERS

When amateur archaeologist John Kenton breaks open a strange stone block from ancient Babylon, he finds himself hurled through time and space onto the deck of a golden ship sailing the seas of another dimension—caught between the goddess Ishtar and the pale warriors of the Black God.

ISBN: 978-1-60125-177-0

Pick your favorites or subscribe today at paizo.com/planetstories

THE SWORD OF RHIANNON
BY LEIGH BRACKETT
INTRODUCTION BY NICOLA GRIFFITH

Captured by the cruel and beautiful princess of a degenerate empire, Martian archaeologist-turned-looter Matthew Carse must ally with the Red Planet's rebellious Sea Kings and their strange psychic allies to defeat the tyrannical people of the Serpent.

ISBN: 978-1-60125-152-7

INFERNAL SORCERESS
BY GARY GYGAX
INTRODUCTION BY ERIK MONA

When the shadowy Ferret and the broad-shouldered mercenary Raker are framed for the one crime they didn't commit, the scoundrels are faced with a choice: bring the true culprits to justice, or dance a gallows jig. Can even this canny, ruthless duo prevail against the beautiful witch that plots their downfall?

ISBN: 978-1-60125-117-6

STEPPE
BY PIERS ANTHONY
INTRODUCTION BY CHRIS ROBERSON

After facing a brutal death at the hands of enemy tribesmen upon the Eurasian steppe, the 9th-century warrior-chieftain Alp awakes fifteen hundred years in the future only to find himself a pawn in a ruthless game that spans the stars.

ISBN: 978-1-60125-182-4

WORLDS OF THEIR OWN
EDITED BY JAMES LOWDER

From R. A. Salvatore and Ed Greenwood to Michael A. Stackpole and Elaine Cunningham, shared-world books have launched the careers of some of science fiction and fantasy's biggest names. Yet what happens when these authors break out and write tales in worlds entirely of their own devising, in which they have absolute control over every word? Contains 18 creator-owned stories by the genre's most prominent authors.

ISBN: 978-1-60125-118-3

ALMURIC
BY ROBERT E. HOWARD
INTRODUCTION BY JOE R. LANSDALE

From the creator of Conan, Almuric is a savage planet of crumbling stone ruins and debased, near-human inhabitants. Into this world comes Esau Cairn—Earthman, swordsman, murderer. Can one man overthrow the terrible devils that enslave Almuric?

ISBN: 978-1-60125-043-8

SOS THE ROPE
BY PIERS ANTHONY
INTRODUCTION BY ROBERT E. VARDEMAN

In a post-apocalyptic future where duels to the death are everyday occurrences, the exiled warrior Sos sets out to rebuild civilization—or destroy it.

ISBN: 978-1-60125-194-7

STRANGE ADVENTURES ON OTHER WORLDS
PLANET stories

PRINCES OF MARS

From fantasy legend Michael Moorcock and master of the pulps Otis Adelbert Kline come these thrilling sword and planet yarns in the adventurous, fast-paced style of Edgar Rice Burroughs.

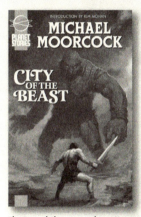

The Eternal Champion reborn, Kane of Old Mars takes on the infamous Blue Giants of the Argzoon.
ISBN 978-1-60125-044-5
$12.99

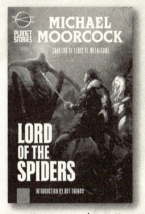

Has Kane returned to Mars thousands of years too late to save his beloved princess?
ISBN 978-1-60125-082-7
$12.99

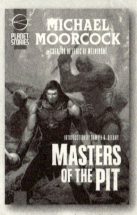

Kane must save the Red Planet from a terrible plague known as the Green Death.
ISBN 978-1-60125-104-6
$12.99

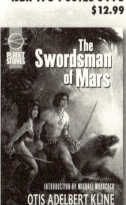

Harry Thorne swaps bodies with a Martian and faces deadly intrigue on the Red Planet.
ISBN 978-1-60125-105-3
$12.99

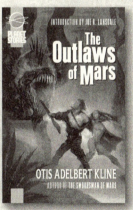

A disgraced American soldier is transported to Mars and must lead its people in a bloody revolution.
ISBN 978-1-60125-151-0
$12.99

"No one has had a greater impact on the field than Michael Moorcock."
Samuel R. Delany

"[Kline's Mars stories are] tall tales in a great and venerable American tradition."
Joe. R. Lansdale

Available now at quality bookstores and **pazio.com/planetstories**

STRANGE ADVENTURES ON OTHER WORLDS
PLANET stories

QUEEN OF THE PULPS!

William Faulkner's co-writer on *The Big Sleep* and the author of the original screenplay for *The Empire Strikes Back*, Leigh Brackett is one of the most important authors in the history of science fiction and fantasy—now read her most classic works!

Eric John Stark finds himself at the center of a mysterious prophecy on the dying world of Skaith.
ISBN 978-1-60125-084-1
$12.99

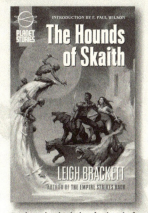

Stark seeks the help of a band of motley revolutionaries to confront the Wandsmen of Skaith.
ISBN 978-1-60125-135-0
$12.99

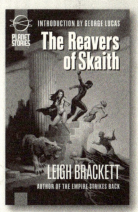

The revolution Stark has longed for is here, but what will he have to sacrifice for it to succeed?
ISBN 978-1-60125-138-1
$12.99

Stark holds a dark secret that could shake the Red Planet to its core! Collected with the bonus novel *People of the Talisman*.
ISBN 978-1-60125-047-6
$12.99

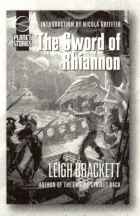

Martian archaeologist-turned-looter Matthew Carse hurtles back in time to battle the super-science of a lost race.
ISBN 978-1-60125-152-7
$12.99

"Fiction at its most exciting, in the hands of a master storyteller."
George Lucas

"Brackett combines the best of A. Merritt and Edgar Rice Burroughs with much that is uniquely her own!"
F. Paul Wilson

Available now at quality bookstores and **pazio.com/planetstories**

PLANET stories
HIDDEN WORLDS AND ANCIENT MYSTERIES

SWORD & SORCERY LIVES!

Planet Stories is proud to present these classics of magic and perilous adventure from three unparalleled masters of heroic fantasy: Robert E. Howard, A. Merritt, and C. L. Moore.

••

"Howard's writing is so highly charged with energy that it nearly gives off sparks."

Stephen King

"[A. Merritt] has a subtle command of a unique type of strangeness which no one else has been able to parallel."

H. P. Lovecraft

"C. L. Moore's shimmering, highly colored prose is unique in science fiction."

Greg Bear

Can a single Earthman hope to overthrow the terrible devils that enslave the savage world of Almuric?
ISBN 978-1-60125-043-8
$12.99

A mysterious artifact from ancient Babylon hurtles amateur archaeologist John Kenton onto the seas of another dimension.
ISBN 978-1-60125-177-0
$14.99

Jirel of Joiry, the first-ever sword and sorcery heroine, takes up her greatsword against dark gods and monsters.
ISBN 978-1-60125-045-2
$12.99

Available now at quality bookstores and **pazio.com/planetstories**

PLANET stories
THE UNIVERSE OF FUTURE CENTURIES

EXPLORE THE WORLDS OF HENRY KUTTNER!

From brutal worlds of flashing swords and primal magic to futures portraying binge-drinking scientists and uncooperative robot assistants, Henry Kuttner's creations rank as some of the most influential in the entirety of the speculative fiction genre.

....

"A neglected master . . . a man who shaped science fiction and fantasy in its most important years."

Ray Bradbury

"I consider the work of Henry Kuttner to be the finest science-fantasy ever written."

Marion Zimmer Bradley

"The most imaginative, technically skilled and literarily adroit of science-fantasy authors."

The New York Herald Tribune

A scientist wakes from each drunken bender having created an amazing new invention—now if he could only remember how it worked!
ISBN 978-1-60125-153-4
$12.99

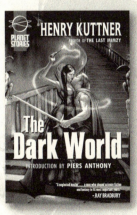

Edward Bond falls through a portal into an alternate dimension only to find himself trapped in the body of the evil wizard Ganelon.
ISBN 978-1-60125-136-7
$12.99

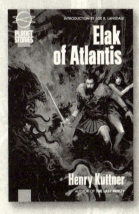

A dashing swordsman with a mysterious past battles his way through warriors and warlocks in the land of doomed Atlantis.
ISBN 978-1-60125-046-9
$12.99

Available now at quality bookstores and pazio.com/planetstories

Read How These Men Got Better Books
THEN FIND OUT WHAT PLANET STORIES OFFERS YOU SUBSCRIBE!

> PLANET STORIES SHIPS A BEAUTIFUL NEW SCIENCE FICTION OR FANTASY BOOK DIRECT TO MY DOOR EVERY 60 DAYS AT 30% OFF THE COVER PRICE. ALL I NEED TO DO IS SIT BACK AND READ!
> **ALEXANDER BLADE,**
> **NEW YORK CITY, NEW YORK.**

> WITH THE GREAT CLASSIC REPRINTS OFFERED BY PLANET STORIES, I'VE LEARNED MORE ABOUT THE HISTORY OF SCIENCE FICTION AND FANTASY THAN EVER BEFORE. MY FRIENDS THINK I'M AN EXPERT!
> **S.M. TENNESHAW,**
> **BOSTON, MASS.**

> THESE BOOKS ARE THE PERFECT COMPANIONS WHEN I'M JET-SETTING ACROSS THE WORLD. ALL MY PASSENGERS ENVY THE TOP-QUALITY FICTION PLANET STORIES PROVIDES.
> **CAPTAIN CURTIS NEWTON,**
> **PATRIOT AIRWAYS,**
> **YORBA LINDA, CA.**

> I'M A TABLETOP GAMER, AND PLANET STORIES GIVES ME AN EXCITING LOOK AT THE ADVENTURE FICTION THAT INSPIRED MY FAVORITE HOBBY. YOU SHOULD SEE HOW I USE THE MONSTERS IN MY CAMPAIGN!
> **DICK AWLINSON,**
> **LAKE GENEVA, WIS.**

> WITH MY PLANET STORIES SUBSCRIPTION, I NEED NEVER WORRY ABOUT MISSING A SINGLE VOLUME. I CAN CHOOSE THE DELIVERY METHOD THAT WORKS BEST FOR ME, AND THE SUBSCRIPTION LASTS UNTIL I DECIDE TO CANCEL.
> **N.W. SMITH,**
> **SCHENECTADY, NEW YORK.**

> I CAN COMBINE MY PLANET STORIES BOOKS WITH OTHER SUBSCRIPTIONS FROM PAIZO.COM, SAVING MONEY ON SHIPPING AND HANDLING CHARGES!
> **MATTHEW CARSE,**
> **KAHORA, MARS**

FINE BOOKS FOR FINE MINDS
SUBSCRIBE TODAY

Explore fantastic worlds of high adventure with a genuine Planet Stories subscription that delivers the excitement of classic fantasy and science fiction right to your mailbox! Best of all, you'll receive your bi-monthly Planet Stories volumes at a substantial 30% discount off the cover price, and you can choose the shipping method that works best for you (including bundling the books with your other Paizo subscriptions)!

Only the Finest SF Books
The Best of Yesterday and Today!

Personally selected by publisher Erik Mona and Paizo's award-winning editorial staff, each Planet Stories volume has been chosen with the interests of fantasy and science fiction enthusiasts and gamers in mind. Timeless classics from authors like Robert E. Howard (Conan the Barbarian), Michael Moorcock (Elric), and Leigh Brackett (*The Empire Strikes Back*) will add an edge to your personal library, providing a better understanding of the genre with classic stories that easily stand the test of time.

Each Planet Stories edition is a Paizo exclusive—you cannot get these titles from any other publisher. Many of the tales in our line first appeared in the "pulp era" of the early 20th Century that produced authors like H. P. Lovecraft, Edgar Rice Burroughs, Fritz Leiber, and Robert E. Howard, and have been out of print for decades. Others are available only in rare limited editions or moldering pulp magazines worth hundreds of dollars.

Why Spend $20, $50, or even $100 to Read a Story?
Smart Readers Make Smart Subscribers

Sign up for an ongoing Planet Stories subscription to make sure that you don't miss a single volume! Subscriptions are fixed at a 30% discount off each volume's cover price, plus shipping. Your ongoing Planet Stories subscription will get you every new book as it's released, automatically continuing roughly every 60 days until you choose to cancel your subscription. After your first subscription volume ships, you'll also receive a 15% discount on the entire Planet Stories library! Instead of paying for your subscription all at once, we'll automatically charge your credit card before we ship a new volume. You only need to sign up once, and never need to worry about renewal notices or missed volumes!

> BEST OF ALL, AS A SUBSCRIBER, I ALSO RECEIVE A 15% DISCOUNT ON THE DOZENS OF BOOKS ALREADY PUBLISHED IN THE PLANET STORIES LIBRARY!
> **WILL GARTH,**
> **CHICAGO, ILL.**

Visit paizo.com/planetstories
to subscribe today!

PLANET STORIES AUTHORS

PIERS ANTHONY	ROBERT E. HOWARD	
LEIGH BRACKETT	OTIS ADELBERT KLINE	MICHAEL MOORCOCK
GARY GYGAX	HENRY KUTTNER	C. L. MOORE